WHITEBEAM

By K.M. del Mara

The caterpillar sees the end of the world.

The Master sees the butterfly.

ACKNOWLEDGEMENTS

I would like to thank Dorian Kincaid, Nancy Dilmore and Lori Rivers Dilmore for early readings and invaluable assistance. Without your encouragement, this rowan tree would be so much firewood.

I owe much appreciation to photographer Chris McLean for old-style generosity to a complete stranger.

And of course no one could have given a greater gift than Henry -- hours and hours of freedom to wander where I would.

Many thanks to all of you,

K.M. del Mara

WHITEBEAM

CONTENTS

The Whitebeam of Arran Isle
SONGS OF THE RENAISSANCE

Prelude
A short piece used by troubadours to test the acoustics of the room in which they will perform.

Chanson de toile
A spinning song in which the central character, always a woman, can be an ill-mated wife or a lovesick girl.

Rondel
A French poem set to music. Also a type of medieval dagger.

Envoi
A short stanza at the end of a poem, standing apart from the poem itself. It expresses the hope that the poem will bring some benefit or enlightenment

Postlude
A concluding piece of music.

THE WHITEBEAM OF ARRAN ISLE

*G*rowing high in the hills of Arran Isle, the whitebeam is a most remarkable tree. "Lady of the Mountains", the Old Ones called it. A type of rowan tree it is, and Arran Isle, off the western coast of Scotland, is the one place in all the world that it can be found.

It promises protection, according to what they used to say, protection from magic. Even the red berry of the rowan was said to have magical powers. Cut it in two, and what do you see there? A pentagram, ai, the very symbol of protection. So, for long ages, equal-sided crosses made of rowan sticks were nailed over doorways of our cottages and barns. And the wood of the rowan, as everyone knows, has always been valued for wands and walking sticks, maybe the odd flute or whistle.

Even before the Old Ones came to Arran Isle, there was another race of people living here. To their way of thinking, the whitebeam bestowed vision. These were a people very sensitive to matters of the spirit. They called the whitebeam "the whispering tree" because it would reveal secrets. But only to those willing to listen, and few their numbers are, in any century.

Stories tell that these ancients organized their calendar around the trees they considered sacred, with a tree for every month, each symbolic of certain personality traits. According to this idea, people born in, say, the Month of the Rowan, January 21st to February 17th by our reckoning, have certain characteristics in common. Charm, cheerfulness – these are typical Rowan traits. Rowan people like to draw attention, and they love life, unrest, even complications, if you can imagine. They are emotional, it's true, but they are artistic, too, often gifted. Fine company, Rowan folk are, without doubt. But they do not forgive. No, they don't forgive, or not easily, at any rate.

So the whitebeam is very symbolic to us islanders. Of course, the question is, did we invent its attributes, or did the tree reveal them somehow, magically, to us? But this is Arran Isle, is it not? Truly, there's not even any need to ask.

Prelude

*A*t the tip of the Isle of Arran lies Loch Ranza, Lake of the Rowan Tree, blue as a sapphire between hills of early green. At its northern end the loch spills into the Sound of Bute. At its southern end there stands, even now in our day, a castle, eight hundred years old, almost entirely surrounded by water.

Now the castle is an empty shell. There are no traces of its former inhabitants. And yet... listen... ...whispers...- do you hear them? Lean your ear to the wall. Faint currents like music waft in and out of the rooms, murmurs of ancient conversations and forgotten stories, never told until now.

The loch itself, Loch Ranza, is named for the rowan tree that has scattered itself all over the hillsides on this island. And the rowan tree of this isle, say the Old Ones, has a peculiar quality. It bestows the gift of sight.

Were you to receive its gift, you might be able to scan the great billowing web of Time to discover who lived the old stories that haunt this castle. Look, do you see? Someone rises there, from long centuries ago. She comes toward us, her carriage stately. Her skirts, of the lightest wool, float in soft gathers at her ankles and a silver pendant dangles from the long sash at her hips. Her flowing sleeves reach almost to the floor. Does she not have thick red hair, bound with ribbons and braids, and eyes the grey-green of a summer moor? We see her lean from a window of the castle. Stray curls blow across her temples. She is watching a boat just entering the loch.

Daughter of ancient Scottish nobility, it is her family, the MacDuffs, who have traditionally placed the crowns upon the heads of Scottish kings. Are we surprised, then, that she is a proud young woman, and willful? But she is charming too, lively and merry. Life is like a dance to her. She twirls and turns and smiles, and for her the music almost never stops. We know, but she does not as yet, that she sashays across a tightrope that will not allow a careless step. When eventually she does stumble, Fate will blindly lead her to the one place she most fears to go. Even so, she must again count herself more fortunate than many of her day.

Perhaps we could use the powers of the rowan to conjure her story. Even with its help, our vision of her may not be perfectly clear. Time, after all, weaves its tales on gossamer threads, into veils so light and fragile that they drift and sway across the winds of the world. Many a story has become shrouded or lost in the far reaches of the years.

However, if that is where our tale lies, that is where we must go, trusting that if we don't find truth, we may at least gain insight.

Chanson de toile

March 1297
Loch Ranza, Isle of Arran, Scotland

From the upper window of the keep a young woman watched a small galley ship enter the loch. She willed herself to ignore it but a minute later was drawn back to the window to look again. The galley came on, prodded gently by the first soft breezes of spring. The woman, Isobel MacDuff, was barely out of girlhood at sixteen years of age. She groaned impatiently.

"Don't fret yourself. Surely it must be a fisherman," said the young man seated near her. "Who else, this early in the year and in this lonely corner of the world?" His grey eyes mocked her.

Isobel smiled ruefully and twisted a curl of hair.

"'Tis a galley, though, Cuinn."

"It's not likely him."

"But it's taking him so long! I've been waiting for over a month! Why doesn't he come?" She turned resolutely from the window once more and leaned against the sill. She looked at the young man and pouted. "You know, I think you like her better than you like me."

"Maybe I do. It's only what you deserve. You're going to leave me soon, after all. Besides, look how adorable she is."

Isobel walked to his side and regarded her own wrinkle-faced infant, held fast in his arms. She ran a finger over her baby's red fuzzy head.

"Red face, red hair. She looks like a little apple," said the man.

"My little pippin apple." They laughed. "What would I have done if you hadn't asked me to stay here this winter, Cuinn? You and your good mother." She rested her cheek against his head and then walked again to her perch on the window seat.

"Then stay here. Stay with me, Iseabail" he said, using the Gaelic form of her name. He opened his free arm in invitation. "You could marry me."

"Cuinn, you know I have to go back. I'm betrothed to a man who would be very displeased if I didn't come home. And betrothed or not, it still terrifies me to displease him."

"Since when does anyone terrify you, Iseabail? You'll have him wrapped around your little finger in a week. After all, John Comyn is old enough to be your father" Cuinn scoffed. "He should be glad to have you."

"I agree, he should," she joked. "But as much as I despise the very thought of marrying him, I have to go through with it for my family's sake. Otherwise, why go to all this trouble, hiding from him here at Loch Ranza until the baby's birth?" She leaned back and gazed again at the loch below. "But I'm beginning to think this child's father is going to leave us here forever."

Down below the boat was closer now. She watched it intently. Framed against the hillsides of Arran, it looked small. It was likely just a fisherman.

Isobel stood abruptly.

"That is not a fisherman! I'm sure it's heading this way! Look! Isn't it?"

Cuinn de Seta got up, careful not to disturb the sleeping infant, and crossed to Isobel's side. He looked grimly at the ship. His heart sank.

"Is it going to anchor here? Is it him?"

"Yes, it looks like that's your man, Iseabail." She squealed with joy and ran from the room.

Abandoned, Cuinn settled himself on the window seat. He propped the baby on his lap. She fluttered her eyes, squinting against the light.

"Here he comes, my little pippin apple" he told her ruefully. "Here comes your daddy."

On the shore below, Isobel ran to the dinghy as it beached. A tall young man leapt out and came toward her, but stopped abruptly in surprise. She stopped then, too, a short distance from him, and put her hands on her hips.

"What? Aren't you happy to see me?"

"What happened to the baby?"

"Oh! She's here." She gestured airily toward the lodge. "A daughter. She's bonny, if you can believe what they say. She was born a month ago. Can't I get a kiss, Rob?" She opened her arms to him and laughing, he twirled her off the ground.

"She's bonny, is she? She looks like me, then?" he teased.

"She looks a little scrawny, I think, but they tell me she's bonny."

The man set her down and looked at her seriously, their arms still encircling each other.

"Isobel, who did you tell about coming to Arran? Somehow your betrothed has gotten the idea that you're here. He's coming after us."

"I told no one, Rob! Absolutely no one! Where is he?"

"He's still on the mainland, I hope. We have warned every sailor we knew not to lend him a boat. And with any luck, if he does get to Arran, he'll go first to Brodick Castle."

"He must know the English have taken it over."

"Hopefully he doesn't know that yet. How is the Lady de Seta doing since they forced her out of Brodick?"

"Sebrina? It's not been easy for her, but she's like a rock. She's had a fair bit of adjustment to make, trying to make a home here, but she's been wonderful to me."

Rob linked his hands possessively around the back of Isobel's neck.

"And how have you been keeping, my love?" He stopped and caught sight of Cuinn de Seta coming toward them, carrying a baby. His brown eyes narrowed. He hadn't known Cuinn had returned to Arran. "Ah, I see you've been well looked after this winter, after all, Isobel." Reminding himself of the de Setas' kindness to Isobel, he covered his ill-humored comment with a smile. He reached a big hand in greeting. "How are you, Cuinn? Is this my own bairn?"

"'Tis, Rob. She's been waiting for you." He handed the baby to the other man who hesitated, then very cautiously took the infant.

"I'm sorry, Rob. I should have mentioned about…" Isobel gestured limply in Cuinn's direction. "You didn't know Cuinn was back from France? He's kept me from going crazy these months, waiting here."

"This little one's a beauty, Rob" said Cuinn, hastily.

"She is. She is so small!"

The baby squirmed again and started to complain. Cuinn laughed.

"Here, shall I take her back? She probably wants her dinner."

"Isobel? Don't you want to take her?"

"Oh, let Cuinn take her to Amie." Isobel waved Cuinn away and took Rob's arm. "I want to hear the news of my dear John Comyn. How is my delightful husband-to-be?"

"I'm not joking, Isobel. You're going to have to move out of here this afternoon. John Comyn suspects, somehow, about us, and was seen down in the village, asking questions. Somebody must have told him that I was coming here. We'll have to move very fast." He dropped Isobel's arm. "I'll speak to Cuinn's mother. We must leave no trace of your stay." He saw he had gotten his message across. Isobel looked horrified.

"You're serious? If John Comyn finds us …" she whispered, "and the baby! After we've been so careful!" She could not bear to contemplate the effect this would have on her family.

"I know it's none of my business…" The other two looked at Cuinn blankly. They had forgotten he was still there, holding their child. "If you leave here today and the baby stays on Arran, my mother could hide her at a cottage in the hills, and you can come back for her in a few weeks."

Rob's face lit up. He immediately began to regard Cuinn in a better light.

Cuinn went on. "That will give you time to make other arrangements. I think we could convince our gardener's wife to continue as the baby's nurse. By the time John Comyn gets here, even if he comes today, we could all be long gone."

"The baby will be absolutely safe? I could come back for her in a month or so. But if anything should happen…"

"I give you my word, Rob, that we will look after her."

"I'd be forever grateful, Cuinn. Seriously, I would, and Isobel will, too. Right, my love? I promised you from the beginning that I would always see to her care. This arrangement would be the best, you must agree."

Isobel tilted her face to him, uncertain. Rob put his arm around her shoulder and she laced her fingers with his. Reassured, she turned to smile at Cuinn.

"Cuinn, you are such a dear" said Isobel. "But your mother will be a little surprised, won't she? What will she say?"

"Everyone here, except my mother, seems convinced that the baby is mine, anyway. I don't think Mother will mind keeping the secret for a few more weeks. We'll take the baby up to a place in the hills that we know of, and…"

"Don't even tell us about it. It will be better if we know nothing. We'll have to trust you."

"All right. We'll come back down to Loch Ranza when it's safe. You'll find us here, Rob, when you return. Or maybe, Isobel, you could come back?"

Isobel went to Cuinn and kissed his cheek. He looked earnestly into her face.

"I doubt I will. But we'll go to Lady Sebrina right now and thank her. And thank you, too, Cuinn. For everything. I'm so grateful."

Cuinn, still holding her baby in his arms, watched her lead Rob away.

*I*t wasn't until she began packing the infant's little gowns that Isobel gave a sober thought to the future. At last she acknowledged, standing dark at her shoulder, the twin specters, Regret and Dread. What would become of this child, raised without a mother? And what kind of household could Rob offer her?

He no longer had much of a household, as far as Isobel could tell, now that his young wife was dead. She had died just after giving birth to a little girl the year before, and the moment her heart stopped, Rob's own heart nearly broke. At that time the English king, in order to keep Rob under his control, had demanded that their newborn daughter, Marjorie, be handed over to him and raised at the English court. Since then, Rob, with no wife and no child at home, had been drifting aimlessly.

*R*eturning with the baby after her dinner, Cuinn found Isobel weeping quietly in Rob's arms. They both turned to give the little one a last kiss. Isobel removed a fine chain from her neck. From it dangled a golden charm, the image of a rowan tree.

"Please, will you make sure that this stays with her, always? I know you gave it to me, Cuinn, and I love it very much, but I want her to have it. For luck. And maybe someday…I don't know…" Her voice caught and she rocked the infant in her arms. Seeing the little furry red head against Isobel's luxuriant plaits, Cuinn silently begged her to reconsider, but she wasn't given the chance. Rob moved quickly to take command of the situation.

"We'd best be going, all of us. If we take time for second thoughts, we'll be doomed. Perhaps things will be different when I come back in the summer."

They couldn't argue. He was right, of course, or seemed to be. An hour later, Cuinn and Sebrina de Seta, his mother, rode out from Loch Ranza lodge. With them were the baby's nurse, Amie, and her own little son Tom, who was too young to be left at home.

Sebrina carried the infant girl bundled in blankets and little Tom, wide-eyed, sat in front of Cuinn.

When they had ridden far up into the glen, high above the lodge, Cuinn turned his pony around, ostensibly to wait for the nurse plodding behind. But in truth he was watching the ship just leaving the loch and turning towards the mainland.

"Iseabail..." Cuinn had his own regrets.

Interrupting his thoughts, Sebrina called to her son from the path above.

"Cuinn, dear, keep up with me. I was just realizing that this baby was never given a name. Are we to keep calling her Baby?"

Cuinn rode up to her side and regarded the sleeping child. He looked around to make sure the nurse could not hear.

"It probably doesn't matter. She has one of the noblest lineages in the land, but she may never know who she really is."

"Poor baby. We might as well call her whatever we like for the next few weeks, until her father gets back. What name would suit her?"

"Isobel said she looks like a little pippin apple." He turned again to get a last look at the boat sailing away.

Sebrina tried to lighten his mood.

"She does!" she laughed. "Little pippin." Her son was hopelessly preoccupied, however.

Sebrina urged her pony forward. "We'd better get going, Cuinn. It will be dark soon and Caela doesn't know we are coming."

Cuinn forced himself to turn his pony and hurry after her, up into the high hills, where they were sure John Comyn of Buchan would not find them.

Cuinn's thoughts were consumed with Isobel's dilemma. She was being forced to fulfill a promise of betrothal that had been made years before by Duncan MacDuff, her cruel and domineering father. Isobel had been the only person ever able to influence that man, but in the matter of her betrothal he had used her as a pawn, as he had used everyone. Her family had gained powerful connections in return for that marriage promise. Now it was impossible for her go against their wishes. Or, if not impossible, it would at least have been very difficult. And, whenever she could, the light-hearted Isobel chose to avoid difficulties.

Why, then, was she sailing back to the mainland with a man that her husband-to-be hated violently?

Perhaps only the Devil himself had the answer to that, and he was laughing uproariously. As well he might. All of Scotland knew what Isobel ignored: that John Comyn and Rob had been bitter enemies for years. So the Devil, being what he was, sat back, crossed his goaty legs, and told himself that all he had to do was watch and wait. The consequences of this day would be regrettable, nay – devastating. It would all be so amusing! Yes, this story was already written. All it needed was the final line, and that he would be more than happy to supply when the time came.

Regardless of what the Devil or any of them thought, Time would unfold their destinies in her own capricious fashion. Of those leaving Loch Ranza lodge that day, some would not come together again for ten long years. Two of these have never been forgotten. The others slipped quietly into the deep hollows of Time, leaving nothing but a tale. Meanwhile, the rowans, the far-seeing whitebeams on the hillsides, whispered regrets, their fruitless regrets.

November, 1299
Loch Ranza Lodge

*T*wo years later, Cuinn's mother, Lady Sebrina de Seta, formerly of Brodick Castle, stood over the child's little bed and looked at her with rapt affection. To the woman who had buried two of her own three children next to their father at Brodick castle, the little girl was as exquisite as any work of art. Dark lashes lay against her plump white cheek. Sebrina touched the red curly head and the child stirred. Blinking sleepily, she put her arms up with a glad smile and Sebrina lifted her from her bed. The little red head dropped onto her shoulder, her nose in Sebrina's neck. Sebrina rocked her and crooned softly for a moment.

"Look, Pippa, someone has come to see you."

She carried her into the room where Cuinn sat beside the enormous fireplace. The only other person in the room was the baby's father, Rob, just arrived from the mainland. The little girl had seen her father exactly twice in her short life. Although he had promised her mother he would raise her, his life had become a confused shambles. He meant to come back for the baby, but his path seldom took him to Arran. So, as way led on to way, it seemed better to leave her at Loch Ranza. He had visited once, but he was a virtual stranger to her. About fathers in general, and her father in particular, the child knew nothing.

"Will she come to me?" Rob held out his hands.

The darling of all the household at Loch Ranza was not shy. As far as she knew, the world was entirely made up of people who adored her. Still, she went warily from Sebrina's arms. She studied the face of the big man with grave misgivings. He had brought her a toy pony and he made it dance along her chubby little leg. She held the pony up for Cuinn and Sebrina to see. The little girl squirmed off Rob's lap and ran over to Cuinn with her new toy.

"You know, Lord Carrick, all this time we have never called her anything but Pippa" said Sebrina. "Have you chosen a name for her?"

"Her mother wants her to have a Gaelic name. She wants her to be called Eshne."

"Because of her hair? It's a pretty name. 'Little fire'. It suits her personality too, believe me." Lady Sebrina took the child onto her lap, straightened her embroidered gown and sighed. "Must we give her up, Lord Carrick?"

"Please, my lady, call me Rob. I do thank you for giving her a home for these years. But Isobel fears for her safety."

"But who would hurt this child?"

Rob sighed. "I can name two immediately who would relish getting their hands on her if they found out about her. John Comyn, her mother's new husband, is no friend to me, and would think nothing of harming her. The other is King Edward. He still keeps my first daughter, Marjorie, at his court in London, though I'm trying to get her back. But Edward knows he can put pressure on me as long as she is there. I worry enough as it is about Marjorie, so I'd rather neither of these men knew about this child. They would use her against me if they could."

Sebrina frowned and looked Rob straight in the eye. "I'm surprised you don't have more influence with the king. We heard you had sided with him against Scotland" she said boldly.

"I was afraid you would be concerned about that."

"Mother! You know Rob's father supported the English and insisted his sons to do the same. What can you expect? Your family, surely, has tried to influence you, Rob, isn't that so?" asked Cuinn.

"Oh ai, truly they have tried. But I've come back to the Scots now. You must have heard that I've burned two of my own castles to keep them out of English hands. I am finally convinced that King Edward is trying to take over Scotland. None of us wants that. But while we quarrel over choosing our own king, he is thinking he can take Scotland's throne for himself."

"I'm glad you've come back to our side, Rob" said Cuinn.

"We have sided against Edward all along" declared Sebrina tartly, "for better or for worse."

"Mother, please."

Rob rubbed his hands tiredly across his eyes, then looked steadily back at the other two.

"I can see that your loyalty to Scotland has never wavered" he said. "You have already been forced to flee your own Brodick Castle, after all."

"If we hadn't owned this old hunting lodge, I don't know where we'd have gone" said Sebrina.

"This is happening all over Scotland. And believe me, King Edward will be making more trouble this summer."

"You think so?"

"I'm sure of it. So if we can find this child a safer place, now is the time for her to go. I promised Isobel I would see to her care. I hope you see my point."

"She'll be near by, Mother, and will be able to visit from time to time." Cuinn turned to Rob. "We've made an arrangement with a woman who happens to be a close kinswoman of the baby's mother. She was brought up with Isobel since babyhood."

"Would I know her?"

"I doubt it. She calls herself Grizel now, but it's not her real name. She came to live with us when she ran away from her uncle Duncan MacDuff. Though he has been dead these many years."

"Isobel's father, would he be? He was a vicious brute, they say."

"His relatives must have thought so too. They are the ones that murdered him" said Sebrina.

"Or so the story goes" corrected Cuinn.

"Or so it goes," Sebrina conceded.

Rob suddenly lunged from his chair to pry a cup of wine from the child's grasp.

"Och! Leave that be!" he cried gruffly.

The child Pippa looked up at him, shocked. She burst into angry tears, but quieted with a little whimper when Cuinn held his finger to his lips.

Rob settled back in his seat.

"So this Grizel lives alone up in the hills, you say?" he continued.

"That's right" Cuinn answered. "Her parents died when she was small. She was forced to rely on her uncle's care for so long that independence means everything to her now. She distrusts most people, which is not too surprising."

"Well she was horribly mistreated! Her uncle spent her entire inheritance yet still resented having her in his household," explained Sebrina. "So you can understand why she is a bit of a hermit. But, to me, she is a very dear friend."

"She makes her living by weaving," Cuinn added. "Our household buys much of what she produces. She is not wealthy, but the child will not go hungry. I will make sure that she and the baby want for nothing."

"No need for you to worry, Cuinn. I would be generous to her as long as she cares for Eshne. Her mother and I would both be very grateful. Then too, if this woman, this Grizel, likes our ideas about the Irish horses, I might be visiting fairly often."

"We'll see. We'll need to convince her."

"I feel badly about leaving the bairn. This is a sorry way to bring up a child of such noble birth, but for Isobel's sake, there is nothing else we could do. We could think of no other place nearby that would be as safe as Arran. Even the northern isles are dangerous."

"Don't you have kinsmen there?"

"Ai, I do. But the family intrigues are, shall we say, complex. A nest of vipers might be more trustworthy, in case you miss my meaning. They could turn on me at any time. But Isobel swears that I can trust you. I keep saying that one day things will be different. I hope someday they will be."

"We are all hoping so" answered Cuinn.

Rob ran his hands over his short beard.

"Isobel wanted me to remind you to send her a portrait of this child. She still has no other children, and she pesters me about this portrait every time I see her. Have you been able to get a likeness taken?"

Cuinn rose to unlock a small casket, and slowly brought out a locket engraved with the rowan tree of Arran Isle. One red ruby was entwined in its branches. Cuinn had designed it especially for Isobel, and had hoped to clasp it around her neck himself. But he relinquished it to Rob and soberly watched him open it.

"This is beautiful."

"I hope Isobel likes it."

"She will appreciate this. I'm sure she will, Cuinn."

"And if her husband asks about it?"

"Should John Comyn ever notice it, she could easily claim it is a picture of herself as a child. She could say the locket was her mother's. The baby has Isobel's hair. And her eyes." They all stopped for a moment to gaze at the remarkable round grey-green eyes that stared contentedly back at them.

"We actually had two portraits done, Rob. My lady mother wanted to keep one. She's become very attached to the child." Sebrina fingered an identical locket she wore on a delicate chain.

"Isobel's was so pretty, I wanted one for myself."

Rob frowned and rubbed his beard again.

"If you are ever in John Comyn's company...."

Sebrina de Seta interrupted him.

"But we never see the man, my lord. We are so far from the rest of Scotland here, I sincerely doubt we'll ever cross paths."

"I worry, too, about your servants talking."

"It's nearly midnight now and the servants are a-bed" said Cuinn. "If you and I take the bairn to Grizel's cottage tonight, Mother will make up a story about you taking Pippa back to the mainland with you. Before we leave here, send your galley 'round to the other side of the island to wait for you. I'll ride down there with you tomorrow to meet it and you can sail from there."

"Don't you fear for Loch Ranza's safety, Cuinn, and that of the Lady Sebrina? Many castles are being threatened. Are you sure you have adequate protection?"

"As Cuinn said, we're in a remote spot here" Sebrina confirmed. "No one would gain very much by taking over this old lodge."

"And we keep a few men-at-arms" added Cuinn. "But the Irish who hold Brodick castle for King Edward are more interested in watching the shipping out on the firth than they are in Loch Ranza. They don't even notice that we still collect rents from our tenants."

"I wish some of these quarrels would get settled" sighed Sebrina. "Maybe the English will leave Scotland soon, and who knows? We Scots just might find a way to stop all our feuding. Maybe it could start with you, Rob, making peace with the Comyns...."

"Mother!"

"Ha! John Comyn and I reconcile? Maybe the sun will set in the east" said Rob grimly, rising from his chair. "Cuinn, it's time we left with the bairn, I'm thinking. Is she ready to go?"

"Yes, she's ready." Sebrina rose. "Come, Pippa."

Rob followed Cuinn outdoors, through the winter-frosted garden toward the stables. A dark figure caught his attention there. A man leaned in the doorway, guzzling from a skin of ale. He had been in a fight recently and wore a black patch over one eye. Rob pulled his hood low over his face.

"You're up late, Dort" remarked Cuinn with surprise. The man shrugged.

"Can't sleep much these nights. Are you going out tonight, Sire?"

Rob interrupted brusquely.

"Isn't it a little cold to be drinking your ale out of doors?"

"Not much warmer at my table."

"Dort lost his wife recently, Rob." Cuinn explained. Rob, tense and wary, gave no apology. "We'll take care of ourselves, Dort"

Cuinn continued. "You've got that boy of yours to care for. Go home. Try to get some sleep."

Dort's good eye slid across to Rob's shadowed face. The high and mighty Cuinn de Seta had called this companion 'Rob'. Dort tucked that piece of information away and turned toward his lonely hut.

*L*ady Sebrina dressed the child for the trip up into the hills.

She had packed the little girl's belongings herself. She tied a warm blue hooded cloak around her, gave her a long tearful hug, and handed her to her father. Cuinn and Rob mounted ponies and Rob settled the child in a sling under his fur-lined mantle. The child's puzzled eyes stared out at the Lady Sebrina with the first shadows of doubt.

"Go with Cuinn, Pippa, and have a nice ride. It will be fun!"

"Don't expect me back before tomorrow evening, Mother. Rob will want to look over Grizel's land in daylight, to see if it will be suitable. We have a lot to talk about with her."

"You're asking her to take on a lot of responsibilities. She will be quite distracted enough, adding a small child to her household. Don't be surprised if she's not enthusiastic about Rob's idea."

Cuinn laughed and nodded toward Rob.

"You don't know how very convincing this man can be."

They rode the ponies across the bridge and headed toward the glen. Sebrina stood shivering, looking after them until they disappeared around the end of the loch. Who could have foreseen how her watchful image would remain forever woven into the fabric of that child's life?

*I*t was black night and a fine snow had fallen. The brooding crags above them were haunted by cold. Rob pulled his mantle tightly about himself, making sure the sleeping child was snug inside. The north wind at their backs blew plumes of snow up into the air like tall, eerie spirits that stalked their ponies. There would be little need to worry about leaving a trail. The wind polished the white landscape and scoured all marks from its pristine surface.

Rob searched the steep terrain ahead. He had expected by now to see a light from Grizel's cottage. Dark sky met trackless snow high above them. Below crawled the black water of the loch.

"You're sure this woman expects us?" Rob called to Cuinn.

"I told her we'd arrive late at night in the first part of the month."

"Maybe she's asleep already."

"Probably."

"Will we have to beat the door down to wake her?"

"Beat the door down?"

"I expect she's hard of hearing?"

"Why would you think that?"

"With a name like Grizel? 'Old gray one'?"

"She gave herself that name."

"I'm a bit worried, truthfully, Cuinn. Will she be too old to care for Eshne?"

"Ah! You're afraid she's too decrepit?"

"I trust your judgment. I do. But I really don't want some old hag taking responsibility for my child."

"No, I expect you don't."

"I mean, I'm sure she's not a hag, but how old is she? Does she have more than three teeth?"

"You'll soon be able to count them for yourself. There, see? There's the smoke from her chimney."

High above them a faint ghost coiled into the heavens. When they finally crested the path, Rob took a moment to look carefully back at the way they'd come. Nothing moved below them. They dropped down into a shallow vale. A white cottage and small stable nestled at the bottom, and directly behind that, the mountain continued its steep climb. Snow shifted back and forth across its face.

A dog, obviously unused to nighttime visitors, was furious at their arrival. They tied their ponies to a rowan tree near the front door. Rob pulled his mantle close around the sleeping child and followed Cuinn.

The front door opened. Cuinn turned with a grin to observe Rob's face. He chuckled when he saw Rob's jaw drop. Grizel, age twenty, stood straight, slim and very beautiful in the doorway, looking at them with sober brown eyes.

She began, in her quiet voice, to speak.

"Hello, Cuinn. Good evening, my lord."

Rob stopped her with a raised hand.

"Please, my lady. Just call me Rob."

"I am honored to have you in my home." She didn't smile. "You–you'll come in?" she asked uncertainly.

The men stamped the snow from their boots and stooped to enter her cottage. Grizel spoke a word to quiet the dog, and offered them a seat on a high-backed bench while she built up the peat fire. Then she perched herself on a stool opposite, her back perfectly straight, her hands folded in her lap. She was fully dressed, even though it was well past midnight, in somber grey as always. A white wimple of exquisite fabric completely hid her hair and neck.

"I was afraid we'd have to wake you, Grizel" apologized Cuinn.

"Actually, no, I've been working late." She gestured to her loom. "I have been restless these last few nights, watching for you. I thought you would be bringing...? Oh!" In Grizel's quiet, composed face, only her eyes showed surprise. She was watching a small pink hand at the opening of Rob's cloak. It tugged at the fur border and the tip of a blue hood appeared. Grizel recognized that blue cloth. She had woven it herself. Beneath the hood, grey-green eyes studied her with a tiny frown that barely puckered the round forehead.

"Ah," Grizel said soberly. "I thought for a moment you had not brought her." Rob opened his cloak and settled the child on his lap.

He pulled off her hood and ran his fingers fondly through her red curls.

The child looked cautiously around the room, then wriggled down and ran to Cuinn, her favorite.

"Look, Pippa!" he said. "Remember Grizel? Grizel, this is Eshne. I shouldn't call her Pippa anymore. Her parents have just given her a name. She doesn't even know she's called Eshne yet."

"Maybe it would be safer to keep the nickname" said Rob.

"Pippa, Grizel is going to take care of you." This information did not interest the child, but the big loom in the corner and the little harp beside it were fascinating. Cuinn stood. "Do you mind if Pippa and I look around, Grizel?"

"Please do, Cuinn. I'd like to offer you some refreshment" said Grizel formally to Rob. "Would you care for some ale?"

"Mother sent some wine, Grizel, along with a bag of flour and some of our cheese" Cuinn told her from across the room. "She sends her love and invites you to visit as often as you can. She'll miss the child terribly."

"I'll make sure to do that. Let me get some bread for the cheese." Grizel rose and crossed to a cupboard. Behind her, Cuinn carried Pippa to where Rob sat. He gestured with his head toward Grizel.

"Do you still want to count her teeth?" he whispered to Rob.

"Actually, I was just thinking that would be a nice way to get acquainted" replied Rob with a grin. "She wears the wimple. Is she a widow?"

"No. She's just modest. She has beautiful hair, actually."

"Aha, so you two have had an amorous relationship?"

"No, but she lived with my family for a while, a few years back."

"So the field is wide open for me, then?"

"Oh, you're thinking you can have all the sonsy maids in the land, eh Robert? I swear, you are right daft, you are!" Cuinn retorted, softly. Rob rolled his eyes and grinned again.

$\mathcal{T}$hey sat at Grizel's table for a light meal. The men pared apples and talked softly, sharing news from the mainland and plans for the future. Grizel was quiet and very solemn. The child soon fell asleep and Rob placed her gently in Grizel's arms. In the first awkward movements Rob had seen her make all night, Grizel walked woodenly to the back of the cottage, laid the little girl on her own bed and covered her. She watched the child for a moment, frowned and turned away.

Cuinn was glad to defer parting until the next day. The men would make their beds in the stable and spend the next morning trying to convince Grizel to join their struggle against the English King Edward.

$\mathcal{W}$hen morning came, Pippa dreamed she smelled something delicious. Then she felt someone kiss her on the nose very gently. She opened her eyes. A black and white dog regarded her from an inch away, his hindquarters swaying rhythmically. He put one paw on the bed but quickly withdrew it. Paws on the bed were not allowed. He licked her little nose again. She giggled. He had never heard a child laugh. He cocked his head and barked.

"Gervaise, come!" The command was stern. Gervaise left.

Pippa sat up. Whose house was this? That Lady came to stand in the doorway. She looked grumpy.

"Kin?" Pippa asked.

"Pardon me?" said that Lady, frowning. She took one hesitant step closer to the bed.

"Kin! Kin!" demanded the child, looking around desperately. She crawled out of bed and ran past the Grumpy Lady. There sat Cuinn, talking with Rob at a table by the window. Relieved, Pippa couldn't get to Cuinn's arms fast enough. Then, her panic forgotten, she turned matter-of-factly to his breakfast and dug in with both hands.

"Hey, wait a minute there!" he laughed. "Grizel will bring you some."

Grizel, standing stiffly by, was glad for his hint. In all her worrying about her new role as guardian, she hadn't stopped to think that this child would be unable to speak plainly. How ever would they communicate?

Making matters worse, Pippa would not say a word to the lady, or even look at her. Cuinn knew better than to insist. When encouraged to thank Grizel for the breakfast, the child squeezed her lip between two fingers and frowned, wondering where Auntie Sebrina could be. She found her toy pony and danced it shyly on Rob's leg, as he had done to hers, and then galloped it merrily around the room. The adults sat and talked again for a long time.

Cuinn was not looking forward to the calamity about to take place. But Pippa was totally unprepared for it. Cuinn was leaving. The Pony Man was leaving, and Pippa was staying with that Grumpy Lady. Cuinn's heart was nearly torn from his body, but he turned away resolutely and left with Rob. Pippa's screams burned in his ear half-way down the glen.

Pippa climbed up and beat her hands on the little window. She was furious. Never in her life had she known more than a hint of anguish.

Grizel, for her part, had suffered much anguish and pain in her youth, both physical and mental. Though that had been long ago, her worst nightmare even now was feeling herself the target of another person's rage. It paralyzed her. Hearing the child's wild screaming brought the old feelings sweeping over her again. The girl was in a frenzy but Grizel was helpless to comfort her. And the noise! She could do nothing to stop the noise. Grizel squeezed her face into her hands. What had she gotten herself into?

The child turned from the window and ran for the door. By a hair's breadth, Grizel got there before her. Pippa refused to let the Grumpy Lady touch her. She fled to the farthest corner and crouched there, hurting to her very quick and sobbing deeply.

*G*rizel's cottage faced the setting sun, but darkness came quickly in early winter. The shadows were gathering and still the child had not come out of her corner.

Nor had Grizel approached her. She felt powerless, weak, unable to move. For the first time in years, she had lost herself in brooding. She imagined herself a helpless girl again. She fell backwards in time, back before she had run away. All over again, her imagination replayed images of her cruel uncle insulting her and punishing her unjustly and painfully, though he always spared his daughter Isobel. All over again Grizel relived her humiliation and loneliness. She felt exhausted, too weak to lift her head. She sat hunched near the table that was still covered with the remains of the morning's meal, but her eyes saw only the past.

There was a scratching at the door. Slowly, in a fog, Grizel rose and opened the door for Gervaise. The dog circled her joyously and pranced to the other side of the room where the child crouched. His tail was a plume of exhilaration, and pennants of fresh air streamed from his coat. He nuzzled companionably at Pippa's inert body, then came to Grizel's knee and sat looking at her expectantly. She didn't even realize he was there, but he never for a second took his eyes from her.

It was, after all, his dinnertime.

Gervaise waited.

He heard a sound behind him. He whipped his head around. The child had stumbled from her corner and was inching toward him slowly, step by tiny step.

But she held no interest for him. He ignored her totally. He focused intently on Grizel, the center of his life.

Grizel had food.

He felt the child's hand on his head but he paid her no attention. He had no use for her. She was nothing to him. He whined quietly and stared at Grizel.

A motion distracted him. He watched the child reaching for a piece of bread from the table.

She came very slowly toward him again. He licked her cheek. She was everything to him and he loved her madly. She offered him the piece of bread and he snatched it. It was gone before he remembered his manners. He glanced, shamefaced, at Grizel, expecting a reprimand but her face registered nothing. The child offered him another piece of bread. He took only a bite this time, polite even though his jaws trembled with eagerness. To his acute dismay, the child ate the rest.

He watched her crawl back up onto a chair, where she reached for a bigger slice of bread. Gervaise opened his mouth expectantly but Pippa gave him only a light tap on the nose. His concentration was a pinpoint as the child walked with the bread, slowly, slowly to Grizel's knee.

Pippa looked up into the Grumpy Lady's vacant face. Maybe the Lady was sad. Maybe she would like to eat something.

She offered the bread. No response.

She stretched higher, made a little sound to entice the Lady to eat. Nothing.

The child tried to crawl onto Grizel's lap.

Then and there the woman's injured spirit ceased its wandering in the past. Grizel recoiled in her chair. Horrified, she realized there was a child here, in her house, touching her. She had forgotten her.

Undaunted, Pippa climbed up and held the piece of bread next to the lady's lips.

"Good" said Pippa. She nudged the lady's mouth with the crust. The Lady's brown eyes were smoldering.

"Come on" Pippa urged. They regarded each other eye to eye.

Grizel took a small bite.

Satisfied, Pippa curled herself into the curve of Grizel's lap and thoughtfully bit off another mouthful. The dog whined very softly so Pippa held the piece of bread out for him. Having spent the entire day pouting, now Pippa was feeling playful. She pulled the bread away each time Gervaise lunged for it. Grizel had always disciplined her dog very strictly, and did not like to see Pippa teasing him. A scolding came automatically to mind.

It faded before she spoke. She could not bring herself to speak harshly to the child.

But Grizel felt sick with remorse. She had made a grave mistake. Why, why had she promised Sebrina that this child could stay in her home? She knew that this would not work. She had no idea how to care for someone. She would have to give her back. A child needed care, attention, needed goodness knew what else. It was more than she could manage.

The child leaned back and rested her head under Grizel's chin. Grizel looked at the red curls lying against the small white neck. They were pretty little curls.

Tentatively, awkwardly, her fingertips touched a lock of red hair. Grizel bit her lip. She let a little ringlet coil around her finger. It attached itself, beginning to possess her now.

She touched the child's shoulder. Just one touch. Slowly, cautiously, she slipped her fingers down to the plump little hands.

What was she doing? What did she think she was doing?

Her body was moving of its own volition. Her arms reached, wrapping themselves completely around the warm bundle on her lap. Her lips touched the satiny red head. How well the child fit the curves of her body.

Grizel's taut body relaxed.

She sat still. Very still.

For the first time in her life she was holding a small human being.

She had not taken this baby into her home because she wanted a child. She certainly did not want a child. She had agreed to the arrangement most reluctantly, and solely because Sebrina de Seta, her only friend in the world, had asked it of her. This little girl, Sebrina had explained, had to be kept safe. Grizel had once begged Sebrina for refuge and Sebrina was asking Grizel to return the favor.

Could she, Grizel, offer that miraculous thing, that hopeless fairy tale from her own childhood – a safe haven? It was a tremendous burden. Was this even possible for her who had lived so long alone, who had never known many adults and no children, ever? When she thought about it, she realized there was much she had never known.

At that thought, something crumbled inside her. A flood of emotion came from nowhere. Tears, unspilled for years, ran over her cheeks and fell glistening among the child's curls. Her embrace tightened. Grizel began to hum and rock gently in her chair.

She vowed with sudden ferocity that she would care for this child and, if need be, protect her with her dying breath.

And she was as good as her word.

1301
Gleinn Eason Biorach

*A*fter that first difficult day, their lives locked together like pieces of a puzzle. They lived on an imaginary border, halfway between the wild mountaintops and the civilized life at Loch Ranza lodge. Their cottage was hidden in a little spring-fed valley high above the floor of the glen known as Gleinn Eason Biorach, in the shadow of the mountain called Beinn Bhreac. The cottage could be seen from the path below, but only if you knew where to look. The folk who lived on the island were aware that it had once, in happier days, been used as a stable for picnickers and hunting parties. But never did anyone need to go there now. Rarely did anyone follow the faint track that passed below the cottage unless they were hunting the red deer. Even sheep never strayed that way. What few travelers there were on the island kept always to the path that skirted the shore.

The high valley that Grizel and Pippa lived in had its own special music. A little burn ran clear and cold, from Loch na Davie all the way down the glen, and they could hear it singing in the spring. In the summertime, the rowans hanging on the sides of their vale whispered all night long. In the winter, they heard only the wind, and it was the only music they wanted.

It was usually just the two of them, all alone except for a goat, a pony, some chickens and the dog Gervaise. Yet they were so busy, they rarely felt lonely.

Their little cottage was covered with pink roses in the summer, and was sheltered all year by a rowan tree, planted near the door to keep witches away. It was a very good tree. The best tree, Grizel said, because they had never once, either of them, ever seen a witch near that house. The old stables had been made into a snug barn for the animals. Fortunately, at least in Pippa's opinion, Gervaise was allowed to stay with them in the house, even though, strictly speaking, he was an animal. His duties, because his ears were very sharp, were to give warning of the few visitors that came along and to terrorize any deer that dared set hoof in their vale. Pippa knew for certain that Gervaise had sharp ears. After all, they came to a perfect point, didn't they?

Grizel thought it was important for Pippa learn to read and write, so there were lessons every afternoon. And Grizel had a harp. At first she hardly ever played it and Pippa was never to touch it. But Pippa begged so hard, and promised to be so very careful, that one day Grizel showed her a little tune. They took turns playing it every evening after that.

Sometimes they went visiting at Loch Ranza. Once Rob visited too, while they were there, bringing horses for Cuinn's stable. They all went outside to greet him when he arrived. He seemed so happy to see Pippa that he tossed her into the air and caught her in his arms with a mighty laugh.

A lad stood watching them from the other side of the courtyard. The boy couldn't take his eyes off the lass with the terrible red hair. He had watched her many times before. He was always surprised at, and maybe a bit jealous of, the attention that Cuinn gave her. Even that tall stern man, that visitor, made a fuss over her. The boy was very curious about the way the grown-ups treated her. If she was ignored, if she was ever punished at random, whenever the whim came over someone, the boy never saw it.

The red-haired girl never noticed the boy. He hovered in the shadows, pummeled by pangs of envy and longing. To step forward and be welcomed into their family would have meant everything to him. It was his favorite daydream. Of course he spoke of it to no one. Dreams were not something most people associated with this lad. He was usually obedient, said little and asked for nothing. To everyone, he was just Tom, always underfoot, a tough, sturdy laddie with no special talents, whose only fault was that he seemed to drag accidents in his wake the way a fishing boat drags a flock of seagulls.

Tom had turned away from watching the de Seta family and slumped against a fencepost. He looked up. Cuinn stood before him, asking him to help with the new horses. Tom's heart flooded with delight. But the girl hardly even looked at him. All she did was run around in that fey little feathered hat the entire day with her huge mane of red hair billowing in the wind. Tom was determined to keep his distance as well. He didn't care about this lass. Not at all. Did the earthworm care for the flower?

She surprised him, though. After he finished helping Cuinn, he turned around and nearly stepped on her.

He stopped short.

She smiled.

Her eyes.... Suddenly he was unable to move a muscle, a rare enough predicament for a lad his age. He tried to turn away but tripped over his own feet.

Her laughter felt like a tickle and made him laugh too.

*U*p in the cottage in the glen, Grizel was always very busy weaving fabric to sell. She and Pippa seldom left home except to deliver Grizel's fabric to someone or to pick up big hanks of wool and flax from the lady who spun the yarn. These trips were wonderful. They would take picnics, and sometimes in the winter they would be invited to stay overnight in the homes of people who lived down by the shore. Some of these people lived so near to each other they could walk from house to house. That seemed very strange. There were children to play with there, which was wonderful, and Pippa noticed that the music in the air down there was different, too. It sang itself constantly, the music of wind over the icy sea.

A few people visited them in their cottage in the glen. Cuinn and Aunt Sebrina came up now and then, and sometimes Rob came too, more for reasons to do with horses than to spend time them, Pippa thought. She had the feeling that Rob did not like her very well. He often chided her for bad manners, which never failed to annoy her. Many times he seemed quiet and too tired or grumpy to talk to her. But after a while he would ask Grizel to play her harp and Pippa to sing, or Cuinn would urge him to tell a funny story. Then Rob wouldn't seem so gruff and Pippa could like him, but only a little.

*P*ippa was happy to find out that the grimy lad with the bright brown eyes lived near Aunt Sebrina. So she could count on him being always around. His name was Tommy. He was two or three years older than she was and he knew how to take care of all the animals and was allowed to ride the ponies with Cuinn. Now whenever Pippa visited Loch Ranza, she followed Tommy as he went about his chores. His father was called Dort the gardener. Pippa wasn't sure what had happened to Dort's face and she was never supposed to stare but she could hardly help it. He wore a patch, a black patch, for the shocking reason that he had only one eye. How that had come about, no one would say. He looked so scary that she simply had to stare, but only from a distance. She preferred to keep away from him anyway. She could tell that Dort did not care for children. He seemed to like Aunt Sebrina's vegetables and animals better than he liked people, better even than his own son Tommy. That's what Pippa thought but Grizel said it really wasn't true.

It was different for Pippa. She never doubted that Grizel loved her very much. Every night at bedtime, Grizel would tell Pippa that she loved her more than Tuncan Tell. Though just who this was, this Tuncan person, this rival for Grizel's love, was a complete mystery.

March 1303
Loch Ranza

𝓟ippa had a clear early memory of Tommy. She had just turned six years old. The moment she laid eyes on him that day, he was doing the two things she would always remember him for: making her laugh and bumbling headlong into disaster. On that particular cold spring morning, Auntie Sebrina said she would take Pippa out for a walk on the new garden path at Loch Ranza. Pippa was told not to step off the path into the mud. They had spread manure on the garden, a necessary evil, as Pippa knew well. But Loch Ranza's manure had a special quality. It made you gag with its terrible smell.

"That's the pig's contribution" explained Sebrina and Pippa's prejudice against pigs began that day.

So they were out taking a dander, looking for the first green shoots of spring. As she and Auntie picked their way along the narrow path through the kailpatch, a scullery maid named Susan came from the opposite direction. That morning Susan had ordered Tommy, the gardener's son, to help her. He shuffled along behind her with his head bent, lugging a large basket of eggs. The wind blowing across the loch was sneaking over the garden wall, so even though Susan held a thin cloak tightly about her shoulders, it billowed out behind her sturdy body. Auntie stopped to talk. Susan turned suddenly to Tommy.

"Set that there basket down afore –Careful with that! Are ye dreich?" In one motion she grabbed the basket from the boy and smacked his ear. She set the basket of eggs on the path.

Tommy skulked behind Susan's ample skirts. At intervals, his impish brown eyes would appear and disappear, peeking out at Pippa. The wind raked waves into his golden brown hair and when he smiled, there was a tiny dimple beneath each eye, right near the top of his rosy-tan cheek. Pippa cocked her head and watched, curious.

Now he had his back to her, his restless hands in his pockets. With his toe, he was absent-mindedly dislodging a flagstone from the path. Susan turned to him without warning and whacked him on the back of his head.

"Leave that rock be, or I'll skelp ya agin" she threatened. "Put it back! Yer father will have a fair-sized fit! He jest put those there." Tommy bent to replace the stone. He stamped on it several times so it would go back into place.

"Quit it out, ye great coof! Stand quiet" ordered Susan, cuffing him so hard she nearly knocked him over. Pippa watched in amazement.

As soon as Susan turned her back, Pippa caught Tommy's eye and smiled. She felt a little sorry for him. He beamed at her, tipped upside down and cartwheeled his feet into the air. He was walking on his hands! Pippa laughed gleefully, but suddenly he crumpled into a heap. Splat! He fell into the mud of the garden. He was on his feet again, quick as lightning. He stuffed his hands back in his pockets and studied the air. Pippa made a face. From head to foot he had bits of manure stuck to him. Tommy glanced over, gawping in alarm at the two women and ready to duck Susan's punishing hand. Miraculously, they hadn't noticed. They had their backs to him and were pointing toward the new garden plots.

Relieved, he looked slyly over at Pippa. She giggled silently. He somersaulted onto his hands again and swung his feet into the air. Unfortunately, the momentum of those large feet carried his legs up and right on over his head. He fell flat on his back and his feet thumped into the big basket that Susan had left on the path. Pippa heard a sickening crunch. The boy squeezed his eyes shut, then cracked them open to peer anxiously at his feet. Not a doubt about it, they were dripping with egg yolk.

Pippa and Sebrina came immediately to crouch at his side. They were afraid he had been hurt. He had landed so hard. Was he sure his head didn't hurt? His back? Susan should take him over to the well, Milady decided, and clean him up, then bring him to the kitchen to have a warm drink and some cake. That would make him feel better. When he was clean, Milady herself would examine his back to make sure he hadn't been injured in any way.

He was afraid to mention, even to the sympathetic lady, that it wasn't so much his back that felt odd at this moment, but the inside of his chest. That look in the little lass's grey-green eyes – that look had stopped his heart.

A glammer! The little witch! She must surely have put a glammer on him.

He looked up, dazed, to confront Susan's scowling glare. She hauled him to his feet and dragged him, covered in egg yolk and manure, off to the well.

When, later, he appeared at the kitchen door of the lodge, he was soaking wet, shivering and scrubbed until he was red. The Lady Sebrina drew him toward the fire and dried his dripping head herself. Milady and the lass seemed truly concerned about him. So he pulled up his shirt to show them another bruise he had gotten yesterday when he tripped over a hoe in the garden. Sebrina was taken aback. He had to point out yesterday's bruise from among a whole constellation of others. Where had those come from? She hid her dismay and instantly offered Tom another cake.

As for Tom, he had the strangest good-luck feeling for the entire rest of the day. He hardly noticed the angry thumps he received later from his father for being a doited show-off.

May 1304
Loch Ranza

*I*t was a cool grey afternoon in early May. A stiff breeze from the southwest beat upon the boat struggling to make its way into the loch. Cuinn stood on the stony beach with his legs spread apart and his hands on his hips, watching the boat's progress. It was so windy, even the loch was running with whitecaps today. Cuinn cursed. They would have to wait until it was calm to unload their precious cargo. The very thought of waiting was torture to him.

Tom, eleven years old, came out through the garden gate and spotted Cuinn down on the beach. He ran across the sand to stand beside him. He spread his legs apart. He put his hands on his hips. He sensed Cuinn's excitement and looked up. Cuinn was grinning.

"That boat, Sire. It comes to the lodge?"

"Yes, it does."

"They be bringing us somethin'?"

"Yes, they are, Tom."

"What is it?" Cuinn was obviously distracted. "Sire, what's on board?"

"Hobbins."

"Hobbins?" Tom's brow wrinkled. Whatever Hobbins was, thought Tom, Cuinn seemed truly fashed about 'em.

*A*h, but weren't they creatures of delight, those hobbins?

When they finally came ashore, Tom was struck dumb. He raced after Cuinn and pulled on his sleeve.

"Sire! Sire!" Cuinn didn't have time to give him so much as a look. Tom yelled. "My lord! Sire! Those're the hobbins? They be stayin' here?"

"No, they're not staying. Can you help me, Tom? Take this whip and urge them through the gate. But just wave it at them. Don't use it on them, no matter what."

When all twelve were safely inside the gate, Tom climbed the fence to watch them roam excitedly in their new paddock. Cuinn came and leaned his arms on the top of the gate.

"What do you think, Tom?"

"They're right lovely, Sire. From Ireland, are they?"

"Mostly, they are. A couple from Wales."

"They're yourn?"

"No! No, they're not mine. We're going to drive them up the glen to Grizel's cottage."

Tom's smile vanished.

"Why?" He had a sudden pang of jealously so intense, he almost fell off the fence. "These be all for Pippa?" he asked in a strained voice.

Cuinn threw back his head and laughed.

"Hardly, Tom. These are very valuable horses."

"Then why take them all the way up into the glen?"

"Because we're hiding them there. It's against the law to bring them into Scotland. The king would have our heads taken off if he knew. He wants all the Irish horses for himself and his armies. We'll keep them up in the glen for a fortnight or so, then some night we'll ship them over to the mainland."

"They're special?"

"Very special. They're Hobbins, meant for battle."

"Battle? They're bitsy little things, though, ain't they?"

"That's just it, Tom. They're much smaller than warhorses, but very sturdy and quick. The Irish and the Welsh archers have been using them for years for scouting and for quick raids over hilly ground. They're ideal for Scotland."

"But why?"

"They can carry a rider right in close to a knight wearing heavy armor. A few quick stabs with the sword before the knight even knows he's there, and then the hobbin is out of reach again. The knight won't even have time to turn his big warhorse before his ghost is roaming over Machrie moor."

Tom waved an imaginary sword in the air.

"But the armor," he pointed out, "ain't it too heavy? Such wee li'l horses can't carry a bloke wearin' armor."

"Their riders, the hobelars, don't even bother to wear armor, most of them. Speed, lightness. Those are the hobbins' assets." He glanced down at Tom. The longing on the boy's face was so poignant, Cuinn found himself making a suggestion before he even had time to think about what he was saying.

"You could help us feed them tonight, if you get your chores done."

"Truly?"

"Then, if your father can spare you, you could ride with us when we take them up into the glen." Tommy's eyes popped. "We must get them all fed before sundown so they can start for the glen as soon as it gets dark. We have to leave before moonrise."

"Tonight? I can go? Does ye mean it, Sire?"

"Only if you finish all your other duties" Cuinn warned sternly. "You can help Grimm with the hobbins but you'll have to do exactly what he tells you. He'll expect you to work hard tonight." Tom turned to climb down from the fence but snagged his foot on a board and thudded to the ground. Cuinn's eyebrows shot up. Tom jumped up and dusted himself off.

"I'll be braw as can be, Sire!"

"No carelessness."

"No, Sire."

"We don't want any accidents. This is serious work. We'll be moving fast. We can't afford to be caught with these horses here at Loch Ranza."

"I ken just what yer sayin', Sire, truly I do."

June 1304
Gleinn Eason Biorach

Summer washed over the island that year in waves of fragrance that intoxicated even the most fousty of souls. Shining white clouds blossomed into cathedrals or sailing ships and then transformed into roses or cows the moment someone turned to look up at them. Near the shore, insects danced up and down grassblade highways and bindweed crawled through the hedges while, up in the glens, pink petals of the wild rose dropped silently into burns and, like miniature coracles, were swept over noisy waterfalls. Vegetables fattened in the kailpatch under the kind old sun and children's cheeks turned to pink gold. Brown trout lazed at the bottoms of their pools and if there were troubles in the land, they touched Arran Isle as lightly as a midge on water.

Pippa, now that she was seven years old, knew right where to find the mint in their garden, since she was the one who watered it with her little bucket. Fat bumblebees swerved out of her way and scrabbled noisily in the ragged-robin blossoms while she picked the very finest leaves and put them carefully into her basket. They smelled so wonderful. It was a special day. Cuinn and Auntie Sebrina were bringing Rob, and Tommy, too, along with a herd of horses. She hoped Tommy liked mint.

Gervaise, sitting nearby, suddenly tore out to the front of the cottage, barking crazily. They must be here already! Overjoyed, Pippa jumped up and dropped her basket. Mint leaves scattered everywhere. She looked down regretfully, but abandoned them in her rush to follow the dog. He could tell when someone was coming, even if they were still far, far down the glen. Pippa flung open the door of the cottage and poked her head inside.

"Grizel! They're coming!" she hollered.

"Yes, I assumed as much from all the racket." She came out to stand with Pippa on the lip of the vale, holding her hand and watching the group plodding up the steep path.

Sebrina led the way on her pony so she could keep ahead of the cloud of dust that coated Tommy, Rob, Grimm the constable, and Cuinn. It rose thickly over another herd of Irish horses, sixteen this time, that were going to stay in their hidden vale.

Pippa jumped up and down, calling to the visitors. Gervaise waved his tail banner and grinned.

"Aren't you two just the picture, with that mass of exquisite rosebuds behind you? And the rowan trees! It's beautiful up here today" exclaimed Sebrina, dismounting. "How are you, Caela?" Sebrina hugged her friend. She always called Grizel that odd name.

Pippa ran to greet Cuinn but stopped in her tracks.

"Why does Tommy get to bring the horses?" Pippa demanded, suddenly irritable.

"Pippa, don't be rude" admonished Rob.

She glared at him. What right did he have to tell her how to behave? Cuinn reached his hand down to her.

"Now don't get all crabbit, me dearie" Cuinn chided her. "Tom's helping us. Come on up here. You can help too. Ride with me." Aunt Sebrina held her foot and Cuinn swung her into the saddle in front of him. Pippa looked archly back at Tommy, who smiled nonetheless. Grimm had opened the gate and they herded the horses through. They were skittish as newts in a witch's garden. Tom rode among them, clucking encouragement.

Leaning on the fence later, Cuinn and Rob watched them like proud fathers. Tom mirrored every move the men made.

Rob had one foot on the fence. "Tom, keep an eye on that one. See? He favors his right foreleg. You might have to bind it."

"I will" Tom assured Rob. His foot went nonchalantly to the fence.

"It's important. Don't forget!" Rob scolded.

Tom shrank a bit.

"Yes, my lord."

"We can't afford to lose even one of these creatures. They cost a fortune."

"No, my lord."

"Dinna fuss, mon. Tom will take good care of them until we come for them" Cuinn assured Rob.

"We'll have to leave them here 'til the solstice, at least" said Rob, turning to Grizel. "I don't know when we'll be able to borrow a boat. We really need to get one of our own. We'll have to wait for a calm, dark night to take them to Ardrossan."

"By the end of this summer, we should have a pretty respectable herd of hobbins, don't you think, Rob?"

"All we need now are the men to ride them."

Tom opened his mouth to speak but Cuinn silenced him.

"You, my good lad, are still too young for battle. Besides, we need you here."

"I can ride them!" Pippa chirped.

Tom looked away to hide a smile.

"Hopefully we won't be reduced to taking wee little lassies to war" said Rob. "Though, who knows, it may come to that." At the time, he thought he was joking. Rob took his foot off the fence. "Did I hear someone say something about supper earlier? I'm starving!"

Grizel and Sebrina were arranging platters on the table under the rowan tree. Tom wandered over to Grizel.

"Have ye seed where I fell and cut me knee?" he asked her conversationally, pulling up his pantleg and beginning a long tale of woe. She knelt beside him, full of sympathy.

Pippa ran to the table and looked up sharply when Rob spoke to her.

"Do you always help yourself before the adults have eaten?" Rob chided.

"Grizel and I eat all our meals together. She never gets mean and bossy about that."

"Pippa!" Cuinn laughed. "That sounds a little impertinent."

Pippa began to protest but he silenced her and she slumped into a pout.

"Whew, it's a warm day today!" Rob pulled off his mantle. Pippa's eyes flew open.

"Oh, you noticed my friend?" Rob asked. From the pocket of his tunic the head of a little puppy stared out at her. A tiny pink tongue made rhythmic motions under a wet black nose. Pippa began to squeal. Gervaise ran back and forth nervously.

Rob told Pippa she must sit near him so he could show her how to properly hold a puppy.

"We'll have to give him a chance to get used to you" he explained. "He already likes me a lot."

"He rode up here in your pocket?"

"I carried him exactly where I carried you when I brought you to Grizel."

"I came in your pocket?" Rob laughed, a rare belly laugh.

"No, but I held you here, right against my heart."

"Truly?"

"Ai, truly I'm telling you."

Pippa frowned at him, puzzled.

He handed her the puppy carefully. He was as soft as a ball of Grizel's finest wool.

"Look how small he is!"

"He's a totty one, for certain sure."

"What's his name, Rob?"

"Since he is going to live with you, you'll have to name him."

"He's going to live with me?"

"Do you think he would like that?" Pippa's eyes were luminous orbs.

"I think Tott will be his name" she declared, "because he's the little one." So Tott it was. "And I will love him" declared Pippa, just as Grizel told her every night, "more than tongue can tell."

*T*om stayed with Grizel and Pippa for several weeks that summer, blending himself skillfully into his adopted family. He slept above the stable and Cuinn came every few days whenever there were horses that he needed to check on.

When they had finished their chores and Pippa had finished her lessons, she and Tommy would ride their island ponies to one of the little upland lochs near the top of the glen.

Pippa, though it would have pained her deeply her to say so, was envious of Tom's riding abilities. They knew a few places in the glen where the rocks were sparse and they could race at a gallop, but Pippa could never catch Tommy. The worst part of that was his constant bragging. He was insufferable. He made her burn with irritation. She tried so hard to do everything he did. If he leaned in the saddle to urge the pony, or adjusted his cap and pushed back his hair, she copied him. If he spit on the ground at the end of a dusty race, she did too. She rose fearlessly to every challenge he issued.

He watched her too, from the corner of his eye. An eager learner, Tom was also a natural teacher. He skillfully coaxed better riding skills from her. She began to improve.

"Your riding is much better now, Pippa" Tom told her. He had just bested her in a race once again. It was high summer and they were riding their ponies at a walking pace along the burn that ran down the glen. Pippa was not enjoying herself.

"What are you talking about? I could always ride much better than you any day, Tommy!"

"I was only saying..."

"You are being so 'pertinent! Again!" Tom rolled his eyes and sighed.

"Whatever that means." Where did she get these words?

"Well, just quit doing it. You are so mean, Tom." She scowled mightily at him and urged her pony ahead.

"Hey, Pippa, hey" Tom called, trying to appease. "Whatever it is, I promise to quit doing it.

"*I*'ve had an idea, Pippa" said Grizel a few days later. She peeked over Pippa's shoulder to examine the embroidery she was working on for Aunt Sebrina.

"Your stitches look nice and even. Pippa. So Tommy tells me your riding has improved a lot this summer. Has he been helping you?"

"He never helps me! I'm doing it all by myself. No one ever shows me anything. Tommy gets riding lessons from Cuinn, but I have to figure it all out by myself."

"Oh? And how do you do that?"

"I just follow Tom and watch him and whatever he does…" She paused and squinted up at Grizel.

"So Tom is helping you, in a way, just by letting you ride with him?" Pippa heaved a great sigh.

"I guess" she growled. "Maybe."

"Well my idea was that, since he's helping you with your riding, why don't you and I help him with his reading?"

"Tommy? He won't be able to do it." Grizel's raised eyebrow spoke volumes. "Grizel, he doesn't even know his letters."

"I'm happy to work with him then. I just thought you might want to help."

Pippa stitched in silence for a minute. Tommy made her tetchy sometimes. Her embroidery floss knotted up and she threw her hoop aside in disgust.

"What does Tommy need to learn to read for, anyway?"

Grizel put a hand on her hip and looked at Pippa pointedly.

"Well, he …he'll never…" Pippa floundered. She knew she was being unkind.

"I was thinking" explained Grizel, "that someday, if Cuinn goes off to battle and doesn't come back .. " Pippa looked up, alarmed. "…just because he is too busy fighting, Tom could help Sebrina with her book-keeping and managing. Tom would be someone she could trust and he would take good care of her."

"All right!" Pippa crossed her arms and thumped them against her waist. "I'll help him. He won't want me to, though. He tries to do everything better than me."

"No harm in just asking him if he'd like to learn. Why don't you see what he says?"

"He'll say 'no'. He will, I know he will."

Two days later, without preamble, Pippa blurted the question to Tommy.

"So. You never said you wanted me to help you at all. I don't suppose you do, do you? Just Grizel?"

"Help me? With what?"

"Grizel told you.'"

"No, she said nowt to me."

"I knew you'd say that." She couldn't bring herself to make the offer. "You just want her to do it." She slumped her shoulders lower.

"What are ye going on about?"

"Helping you learn to read, you great galoot."

"Read? Truly? Would ya learn me? I'd like that, Pippa."

Pippa scowled darkly, hunching her back into a U-shape.

But thus inauspiciously they began. In a month, Tom could pick his way along haltingly, following words with a grubby forefinger. By the end of autumn, he could read and write with ease anything Pippa could manage.

Also by the end of that autumn, Pippa actually passed Tom in a race up the glen on their ponies. She was amazed, and maybe a little humbled, to hear Tommy tell everyone about it.

August, 1304
Loch Ranza

A visit to Loch Ranza lodge was always a treat for both Grizel and Pippa. At home in their little cottage, Grizel worked hard. She grew and preserved their food, kept the house, themselves and their clothing clean. She wove the cloth that she delivered to several tiny villages on the island. Loch Ranza lodge, on the other hand, had a staff of servants. Although the English army had forced the Lady Sebrina from her large, comfortable home at Brodick castle on the east coast of the island, she had managed to take her most loyal servants with her to Loch Ranza. They worked devotedly for her, trying hard to make a home out of the bare hunting lodge at the edge of a wild loch.

Sebrina invited Grizel often to Loch Ranza, partly so she could visit with her and Pippa, and partly so Grizel would have at least one day of rest now and then. They went for long walks on the shore, and talked endlessly by fireside and table. Grizel's face lost some of its gaunt tiredness after a couple of days there.

For Pippa, too, these visits were high points. To her surprise, she seemed to enjoy seeing Tommy every day. He always had something interesting to tell her. One muggy summer day, for example, he told her some fascinating news about herself. The two of them were wading in the river, near where it flowed into the loch. They stopped to watch a family of otters splashing about.

"Look, the big one never leaves the little ones." Pippa pointed with a stick. "He's taking care of them."

"That's the mother, that's why."

"Do you think?" They watched for awhile then perched on a log on the sandy bank. Pippa decided she wanted to share a secret piece of family history. "I don't have a mother. Did you know that? Grizel is really my guardian."

"Everyone has to have a mum."

"No, I don't think everyone has one. Cuinn told me so. You don't have a mother."

"I did have one, but she is gone to the graveyard."

"Was she nice?"

"I 'member her only a wee bit."

"Too bad she had to die."

"Ai, I wish she didn't. It's nice to think about her."

"So who takes care of you? Just Dort?"

"Yeah, me dad."

"I don't have a father, either."

"Sure ye do."

"No. I don't."

"Everyone has to have a father and a mother. Cuinn is probably yer father."

Pippa sat back, her eyes wide.

"Cuinn?"

"Sure. It's what everybody knows. They all say it."

"Do you think so?"

"How is it they don't tell you these things? What, it's a big secret? Everybody else knows."

"Knows what?"

"Who your mother and father is."

"How do they know?"

"'Cuz everybody says so. You were born here at Loch Ranza."

"I was?"

"And me own mum was your nurse, 'fore she died. And then one night Cuinn took you up to Grizel's cot to live. My dad saw him take you. And Rob– Lord Carrick was with him. So me dad figures it had to be –"

"Why doesn't Cuinn stay with us all the time then, like your father does?" Pippa demanded, beginning to feel resentful.

"I don't know. Ask the old ladies. They know ever'thin'."

"What old ladies?"

"The old ladies in them fishing huts. They get their heads all close together and have a clash about it many a time. I heerd 'em."

Tom saw Pippa struggling to understand. She got up and wandered down the beach a way. He wondered what it would be like to have Cuinn for a father. He wished Cuinn were...no, better not say that. Pippa was very lucky. Tom swished his toes through the water. He lashed the river with a stick.

Maybe one day when he grew up Cuinn would ask Tom to be his squire. Tom whapped the water hard. They would go off to the mainland to fight and hunt. Tom's stick sliced the air. He would call Pippa "my lady". Pippa was a girl so she would never be able to go with them. He stabbed a tree stump on the shore and whipped it soundly. Just Tom and Cuinn and the other men. If they ever came home to Loch Ranza, though, Tom would never scold the children who lived here, and he would make sure Pippa gave them cakes every day.

Whoosh! He slipped on a rock and soaked half his tunic. He would never let anyone drink so much ale he would get himself blootered and beat children with straps.

Tom stood quiet at last, up to his calves in cool river water. He looked back toward the lodge.

And Pippa would come out every day to watch him ride around on his own horse, a beautiful hobbin, with his own bow and arrows on his shoulder. Maybe he would even wear a hat. With a big brim. And maybe one of those big feathers.

Well, maybe forget the feather.

$\mathcal{P}$ippa decided she would ask candidly what she wanted to know. She and Grizel had returned to their cottage in the glen, and were sitting at the table under their rowan tree after dinner. The tree's berries were fattening and the evening was plump with summer's scents. Even the early stars hung, like ripe fruit, heavily in the lavender sky.

"Grizel, remember when you told me you weren't my mother?"

Grizel's heart thumped once, but she tried to answer calmly. "I'm your guardian, my love."

Disappointed, Pippa couldn't bring herself to be forthright after all. She had so wished Grizel had not been telling her the truth before. If Grizel wasn't her mother, she couldn't think of anyone else that she would like to belong to, except Aunt Sebrina.

"Is it true, Grizel? You really aren't my mother? Are you sure?" Pippa blinked when Grizel laughed.

"We're related, but I'm not your mother. I'm very sure."

"How can you be sure?"

"Because you were born in the Rowan Month but I never laid eyes on you until the Month of the Alder. You didn't come here to live until you were almost three years old."

"But I could still be yours."

Grizel put her cup down.

"Pippa, you are the child of my heart, and if I had ever had a child, I would want her to be you. But, sadly, I never did. Someone else is your real mother."

"Who? Auntie Sebrina?"

Grizel shook her head.

"No, not Sebrina. Remember we agreed to talk about this when you were a little older?" She could hardly bear the puzzled look on Pippa's face. Why couldn't she just leave the subject alone? Grizel wanted to go on just as they always had. No explanations, no difficult questions. And no choices. Please, no choices. Feeling a bit sheepish for being so evasive, Grizel rose from the table. "Come inside. I have something to give you."

At the back of a cupboard she found a little black enameled box. She handed it to Pippa.

"I think you are old enough to have this now."

Pippa opened the box. Inside was a fine gold chain. She lifted it out. A tiny golden charm dangled from it, a little rowan tree.

"This was a gift given to your mother from her close friend, and she wanted you to have it when you were old enough." Grizel hung it around Pippa's neck. "Isn't it nice to have a gift from her?"

"I guess so. Yes. It's nice."

"You must keep it forever."

"But why did my mother give me away?"

"When you're older you'll understand better."

"Well anyway, I know who my father is."

"Oh do you?"

"Tommy told me."

"Tommy told you." Grizel regarded her thoughtfully. "And how does Tommy know?"

"His father told him."

"His father told him?" An angry look flashed across Grizel's face. "He had no right to do that."

"I don't mind. I wanted Cuinn to be my father anyway."

"Cuinn?"

"He should be here, living with us, though. Do you think I should call him 'father', Grizel?"

Grizel was upset. She thought they had touched on enough sore subjects for one night. "It is not a good idea at all, Pippa. Cuinn is not going to live here. And you should just call him Cuinn." She went to clean off the table.

Pippa was miffed at first, then she smiled to herself. Grizel hadn't actually denied that Cuinn was her father, had she? That could only mean one thing! Now she knew for certain. She had very cleverly tricked Grizel. She would wait a few days, then try to find out why it had to be such a big secret.

The whole question of fatherhood was confirmed in her mind when next they saw Cuinn. Pippa was sure that he was her father because right away he took special notice of the gold chain around her neck.

"What do we have here?" He held the golden rowan tree on the palm of his hand. How long ago had he given it to Isobel, he was wondering? Seven, maybe eight years ago? All that time gone by, and he still had not found anyone who measured up to that woman.

Pippa watched his face carefully. He frowned, lost in thought for a minute. She put her cheek against his arm.

"You look sad. What are you thinking about?" she finally asked.

He looked at her and suddenly his face cleared.

"I'm thinking how lucky it was that you came here to live with us."

Pippa hugged him hard. She loved knowing that Cuinn was her father, even if he was a secret.

September 1305
Gleinn Eason Biorach

The shrieking wind whipped a furious deluge of rain from the stormclouds that cowered over the glen. Cuinn and Tom ran into Grizel's cottage, stamping their boots on the stone floor. They had ridden up just ahead of the storm, dragging a small wagonload of fodder behind a pair of oxen. Fortunately they had managed to get it all safely stowed in the stable just before the rain started.

"It's dreechit out there" said Tom.

"It's pouring cats and dogs!" exclaimed Cuinn.

As if on cue, the dogs, Tott and Gervaise, began to bark at the door. It might seem unlikely in this weather, the dogs insisted, but heed our warning! Someone is riding through the glen. In some things dogs are experts, and their certainty gave them authority. Someone was definitely out there.

If this were indeed true, no one should stay in the cottage. Without a moment's hesitation, they all dropped what they were doing. They frantically grabbed what wraps were to hand and ran out the back door. Commanding the dogs to wait in the stable, they pounded up a path hidden in the rocks behind the cottage. It was running with mud and Pippa's boots were filthy in a moment. The wind tore savagely at the cloaks they held over their heads. They climbed a light ladder hidden under a narrow rock ledge. By the time they had all reached the ledge, drawn the ladder up and wedged themselves into a tiny cavern between the boulders, no one had yet ridden into their vale.

Inside their dark cave in the rocks, the sounds of the storm were muffled. The four of them sat on the ground, shoulder to shoulder, panting and soaked to the skin. Their ears strained for the sound of hoof beats.

"The dogs will be ..." Pippa began to whisper to Tom.

"Shh!" Cuinn cautioned.

He had often warned them that, in these unsettled times, they should assume that anyone riding through the glen might be dangerous. Bands of men, not only English soldiers but others too, roamed the countryside. Unless the visitor signaled them, they must run to the cave immediately. Nowadays, almost everyone in the Scottish countryside kept a hiding place stocked with food and blankets. Most families, unless they lived within castle walls, had neither weapons nor enough people to fight off marauders. Their only defense was retreat. Many times, though, families had emerged from their hiding places to behold a tragic sight: their homes and barns in flames and their livestock stolen.

Of late, even the island of Arran was no longer safe. Cuinn had learned that the English were trying to put a stranglehold on Scottish shipping. They had now moved a much larger garrison of soldiers into Brodick castle, his former home overlooking the waters of the firth. Could some of those English soldiers be searching up through the glens today? What would bring them up here in this weather? Cuinn went through a half dozen scenarios in his mind.

Perhaps the English knew more about Loch Ranza than he realized. Maybe someone had told them about the comings and goings in Gleinn Eason Biorach. Cuinn brought his small herds of horses up into the glen only at night now, and as soon as he received a signal, he and one of his trusted men would run the horses back down to Loch Ranza and ship them off. It was just a quick sail across the firth to the mostly-deserted castle at Ardrossan. Fergus, awaiting them there, would help them unload so quickly that Cuinn's boat would be heading back to Loch Ranza in mere minutes. So far, their scheme had worked brilliantly.

But there was a possibility that one of the fisher folk had reported them. Nowadays information was valuable. It could be used to bargain for anything. Even though there weren't that many people living here, even though Loch Ranza was a remote castle almost entirely cut off by high hills from other parts of the island, Cuinn still allowed himself to trust no one. It was best, he knew, to be careful. He held his breath and tried to hear above the howling of the storm.

A familiar horn call pierced the wind. They all sighed in relief. Their taut bodies relaxed and they grinned at each other. Still cautious though, Grizel stood on tiptoe to peer from behind the boulders guarding their cave. Barely able to see against the rain pounding her face, she could just make out that it was Rob, riding alone into the stable yard. They ran back down the path and beckoned him inside as he dismounted. Cuinn gestured to Tom to stable Rob's pony.

"Did you come from Loch Ranza, Rob?" asked Grizel, breathless.

"Yes, and I have to go back tomorrow. I've left a few men down there. They're camped on the hill in the ruins of that old fort." Grizel spread their various wraps near the fire while Rob continued. "Truth be told, I'm here to get an army together. Cuinn, I'm begging you to give us some help. Is there any hope you could join us, bring some of your men?"

Cuinn rubbed his forehead but didn't answer right away.

Rob leaned on the table, exasperated. "King Edward is piping us a fiendish tune, man," said Rob, "and he wants us all to dance. If he gets the Scottish throne, you'll be in the same situation as the rest of us – you and all your property won't be worth a basketful of thistledown."

"I hate leaving the women alone here, Rob, and no one to defend them. But I knew it would come to this someday. Ai, you can count on me."

"We're desperate. We could use as many men as you can bring."

"Can I come too, Cuinn?"

"'Sakes, lass, you're just a bit young."

"I'm almost nine years old!"

"Pippa, go out and get a pitcher of water so Rob can wash" said Grizel.

"It's raining!"

"And you can't get much wetter than you are. So go on, be quick."

"Pippa! Do as Grizel asks!" ordered Rob.

As soon as Pippa had slammed the door behind her, Rob collapsed against the back of his chair. Grizel threw a blanket over his wet shoulders. She and Cuinn came to sit on either side of him.

"Rob! What–?"

Rob's head was in his hands. "It's our leader, William Wallace. King Edward executed him last month. A traitor's death."

"Oh, no! Not Wallace! How did they catch him?" Cuinn gasped.

"He was betrayed" Rob said darkly.

They gawked at Rob in disbelief.

Grizel broke the silence. "Do you know who betrayed him?"

"Yes, everyone knows. It was one of our own bloody men, John Monteith, purely for revenge. He knew Wallace was hiding in a house in Glasgow." Rob was so distraught he had to struggle to get the words out. Cuinn and Grizel looked at each other. They had never seen him so upset. "They took Wallace all the way to London for the trial. Dragged him through the streets to the gallows. Scotland's leader, dragged through the dirt like an animal. They tortured him in the town square before they …"

"Please," said Grizel, turning her head. "I don't want to know what they did to him." No one heard the back door open and close.

"Do you want just a rough idea?" Rob breathed raggedly through pursed lips. "Sure, I'll give it ye. There are pieces of Wallace's body nailed over the gates to all the towns in Scotland."

Cuinn spread his hands over his eyes. They were all quiet. A few drops of rain slid down the chimney and hissed into the peat fire. Cuinn raised his head and stared across the table at Rob. He spoke softly.

"So William Wallace is gone. Our leader is gone. This changes everything, doesn't it Rob?"

Rob glowered at him. "Everything! Everything is changed now!" He sat up and clenched his hands. "Do those foul English rats think that this will kill the Scottish uprising? Never!" He pounded a fist on the table. "Do they think they can kill what is in our hearts? No, they cannot! They can humiliate us one by one, they can tear us to pieces on the gallows, but they can't kill our spirit. Not as long as I have breath in my body. The crown of Scotland will sit on the head of a Scotsman, I tell ye, and a MacDuff will place it there!"

"I swear to you, Rob. I'll get you those men for your army. The English will pay for this."

"That's not all we need. We need supplies of all kinds, too. And I'll get them if I have to raid every kettle on every hearth in the country!"

They turned in surprise. Pippa stood stiffly by the door with a pitcher of water, watching them with frightened eyes.

Who was William Wallace? What they were talking about? She was rooted to the floor.

They tried to turn the talk to less weighty matters, but they couldn't shake the heavy cloud that had settled over them. Much of Scotland, though not every Scot, would mourn their dead leader. And who would lead them now?

Tom came in from the stable.

"I'm drookit!" he said, peeling off his dripping clothes. No one paid much attention. He looked at the gloomy faces around the fire while he unrolled a dry tunic.

Grizel got up and stirred the soup kettle thoughtfully. Tom came immediately to peer over her shoulder.

"Cuinn."

"Yes, Grizel?"

"Remember when I helped you pack up to leave Brodick in such a hurry that last time, and we hid the…" Cuinn raised his head, amazed.

"You're right! We hid the silver. In that dungeon room in the castle."

"Remember? What chance is there that it was ever found?"

"I'd say there is a very slim chance."

"What chance is there of getting to it?"

"That's another matter entirely. And getting it out of Brodick would be even more difficult. Is that what you had in mind, Grizel?"

"Exactly. Not that the silver is mine to remove. But, I just wondered. What would it take?" She reached for wooden bowls absent-mindedly. "First you'd have to get all the way across the grounds and into the castle without being seen. But the little passage is near that western door, remember?"

"Once you're inside the castle, and through the secret door, you could stay for a week and they would never know you were there. But then of course you'd have to get the loot out of there. If the English haven't already found it themselves."

"How about late at night? The guard would be lighter."

"Och, they'd have sentries on duty all night, I'm sure. I mean, you could observe them for a couple of nights to make sure, but you would still never know what you'd find once you got inside. If you could get inside."

"I'll wager I could get in there." Pippa looked at the adults matter-of-factly. "They wouldn't be looking for a child."

"No, dinna send her!" Tom butted in. "It's too dangerous. Send me instead. I'm stronger, and a lot older."

Pippa's jaw tightened with a loud intake of breath. She frowned darkly and had to bite her lips to keep back an angry retort. She was glad she did, for in that moment of hesitation, an idea bloomed in her mind – an idea that would prove just how big and brave Tom really was.

"You're both too young. It's much too dangerous" Cuinn asserted.

Tom started to protest but Pippa caught his eye. He hesitated, then saw Pippa's sly smile. He grinned at her.

Good. Tom had taken her bait.

"How do you find the secret door?" Pippa asked lightly.

"It's a very clever arrangement" explained Grizel. "When you press on the molding around a certain wall panel, the latch opens."

"Molding?" Pippa looked at Tommy quizzically. She could tell that he had no idea, either, what molding was.

"Anyway, Cuinn," continued Grizel, "we can't really make any promises about silver without speaking to your mother. We can do nothing without her consent. It is her silver, after all."

"Don't even bother to ask her", said Rob. "It's impossible. No one could get in and out of Brodick. And I couldn't abide another hideous execution if someone got caught."

"Ai, 'twas a dumb idea, it was" admitted Grizel. The men nodded ruefully.

Outside, drumbeats of rain pelted the thatch of the cottage roof in an endless tattoo. But inside, as Grizel handed round bowls of hot broth and some fresh bread, Pippa brushed Tommy's shoulder and murmured a few words.

He caught her idea immediately and committed himself to it whole-heartedly. He was so eager to prove himself to Cuinn and Rob.

Pippa only wanted to make a fool of Tom, to send him down to Brodick castle and then watch his courage crumble before he ever got inside. He would fail miserably.

Neither of them said anything of these ideas that day, but they nodded wisely to each other.

Of course it was not a wise thing that either of them was planning. In point of fact, it was downright daft.

October 1305
Brodick Castle

$\mathcal{B}$ut that was how it came about that, late one night while the moon peeked from among the clouds, Tom and Pippa stole out from Loch Ranza castle and rode up into Glen Cloy, as far as the Faeries' Mound called Tornanshiain. This was the farthest east either of them had ever ridden. They tied the ponies there, safely hidden behind the thick walls of the old camp.

Tornanshiain had been a hiding place since ancient times. Women and children would retreat to the camp nestled high in the glen, while their fathers and brothers defended the beach below against invaders. Tonight, unbeknownst to anyone, Pippa and Tom were following the directions they had beguiled out of Dickon, Sebrina's unsuspecting steward. They crept out of Tornanshiain and began to descend the narrow path to Brodick castle.

It was a long walk down to the castle. Pippa and Tommy warily picked their way along, following the stream to where it gurgled into a grove of trees. Dry leaves clacked and whispered overhead. The moon had begun her downward path also. Her shadows swayed exotically in the wind. Where her light fell was silver brightness, but the shadows were dark and deep.

Pippa and Tommy stopped and held their breaths. There it stood, just below them, a black hulk like a huge beast.

Brodick Castle.

They had never seen it before, either of them. They stood under the trees, studying the castle across the dark garden. Pippa didn't realize she had her shoulder pressed into Tommy's ribs until he stepped away. They heard no sound save the sighing trees. They knew there were guards somewhere. There had to be. But where?

All was perfectly quiet.

Who was out there? Surely someone guarded Brodick Castle.

"Tommy..." Pippa gripped Tom's sleeve. The brooding silence was nerve-wracking.

"Wheesht!" Tom hissed, his finger to his lips. He pointed and they slipped along the perimeter of the garden, not daring to risk the bright open ground. They stopped again to listen.

Pippa was suddenly aware of the sound of her own heart thudding thickly in her chest. Something boiled sickeningly in her stomach and made her legs wobbly. When would Tommy confess that he too was scared? When would he say they should give up and go back? She was determined that he be the first to suggest it.

Tom dropped to his knees and pointed to himself. He would crawl forward, across that moonlit patch, to a huge beech tree. She should follow after.

He was leaving her all alone at the edge of the woods? He was really going on?

He put his face to the ground and moved over the grass on his belly, so slowly that he looked like nothing more than a long shadow. Pippa couldn't abide waiting by herself. She moved the empty sack that was wadded under the sash at her waist, dropped to the grass and began to follow. Moving by inches, it took them a long time to cover ground.

They were getting near, perilously near. Pippa never thought they would get this close. The closer they got, the more the castle swelled in size, bloated like a giant reptile, larger and darker than ever. Maybe there were a hundred soldiers in there, carrying a hundred swords, and at any moment the maw of the black castle would spew forth hordes of them. With every second, Pippa and Tom were farther from possible escape.

This had all gone too far. Pippa had to give up. Deeply shaming though it would be, she crawled faster so she could reach Tommy and confess that she did not have the courage to go through with this.

Then they heard a long, loud creaking sound and knew they had been discovered. It was all over for them. A door opened, the very door they had planned to enter. The flickering light of a lamp fell across the grass in front of them. Guards!

No, only one guard. He had seen them, certainly. Pippa dared not turn around to see if there were others behind her. Had they sent only one man? Well, if they had, he would never catch them both. But Tom could run faster than she could, she told herself dismally. Her goose, as Sebrina would say, was cooked. They would torture her, tear her fingernails out.

The guard stepped outside and closed the castle door. Tommy had been able to curl up in a shadow behind a huge tree, but Pippa was caught, caught in the open and fully visible in the moonlight. She panicked. She should get up and run for it, but she couldn't move. She watched stupidly as the man raised a jug and took a long swig from it.

Had he not seen them? Was it possible? She forced herself to lay quiet and slowly brought arms and legs together. She lowered her head to the grass and kept her eyes half closed so he would see no glimmer of life. She realized she was panting. She tried to take smaller breaths, as small as possible. It was so difficult trying not to breathe. Barely, barely breathing. A shadow – she wished herself a mere shadow, cast by the moon.

Tommy crouched in relative safety. He looked back at Pippa. There was terror on his face, she could tell, terror for her.

Oh, no, the bad luck! The man with the jug settled on a bench, leaned back and crossed his legs. He put his face to the heavens and let out a long, loud belch. How long, for pity's sake, Pippa wondered, would he sit on that bench venting obnoxious noises? She had to concentrate on stillness, perfect stillness. She was trembling slightly. She wished she were smaller.

To her left, she heard a scratching noise, high in a tree. Now her whole body began to shake. They kept sentries in the trees! Of course, why didn't she think of that? She hadn't a chance now. The sentry must have seen her, though she was paralyzed and couldn't move her head to look. He was climbing down. She heard his boots scraping on the tree trunk. Now she could hear his feet, sliding slowly over the grass. She could not look at him. She might as well give herself up, she knew, but she was frozen. She managed to swivel her eyes to the left. It was not a sentry.

A raccoon. He was huge. Pippa had never been frightened of a raccoon before but this one towered over her as she lay there. His inquisitive eyes were large and bright over a miniature, narrow nose. He waddled closer.

Please don't come near me, she begged silently. He stopped and stared at her. His long claws shone in the moonlight. Pippa gaped at those claws. They looked very sharp. She tried to stay still. Then both she and the raccoon gave a start. The man on the bench had noticed the raccoon and clapped his hands to scare it away. It hunched its back and loped off, never taking its eyes off the man. Pippa lay as still as death.

The man laughed and got up. She heard his sword clanking on his hip. He stretched noisily and ambled across the grass, fumbling with the ties on his breeches and coming straight toward her. Fortunately he was not sober enough to walk very straight. Unfortunately, he swayed on his feet as the strong, steady stream hit the grass. Fortunately, she was out of range. Unfortunately she was not able to fight down an insane giggle.

Someone opened the door at that exact moment and called to the man. That squelched that giggle.

"Brock!"

"Aye."

"You gonna play some dice tonight or not?"

"Aye. I'm a-comin'."

"You sure you got the stomach for it, after last night?"

"Ye must be jokin', ain't ya?" blustered Brock. "But you gotta lend me some coin, buddy."

"I ain't lendin' you nothin', you smuck fuster."

"You owe me..." They began arguing. They headed back inside the castle. The door thudded shut.

Nothing moved or made a sound. An iron hand released its grip on Pippa's stomach. She let out a small whimper and inched forward again across the grass. She reached the tree where Tom crouched and leaned against him until her strength returned. Her plan to embarrass him seemed to have backfired somehow. Tom patted her shoulder sympathetically.

They looked warily around the park behind them. All was quiet, still but for the swaying treetops. They could see no other movement. Without warning, Tommy grabbed her hand and forced her up. He pulled her into a crouch and they ran across the grass to hide in the shadow of the bench beside the door. Tommy gestured for her to wait. He went to the door to listen, but quickly ducked into the bushes. They heard determined steps and the door was flung open with another loud groan of hinges. Pippa's heart – or some other miserable part of her insides – flew to her mouth. She felt sick. They had been seen! Here was the same man again. He walked with his head bent forward, looking left and right. Pippa folded herself up as small as possible behind the bench. She hadn't even had time to find cover. The man came near, stubbed his toe and stumbled against the bench. His face was inches from Pippa's. He swore, then searched the seat of the bench and the ground underneath. Pippa could smell his dirty clothes and oily hair, he was so close. She could have reached out and touched him. Crouching in the darkness, she felt so very visible. She could see Tommy clearly, even in the dark, there behind that bush.

"Ah!" the man exclaimed. Pippa's heart stopped.

He had found, not Pippa, but his purse on the ground under the bench. It seemed like a very thin purse to Pippa. Nevertheless, he looked pleased to find it, and hurried back inside. The hinges croaked and the door slammed.

It was quiet again.

Pippa's nerves were ragged. She reminded herself to breathe. She imagined Tommy trembling on his side of the doorway, as she was on hers. By some miracle, probably because the man had not expected to find them there, he never noticed them.

Once again she made sure the big bag was secure under her sash. Tommy motioned that he would try the door again. He listened intently for a minute and reached for the handle. Slowly he turned it. Remembering the hideous squawk of the hinges, Tommy pushed the door open just a crack. It made nary a sound. Pippa sprang to his side.

"Do you want to go home?" she whispered.

His face could not have been more incredulous if she'd asked him to join her, just then, in a boisterous display of fire-breathing.

"What? Have ye barley-oats in yer haid?" he hissed.

"No, it's just...."

"Well let's go then!"

He allowed an opening of a hand's width, no wider, in the doorway, and they slipped through noiselessly.

They were inside Brodick Castle.

At first, a deep hush prevailed. They were in a passageway, tall and shadowy, unfurnished but for a long table near a hanging tapestry. Thrown on the table in disarray were helmets, gloves, a few battered weapons, even muddy boots. In a room to the left down the passage, the sounds of a game erupted, alternating curses of the players and the clatter of dice. Someone called for more ale.

Tom and Pippa began to search the wall beside them. The secret door was supposed to be near. It was on the south wall, Dickon had confided to them, although they could see no sign of it. You wouldn't be able to see it, he had said when they prodded him. It was cleverly hidden, small, part of the paneling. It only required one touch on a certain piece of molding to open it. They ran their hands along the wall, along what they guessed was the molding. Even Loch Ranza lodge, the only castle either of them knew, had no such thing. Molding was trim, carved of wood, to ornament paneling, Dickon had said. He hadn't told them how much molding was here, though. A lot! Brodick was a much bigger and more luxurious castle than Loch Ranza. They hunted in a panic for the little door, probing and pushing. Nothing anywhere.

Down the passage, they heard one of the dice-players scrape a chair back. Footsteps! Their fingers flew frantically.

They had no time. Tommy tried to pull Pippa down beside him, under the table. She wasn't quick enough. She slipped in behind the wall-hanging. The tapestry was huge but it did not reach the floor. Her boots showed beneath. Under the long table, Tom pressed against the wall, trying to blend into the shadows. All they could do was to flatten themselves against the wall and try to ignore the urgent need to breathe.

Someone came along the passage. Leisurely footsteps taking an agony of time. Suddenly, snick! There was a sound in Pippa's ear, deafeningly loud. Stupid Tommy! He had banged something against the wall. Trust Tommy to do something clumsy at a moment like this. She was sure Someone would hear. She stood very still. A cold, dank breath of stale air blew from somewhere. It rustled the tapestry. She was sure Someone would notice. Where was this draft coming from? The footsteps were near, they were right in front of them. Someone had only to glance down to see either of them. Would he look under the table? Notice the tapestry rippling evilly? Hear their hearts bashing in their chests, their lungs begging for air? Someone went right on past, opened the back door and closed it again.

They waited. Had he actually gone out? Was he coming back? Under the table, Tom began to push against the wall behind him. There was again a horrid creaking of ancient hinges.

Tommy had found the door!

His head had bumped against the secret panel accidentally. If he hadn't crawled beneath the table, they might never have found it. Pippa crawled under the table and ducked through the door after Tommy. They slid into a tiny space and pushed the door closed behind them. Again, the relief of being able to breathe. Tremendous relief.

The darkness now was total. They had forgotten to light the torch Tom had brought. Pippa, her finger still on the little ring inside the door, pulled it open a crack. They listened again. Tommy crept back into the hallway, touched his torch to the lamp burning on the wall there, and covered the flame with his hand.

Pippa held the tapestry aside until, in the time it took to turn an hourglass, Tommy was back behind the secret door once again. Now, with any luck at all, they were safe for a while.

They looked around. There was absolutely nothing to see but an exceedingly narrow, curving stair. They began quietly to descend. At the bottom they found a very small room. Dickon had told them that no one knew for sure why this room had been built. Some said it had been a prison cell. But Sebrina had managed to put it to good use, hiding her valuables here before she was chased out of her home by King Edward's men. In this tiny room, Pippa and Tommy found several chests piled together, each with locks as big as Pippa's hand.

She had swiped Sebrina's giant key ring. The Brodick keys were fortunately separate from the keys for Loch Ranza castle. But which key went to which chest?

It took a long time to find the right keys, and they were appalled at the loud scraping noises that the old locks made. The first one groaned as if in pain. Their heads came up. They listened. But there seemed to be no answering commotion from upstairs. Slowly they opened the first old chest. Its lid, as though under a spell that protected its contents, had its own set of screeches and growls. Pippa lifted the torch. Inside were several carefully wrapped bundles. Tommy lifted one and began to unwrap it. He held it up. Silver gleamed in the torchlight. Pippa snatched it from him in panic and dropped it into her sack. They had to hurry! With so many chests to open, there was no time to be curious. They began to work.

As it turned out, they had only unlocked and emptied three chests when they realized the torch was dangerously low. There were still more chests of varying sizes crammed into the little room. Pippa made a face like a silent wail.

"Our sacks are almost full. We can't carry any more anyway" Tommy whispered. They looked longingly at the other chests. Rob desperately needed the silver, thought Tom. But if anyone ever had to come back for more, Tom and Pippa hoped fervently it would not be them.

And that was assuming they would get out of Brodick castle tonight.

Carefully they pulled the drawstrings to close their sacks, and tried to shoulder them. They were impossibly heavy! They hadn't considered how much this silver would weigh. How were they to get into the hallway, out the back door and across the park with bags that they could barely lift? It was then that the torch sputtered out and they were in pitch blackness.

Pippa reached for Tom. "Where are you?" she moaned. She clawed madly at the darkness.

"Here, take my hand."

"I can't find it!" She felt his hand bump her waist and Tom took her arm. She had to fight to keep down her panic. She fumbled so she wouldn't lose the string of her sack. They were blind, blind as stones.

They bumped clumsily into chests, into each other, into the walls, trying to find the stairs. Fortunately the room was so small and the stairway so narrow, they were not lost for long. But it was unbearably creepy all the same. Pippa gripped Tommy's sleeve. She was ashamed to cling to him, but she couldn't help herself. In response, he took firm hold of her hand and this steadied her. They began to work their slow way to the top of the stairs. Tommy stumbled and tripped over his bag. There was an immense clatter of noise.

They froze in terror. Waited.

No response.

But who knew what might be waiting on the other side of the secret door? They were damp with fear and effort by the time Tommy touched the door. They settled their bags on the steps and took a rest, trying not to pant too loudly. Their chests heaved in and out. They needed time to prepare for the worst.

Finally they had gathered strength and a little courage. They could hear nothing from the hall. Tommy felt for the little ring on the door and turned it. The door opened the tiniest crack. They would be able to see now!

But no ray of light appeared from the hall lamp. Had they taken the wrong stair or a wrong turn, and ended up in a different place? Cautiously Tommy put his eye to the crack, then slowly leaned his head out. He could barely make out the hallway, but it was indeed the same hallway, the same table piled with dark shapes. Had they been in the secret room for so long, that everyone had gone to bed? There was an entire army living in this castle. Armies never slept without guards!

Pippa and Tom crawled out from under the table. Cautiously they dragged their sacks loaded with silver after them. Still there was not a sound to be heard. Where were the sentries? Were they all asleep? How could that be? Tom and Pippa didn't want to wait to find out. They slipped as quietly as possible out the back door while they had the chance. Outside, they crouched behind the bench again, this time feeling even more visible because of their huge sacks of booty. Hurry, they had to hurry! They took only a minute to survey the lawn of the park. The moon had disappeared. It was full darkness now. They waited a little longer but still no one appeared. The treetops sighed, falsely encouraging them to throw caution to the winds. The thought of creeping slowly across that lawn again was agony.

"Run for the big tree" whispered Tommy, willing as ever to take a chance. He took her hand again. They bolted. They staggered. They could barely run. Their sacks were too heavy. They finally reached the tree, desperately out of breath again. They looked frantically around, hitched their bags over their shoulders, joined hands and ran the rest of the way like crazed deer. This is ridiculous, Pippa's mind screamed. We'll be caught! But neither could she bring herself to stop running until they reached the border of the garden.

They passed the border. Here was the stream. The ground was muddy near there, wicked and spiteful. It sucked at Tommy's boot with such determination that it pulled it completely off. Terrified of turning back, he hopped on one foot for a few steps. He finally was forced to run lopsided, one foot bare, making him yip in pain every few seconds. They didn't stop until they found the narrow path to the glen.

Once there, they paused to catch their breath and listen. It seemed they had disturbed nothing and no one. The loss of one boot was apparently the only calamity.

Or so they thought. Grinning broadly at each other, they were trotting triumphantly alongside the stream when two black figures stepped out of the trees ahead and blocked their path. Pippa and Tommy gave little terrified screams and clung to each other. Their bags crashed to the ground. They had been found, and with a huge stash of precious silver! They would be dragged behind horses to the scaffold and little pieces of their bodies would be nailed...

But it wasn't soldiers. It was Grizel and Cuinn, laughing silently at them. They opened their arms and Pippa and Tommy slumped against them, weak with relief. They whispered a hundred questions.

"We were looking everywhere for you two! We were sick with worry."

"How did you know we were here?"

"Sebrina's hound found a trail and led us to your ponies. Don't say you were inside Brodick?"

"We got some of the silver!"

"What? Truly?"

"You found it? How did you know where to look?"

"Oh... we just... took a chance." How could they admit that they deceived Dickon into giving them directions?

"Wonderful! Though we should be angry with you!"

"Where's your other boot?"

"How many sentries were there?"

"Maybe they guard only the front of the castle, never imagining that any danger could come out of the hills behind Brodick."

Cuinn and Grizel relieved them of their black sacks and were amazed at their weight. To save his bare foot, Tom rode on Cuinn's back until they reached the Faeries' Mound. They found the ponies and headed back to Loch Ranza. Dawn had already flushed the sky by the time they arrived. To Pippa, the morning sun was like a celebration. She was light-headed with relief.

At Loch Ranza they amazed Sebrina with the tale of their theft. She was too shocked to scold them, even when they interrupted each other in their euphoria. She gasped throughout their tale, with her hand on her heart. She had forgotten that she had hung a tapestry on that wall just before she fled from Brodick.

Rob insisted that Sebrina look over the silver before he took any. He refused to sell her dearest pieces. She selected a couple that she felt she could not part with, and was more than happy to give him the rest.

It was a start, but only a start for the army he was building. It was a blessing that Rob could not look ahead and see the battles that were to come. If he had known, he would never have begun. But, on the other hand, if he had not begun, the world would have been a different place.

So Rob did begin preparing for battle. And the consequences began to ripple outward, amplifying, widening, and finally gorging on the lifeblood of Scotland.

Late October 1305
Loch Ranza

*I*n the yard at Loch Ranza, the old sow trotted daintily to the side of her pen. With great delicacy she scratched herself on the fence. Her sensitive snout swiveled from side to side. Ah! The scent of rotting apples was perfuming the morning breeze. Rotting apples, her favorite!

Like all her kind, the pig's eyesight was poor. She couldn't see the orchard where the apples lay, even though it was just across the yard. But she did hear a sound she had been waiting for. Someone was coming towards her pen with a full bucket: breakfast. She snorted grumpily. The boy was bringing it, the one she had come to despise. She could tell it was him from the halting rhythm of his step. The man could carry a full bucket and maintain an easy stride but the boy wasn't strong enough. She had gauged his strength exactly on a day last summer when she had raked her sharp teeth up the side of his leg. A triumphant half-second later she had thrown him to the ground. He was a puny weakling. She could have hurt him very badly that day, and she wished she had, because since then he tormented her mercilessly. She would bide her time until the chance came to finish what she had started. He wouldn't last long, scrawny beggar that he was!

Tom came through the gate and let it bang closed. He dragged the heavy slop bucket to the trough and perched it on the end. Then he leapt up and stood with his feet straddling the trough. He was out of the sow's reach up there.

He knew that this pig was a tetchy creature and should be treated with caution. She had been born the runt of her litter and had always had to fight for everything. The long scar that ran from Tom's ankle to his knee was proof that she had battled him once and won. He glowered down at her, and teasingly touched her snout with his long stick. She backed away and protested with a cantankerous grunt. He jabbed the air and said something in a rude voice. She backed further while he poured the bucket of kitchen scraps into the trough. Saliva dripped from her mouth.

Suddenly distracted, Tom raised his head and looked toward the road. He heard horses coming round the end of the loch and the voices of riders bantering back and forth. He jumped backwards to the ground and the pig dove noisily into her breakfast.

Always wary of his enemy, Tom knew to stay out of harm's way. Even if the pig was eating, he dared not turn his back on her. He jumped up to sit on the top of the fence, out of her reach, so he could watch the horsemen as they came thundering across the bridge. It was Cuinn, bringing Rob and a few others for a couple of days of deer hunting. Simon Fraser, Robert Boyd, Christopher Seton – they were all close friends and joked easily among themselves. Tom gaped, his heart yearning, taking in every detail of weapon and horse-trapping, the proud straight backs and the strong, easy grace of the horsemen. Pippa, Tom instantly noted with envy, was riding with them, wearing some sort of absurd little jeweled cap on her red curls. Lady Sebrina came outdoors to greet them.

The gate to the pigpen made just the slightest creak. Tom was in another world but the pig heard it. She edged slowly around the trough while Tom's attention was on the horsemen. She squinted up at the gate. Yes, she was positive it was open a crack. Even though her trough was still full, the smell of those apples was overpowering. It was apples she wanted in the worst way. She gathered her strength and charged the gate, muscled it open, and took off across the yard. Horrified, Tom leapt after her.

The men hadn't even dismounted when Christopher Seton noticed a determined sow lumbering toward them, and Tom racing full tilt behind her, waving his stick and shouting. Tom's father, Dort, in the garden near the orchard, grabbed a shovel and began shouting as well. Cuinn turned his horse but it shied at the pig and reared in terror, exciting the other horses. Christopher Seton handed his reins to Robert Boyd, jumped to the ground and joined Tom, who had managed to corner the pig by a shed.

Dort ran up. He was furious! Here was Milady's only sow, panting feverishly, swinging her head back and forth in fright. Dort pushed Tom, useless boy, to the ground.

The pig was panicked, and Dort could see she was dangerously overheated. He could hardly contain his anger. This kind of stress could kill a pig, and Dort did not want to be blamed for that. No, this was not going to fall on his shoulders. This was all Tom's fault. Dort was sick to death of Tom making trouble. Tom, his own son, made nothing but trouble for him.

Christopher Seton had less of a grudge and more presence of mind. He tore off his mantle and twirled it in the air. The pig saw the dark cloak swinging above her and screamed. It dropped over her head and she froze in terror. If she couldn't see, she dared not move. Pigs were like that. Cuinn and the others were beside her in an instant. Someone found a rope. They quickly had her trussed up. Grimm, the constable, brought a bucket of water to pour over her. It cooled her and she lay panting for a while. Finally they were able to coax her gently up and lead her back to her pen. There they fed her some of her own kitchen scraps to try to calm her. She was so frustrated that she came as close as she ever would to losing her appetite. She did manage a few noisy mouthfuls, but what she really craved was a nice little dozen or so apples. Not to mention a big bite of that nasty boy.

*A*s soon as Dort saw the pig being led safely away, he turned wrathfully on his son, still sprawled in the dirt.

"You daft imbecile! What were you trying to do, kill her?" Dort gestured threateningly with the shovel-handle.

"She got out! It wasn't my..." Tom tried to get up and stumbled against his father. Dort, in a temper, shoved at Tom again and that is how the accident happened. The handle of Dort's shovel banged hard across Tom's face. Blood spurted down the front of his shirt. He collapsed again in the dirt. Cuinn wrestled the tool out of Dort's hands and threw it to the ground.

"Do you want to kill your own boy over a pig?" he screamed at Dort.

Dort's face withered to a mask. This wasn't his fault! That foul git should know that. He glared at the men encircling him. They had him cornered, just like his sow. He bared his sharp little teeth, breathing heavily. No one else moved. Dort wiped his mouth on his sleeve and lurched backwards, muttering vile oaths. He stumbled away without a single glance at his son lying unconscious in the dirt.

The Lady Sebrina, closely followed by Pippa, ran to where Tommy sprawled motionless. The lady tried unsuccessfully to sop up some of the blood with her scarf. Pippa was sickened by the sight.

"He's still breathing," said Sebrina with relief. "Take him inside." Cuinn very gently gathered the boy in his arms.

"Dort is a madman" he barked. "We have to get rid of him, Mother."

"And if we do, then what will become of the boy?" his mother spat back.

"Let's see if he lives through this, first. If he does, we'll talk about it" said Cuinn.

Pippa reeled in shock. She hated that pig. She pressed her hands to her mouth. Tommy might die. Every terrible thing she had ever said to him jangled mockingly in her ears.

*H*er face ashen, Pippa sat near Tommy's bed and refused to leave. Sebrina insisted that his body be washed if he was going to lie on one of her beds. His skin was embedded with the deep grime of someone who seldom bathed, but it was the bugs he could be carrying that worried her. Cuinn refused to let her touch him.

"Let him rest quietly until we see if he regains consciousness."

"I don't want to have to lay him out for burial looking like that!" Sebrina insisted, then regretted it immediately. Pippa ran from the room.

Cuinn reached for a clean cloth to hold against Tom's face and asked someone to run down to the fishermen's huts to fetch Devorgilla. She had skill with herbs and healing.

Devorgilla came. She gently raised Tommy's inert body so his head was tilted back against a pile of cushions. She washed his broken face with saltwater. Then she folded crushed oak and yarrow leaves into a cloth, dipped it in cold well water and pressed it to his face, changing it for another repeatedly. She called for more cool water. After a while the bleeding slowed. She produced a small box. It held balls of cobweb which she laid over the wounds on Tommy's nose and cheeks. Then she wrapped a cloth in a band around his head. The bleeding finally stopped but the boy still hadn't opened his eyes. His nose had swelled horribly and his eyes were ringed with deep purple bruises. Devorgilla carefully searched his head for other cuts but found none.

The women moved to the other side of the room. Pippa could hear the healing-woman murmuring answers to Sebrina's questions but she couldn't make out what they were saying. Tommy's legs stirred a bit. Pippa grabbed Tommy's hand and called his name. His swollen eyes opened a crack but didn't seem to focus.

He didn't regain full consciousness until the next morning. Pippa had fallen asleep at the end of the couch, but Cuinn got up immediately and went to Tom's side.

"How are you, mon?" asked Cuinn softly, leaning low.

"Nnn baaa." whispered Tom, his eyes fastened on Cuinn's.

"Does it hurt much?"

"Nnn muu." answered Tom.

"You're a real hero" smiled Cuinn. Tom could make no answer.

Cuinn touched his brown tousled head. Looking at Tom lying there prompted a memory of Amie, Tom's mother, thin as a reed on her sickbed years before. Cuinn and Sebrina had visited her, taking some food that they hoped would be nourishing. She had urgently begged a promise for her little son.

"You won't forget him, no matter what?" she had pleaded. "You'll make sure he's cared for?" Cuinn had never forgotten that promise and had never yet regretted it.

Cuinn sent a message to ask Dort, Tom's father, to come to the house. When Dort arrived, Cuinn made an effort to be hospitable. He invited him to sit beside the fire and offered him a cup of wine. But he couldn't refrain from chastising the man.

"You haven't come to see your son once in the three days since he was hurt. I should think you'd be concerned for him."

Dort didn't answer.

"You have already lost your wife and another child. Tom is all you have left."

Dort downed his wine in one gulp. As if he had to be reminded of losing Amie. He only wished he could forget for one single day. He puffed out his lips, grunted and shrugged. He didn't answer or look at Cuinn.

"I take it that you won't mind then, if we make a place for Tom to work here in the kitchen from now on? We could use his help."

Dort looked up. Again he said nothing. He twirled his empty cup.

"'Tsall the same to me" he growled, finally. "He's nothin' but a nuisance. Ye'll see that for yerself soon enough."

Cuinn fought to keep his voice calm.

"We'll take our chances with him."

"Ye'll change yer mind soon's he breaks a few things. He's always breaking everything. Ye'll send him back in a week."

In a couple of days Tom was able to sit up without getting dizzy, and they helped him to stand a day later. All Cuinn's visiting friends came in to see Tom before they left Arran, trying to joke him into feeling better. Christopher Seton, who was married to Rob's sister, had visited him every day. Tom tried awkwardly to thank him for his help with the pig.

"'Twas nothing! You can do the same for me someday, Tom. Hey, I hear you're pretty good on a horse!" Tom waved off the compliment with his crooked version of a smile, all that his swollen face could manage just then. "Next time I come we'll have to have a race. Are you up for that?"

"Sure" exclaimed Tom, nasally.

"I'm going to bet a lot of silver that I can beat you. What do you say? Do we have a deal?"

Tom's face was tragic.

"I dote hab eddy muddy!"

Christopher Seton laughed in delight.

"Well you'd better start earning some. Or start perfecting your horsemanship, one or the other."

To Tom, if it was silver that allowed him to be accepted by the likes of Cuinn's friends, he resolved to find it somehow. He needn't have worried overmuch, though. The handsome and vivacious Christopher Seton would be dead, captured by the English king, tortured and executed horribly before a year was gone. Tom was never to see him again.

As Tom recovered from his injury, he was swept as if by a torrent to the far edge of boyhood. He thought about the circumstances of the accident often, and firmly believed that his father had not meant to hurt him. Nevertheless, his face was a riot of color. His nose would be permanently disfigured, and his voice sounded like someone was pinching his nostrils shut. But at first, his spirits were as lively as ever. Possibly more lively, surrounded as never before by people who worried so gratifyingly about him.

Sebrina, though, began to wonder if perhaps Cuinn had been right when he suggested they get rid of Dort. Her suspicions about Dort's temper tantrums had certainly been confirmed. She toyed with the idea of asking him to leave. Unfortunately for them all, she never put her thoughts into action.

When Tom was stronger, Cuinn told him that they had decided to give him a job working in the lodge. He could live in the lodge and work in the kitchen. Cuinn was amazed at the boy's response, however.

"No! I'm sorry, my lord, but no. I need to bide with my dad."

"But Tom," Cuinn insisted, "there is work here that needs to be done. Your father doesn't..." He stopped. He couldn't bring himself to say what he had been thinking.

"I canna bide here." Tom pressed his hands to his aching head. A hammer began to pound his swollen face from deep inside.

"Your father thought you'd be excellent help in the kitchen" Cuinn fibbed.

"No, I canna live here. My dad needs me. He'd miss me. Didn't he say so? Didn't he tell you he'd miss me?" Suddenly Tom couldn't help the tears. They just came. "My dad, he – he needs me with him. Especially at night. He's bad at night. He – it's not easy for him. He wants me home." His words came hard. It wasn't that Tom didn't realize the truth. He knew it very well. His father only needed him for one reason.

"What is it?" Cuinn asked gently. "You get him to bed at night, is that it?" He strained to hear Tom's answer, it was so soft.

"I have to try to take the jug away."

"It's the wine?"

Tom hated himself in the worst way. It was a gross betrayal and he would never forgive himself. And now he was crying in front of Cuinn. He held his breath locked inside himself but his shoulders still shook like a girl's. He wished he could disappear.

Ignoring Tom's dignity, Cuinn covered the boy's head with his big hand and pulled it toward him. Tom sobbed against Cuinn's chest. Pain pulsated cruelly behind his face. Cuinn felt an unbearably tight lump in his own throat. His voice was hoarse.

"I don't blame your father for wanting you at home. Anyone would miss having a lad like you around." Tom leaned so heavily on Cuinn's chest that he had to be pushed to a standing position.

He stood limp in Cuinn's hands. So Dort had been right. Tom would be drawn back home.

"I think I understand. You don't want to be a kitchen boy. That's it, isn't it, Tom?"

Grateful for any excuse for bawling like a baby, Tom shrugged and nodded.

Cuinn suddenly had an idea. He hesitated. Perhaps it was foolish. Perhaps it would put too high an expectation on Tom, but Cuinn made a quick decision. After all, he reasoned to himself, many a ragged colt has made a fine horse.

"I think we can do better than the kitchen for you, Tom. How old are you now?" Very gingerly, Cuinn mopped Tom's bruised face.

"I'll be thirteen in the summer, my lord."

"Thirteen, already? All right, laddie. I think I have the perfect job for you."

"You do?"

"Can you use a bow and arrow?"

Crestfallen, Tom whispered "No, my lord."

"Well it's time you learned. Meet me in the stable tomorrow, after your morning chores are done. You'll have your first lesson."

Tom blinked hard. Archery! It had become a symbol for Tom of all that he had ever wanted. His brow was furrowed so tightly he felt it might never come unknotted. He dared not open his mouth and had to struggle to hide his trembling.

"I have something in mind for you. I think you'll like this job. 'Til tomorrow, then."

Cuinn left the room and Tom watched him close the door. He had forgotten to thank Cuinn. Tears came again, and now Tom did not even try to hold them back. But he vowed they would be the last tears he would ever shed in his whole entire life.

They weren't the last tears he ever shed. He did go back to live with his father. He never, after that, asked Lady Sebrina to console him for his various hurts and bruises. But, as though he had crossed into a different country, his whole life changed the day after he spoke with Cuinn. He could hardly believe it himself.

Tom found what he had been born to do.

*T*om was in the stable waiting for Cuinn the next morning. When he heard Cuinn come in, he hastily replaced the bow he had been examining. In the process he knocked over half the collection.

Cuinn groaned inwardly. What had he started? Was this idea going to work or was he making a mistake? Archery required a great deal of precision and discipline. The only reason Cuinn didn't turn around and walk away was the unbearable thought of disappointing the boy. He was afraid, though, that Tom's father might have been right. Maybe this would be too much for Tom to handle. Well, they might as well go ahead. Maybe the boy would get discouraged and quit on his own. Cuinn looked down at the skinny, broken face. The eager brown eyes burned into his.

"Do you think you're ready to —?" He didn't have time to finish his sentence.

"Yes, Sire."

Cuinn picked out the smallest bow he owned, and a quiver of arrows.

"This was the bow I learned on, when I was your age. Old as the hills, is this bow!" Cuinn laughed at his own joke. Tom stared at him earnestly, apparently in full agreement that the bow must be extremely old.

Cuinn, somewhat deflated, handed it to him. "So be careful of this! I'm afraid it may be a bit big for you."

"I can handle it, Sire."

"It's pretty heavy." Cuinn looked up. Tom, with the bow wedged tight against his instep, was just slipping the string into place.

"That didn't take you long."

"I've seen you do it lots of times, sir." For the rest of the morning, Tom concentrated carefully on everything Cuinn told him. Cuinn allowed him no slack. He straightened Tom's stance, corrected his elbows, commented critically on every single move, and supervised exercises for strength.

Tom required no slack. He kept working until his cheeks were pink with effort under his purple bruises. The morning wore quickly away. Cuinn finally complimented Tom briefly, privately amazed at his progress.

It was Pippa's turn to hang on the fence and watch enviously, and Pippa wasn't used to being an onlooker. She had no words to describe her feelings, but they were painfully intense. She could say only that she was not happy.

The following day, early, Tom's arrow hit a target for the first time. Pippa watched again. By the end of that morning, he could hit the target every time. Tom had no words to describe his feelings either but for the first time in his life, he felt a new kind of gladness flickering inside him. He had never heard of anyone having a sense of accomplishment, but something was, indeed, making him feel vastly happy.

Then Pippa came stomping into the yard.

"I want to try that." Tom, who was lost in a daze of imagination, only looked at her blankly. He was riding through a forest, at the head of an army, aiming his arrow at....

"It's my turn" Pippa demanded. Cuinn reached to take the bow she had just snatched from Tom's distracted hand. She pulled it back.

"Pippa, that bow is too heavy for you."

"Tom can use it."

"Well Tom is older and stronger than you."

"Let me try!" she insisted.

"You'll need this." Tom handed her his leather hand guard. He tried to show her how to place her fingers.

"I'll do it!"

"Keep your shoulders down" Tom advised.

"I am."

"Dinna be so tense. Relax them. Keep your head up."

"I know!" Her scowl was ferocious.

"Have you figured where the wind is coming from?"

"You're really bothering me, Tom!"

"Oh, oh" laughed Cuinn. "What do we have here, a bit of rivalry?"

Pippa struggled but could not draw the arrow. She groaned mightily and gave it her most supreme effort, to no avail. Tom laughed. She glowered at him.

"Just shut up!" she howled. She held the bow in two hands above her head and raised her knee. Cuinn grabbed it from her just in time.

"Hey, what are you doing, Pippa? This is a very valuable weapon. It takes four years to prepare the wood and carve a decent bow, and you're going to break it over your knee in a fit of pique?"

"Well if someone as stupid as Tom can do this, why can't I?"

"That is very mean, Pippa. Tom is not stupid."

"He is too. He couldn't even read until I taught him."

"That doesn't mean a person is stupid. I'm shocked at you, Pippa. I think you should apologize for that heartless remark."

"I will not. I'm not even sorry. You're both stupid!" She threw down the leather guard and stalked out of the yard.

Tom and Cuinn stood together and watched her go with their mouths hanging open.

"Och!"

"Tom, my man, I hope you've learned an important lesson today." Tom stared and nodded, totally mystified. "Just when you think you can trust a woman, she threatens to break your bow in two."

"Ai," said Tom knowingly.

"You never know what they will do next."

"Nope."

"But always remember this: it's better to eat hot coals than to let a woman get you too worked up."

"Ai. Lots better."

"You can't let them bother you."

"Nope."

"Now you know why I'm not married."

"Ai," said Tom, trying to swagger. "Me neither."

Tom learned to hit moving targets with the bow and arrow, even while riding. For a boy who could not walk through a room without banging into something, his skill amazed everyone. He got his first bird that fall and his first deer shortly thereafter. He had earned a place next to Cuinn on almost every hunting expedition now.

"You know what, Tom?" Cuinn asked casually as they led their ponies into the yard one afternoon. "I just realized you don't have a bow of your own yet." Tom sucked in his breath. "You'll soon be a man. Every man's got to have his own bow." Tom grew nearly an inch taller in that very moment. "I'll ride down to see Johnnie in Kildonan next week, and ask him what he can do for you. You'll have to come along so he can measure you."

Tom's face split from ear to ear under his crooked nose. Cuinn put a reassuring hand on Tom's shoulder.

"I'll even lend you the silver to pay for it." Tom's smile faded. He looked slightly ill.

"You can pay me back with a dozen duck, two deer, and, oh, let's see, some couple dozen partridges would be fine. Not all at once, of course. What do you think?"

Tom was grinning again.

Grimm the constable came out to help with the ponies and Cuinn followed him into the stable. Out in the yard, Tom turned a neat cartwheel. And then, with joyous abandon and perfect form, another.

April 1306
Gleinn Eason Biorach

𝒫ippa was up near the little woods above their cottage, searching, but not very hard, for stinging nettles for their soup. Spring had touched their glen and the whitebeams wore their new leaf buds like green-gold ornaments. From up here, she could look down on their cottage, finally wearing a new coat of whitewash. The afternoon was so quiet and peaceful that when Tott leapt up with a frenzy of barking, Pippa started in surprise. Tott was usually the first to sound the alarm nowadays. He ran barking out of the woods and down to the lip of their vale, scattering the chickens in all directions. Old Gervaise, lying in the yard, got up slowly and added his voice uncertainly. Pippa peered from behind a tree, then tore down the hill.

"Grizel! It's Rob and Cuinn and someone else!"

"You're sure?" Grizel ran out to peer down the track. "All clear, then, Pippa" she called. She pulled a veil over her hair and they watched the men anxiously. Who was this third person? The men were riding the ponies hard.

Grizel knew it had been a difficult year for Rob and Cuinn, but she had mentioned none of the details to Pippa. She could sense the men's weariness as they rode up the track, just by the way they sat their ponies. Grizel, who had at one time been perfectly content to be alone, now found herself hoping the men could stay for a couple of days.

Cuinn looked exhausted. She watched Pippa's delight in greeting him and went herself to hug Rob as usual. She hung back suddenly, a little afraid. Maybe she should kneel. Everything would be different around Rob, in so many ways. Rob himself was different now.

But he didn't hesitate a bit. He pulled her into a big bear hug, and bent to scoop Pippa in as well. Then he put his arm around

Grizel's shoulder and turned her toward the stranger who had ridden up with them. Rob stood for a moment, watching his new dark-haired friend and grinning, exactly as Cuinn had grinned when he introduced Grizel to Rob almost seven years before.

"Grizel, I'd like you to meet my friend Jamie Douglas, just back from England. Jamie, this..."

"I expected...I thought...you told me..." spluttered Jamie.

"We told you what?" asked Rob and Cuinn together, smirking. "Jamie, lad! I've never known you to be at a loss for words. Especially around the ladies!"

Their friend pulled himself together. "I beg your pardon, my lady, for my deplorable manners. I am very pleased to meet you." Jamie took Grizel's hand politely. It took him a little time to notice Pippa. He made up for that by giving her the warmest smile she had ever seen. "And you must be ... I have no idea who you are." Pippa giggled.

"I'm Pippa." Jamie had bright black eyes. He was almost as handsome as Cuinn, but not quite.

"Will you be able to stay for a while?" asked Grizel.

"We were only waiting for you to ask." Delight lit Pippa and Grizel like two lamps. The men looked dog-tired. Rob was as tense as a bowstring.

"Come inside and tell us all the news."

Pippa drew some water for them to wash and took their ponies to the barn. She carried their packs upstairs to the loft above the stables.

While Pippa worked in the barn, Grizel invited the men into the cottage. She poured water so they could rinse the dust from their faces, then sat them at her table.

"I expect you have heard about the Red Comyn, Grizel?"

Of course she had heard but Grizel would not have dared to bring up the subject, though it was on all their minds. Rob not only went straight to the point, but looked her defiantly in the eye as he did.

"Yes, Rob, I heard. Cuinn was here a few weeks ago and told me about his ... his death. I'm sorry things had to happen that way."

"I would have been sorry too, if he hadn't betrayed me to King Edward. The scum! I knew it would happen. You can't trust anyone in that family. They're rotten and slimy, all of them."

"Are you saying you didn't plan to kill him? Him or his uncle?" She might as well be blunt. She had known about Rob's lifelong feud with the Comyns, but had prayed that Rob could shed a different light on all the latest rumors. Cuinn and their new guest, Jamie, shifted in their chairs, wondering how far Grizel was going to push Rob before he pushed back.

"It wasn't my plan to kill them, no, of course not. Actually, although I wounded them both, it wasn't I who killed them. It was one of my men."

"But in a church, Rob! A church is supposed to offer refuge from any harm. Murdering someone, even your bitterest rival, is bad enough. How can you expect people to support you when you have committed murder – two murders! – in a church?"

"It wasn't planned that way" Cuinn insisted. Grizel shook her head.

"I'm sorry, but I can't help but wonder what terrible price your men, and maybe all of Scotland, will have to pay for this. If I didn't know you, and admire you as I do, Rob, I would certainly think twice before I gave you my support. I'm sure many other people will feel the same. Both those murdered men were from the same family, too. What were you thinking? The Comyns! Now you've offended one of the most powerful families in Scotland."

"But Grizel, don't you see? There was such a slim possibility of the Red Comyn and me ever reaching an agreement. One of us would have ended up killing the other, sooner or later. The rat betrayed me. So it was kill or be killed."

"I worry so for you, Rob, and for all of us."

"I know, I know. Now more than ever the Comyns want my head on a pike. And, what is worse, they've sided with the English against me."

"That's terrible!" She shook her head. "Well, so much for bringing Scotland together. Wasn't that what you said you were trying to do? Wasn't that supposedly your plan?"

Rob leaned his chin on his hand.

Grizel sighed heavily. "I just wonder what we have begun here."

At that, Jamie Douglas decided to jump into the conversation, hoping to lighten the mood. This woman wasn't talking to just any common soldier, after all. She was gorgeous, but he would not have guessed, at first, that she had such spirit. Oh, these MacDuff women, they were a strong, hard-headed breed. Rob had recently introduced him to Isobel MacDuff, but this one sitting here was even more beautiful. So fair a lass! Jamie Douglas was pretty sure he was falling in love again, albeit for the hundredth time.

"If you don't mind me answering that question, my lady," said Jamie, "I think you're being a bit unfair here. Mayhap you have no idea of how badly things have been going for us. How many battles we've been losing. People are feeling they can't get behind us, can't help us out. And even if they did, the English would string them up by the neck. Them and all their families, down to the smallest bairn. That's bloody frustrating! How can Rob hope to beat the English when no Scotsman will stand up to fight beside him?"

Grizel frowned and nodded.

"I guess I was hoping the situation would improve, not get worse."

"It's a black pit of despair we're in, to be sure. Rob is despised in England and in Scotland both, at this moment."

"Do you have any idea how much suffering the English king has caused this country, Grizel?" asked Cuinn. "You don't see it as much out here on Arran but he has our entire country by the throat."

"I hear what you're saying" she admitted.

Cuinn tried to explain their dilemma. "We've got to somehow find people to join us. Half the country is sick of war. The rest are clansmen who never get tired of war. But the clansmen only want to battle each other. It's what they've been doing since the beginning of time. They don't give a pence for what Rob is trying to do."

Grizel put a sympathetic hand on Rob's arm.

"If the people of Scotland are at war with each other, you're going to have to do something about that, don't you think?"

"Sure, and what's that to be?" Rob asked. "I've tried everything but it's all going to Hades in a hand basket." He swung away from the table. "We're fighting each other here, we're fighting the English there, and we're getting nowhere at all. Truthfully, I don't even know what's right anymore."

"War ruins our good sense. We make ourselves believe the enemy is entirely wrong."

"Och! Well, apparently I don't know the difference between right and wrong anyway. I'm such a sinner, I'm not even allowed to set foot in a church anymore. The pope has excommunicated me."

"Doesn't he care that Scotland finally has a new king?"

"The pope cares about whatever Edward of England tells him to care about, as far as I can see. Did Cuinn tell you that your cousin, Isobel MacDuff, came to Scone for the coronation?"

"We have a real king, properly installed on the throne" said Cuinn.

"So the old tradition was observed" Rob continued. "A MacDuff was there to make everything legitimate."

Grizel felt a pang of resentment. She stared at the table. "Yes, Cuinn told me. That was very brave of Isobel. But it's a wonder her husband hasn't had her chained to a dungeon wall for going against him like that. You had just murdered his cousin, after all."

"Oh, John Comyn is madder than the devil with his tail caught in a winepress. But Isobel wasn't planning on going back to live with him anyway."

Grizel hesitated. She wanted to ask Rob more about Isobel, but she was afraid to bring up another difficult issue.

"Isobel has left her husband?" she finally asked timidly. So full of strong opinions a moment ago, Grizel now had to struggle to keep her panic under control.

"Yes, she has at last."

Grizel hunched in her chair. Finally she got up the courage. She glanced quickly at the door.

"So, what about Pippa?" Her voice caught. "Has Isobel said anything about Pippa?"

"She always asks after her. She has borne no other children. She would love to have her lass with her."

"I ... Do you think Isobel would ever want her to...? I mean, I know Pippa is not my child, but we've been together for so long now."

"To tell you the truth, Isobel and I have talked about my taking Pippa back with me. We both think Pippa should be with her mother."

The color drained from Grizel's face. How was it that Isobel always managed to get exactly what she wanted?

"Back to the mainland?"

"But we changed our minds. We have decided to wait until Isobel and the rest of my family are settled somewhere."

"Oh."

"Isobel knows how dangerous it would be for the child if her husband found out about her. He would be furious, even after all these years."

"John Comyn is only part of the danger" argued Grizel. "At least here on Arran, Pippa is relatively safe from King Edward."

"Grizel, stop worrying. We're trying to take things one step at a time. Isobel has gone east now with my wife and kinswomen. They are under my brother Niall's protection. We'll see how things go before we decide what to do."

Grizel tried to see that in a positive light. She changed the subject.

"Cuinn tells us the English king is furious with you too."

"Edward? Of course he is furious. He doesn't want Scotland to have its own king. He wanted to rule us himself. But I am sick of fighting his wars and paying his taxes and getting nothing in return." Rob took Grizel's hand. "I might as well tell you that there is another reason why I wanted Pippa with me, Grizel. King Edward has proclaimed that I am a traitor and any member of my family, or anyone who supports me, is also a traitor. You know what that would mean, if he captures any of them."

Grizel's face was grey. "It means a terrible punishment."

"It means a hideous death."

"This is so horrible. What will you do?"

"I'm making sure that the few castles I have left have enough food to withstand a siege, in case I have to retreat to one of them. I'm leaving for Dunaverty tomorrow, to get it stocked with provisions."

Pippa interrupted. They hadn't even heard her come in.

"You're leaving tomorrow? Cuinn too?" she piped up, incredulous. "So soon?"

Rob smacked the table with his hand and forced a smile.

"But not until you ladies give us some dinner. Och, lassie, I'm starved! What do you have to eat?"

Grizel got up. "I believe I'll make a celebration dinner tonight" she announced.

Pippa danced a little jig. "What are we celebrating?"

"Well, we have to celebrate Rob's king..." She caught a warning look in Rob's eye. He shook his head slightly. For now, the less Pippa knew, the safer they would all be.

"Let's celebrate that we're together, for tonight at least. What could be better?" She put a jug of wine on the table. "What happier occasion could there possibly be?"

Cuinn got up and pushed back his chair. "One of your feasts would be wonderful, Grizel. What have you got in the way of food? We're so hungry."

Their new friend, Jamie, got up as well. He rolled up his sleeves. "Sit down, sit down" he said to Cuinn. He turned to Grizel. "May I assist you, my lady? You have no idea what a great cook I am. Didn't I see some fat poultry in the yard when we came in?"

*N*o mercy for poultry that night! Soon there were three fewer chickens in the flock. Pippa had found a clump of nettles and she raided the garden to dig some young onions. She and Grizel baked a tart with butter and sugar and raisins. Even though the spring evening was cool, they decided to eat in the garden. They built a huge fire in the pit outside and pulled the table out under the rowan tree. And best of all, no, second best of all, thought Pippa, Jamie had a small flute in his pack. After dinner, he played and they sang their hearts out.

Oh rowan tree, oh rowan tree, thoul't aye be dear to me,
Entwin'd thou art with many ties, of home and infancy.
Thy leaves were aye the first o' spring,
Thy flowers the summer's pride
There was not such a bonnie tree, in all the country side.

High up on the slope above their deep, lonely glen, their fire was a mere spark of light, their song only a thread of music. No one heard them but the owls and the numberless deer. Overhead the night sky was a glittering shawl, flung over the black mountaintops to hide their little company from harm. The great silent dark refreshed and quieted their troubled spirits. They felt safe, each from different demons. The very best thing about it, though, to Pippa's mind, was the smile on Grizel's face that evening. Her cheeks were rosy and she laughed all night long. Pippa had never seen her laugh so much. Many times, in memory, Pippa would return to that night.

*N*o one suggested that Pippa go to bed early like a little child, thank goodness, but the next morning, she found that someone had tucked her into bed. She must have fallen asleep. She crept out at first light, milked the goat and gathered some eggs.

Rob was the first one up. He wore his worried face again.

"Cuinn and I are going to ride over to the other side of the island today. Jamie wants to stay here."

"Can I come with you, Rob?" Pippa asked eagerly.

He considered for a moment, then shook his head.

"Not this time, Pippa. But next time, I promise you."

She slouched in disappointment. She knew he'd say that. Grizel had never taken her to the western shore of the island. Few people lived there and anyway, Grizel could not hope to do business there. None of those folk had any use for, or could afford Grizel's fine fabrics.

After Rob and Cuinn left, Grizel asked Pippa to go up to the woods to find more nettles. When she got back with a basketful, Pippa was surprised to find Grizel sitting in the garden, chatting and laughing with Jamie. Pippa could hardly remember Grizel ever lounging idly on a spring afternoon. But most surprising of all, her head was bare. She wore no veil. She had plaited her dark auburn hair and twisted it neatly behind her head.

When Cuinn and Rob came back the next day, Rob was as shocked at this as Pippa was.

"I had no idea that you had red hair!" he said, frankly staring. "Or more auburn, I guess."

"Beautiful auburn hair, Grizel" said Jamie appreciatively.

Grizel glanced at Pippa. "It does run in the family" she replied.

Pippa pondered that for a moment, wondering what 'running in the family' meant. She was about to ask when Jamie took Grizel's hand in his and kissed her fingertips. Pink flamed Grizel's cheeks again. Pippa stared.

"Why do you call yourself Grizel when your own name is so lovely? Caela. It's a beautiful name." Jamie asked.

Grizel fidgeted. She rarely spoke of her past. "Well, I told you I was running away when I first came to Arran. My childhood was painful. When I came here, I wanted to leave all that behind.

Later, when I began living by myself, I just wanted to be left alone, to disappear from the world. So I took a new name, a name with no past."

"Caela is a good Gaelic name, though. From now on," Jamie announced to everyone, "we should call Caela by her real name."

Grizel put her fists to her cheeks. Just for a moment, her eyes were bright with tears.

Pippa threw her arms around her waist.

"What's the matter, Grizel?"

"It's been such a long time …I don't even feel like I am Caela anymore."

"You'll get used to it" Jamie assured her, kissing her hair. "And do you have to wear that head-covering anymore? You said that the man you were running away from is dead. Your uncle?"

She nodded.

"My uncle, Duncan MacDuff."

"So there's no longer any need to disappear. All the rest of us need to hide from the English, but you, at least, are safe now, my Caela."

Grizel—Caela—nodded and held Pippa's head tight against her body.

Pippa pulled out of her embrace. "I'm not hiding either. I'm just plain old Pippa."

She looked around but no one met her eye. No one could bring themselves to mention the child, Eshne de Bruce, who was known to no one, not even herself.

*I*t was certainly surprising to Pippa how a new name (even though Pippa could never get accustomed to using it) could change a person. Several times that spring Jamie came to visit them. Grizel always ran joyfully to meet him. She laughed and smiled and chattered more than Pippa had ever heard before. Grizel seemed to be getting younger before their very eyes. When Jamie was away, Grizel would sit while Pippa brushed and braided her hair, and just for fun they tried all sorts of ways of pinning it and twining it with ribbons and nets. Then Grizel would do Pippa's hair. In the old days, they would never have wasted time on their hair. They didn't even own a looking glass, although Auntie Sebrina had one, so Pippa knew what she looked like to other people.

Whenever Jamie came back, he repaired the well or mended the loom or trapped birds for their supper. He always prepared the dinners while they sat and watched like two gentlewomen. He entertained them with stories while he chopped and baked, and after dinner, what music they had! He would play his flute for them, or ask Pippa to sing. Grizel played her harp. But Pippa's favorite times were when Jamie and Grizel sang together. Pippa loved to listen to them. And after she went to bed, she liked hearing their voices murmuring on and on, talking long into the night.

July 1306
The Sound of Bute

$\mathcal{T}$om sat in the prow of the cog boat *Chevalier*, steered by John Dimond, a fisherman who lived down the beach from him. The *Chevalier* was heading north up Loch Ranza. Tom carried his dagger and was told to keep his arrows close at hand. It was nighttime. Hundreds of stars winked in and out through thin clouds. A cool west wind prodded little flags of mist that hung over the waters of the loch but didn't manage to disperse them. Beneath the deck where Tom sat, twelve hobbins stamped restlessly, not pleased either with their confinement nor the fact that the floor pitched beneath their feet.

When they left the loch behind and sailed out into the Sound of Bute, the seas were higher. They rounded the Cock of Arran, a promontory that looked like a crowing rooster hanging over the sea, and the breeze was stronger too. The sail filled nicely but their cargo was heavy. The bow plunged deeply from time to time.

They were headed for Ardrossan castle. Cuinn came forward to stand behind Tom. Besides the three on deck, Grimm the constable was also on board, and he was below with the horses.

"Seen anything, Tom?" asked Cuinn.

"Nothing, Sire."

"It's quiet tonight but the breeze is good. We should make pretty decent time. I'm going to get the signal lantern, and see if I can raise Fergus's men." In a few minutes, in immediate answer to Cuinn's signal, a tiny speck of light appeared and disappeared twice across the water.

"Fine. So far, everything looks good. Keep a close watch, though, won't you Tom? Sing out if you even think you see a sail."

Cuinn went back to sit with John Dimond and Tom stared hard into the darkness. Ahead, he could just make out a dark outline that was Horse Island, or what Cuinn had named Horse Island, near the Ardrossan shore.

Tom whistled softly and Cuinn came instantly.

"See something?"

Tom pointed to the south.

Cuinn cursed. "Looks like we'll be playing cat and mouse again tonight. I'll tell John."

"Can they catch us, Sire?"

"I hope not. We have a few tricks up our sleeves."

Tom wasn't much comforted. The thought of being captured by the English, after all the stories they had heard, drained the strength right out of his limbs. He gripped the gunwale and tried to gauge how fast the English boat was moving.

Fortunately, the wind didn't favor the other boat, sailing in the lee of Arran Island, and Horse Island was coming up fast for the *Chevalier.* Tom could hear the waves breaking on its rocky shore. Cuinn came forward again and spoke softly.

"We're going to turn around the northern tip of this island. Ah, there's our decoy." He pointed. A boat with bare poles sat at anchor in the narrow channel between Ardrossan and Horse Island.

"Whose boat is that?"

"Those are some of Fergus's men. Keep your eyes peeled now."

"Where can we land, Sire? It looks like the shore on that island is all rocks."

"Right, Tom. There are rocks underwater too. There is only one channel. If we miss it, we're done for. We'll be sitting ducks. Help me watch for a light."

John Dimond had stumbled forward to join them. He wanted to make sure Tom kept a sharp lookout.

"Don't you miss that signal, Tom, or I'll feed your living entrails to the fish" he hissed nervously, and lurched back across the heaving deck to his post. Cuinn was tense, too. Tom could sense it. Tom himself was terrified.

A small light shone briefly from the tip of Horse Island. John Dimond changed course and headed straight towards it. Tom really started to panic. Ahead was a cliff of rock, twelve feet high, just visible in the darkness. There was no safe place to land. Then the light shone briefly again and Tom could barely make out a narrow inlet that opened to the north. John Dimond threaded his way toward it. He looked over his shoulder and was reassured. There was the other signal fire, on the island of Bute across the channel. He kept that fire centered on his stern. Cuinn ordered Tom to help him drop the sail. Ahead, four men stood on a miniscule patch of beach in the dark and caught the lines Tom threw. They drew the boat in close and took great care turning it so it was kept off the rocks. Now the bow pointed out. The *Chevalier* rocked in its tiny berth, almost hidden between the rock cliffs. They waited. No one was allowed to speak. Voices carried easily over water. Below deck, Grimm's job was to keep the horses as quiet as possible.

At the very moment that the *Chevalier* dropped her sail, the boat belonging to Fergus, out in the channel, sprang into life. Its sail billowed and it began to move north.

"Watch this, Tom" said Cuinn very quietly. "The English know they'll have to sail to the west of this island to avoid the rocks."

"Many and many a boat" whispered John Dimond, "has had its hull torn out on the rocks around Horse Island."

To the south, the English ship advanced on Horse Island, attempting to follow the boat that sailed along the coast. They seemed to know these waters were treacherous because they were giving the island a wide berth. All on board the *Chevalier* watched intently as the English ship came into view on their port side. They quietly took up and adjusted their weapons. Tom had never been in a fight in his life, but if the *Chevalier* were seen, it would be a fight to the death.

The boat belonging to Fergus, carrying nothing but a few bolts of woolen cloth, sailed on to the north and the English took the bait. They sailed past Horse Island without a backward glance.

The men on the *Chevalier* watched them pass with relief. Grimm the constable came up from below and stood behind them with a smile.

"Just about ready, Sire?"

"Let's push off." The English boat had almost disappeared, lured to the north by Fergus's decoy. Tom drew in their lines and the men on the little beach waded into the water and shoved them carefully back into the harbor. John Dimond steered straight for the signal fire across the sound, until he came level with the wide sand beach at Ardrossan. Then he put the wind behind them and headed in. Fergus of Ardrossan was waiting on the sand with more men, some of them on horseback. It was the work of a quarter of an hour to drop the *Chevalier's* ramp and unload the horses. Fergus's men rounded them up with quiet yips and, before Tom knew what was happening, they too had disappeared into the night. The Scottish rebels now had a few more precious horses to add to their cavalry.

"Tom, get a bucket of seawater and a shovel. Go back inside and swab out the hold. We don't want any trace of horse in there."

"What? Muckin' out manure? Aw, that was supposed to be my job!" bawled one of Fergus's men. Everyone laughed and some of the tension melted away.

"You can clean up the beach. There's more than enough horse manure to go around" Cuinn assured him.

When the hold was clean, they closed the ramp.

"It takes a lot of men to pull this thing off" commented Tom to Grimm.

"Och ai, but there's the Scotsman for ye. Cuinn's got twenty, thirty men lined up wantin' this job, don't ye know. There's no' a bluddy Scotsman born who don't love runnin' around in the dark, makin' fools of the English. Gives the heart a rare glow, don't ye think?"

"Ai, that it does!" smiled Tom.

They pulled up the anchors and eased back out into the channel. Grimm sat with Tom, glad to be out on deck. Tom shared his relief as they breathed the fresh sea air.

Their stay at Ardrossan had been short. They gave Horse Island and its treacherous rocks a wide berth and John Dimond steered the *Chevalier* by the stars across the dark water. The night was moonless and the black mountains of Arran Isle, though close, were nearly invisible. It was into that invisible land that the *Chevalier* would disappear, a mere will-o-the-wisp, a wee Scottish fantasy with nowt but ghosties for crew.

August 1306
Gleinn Eason Biorach

On another night a month later, Pippa and Grizel had just gone to bed. Tott the dog heard the horsemen first and began a terror of barking. Gervaise, nearly deaf now, saw rather than heard the commotion and began to yowl. Grizel and Pippa sprang from their beds and ran out the door of the cottage. Now they could hear riders, too.

"Listen!" Pippa put a hand on Grizel's arm. "There's a horn." They paused in the dark garden. "It's Rob's horn!" Still cautious, they lit no lamp but hid in the rocks until the men rode into their vale. Tott's eager greeting reassured them. It was indeed Rob, with Cuinn, Jamie Douglas, and Gilbert de la Haye, a close friend of the men. Gervaise continued to howl, but delightedly now. They had company!

Caela ran to kiss Jamie.

"I hope we didn't frighten you" he said. "Were you asleep?"

"We had just gone to bed. We're glad that you're here. Pippa, why don't you get some clothes on so you can take care of these ponies. What brings you here in the middle of the night?"

"Aside from seeing you" said Jamie, "we needed somewhere safe for a night or two."

Jamie seemed to be the only one able to smile. Caela had never seen Rob and Cuinn looking so sober. She was barely acquainted with Gilbert de la Haye, but she knew a depressed man when she saw one. He walked to the edge of the vale and stood gazing out. Rob went out to stand beside him.

"What a lovely spot" said Gilbert quietly. "It's so peaceful here."

"It's one of the few places in all of Scotland where I can feel somewhat safe" declared Rob. "And Caela seems happy to have us, though I don't know why. We usually bring nothing but bad news. She'll probably have something for us to eat. Are you hungry, Gil?"

"I didn't think I'd feel like eating, but now that I'm here, I'm famished."

Caela drew them to her table with a platter of food. She sat down close to Jamie.

"How are you?" he asked softly, full of concern. "Have you been feeling well?"

"Yes, I feel wonderful." She smiled at him. "And you? All of you look so thin and tired." The four men sat, turning their horn cups speculatively on the tabletop. Jamie roused himself to answer.

"We're running for our lives this time, Caela. We've had a disastrous summer."

"Things are not going well?"

"Things couldn't be worse."

Caela waited expectantly. With a sigh, Cuinn looked around the table. He saw that the other men could hardly rouse themselves to explain.

"We saw an English ship in Brodick harbor" Cuinn said to her. "Have they bothered you or my mother at all?"

"Never. I only found out they were here when I went down to Mo Las to sell some fabric."

"You're careful that no one follows you home?"

"Very careful. " She looked around. "What has gone wrong for you? Why are you on the run this time?"

Rob answered her with bitterness in his voice. "Between King Edward and his troops, and the Comyns and all their supporters, there is hardly a place in Scotland where we feel safe anymore."

"Has there been much fighting?"

"Too much. Much too much fighting. And we have been soundly defeated in every battle."

"Defeated!"

"For the past few weeks we haven't even been strong enough to fight. All we can do is keep running. We've been hiding in the hills on the mainland, trying to protect my family – oh, it's been one disaster after another."

"Your family? You don't mean your wife .. "

"Yes, my wife and my daughter and sisters were with us for a few weeks."

"On the battlefield? Why? I thought they were somewhere safe. At Kildrummy, with Niall."

"They were. I had them brought back to me because I was afraid Edward would chase them down. If he catches them, he has threatened to hang them. Or worse. But it was difficult, having them with us. The battlefield was no place for them. We had nowhere to stay, very little food. We had to hide in the mountains and sleep on the ground. We would have starved, but for Jamie here, who managed to trap game for us almost every night." Caela smiled at Jamie but he didn't notice. He was staring at the tabletop. A thought occurred to her.

"Where are the women now?" she asked anxiously. "Have you brought them to Loch Ranza?"

"They convinced me, against my better judgment, to send them back to Kildrummy. I made them promise to head farther north after that. I'll feel better when they get to Orkeny."

Caela felt a guilty flicker of relief. They had gone north. Pippa would stay here for now. She hesitated.

"Is Isobel still with them? I was wondering ..."

"Yes, she's with them. You still worry about her taking Pippa? I know you do, Caela. But Isobel knows that is not possible right now. She knows what would happen."

Caela couldn't help but sigh. Rob continued.

"Anyway, her husband, John Comyn, knows I have had a disastrous summer. So many of my men killed ..." He paused, shook his head. "Our army has been decimated. So many friends dead. The rest of us have been running for over three months now. Never enough food, nowhere safe to stay. You can't imagine how narrowly we escaped from the mainland yesterday." His face was bleak, he sagged in his chair. The other three men put their elbows on the table and watched him in silence.

"I'm so sorry, Rob" said Caela.

He took a ragged breath.

"At Strathfilan they surprised us; at Dal Righ they got almost the whole lot of us, including me. Simon Fraser barely managed to save me. Ha! That's three times that man has saved my life. And now, what do I have? What have I accomplished, after all this?"

Cuinn spoke up. "This is why we're hiding, Grizel. They've mounted a serious search for us. We just pray that no one knows we're here. We, and what is left of our men, are all hiding on the island."

"Here? Where?"

"Don't even ask where. Hopefully it's only for a short time. We have to give the men a chance to recuperate, and we have to figure out how we're going to get out of this mess. We've been beaten too many times. We hardly have an army left."

Caela looked from one dejected man to the other.

"The die is cast, though, isn't it? You can't give up now" she said, "now that…" She looked up to notice Pippa standing at Cuinn's elbow. "I thought you were outside with the ponies."

"What can't you give up?" Pippa demanded, her arm around Cuinn's shoulder. She looked soberly at Rob. She had heard whispers. Rob had murdered two men. Their friend, Rob, a murderer.

Rob tried to shake off the somber mood.

"We couldn't give up the chance to visit. And you might be seeing a lot of us for the next few weeks."

"Did you bring Tommy home with you? He's okay?"

"Oh, Tom! Yes, he's turned into our best messenger boy. He'll make a fine soldier if we can keep him out of battles 'til he's strong enough to handle a sword."

Pippa turned to Jamie and Cuinn.

"And you'll be staying for long?"

"We'll be visiting now and then, while we sort some things out. If it's all right with Caela."

"I'd like to take this opportunity to say something, if I might. This visit suits Caela and me just fine, actually" proclaimed Jamie. He was smiling again. "This is a good time to tell you gentlemen, in case you haven't guessed." He looked proudly at Caela. "Last time I was here, Caela and I had the priest marry us. We are having a baby."

"A sister for me," Pippa spoke up.

"Oh, no! Uh, uh!" roared Jamie. "I'm planning on you having a brother! No argument! I've decided."

Thinking about Pippa having a sister, Rob opened his mouth to say something about his other daughter, Pippa's half-sister. He thought he should say something. But tonight he was just too tired. He let it go.

Amidst the congratulations and manly back-slapping, they ate a late supper. Then Pippa and Caela curled up together and fell asleep while the men sat at the table talking on and on. And in the middle of the floor, where they could benefit from the cool night breezes, the two dogs slept. Or rather they drifted in and out of sleep. In the early hours of the morning they got up several times. They yawned and stretched noisily. They stared reproachfully at the men whenever the scheming and plotting at the table grew heated. Now it was nearly dawn. These humans talked so much, discussing this angle, discussing that angle. As every dog in the world knew, there were ways to handle problems with other creatures of the species. All that was really needed was a polite sniff or two in greeting, perhaps a bone to share. Diplomacy, compassion, and problem solved. After which all parties could stretch out on the floor for a nice, long, companionable nap. So simple.

Finally, the men slept too. In fact, as the sun rose higher they proceeded, in their exhaustion, to sleep the entire day away. The dogs went out, came back in. Went out, came in. Then, thinking how therapeutic another nap might actually be, how very companionable, the dogs threw themselves down on the floor to join them. So men and dogs slept and for a little time, all their worries slept too.

October, 1306
Arran Isle

"Jamie Douglas! You're such a joker!" Caela put her hands on her hips.

"He's king of Samhain" giggled Pippa. "Do you like his crown?" The two of them cavorted around the garden wearing wreaths of red-berrried rowan twigs.

"I'm wearing this to keep witches away. You're not a witch are you, Caela?" He galloped by with Pippa on his back and gave Caela a peck on the cheek. "You've bewitched me, I swear you have!"

"I'll put a spell on you both if you're not ready to go soon. I want to get there before dark."

"We have to obey her," said Jamie, setting Pippa on the ground, "or she'll put a hex on us. Or complain that she's not well enough to go. Then we'll all have to stay home."

"I'm feeling fine! Most people can't even tell I'm pregnant." She displayed her profile for their benefit. Her baby was due in three months, but she had gained very little weight and was as strong and energetic as ever.

"We are ready to go!" exclaimed Pippa.

She was wild with excitement. It was the festival of Samhain, and for the first time, Grizel was leading them down to Machrie Moor. All the islanders, what few there were, gathered at the ancient stone circles for the feast that marked the end of the year and the ritual lighting of the last great fire. Pippa had convinced herself that it wouldn't matter if Tommy were there or not. They would see other people they knew, children of Grizel's customers, the families of fishermen, the woman who spun Grizel's wool. Their ponies stood ready, laden with food and a small tent.

It was late morning when they set out. Tott the dog had to stay home all by himself to keep marauding animals away, sadly no longer, indeed never again, to be assisted by the noble old Gervaise.

Caela led the way high into the hills. Near the top of the glen they spread their lunch on a rock that was sheltered from the wind. From here they could see the mainland of Scotland.

"That's where I was born" said Jamie, pointing. "Someday you'll both come back with me to Douglasdale, after we drive the English out." He had been but a boy when the English confiscated the castle belonging to his family.

"I don't see why you don't just stay here with us, Jamie" Pippa said.

"That's a very appealing offer. I'll have to think it over. I wonder if Caela would mind?" Caela's eyes, Pippa noticed, were very wide. She was looking at Jamie, saying nothing. Then she turned to examine the view.

"She wouldn't mind. And I'd like it" Pippa assured him. "Why do you bother to fight the English, anyway? It's really a waste of time."

"If they ran you out of your home, put most of your family in prison and killed your father, wouldn't you fight them?"

"They killed your father?"

"And gave Douglasdale, our home, to Robert Clifford, that .. that rotten pile of pig guts. He's getting rich off my property, and here I am, with nothing but the clothes on my back."

"The English took Brodick Castle from Aunt Sebrina, too."

"They've taken over many castles in Scotland. They burn peoples' homes to the ground, steal their crops. They are trying to weaken us, Pippa. King Edward is trying to hammer us into submission."

"Do you miss Douglasdale?"

"Yes, I do. It was my family's home for a long time. One day I'm going to take it back." Pippa had never seen Jamie's face look so dark. When the smile left his face, it drained all the light from the afternoon.

He lay back and laced his fingers over his eyes. "They'll pay, one day, for what they've done to us. For what they've done to Scotland!"

Quietly, Grizel rose and began to repack the lunch foods. Pippa bounced up to help her, wondering what had changed her mood. After a bit Jamie got up and went to speak to Grizel. He put his arms about her wide waist. Grizel began to smile. Ah, the sun began to shine again. It was time they set off for Machrie Moor.

When they came out onto the high plain of the moor, Pippa had her first view of the double ring of standing stones.

"Here it is, Suithi-Choir-Fhionn" Jamie said softly. "Cuinn showed me this place. This is the cauldron seat of Fionn, where the Fianna once hunted and the ancient tribes used to meet. They were great warriors, Pippa. Do you know the tales of the Fianna?" Pippa shook her head. "See that stone with the hole in it? That is where Fionn tied his wonderful dog, Bran."

"Look!" shrieked Pippa. She raced her pony across the moor and leapt off, into the arms of Cuinn.

"I didn't know you'd be here!" she yelled. She looked with disdain at the lady clinging to his arm. Her clothing was magnificent. Little bells were sewn into the embroidery of her cloak. It was lined with blue fur and her hat was pinned with a sapphire. It was very obvious that she was from away, not from the island. Cuinn held Pippa's shoulders.

"You've grown since I've seen you last! Look at you!" he exclaimed. He greeted Jamie and Caela and introduced them to his companion.

"Is our great leader coming up here for the festival?" Jamie asked, warily. Given the high price on Rob's head, Jamie didn't refer to him by name when they were in unfamiliar company.

"Yes, he'll be here after dark. He went off on his own somewhere. He didn't say where, but he was smiling when he left, so it probably involves a lady." Jamie stirred warningly. Cuinn's eyes flicked down to Pippa and back to Jamie. "He's looking for, uh, adventure..." he added.

"Oh oh. Adventure!" said Jamie, ruefully.

Caela looked up. For the second time that day she was suddenly overcome with dread. Who was Rob bringing to Arran?

"We may see him and his friend, and then again, we may not" said Cuinn, returning Caela's questioning gaze with a frank look. Caela couldn't guess his meaning. Anxiety caught her unawares and wouldn't let go.

Cuinn turned quickly to Pippa. "I brought Tom along, Pippa. Why don't you see if you can find him?"

Tommy soon showed up, making Pippa's day complete, if she were admit it, which she did not. Jamie found some men to help set up their tent. The place was full of people and Pippa was a wild thing, running here and there, helping one moment, and horsing around with friends a moment later. Finally Grizel told her she and Tom could go off to help the men piling the wood for the night's fire. The ritual bone fire was to be immense. They were bringing in logs from each of the nine sacred trees.

Caela spread out their food and Pippa reappeared as if by signal. They invited Tommy to eat with them. They set a place for the dead at their makeshift table, as tradition demanded, and Cuinn and Jamie were sober for a moment as they honored the departed. Since custom encouraged talking about the dead at Samhain, someone took up the telling of a story. The sober mood lifted. Little lanterns made of carved turnips made faces glow. Fires, lit for warmth as well as for cooking, crackled merrily all across the moor and people gathered in groups to sample food and gossip. There were several men there that Cuinn and Jamie knew from the mainland. Pippa suspected they were all part of Rob's army. They roamed around, sharing jokes and stories at each gathering. Children ran from one family group to the next, were welcomed at each, and accepted traditional handouts of sweets and nuts at every fireside.

Samhain marked the end of the harvest season and the beginning of the dark of the year. This would be the last fire festival, probably the last time that everyone would come together until the spring feast of Beltane. The summer's work was over. Crops had been harvested and stored carefully, and all the fruit trees had been picked bare. Whatever food people had put away by this night would have to last them for the entire winter. By now they had chosen which animals would be slaughtered for the stewpot, and a bone or two of these would be saved for the Samhain fire. Only the strongest animals would be kept alive and fed through the long winter. Tonight no lights showed in any cottages. All hearth fires were extinguished, to be relit from the great fire they would set alight that evening.

Nothing would be renewed until Candlemas. Now, in the dark of the year, everything came to an end.

The old ones told that on this one night of the year, ghosts of the dead might mingle with the living. They might leave a sign, a portent, a warning from beyond. One must walk carefully. Carry a turnip lantern wherever you go, for without a light it would be easy, far too easy, to stray across the treacherous boundary from which there was no return. Tonight, only a veil, the thinnest of veils, separated life from death. This was the Night of the Dead.

*T*he feasting was boisterous. But just beyond in the darkness, out where impenetrable silence muffled the night moor, out there stood the tall standing stones. It was said they towered over ancient graves. No one remembered who had been buried beneath them, or why, but they were certain no Christian bones lay there. Out of superstitious fear, people shivered and hurried as they passed the stone circles. White mists, like serpents, undulated just above the ground there and coiled themselves around the tallest standing stones. They licked the cold rock with frosty tongues and stared menacingly with their silver eyes at the intruders below. Living beings kept close to each other and avoided walking among the stones. But the dead waited there surely, perhaps even the beautiful Sidhe on their fair horses.

And there, as well, waited Ailliol. Silent, she seemed, because she communed wordlessly, but not with the living. More ancient than any old crone, she had directed the preparations for the annual fire festivals since time out of mind. She carried a stout rowan stick, itself a sacred relic that had come down through four centuries of seers.

For Ailliol could foretell the future. The islanders depended upon her to do so, and with good reason. Their very survival depended upon the choices they made and Ailliol's predictions helped them decide wisely. Would there be much rainfall, and should Bette marry Dick?

It seemed perfectly natural to them that there should be someone amongst them who could predict what would happen. For four hundred years or more, stories told, there had always been one woman on the island with a remarkable gift of vision, who led their sacred festivals and, miraculously, was able to see into the future. No islander thought it odd that each of these women had been blind. Some said it was coincidence, some said it happened by other secret means.

So when the full moon began to rise, a little crowd gathered around Ailliol at the inner stone circle. They carried bones to throw into the fire, as ancient custom required. The ground nearby had been brushed clean with branches.

The orange moon began her procession into the temple of the sky. She was lifted free of the horizon by grey clouds that hung at her elbow. Like priestesses, they followed her into the heavens. The people were silent, watching the moonrise for a sign. The old woman, Ailliol, held a torch and began to chant in a low voice. Everyone turned toward the great pile of wood. They watched the woman. She moved slowly, as if in a trance, and though she could not see, no one needed to guide her torch towards the kindling. A sudden gust of wind blew across the moor just then, sharp and cold. It blasted the standing stones with its bitter breath and the serpents of white mist hissed and recoiled. The old woman's torch fluttered and almost went out, but suddenly the twigs caught in a burst of flame. Fire roared through the pile of brush and the wind, in a fury, tore sparks from the flames and flung them into the blackening sky.

"That's an evil sign, that is, that north wind" muttered one bent old man. Pippa moved closer to hear what he was saying. "Just ask Ailioll. She'll tell ye. There'll be no good to be foretold for this year, if the cruel north wind comes up just when the bone fire is lit."

"Augh, Ailioll never has any predictions but evil ones. Ye shouldna listen to her" claimed another.

"Yeah, well, ye notice, don't ye, that she's right most of the time, and for nigh on a hunnerd year."

"Too long a time, says I. I heerd she's just bidin' her time 'til she finds someone to take her place. She can't leave us 'til the new seer is borned."

"Strange to think on, ain't it? Now look at that moon, wearin' a grey cloak. That's not a good sign neither."

"Throw yer bones on the fire, then, old man. Come on," encouraged his neighbor. "It'll keep the evil spirits away. That's what ya came fer." They trudged away to toss their cattle bones onto the fire and Pippa and Tommy did the same.

"Do you think those old men are right? Is it going to be a bad year?" Pippa asked, not taking her eyes from the fire.

"We'll have to wait and see, I guess. Who knows?" Tommy tried to sound nonchalant. His back felt suddenly vulnerable. He told himself that at his age the Feast of the Dead should be losing its terrors. There couldn't be cold, dead hands running fingers down his spine. Impossible. He and Pippa both glanced quickly behind them. The standing stones loomed taller than before, and closer. Who moved among them? Only the mist?

The moon rose overhead, but still she hadn't shed her mantle of grey clouds. On the horizon, lightening flashed and they heard a faraway rumble of thunder. The restless crowd groaned. The wind wailed. People held tight to hats and hoods and averted their eyes from the talismanic stones on the moor. Before the keening wind, the white serpents of mist fled in terror, in their haste shedding vaporous tatters like skins.

But a moment later, all was quiet. The wind was gone and an evil spirit with it. Smiles loosened anxieties and began to ease wrinkled brows. Relaxed banter rippled here and there. People put their arms on each others shoulders and gathered again at their cooking fires. Jamie took out the new rowanwood flute that Caela had given him and the dancing began.

*T*ommy looked restlessly over his shoulder again.

"I'll see you later, ai?" he said to Pippa.

"Where are you going?" Tommy pointed toward a rowdy group of lads close to his age who were flinging one another to the ground for sheer boyish joy.

"Can't I come with you?"

"No Pippa! Find some girls to play with." Stung, Pippa watched him run off. Slowly she turned in a circle, surveying the crowds. Jamie and Grizel were smiling and chatting with some dull-looking people. She ambled over to where the girls were focused on disregarding the boys. Likewise the boys ignored the girls, making a boisterous show of breaking each others' necks. Just beyond them, the dancing couples caught Pippa's interest.

Cuinn and his lady friend were sometimes in the middle of the frolic and sometimes whispering together on the sidelines. And there was Rob! He had come after all. Tall and commanding, he captured everyone's gaze, but he had eyes only for his partner. She was small with thick red hair and a green gown unlike any the islanders wore. Pippa wondered who she was. She couldn't see her face.

Meanwhile, Caela and Jamie were holding hands and walking slowly through the crowd, talking to people and idly watching out for Pippa. Jamie could mingle among the people of the island more freely than Rob. As yet, he had no price on his head. At this point and for the next couple of months, King Edward I was perhaps only vaguely aware that Jamie Douglas was even alive. So Jamie laughed and joked with all the islanders and Caela basked quietly in his glow.

Pippa was losing interest in watching the boys fight as it became clear that, though the battering would go on at some length, nearly everyone would come out alive. She stood on one foot, then the other, then turned to make her way over to where a bagpiper was pumping his instrument with air. Busy watching the piper, she forgot to watch her step. She collided hard with the old blind woman, the one who had lit the bone fire.

"I'm so sorry" Pippa cried to the fragile old soul. "Are you all right?"

"Yes, I'm fine, dear lass. Perhaps I walked too close." Her voice was as resonant as a girl's.

"I didn't know you were there. I'm really sorry."

"No harm done, but if ye would help me find some place to rest, I'd thank ye. Is there a seat nearby?" Pippa guided her to the back of a cart and held her arm as the old woman eased herself down. The woman kept hold of Pippa's hand for a moment.

"Thank you kindly." She touched Pippa's palm with her fingers, and nodded silently. She seemed very absorbed with some thought of her own. Then she sighed and reluctantly loosened her hold. "So, my girl. You are Isobel's child, I understand."

"No–" Pippa thought for a moment. She straightened suddenly and peered at the bluish-white eyeballs in the woman's deeply wrinkled face. "Or – I don't know."

"Ah, I'm sorry. I didn't mean to pry."

"No, it's all right." Pippa sat down quickly. She found herself out of breath. "I don't know any Isobel. Who is she?"

The woman shook her head and quickly put her hand on Pippa's arm.

"I really don't know why I said that. These things just come to me sometimes. And it's often embarrassing." She laughed a deep rich laugh. Pippa had half-expected a cackle. "I must have you confused. Who are your parents then, lassie?"

"Well, I don't really know. I live with my guardian."

"Oh yes, yes, the woman who weaves. Of course. Ah ha." The woman's smile disappeared.

"Maybe you know who my real mother is? Tommy said the old women knew…oh, I didn't mean to say that. I'm sorry. Again!"

"Believe me, I am fully aware that I am an old woman, a very old woman, in truth. So you needn't apologize." She became serious all of a sudden, and changed the subject abruptly. "Now my sweet, a young lass like yourself would much rather be with her friends. You can run along. Thank you for aiding an old woman. I'll be fine here on my own."

Pippa looked hard at the woman for a moment. "If you know something about my parents, I would really like to hear it" she pleaded.

"I'm sorry. I can tell you nothing." The woman leaned forward to grip her staff with two hands. She rocked gently. "Nothing. I can tell nothing, nothing." she crooned softly.

"Oh, I was just hoping" Pippa sighed. "I keep wondering. I don't know who my mother is, but I have, you see, this little charm. It's all I have from her." She pulled the necklace from her tunic. She took Ailioll's hand and placed the charm on her upturned palm.

Ailioll's eyebrows twitched. She touched the charm with delicate fingers.

"The whitebeam of Arran Isle. Yes. It is well that you wear this. Keep it with you."

"Why do you say that?"

Ailioll released the charm and Pippa tucked the chain back inside her tunic. Ailioll shook her head.

"For protection. But there I go again, rattling on. You must forgive me."

"But you don't understand. I really want to find out about my mother" Pippa insisted.

"And in time, my lass, you will, you surely will." Ailioll lifted her head. "Ah, someone is looking for you, I believe." Pippa stared at the sightless woman again, then looked out at the crowd of people. Sure enough, there were Jamie and Grizel, craning their necks and looking around. Pippa stood and called to them.

"Here you are! We were just wondering if you were having a good time." Grizel held her lantern in front of Pippa's nose and laughed at the face she made.

"Oh, yes. I was talking with this woman," Pippa replied, turning back to where Ailioll sat. She was gone.

"Did you see that woman sitting here?"

"No, I didn't."

"She was right here." Pippa whirled around.

"Maybe you'll find her later. Shall we walk around? Cuinn is playing the mandolin over there, I think. Let's go listen." They dragged Pippa reluctantly away.

She had been close to finding some important information. She said nothing more to Grizel, but her eyes darted everywhere, looking for the old blind woman.

Pippa touched Grizel's arm and they stopped to watch the dancers. Suddenly, Grizel went rigid. Pippa looked up. Grizel's face was snow white. Jamie, standing on the other side of Grizel, felt it too. He turned quickly to see what had disturbed her.

"Oh, no!" Grizel's hand flew to her mouth. She stared at the small red-haired woman dancing with Rob. Pippa stood on tiptoe to try to see over the crowd.

"What?" cried Pippa in alarm. Just then the red-haired woman turned and happened to look in their direction. Grizel went limp with relief. Freckled skin, not creamy white. Brown eyes, not grey-green. She leaned on Jamie's shoulder.

"I thought for a moment..." was all she could say.

"I thought so too" Jamie answered. "I was sure of it. He seems to like redheads, doesn't he?" he added softly. "Are you okay?"

"Grizel, what's the matter?"

"Oh, I thought I saw someone I knew in my childhood."

"Who?"

"It wasn't who I thought it was. I...I'll be back in just a moment. I want to....um, Nature calls. I'll be right back."

Jamie was concerned. "Are you sure you don't want Pippa to come with you?"

"No! No, I'm fine. I won't be a moment." Jamie grinned at Pippa and steered her toward the dancing.

"Let's get closer, shall we? And, hey there, I'm a-wonderin', my bonnie lass. Would ye dance a step with me?" Pippa followed him happily through the crowd.

Caela pressed her fingers to her forehead as she made her way to the edge of the crowd. She saw an empty seat and took it. She had had a bit of a scare. She had been sure the redhead was the cousin she had been raised with, Isobel MacDuff, and sure that she had come to take Pippa away.

She reprimanded herself for being so anxious, worse than an old hen. She sat quietly for a few minutes, feeling her heartbeat return to normal. The whole issue of Isobel MacDuff would have to be settled, she decided. Pippa was getting older, and was asking questions. What to tell her, though, what to tell her? She didn't want her to feel she had been abandoned by her mother. On the other hand, she didn't want her to go away to live with her, either.

Oh, Caela, she said to herself. Caela you fool, you are the one who doesn't want to be abandoned. That's the real problem, isn't it?

"Oh, Caela" echoed a voice by her side. She looked around in astonishment. She recognized the ancient woman who had lit the ceremonial bone fire. The blind woman smiled into the air. "Caela. It's a fine Gaelic name. 'From the forest', it means."

"Yes. Yes, I knew that" she replied politely. "I'm sorry. I didn't see you sitting there. Was I speaking out loud?"

The old woman, instead of answering, turned her blind eyes toward the moon and began to hum tunelessly. She stirred the dirt with her stout rowan stick. Then she was still as stone. "So you are a MacDuff, are you not?" she finally asked Caela.

"How did you know that?"

"Well, I have known of you, haven't I, and the remarkable child you care for? Ailioll sees with more than her eyes, you know."

"I'm sorry that I don't remember having met you. Remarkable child? Why do you say that?"

Ailliol ignored the question. "We have never met, my dear. Hmm, MacDuff, MacDuff" said Ailioll, musingly to herself. "Yes, the red stag comes for the MacDuffs, I seem to remember." She turned toward Caela. "Do you believe in the Sidhe?"

"Well, I've heard the stories."

"Have you heard of the signs they send us, portents of death, in the form of an animal? The same animal for everyone in the family."

"Yes." Caela tried to laugh. "Those creepy stories." Looking around for Jamie, she was not paying close attention.

"They are strange stories, sometimes. Still, I've heard them told, many and many a time. I trust you'll watch for the stag" said Ailioll. She sensed now that Caela, sitting with her head in her hands, was not listening.

For some reason, a sick anxiety had gripped Caela all over again. She wasn't feeling well.

The woman spoke softly, close to her ear, secretively.

"There are certain things that need taking care of, before your new little bairn is born, my dear. Secrets that must be told."

Caela looked at her, stunned. Her chest felt tight.

"I was just thinking about ...about that very thing."

"I'm glad." The old woman thumped the ground with her walking stick.

Caela gripped her stout waist and slumped forward. She was very hot, burning hot. And what was this vision she saw before her?

The woman seemed unconcerned. She leaned over and whispered again.

"Your story is part of a long tale, Caela MacDuff, a very long tale. Do not be afraid. Let it be as it will be."

Caela heard the old woman's words but she was afraid, very afraid, of some nameless thing. She slipped forward and fell hard to the ground.

Pippa jumped violently at the sound of a scream. People were exclaiming, moving, gathering. She and Jamie pushed through the crowd to see what was happening. There on the ground lay Caela, unconscious and white as a ghost.

"Grizel!" she shouted. She dropped to her knees beside her. "Grizel, wake up!" Caela stirred faintly. Jamie lifted her in his arms. She began to come round.

"Are you all right?"

"Yes, I – I'm fine. Just a bit..." Caela struggled to sit up. Pippa threw her arms around her.

"You'd better let her get some air, Pippa" warned Jamie.

"No, no. I'm fine." Caela put one weak arm around Pippa. "I don't know what came over me."

Hearing this, the old blind woman at the edge of the crowd backed away and walked off alone, in a straight line between the standing stones and over the dark, empty moor.

"Grizel, what happened to you?" Pippa cried.

"I don't know. I was sitting here for a moment." Caela shook her head hazily. "What was I doing? I don't remember. Can you help me up?" She laughed as she struggled to her feet. She had to lean against Jamie, she felt so weak.

"You're freezing cold" exclaimed Jamie. "Come sit beside the fire. Pippa, sit close to keep her warm." Sandwiched between the two people most dear to her, Caela finally began to feel her strength returning. One of the women brought her a hot drink.

"Shall I sing to you, Grizel?"

"That would be lovely, Pippa."

Jamie would have taken out his flute but Caela had her arms wrapped so tightly about him, he could hardly move.

Pippa stood and began to sing. Cuinn took up his mandolin and strummed it lightly. It was a song they all knew.

Oh rowan tree, oh rowan tree, thoul't aye be dear to me,
Entwin'd thou art with many ties, of home and infancy...

By the second line of the song, Caela began to tremble violently in Jamie's arms.

"What is it, Caela?"

"Please, not that song."

"That is one of your favorites."

"No, not that one! Please, not now."

"Pippa, do you know a happier song? How about 'If All the Young Ladies'?"

Pippa started over. Cuinn followed suit, and soon everyone had joined in with instrument or voice. People began to dance again. Caela soon sat up and laughed and clapped with the rest.

Meanwhile, the moon skulked across the heavens, swirling her tattered old grey cloak high above the moor.

'Twas thus that the Night of the Dead closed the old year. The veil between life and death ceased fluttering and it too drew closed. The old woman, Ailioll, tapped her rowan stick as she made her way alone across the black moor, wishing she did not know what she knew. Another life would soon be gone, like a dream forgotten the moment we awake.

Tonight she had learned her own destiny too. It wouldn't be long for her now, either, not long at all. That made her sad, not for herself, but for the one who would succeed her.

December 1306
Gleinn Eason Biorach

*I*t was late at night when Jamie rode up their mountain path the next time. He had been away for a couple of weeks with Rob and his army, staying on the move, never in any one place for long. Pippa didn't know for sure where they went, but she had heard them talking about Ireland and the western isles. Jamie, still able to move about more freely than many of them, had come up by himself several times, to be with Caela. This time he was on his way to the other side of the island.

"Rob and Cuinn should be on their way here already, Caela" Jamie had said on that visit. "Are you feeling up to giving them a little of your famous hospitality? They are in pretty low spirits right now."

"Things are not going well?"

"No, things are not going well at all. I'm really worried for Rob. With all his concerns about his family and what to do next –he's very discouraged. I'll be going down to help him, but I'll come back in a couple of days. You'll wait for me, my Caela?"

"You know I will."

"In the meantime, you'll ride down to Loch Ranza if you think for even a minute that the baby is coming?"

"Yes, but it will be a few weeks before that happens. I'll be here, Jamie. I'm always here."

And Jamie had gone.

*B*abies do not always do what is expected of them. Caela and Jamie's baby decided to arrive rather inconveniently early. Pippa, alarmed at finding Caela so helpless, saddled the ponies and hastily packed a few things into panniers. She didn't know how long they would be gone so she summoned Tott the dog to lead them. It took them a good four hours to pick their way slowly down the glen. Grizel kept assuring Pippa that the pains that tore through her body were perfectly normal, but Pippa was worn with fright when she saw Grizel slide from her pony to crouch, groaning, on the frozen ground. Tott lay next to her with his head on his paws, distressed and anxious, his eyebrows flicking nervously. Pippa mopped Grizel's face and crooned softly to her until the pain subsided and they could continue on their way. But Grizel seemed weaker each time she remounted her pony. The wind howling up the glen gave them no comfort at all and winter darkness fell early. Both of them were frozen blue and numb with fright by the time they saw the lights of Loch Ranza lodge below them.

Sebrina hastily ordered the fires built high and a bed warmed with hot pans. Grizel crawled gratefully under the blankets. When Devorgilla, the healing woman, came sweeping in she sailed into Grizel's chamber and slammed the door. Pippa was left shivering in the hall, chilled to the bone, frightened out of her wits, and totally ignored until, through some miracle of telepathy, Jamie arrived. Now Pippa's misery had company.

They couldn't sleep. No one in the house slept. Jamie and Pippa paced outside of Grizel's chamber all night, waiting in anguish for the beautiful Baby William, named for Jamie's father, to decide to make his appearance.

Very early the next morning, Pippa and Jamie were finally allowed into the warmth of Grizel's room. Stiff with cold, they came, awestruck worshippers, to her bedside. The black-haired stranger, unbelievably tiny, was cuddled with his mother. Perfect in every way, he instantly became sovereign master of all their hearts. It was soon completely beyond understanding how they had ever lived without him.

Holding his son that morning, Jamie became very solemn.

"My boy must have a home" he declared, as though the realization had just come to him. "For his sake I am more determined than ever to recapture the Douglas lands." Jamie put his hand on Pippa's head. "Then we will all have a proper home of our own."

"A castle?"

Jamie nodded. "And an income!" he added, jubilantly. It all sounded so promising.

January 1307
Loch Ranza

*J*anuary came and they knew, rather than felt, that the days were beginning to lengthen. The weather was wintry, though, and Pippa and Caela were grateful to stay at Loch Ranza and let Sebrina care for them. Sebrina was more than happy for their company. They kept close to her huge hearth, sewing and chatting while their lives for the next month revolved almost entirely around little William. He, all oblivious, fattened and grew. And steadily, Caela regained her energy. In spite of her brisk recovery, Sebrina was concerned for her. She warned Pippa to be especially helpful to Caela in the next few months.

"She's not that young, you know. Twenty-seven is quite an advanced age to be having her first child."

"Twenty-seven?" Pippa breathed. "I didn't know she was that old."

Sebrina laughed. "Oh? And how old do you think I am?"

"I don't know, Aunt. Pretty ol-.... Uh, thirty?"

"I'm forty-one."

"Forty-one!" Pippa squeaked. "Forty-one?" She pushed a chair closer to the fire and took Sebrina's arm. "Here, sit down. Careful, Aunt. I'll help you. Let me get a robe for your lap."

"All right now, that's enough, Pippa" growled Sebrina irritably. "Let's not get carried away. I'm old but I'm not ancient."

Wisely, for once Pippa held her tongue.

*B*y the middle of the month, the cold weather broke. Even Loch Ranza, huddled in chill shadow on the north side of the mountains, reveled in the first sensations of spring, though everyone knew it wouldn't last. Soon came a day when Caela felt she was ready to ride back up the glen to her own cottage. She had so much work to catch up on. Pippa was eager to show Baby

William, if he would just stay awake long enough, his home and the stable where his pony would someday be, and the mountain peaks above their glen where they would go exploring together. Sebrina de Seta stood at her window and once more watched them cantering gaily around the end of the loch before disappearing between the high steep walls of Gleinn Eason Biorach.

One night a little while later Jamie rode up to Caela's cottage just as they finished their evening meal. His arrival upset Tott the dog, as usual, and so Baby William felt obliged to add his voice to the uproar. Jamie was restless and when everyone had settled down, he was finally able to tell them his news.

"First the good news" he said, "but then some very bad news." Pippa watched Caela fold her hands as though gathering her strength.

"We left … a certain hiding-place yesterday, Robert Boyd and I with some thirty others. Boyd knows Arran Island well, and we were hoping we would find Brodick lightly guarded so we could steal a little food. The men hadn't eaten decently in weeks."

"Brodick!" exclaimed Pippa. "Are you going to fight to get it back for Sebrina?"

"Just a minute. I'm getting to that. We hid our boat in the loch and after dark we moved up close to the castle through the woods. There's an old fort in the glen…"

"We know" declared Pippa.

"Tornanshian," nodded Caela.

"Oh? All right. So that's where we were last evening when we saw three big English supply ships just coming in to Brodick Bay. It was dark already, and it looked like they were going to wait until morning to unload. So we hid there all night, and in the morning, just when they finished bringing all the supplies ashore, we ambushed them and very handily relieved them of food, weapons, ammunition, all kinds of things that we really need. It was a great haul! They were in an uproar, completely unprepared for us. Even though there were so few of us, we managed to fight them back into the castle. Robert Boyd knew his way through the glens and up into your mountains, so we managed to get away with all of it!"

"Well that's good news for a change!" said Caela. "Where is everybody—all your men? Are they coming here?"

"They are farther up in the hills, having a fine old celebration. I didn't want them near here, in case the English try to come after us. In fact, I don't think it is safe here anymore, Caela, for you and the children. You'll be better off at Loch Ranza for the next few months."

"All right, Jamie, if you think that is best."

"Will you come with us?" Pippa asked.

"Yes, or I will stay with you, at least until Rob gets here. He's…well, I shouldn't say where he is right now." He looked at Pippa. She was leaning on the table, all ears. He turned to her.

"Pippa, sweetheart, would you bring in a basket of peat? The fire is getting low."

"But I want to hear what else happened."

"Pippa, please do as Jamie asks" ordered Caela quietly. Pippa slumped to the door, swinging her arms in high drama. When she had gone out, Caela turned again to Jamie.

"Go on" she said again.

"Rob has had some very bad news. Robert Boyd has come back from the mainland." He propped his chin on his hand. "You remember that last fall the ladies of Rob's family were all traveling with our army?"

"Yes, that was when Rob wanted Pippa to go with him. Of course I remember."

"That's right. Rob thought his family would be safer with him. So they dragged around after us from one hideous battle to another, until no one could stand it anymore. Remember, we told you about it? We were losing every battle and so many of our men were getting killed, that Rob decided the ladies should go north."

"He wanted them to go to Orkeny. Yes, I remember."

"That's right. He had asked Robert Boyd to go with them, and the Earl of Atholl, and Rob's brother, Niall."

"I get his brothers mixed up. Niall is the good-looking one?"

"Yes, now that you mention it, I guess he is. He's the youngest. Anyway, we didn't know it when they left us, but the English were hot on their heels. They chased Niall and the ladies as far as Kildrummy castle. Niall thought they would be safe there, but the blacksmith at Kildrummy betrayed them. The English had apparently promised him a bag of gold if he would set fire to the castle keep so they could sneak in and attack. He set the fire and did his part and, oh yes, the English kept their bargain. They gave the blacksmith his gold. But first they melted it. And then they poured it down his throat."

"How absolutely hideous!"

"There's worse. They captured Niall. We don't know what has become of him."

"Not Niall!"

"But Robert Boyd escaped. He says that John of Atholl got the ladies out of Kildrummy in time, and headed north again."

"I hope they are safe. Jamie, do you realize that if Pippa had gone with Rob last spring, she would be running for her life right now, too?"

Jamie sighed and nodded.

"What will become of Niall?"

"No one knows yet. We are waiting to hear what ransom they will ask."

"This is getting to be too much to bear."

"You're right. It is too much. We're going to put an end to it. Rob is making plans, Caela. I can't talk about them, but he's determined, finally, to make a move. And it's about time, I say. We've been hiding for weeks. You'd think we were cowards."

"Hasn't there been enough blood shed, Jamie?"

"You can't let a thing like this go. You can't fight a half-hearted war. Edward the First has to realize that he can't do whatever he pleases in Scotland. We do not belong to him. I, for one, will be glad to get out there and fight. I want my lands back. I want them for my son and for you and Pippa."

"You hardly have enough men to take a castle. How will you ever defeat the English nation, not to mention all the Scots who are Rob's enemies?" She gripped Jamie's arm where it lay on the table, and rested her head there.

"No, listen! We have been promised gallowglasses from Christiana of the Isles. Gallowglasses! They are amazing fighters, Caela. You should see them."

"No thank you."

"Rob is working hard to get more support from the earls. And there are more and more men, like me and like Cuinn, who have had their ancestral lands taken away. They are starting to join us. Rob's other brothers have come here to help. We are ready to fight. It's now or never." Jamie looked up as Pippa came in dragging a big basket of peat. He lifted Caela's chin. "Our past defeats are like that peat – fuel for our fire. We will fight now with everything we have so we can defend our families."

"Are you going to fight in a war, Jamie?"

"I hope so, Pippa."

"I wish you didn't have to."

"Pippa, let me tell you something a Roman philosopher once said. He said 'The desire for safety stands against every great and noble enterprise.'"

Pippa rolled her eyes. She'd heard these philosophers' remarks in the past. They never made much sense.

"He meant that people are sometimes afraid to do important things because they might be dangerous. But we can't afford to worry about danger any longer. Getting the English out of Scotland is more important."

Pippa pouted. "Those old philosophers wanted to make everyone suffer and be miserable."

"No, their advice is to be strong. You'll see," Jamie prophesied. "Someday you'll see that we have done the right thing."

*J*amie went away again with Rob's army. No one ever knew where they went or when they would be back. Tom told Pippa it was very dangerous for them now because the English had offered a big reward for news of either Jamie or Rob.

"The English hate them that much? Rob has done some very wicked things, but Jamie has certainly not done anything terrible," said Pippa.

"The English despise Jamie almost more than Rob. You would have seen why if you'd been with us when we were fighting on the mainland."

"Did the English run when Rob and Jamie came?"

"Oh no, not at all. No, they beat us. Beat us badly. We were the ones that had to run."

Pippa became very quiet when she heard this. She finally turned to Tom again.

"Will Baby William have to grow up without a father, too, like me?"

"I don't think so. Jamie's a great fighter! You should see him. He is so fierce, you wouldn't believe he was the same person we know."

"Ai?" Pippa was doubtful. "But still, the English beat us?"

"Well, Rob is trying to change all that. They are getting ready to fight again, and they're going to try a new way of fighting."

"When will that be?"

"I don't know. They don't tell us. But I think it will be soon. That's a secret, though. You'd better not tell anyone."

"Who do you think I would tell?"

"I'm just warning you not to say anything."

"You're the one that is telling all the secrets. You're the one with the big mouth, not me. Some soldier you are!" She laughed at the angry red that suffused Tom's face and jabbed his shoulder with one finger.

Why did she always have to make him feel like such a horrid …well, so very horrid? Tom fumed, too annoyed to finish putting his thoughts into words.

February 1307
Gleinn Eason Biorach

Rob and Jamie came to Caela's cottage, and Rob brought his brother, Alexander, with him. Rob introduced him to Caela and then they turned to Pippa. Alexander took Pippa's hand and smiled.

"You do not have to tell me who this is. I would have known her anywhere."

Pippa laughed.

"How would you know me?"

"Well, I was pretty sure you weren't Baby William. And you're the only other child in the house." He didn't mention how very like her mother she looked.

"Pardon me for saying so, but I don't think I should be called a child any longer."

"I wouldn't get into an argument with Alexander if I were you, Pippa" warned Rob. "He's the brains of the family. A distinguished scholar, the dean of Glasgow."

"The only reason Rob takes pride in my accomplishments" joked Alexander, "is that he has had to pay most of the bills for my education."

"You worked hard for your learning, Alexander" said Rob. "We're proud of you. It's too bad you have to take time out to fight a war."

"You are not going back to fighting, are you?" interrupted Pippa. "I don't want you to!" Already, she liked this Alexander de Bruce better than his brother Rob.

"But we've begun now" Alexander answered. "If we don't finish, everything will have been wasted."

"I know" she said, resignedly. "Jamie told me you won't accomplish anything if you only worry about your safety."

"That is very true" said Alexander, taking a seat close to Pippa. "And I'm sure that Caela has taught you that he who hesitates is lost."

"Yes, she's told me. But she also told me that fools rush in where angels fear to tread."

Alexander threw back his head and laughed. He turned to Rob. "I like this girl!" He held Pippa's hand lightly in his. "We are hoping to return to battle smarter and better prepared this time, Pippa. Rob and I have two other brothers, Thomas and Edward, who are helping us now. We're getting support from many more Scotsmen, and Rob has some interesting new ideas about fighting the English. We might just win a few battles this time. And surely you've heard about our great new king?"

"Uh-uh. No, I haven't. Does Scotland have a new king?" Rob, Jamie and Caela stopped talking and turned as one to listen to Alexander's conversation.

"Yes, indeed. He's absolutely brilliant and determined…"

"And fearless!" insisted Jamie.

"And noble!" said Cuinn.

"And handsome!" interjected Rob.

"And modest" said Caela. "Come on, everyone, it's time for dinner."

While Pippa helped Rob and Jamie in the stable after dinner, Caela fed Baby William and laid him in his cradle. Then she joined Alexander by the fire, grateful for a peaceful moment. Alexander looked at her sympathetically.

"Is your life up here very difficult, Caela?"

"We're busy right now. The baby needs me all the time, and I've finally finished working on some fabric that Jamie asked for. That was a big project. He wants thirty black cloaks made for his men. Heaven knows what he has in mind. It took me days to dye all that yarn with rowan bark, weeks to weave it. Look at my hands!"

"That is a lot of work, but very important work. I've heard about some of Jamie's plans. He's an inventive fellow."

Caela face glowed. "He is that. But I simply won't have time to sew the fabric into cloaks for him. We know a woman down in Catacol who we can trust. She's going to finish them."

"Caela, do you mind if I ask something personal?" She nodded. "Rob tells me Pippa has never been told who her father and mother are?"

Caela sighed. Not this again. "When she was a little girl, it was too dangerous. We were smuggling horses. Rob had a price on his head. If Pippa had said one word to the wrong person, Rob could have ended up in prison, or worse. We all could have. Now, I know, she's getting older. She is wondering about her parents. I have told myself many times I should tell her and get it over with."

"How old is she now?"

"She turned ten in the rowan month."

"I'm not trying to tell you what to do. But what if she hears it from someone else? It could be upsetting for her."

Caela sighed again. One more thing to be taken care of. She was exhausted, and not prepared for this, though she knew Alexander spoke the truth.

"You're right, Alexander. Pippa would be devastated if she heard this from someone else. She has a flair for the dramatic as it is. I'd never hear the end of it from her."

"Is this a good time to tell her?"

"Yes, yes, I get your point! I'll do it this week, as soon as Rob leaves." She sighed again. "It will give her time to get used to the idea before she sees him again."

"If you want, I could tell her. I wouldn't mind, seeing as how she is my niece."

"Thank you, but no, Alexander. I would never forgive myself if I didn't tell her. I want to be sure she understands why...." She looked up quickly at the sound of the door opening.

Rob came in alone. He wanted a moment to mention something he had in mind for Pippa. "Caela, Alexander and I have to leave here to help bring in some supplies that should be coming from the northern isles. We'll be gone for about two days. We won't be far away, though I don't want to say exactly where. I did promise Pippa she could come with us this time. I thought I'd better let you know."

Caela was weary of other people informing her about what was going to happen in her own household. "Oh, thank you. That's very considerate, Rob!" she snapped.

"You sound angry. It's only for two days."

"Rob, how can I allow that? No, she can't…"

"She can't stay cooped up here for the rest of her life, Caela. Let her get out to see a bit of the world. We'll take very good care of her, I promise."

Caela stood up to face Rob.

"It's not proper for her to mingle with all those soldiers when there are no women around! She's only a girl. She's never been away from me." Amazingly, Caela had never put that thought into words before, but it seemed like a good strong argument to her. "And who will take care of her?"

Pippa came in and stopped short, but no one seemed to notice. She knew immediately that there was an argument going on. What was it about? Grizel hardly ever raised her voice. Rob sounded angry too.

"She'll be with me, Caela. Me, Rob! And Cuinn. I would never let anything harm her. And I did promise her. She's ridden out with us before. I'd like a chance to spend some time with her. "

"No, I can't let her go."

"You forget" said Rob, suddenly adamant, "who she is." He stood glaring down at Caela.

Pippa straightened up, alert. She wondered herself, when he said that, who in the world she was. But the thought flitted in and right out of her mind. The anger on Rob's face stunned her. She looked quickly to Grizel. Most people would have cowered in front of that look, but Grizel stood her ground like a blackbird defending a tree full of rowan berries.

She answered Rob firmly. "I know very well who Pippa is, Rob. It's in my mind, perhaps more than you know." Grizel glared right back at him. Pippa, who had been about to interrupt in her own behalf, was speechless.

"And you should continue to keep it in mind, Caela. It is my plan for her that we will follow, not yours."

Everyone was silent. It was Caela who finally backed down, but her burning eyes never left Rob's.

"All right, then" she said slowly. "If that is what you want. I have to go away anyway, to take Jamie's black wool down to Catacol. I could do that tomorrow. Maybe it's as good a time as any for Pippa to get away for a bit."

"I can go with them?" shrieked Pippa, surprising them with her presence. She was ecstatic. She threw her arms around Grizel's stiff body, and counted the hours until morning. She could hardly wait to leave.

It was a sentiment she would forever regret.

*T*hey all left at the same time early the next morning, all going in different directions. Och, it were quite a muddle, as Jamie put it, it really were.

With all the preparations, though, certain things were inevitably forgotten, or left unsaid, or maybe postponed once again.

Pippa got to ride with the men, west and up over the mountains. Caela and Jamie went in the other direction, taking Baby William down to Loch Ranza to stay with Sebrina and a nurse. Jamie would help Caela deliver her heavy bags of wool, then go on around the coast road to meet up with Rob's army. Caela had a long day of riding before her. After she delivered the black fabric to Catacol she would load her panniers with yarn and take that back up to her cottage. Then, probably the next day, she would return to Loch Ranza for Baby William. That way, she would have stockpiled all the wool she would need to see her through the rest of the winter.

Meanwhile, when Pippa arrived on Arran's western shore, there was more to see and do than she had ever imagined. Here the mountains cooled their stony feet in the sea and beneath these mountain cliffs were long caves. Ages ago these caves had been inhabited and now they were again full of men, horses and supplies.

Pippa had not realized how much preparation it took to get ready for war. Rob carefully explained some of it to her. But there were so few men in his army that Pippa hoped ardently that England was a very tiny country. She had heard that King Edward was getting to be an old man. Maybe he was so feeble that five dozen Scottish men would be enough to defeat him.

Then the gallowglasses began to arrive from the northern isles. They were fierce fighters, each man of them accompanied by two boys whose only responsibilities were to carry and prepare all their master's weapons. Pippa shrank from their rough ways and coarse manners, and shuddered to envision them on a battlefield. She was glad they were on Rob's side. The camp was suddenly crowded. Rob's band of men began to look like an army.

Tom was at the caves too, working all day long just like the men. They gave him jobs unloading supplies from the boats. Rob even set Pippa to work, running here and there with messages or water jugs, or helping to serve food. Some of the men's clothing was badly torn, and though she spent an entire afternoon mending, she barely made a dent in the pile.

Here by the edge of the sea they might have watched the red ball of the winter sun disappear into the mists of Kintyre. But there was no time. Work continued, even after dark. The men were chilled and exhausted by the time they had their evening meal. Fortunately it was hearty fare. Rob saw to that. They had starved for long enough. The excitement and busy-ness and strangeness exhausted Pippa too. She would be more than ready to return to their cottage the next day.

*E*arlier that same day, from around the northern tip of the island, a trio of horsemen rode into the yard at Loch Ranza lodge. One of them, John the Black Comyn of Buchan, was on a mission for King Edward I of England. He had been charged to do everything in his power to find the outlaw, Robert de Bruce. Because of his personal enmity, that suited John Comyn to a fare-thee-well, but he had searched the whole of Scotland and found not a trace of the man. Then, acting on an old suspicion, he came to Loch Ranza and demanded to see the Lady Sebrina de Seta.

By great good luck, Caela and Jamie had left just hours before to go their separate ways, Caela to Catacol and then home, and Jamie to the caves to help Rob. So it happened that, except for the servants, only the mistress was at home. When her steward found her in the garden, she gave permission for John Comyn of Buchan to be admitted.

He strutted down the path to where she was giving instructions to Dort, her gardener. She did not turn immediately to her guest.

"As long as it's staying mild, Dort, I'd like to move these roses closer to the wall to make more room for vegetables. Trim them back just a bit before you dig, will you?"

"Yes, Lady." Dort picked up his cutters and set to work. When she saw that he was clipping to her satisfaction, Sebrina finally turned regally and peered down her nose at John Comyn.

"Hello, my lord. We met long ago, but I doubt you'd remember. I was just a girl at the time. It was when you came here to hunt with my father. Am I to assume you have come to ask permission to do some shooting?"

"I would like to do some shooting, but I'm not here for red deer, Lady."

"You've come from Brodick?"

"I have. Your former home, I know."

She was certain he leered. She lifted her chin. Her smile did not falter. "How have your English friends been taking care of my castle? I do miss the gardens and the views."

"If certain hard-headed Scots would come to their senses, Lady, you could be back at Brodick someday very soon." His smile showed brown teeth. "If you like, I could make certain that King Edward hears of your willingness to assist us."

"Assist you, my lord? How do you mean?"

"To get to the point of my visit, I heard a rumor that Robert de Bruce is here with his men."

"Oh" said Sebrina pleasantly, "the things one hears."

"I heard they were hiding here. Is this true?"

"There are no men hiding here, my lord, I can assure you."

"But you know their whereabouts?"

"I'm sorry. I do not." She batted her eyelashes and smiled down at him.

"What can you tell me of their plans? Surely you can give me some information."

"John, I'm only an old woman. Men do not confide their plans to women. I'm sure it's the same in your family. You have a lovely wife, yourself. How often do you confide in her?" Sebrina smiled winningly. She knew very well that his wife, Isobel MacDuff, was at the moment living with the women of Robert de Bruce's family.

John Comyn of Buchan bristled in an instant.

"We will not speak of my wife." He spat and Sebrina raised her eyebrows at the gob of spittle on her garden walk. "My lady, there are men searching throughout Scotland for de Bruce. We will find him. I do not intend to leave Arran without some useful information."

"Indeed, I hope you shall not."

"So he is here, then?"

"De Bruce? I haven't the faintest idea where he is."

"May I speak with your son?"

"He is not here at present, either, John. I'm sorry to disappoint you."

"Tell me where your son is, then."

"John, you must know how it is with grown sons. Or mayhap you do not. You have no sons?" Buchan shifted testily from foot to foot, but Sebrina breezed on. "Well, I'll tell you something." She flipped a laugh at him. "Mothers are always the last people to find out where their sons are at any given time. But you and I needn't stand out here in the garden with this fog rolling in. Would you care to come in for some refreshment?" She thought of Baby

William asleep in his cradle and prayed that she would not have to explain him to such a horrid little man. Buchan followed her toward the courtyard, snapping his riding crop impatiently.

"I do not want anything to eat. But I am losing my patience, Lady, with women who do not know how to cooperate." She turned, amazed. His voice was trembling. She feared she had goaded him a little too far. He waved the crop in her face. "You are being foolish, my lady. You think you are smart, but no! You are foolish."

No wonder you're touchy, thought Sebrina. Your own wife defied you by siding with your mortal enemy, Robert de Bruce. And he keeps disappearing, slipping right through your fingers.

Sebrina said nothing however. She was afraid she had said quite enough. Buchan stared at her in fury. He waved his crop in her face and tried to goad her into speaking.

"I think your son and his ilk are hiding somewhere in these hills, too cowardly to come out and fight like men. Are they licking their wounds because they lost too many battles? Or are they terrified because so many of their friends have been executed? There can't be many of them left, at the rate they're being drawn and quartered by King Edward. Personally, I think that executing that pack of vermin is the best thing to happen to Scotland for a long time. We needed to get rid of them."

Sebrina, never one to curb her tongue, could stand no more. "You have the nerve to talk to me of cowardice? You? Everyone knows you literally ran from the battle at Falkirk and let hundreds of your own countrymen die!"

He had shown himself a coward in war, perhaps that was so, but John Comyn was not too cowardly to strike a woman. He grimaced fiercely and struck, actually struck at her with his riding crop. The blow took Sebrina unawares. She stumbled backwards and lost her balance. If her head had not cracked against the edge of the garden well, if she had not blacked out and fallen to the ground, the Black Comyn might never have noticed her locket on its fine chain. But when she fell, the locket slipped out. The man took a step forward.

The locket was unique, with its engraving of a rowan tree entwining a single ruby. Otherwise, he might not have taken a second look. But he thought it odd that he had often seen an identical locket on his wife's neck. Sebrina hadn't moved. He reached down, yanked on the chain and broke it. When he opened the locket, he gasped. Not only was the jewelry identical, but the same little face looked out of this locket. He had been told it was a likeness of his wife as a child. Why would Sebrina de Seta be carrying a portrait of Isobel MacDuff? It made no sense. John Comyn's hand began to shake.

Lying with her cheek against the ground, Sebrina swam to consciousness through a thick brown sea. She surfaced in a brown mist and opened one eye a slit. The world reeled sickeningly and she quickly closed it again and lay motionless, holding herself as still as she could until the spinning stopped.

John Comyn heard a sound behind him and whirled around. A man slumped obsequiously near the gate. He had a patch on one eye, and his dirty fingers clutched his cap. He had not missed what had just happened and John Comyn knew it. He would have to deal carefully with this man.

"Beggin' your pardon, sir," said Dort the gardener, his eye on the locket in John Comyn's hand.

"What is it?"

"It may be that I could help yuz."

John Comyn of Buchan took a step closer.

"You know something of de Bruce?"

"I know somethin', sir. I seen him on this very island."

"When was this?"

"I could tell you exactly, if you could make it worth my while."

John Comyn was desperate and didn't bother to hide it. "How long ago did you see him?" Dort shrugged. "All right, all right."

John Comyn fished out his purse. Dort's eye bugged at the sight of it. Jewels studded the colored leather and it was fat with coins.

"It were Samhain, sir. Down on Machrie moor."

"Samhain was four months ago. He could be anywhere by now."

Dort pursed his lips in thought. His one eye slid sideways.

"As ye say. But there is something else, sir, what ye might be interested in. Someone, I should say."

"So? Talk." John Comyn tossed him a coin.

Dort looked at it. He tongue flicked across his upper lip.

"This might be worth more 'n that, when I tell ye who she be." John Comyn looked at him hard.

"She?" he asked, finally. His chest rose and fell rapidly.

"That's right. A little red-head, she are." He paused and looked at the ground. "A red-haired child what looks a great deal like someone ye knows. Someone close to yuz."

John Comyn's breath was strangled out of him. He couldn't answer for a moment. His voice nearly failed him.

"What do you know about a child?"

"I knows that my wife, God rest 'er soul, nursed the girl from birth. She knew the child's mither, and you knows 'er too. And I knows who fathered her. And I knows where the child are now. It may be you'll find others yuz're lookin' for too, in the same place." Buchan took more coins from his purse. Dort held his silence. John the Black Comyn handed across the entire purse and bent his head to listen attentively.

Sebrina heard Comyn's footsteps recede. Dort came near her but she was so violently dizzy she dared not move or even open her eyes. He trod purposefully and nonchalantly on her hand as he walked slowly away, going on a leisurely search for Dickon the steward, to tell him about his poor mistress's fall.

*T*hrough the wet fog, Caela let her heavily-laden pony walk back up the mountain later that afternoon, even though she was eager to get home. She hoped that Jamie had gotten to the cottage ahead of her. She would love to walk in her door and find him there, his grin big and warm, and maybe with Baby William in his arms. She smiled at the picture.

By the time she rode over the lip of her little vale, it had begun to rain. She confirmed that, sadly, only the thinnest curl of smoke came from her chimney. When she noticed a red stag watching her impassively from her own dooryard, she knew there must be no one around. Tott the dog usually took passionate care to harass intruding deer, though. How odd. Where was Tott? The stag looked at her knowingly for a long moment, then turned and loped up the mountainside. Caela paused. A ghost of a memory flitted across her mind and disappeared.

She was full of happy anticipation. Perhaps Jamie might still arrive in time for supper, she thought. What could she prepare that he would like? The rain was becoming a downpour. She dismounted quickly, humming, and headed the pony toward the barn.

It was then she noticed the hoof prints in the yard. Horses' hooves. Not stag and not pony hooves. It couldn't be Jamie, could it? He never rode a horse into the glen. She tied her pony to the rowan tree and went to the door eagerly. Just as she put her hand on the latch, she was struck with a terrible feeling of foreboding. It took her breath away. She jerked her hand away from the latch, but too late. The door was flung open and a man stood there. She recoiled in surprise. The man pulled her roughly through the door.

He was very short. She thought she might be able to overpower him. But he wasn't alone. There were two others with him. She had no idea who they were. She struggled and kicked but they held her easily. Were they looking for Robert de Bruce? How had they traced Robert to her? The man forced her into a chair. She almost gagged. The body of Tott lay dead on the floor, a dark red gash across his neck. The man leaned over her. His breath came foul from the brown cavern of his mouth.

"A girlchild lives here." The man drew out his words slowly. Her heart stopped beating, then began again with a tremendous jolt. She felt the blood drain from her face. No, please dear God, no.

"Where is she?"

"There is no one here but me. I live alone."

The man held up one of Pippa's gowns. "This is a bit small for you." Panic churned cruelly inside her. She tried desperately to piece together who this man could be.

"I make clothes for people. I sew clothes and weave for a living. I've been away buying some wool…" The man hit her very hard. She tasted blood and was sure her jaw was broken. So this was to be his game. This sort of treatment she had known since childhood. Now she was on familiar ground. She knew how to get through this. Pain was a good distraction. She settled back in her chair and willed her mind to go blank.

The man dangled a gold locket in front of her face. He opened it, watching her expression, and held up a small portrait of a red-haired child. She knew that dear little face immediately but she never showed it. She knew also, of course, whose locket it was. What had become of her friend Sebrina? Caela struggled to keep her face blank. Her childhood punishments had not been quite the same as this, after all. She had had no one to protect then, but herself.

The man bared his rotting teeth in something similar to, but not the same as, a smile.

"My loving wife, Isobel, has a locket like this" the man said softly. "Exactly the same. She said the locket had belonged to her mother. She told me the painting was her own likeness, herself as a child." The man's lips smiled. His voice was ugly. "I now know she was lying. This is not Isobel's portrait. And I know who this child's father is, and whom she was trying to protect. She will fail in that. She will never be able to protect him or their child. Not from me. When I find him, I will tear him to pieces."

Now Caela knew this man. He was John the Black Comyn of Buchan, Rob's arch-enemy for long years. He was cousin to the man Rob had helped to murder last winter. And husband to Pippa's real mother, Isobel.

Somehow John Comyn had found out that his wife had given birth to a child. That was not all. Last March Isobel had openly defied her husband. Against his wishes she had carried out the

MacDuff tradition, placing with her own hands the crown of Scotland on the head of the new king. The same king her husband refused to support. The king he despised. As a particularly stinging insult, Caela had heard it said, Isobel had stolen her husband's favorite warhorse and ridden all night so she could be with the king at his coronation.

She had sided against her husband and with his mortal enemy. This was Isobel, just as Caela had always known her, completely careless about the consequences of her actions. Caela felt the bottom fall out of her world.

The new king. And Pippa. They must be protected. Caela kept her face like a stone, her eyes as dull as dead leaves. John Comyn spoke harshly in her ear.

"This child is here, I know it. No? You think I don't know what I'm talking about? I have it first-hand from the gardener at Loch Ranza Castle. He was only too happy to give me this information. Just as you will be more than happy to tell me where she is hiding." He whipped the locket across Caela's face. It opened a gash that bled instantly. The locket clattered to the floor.

So Dort had told. He had told about Pippa, even though Cuinn paid him for his silence, payment that Dort demanded each Candlemas. She stared hard at the little bouquet of dry weeds that Pippa had arranged days ago in a small pitcher on the table. John Comyn breathed his stench in her face.

"Where is this girl? You will tell me, sooner or later. It might as well be now, before you learn the real meaning of pain."

John Buchan stomped, screamed and finally made good on his hideous threat. Incandescent with anger, he had Caela tied to her chair. Through all the pain, not a word escaped her, nor any sound at all. Frustrated at her silence, he bellowed for his men.

"Light a torch!" he demanded. The man brought him a flaming brand. He touched it to the thatched ceiling of Caela's beloved cottage, across the room from where she sat. Caela prayed only that John Comyn would be gone before Pippa returned. Suddenly an old crone's whispered words came to her, from the night of the Samhain festival. She had forgotten Ailioll until now.

"Your story is part of a long tale, Caela MacDuff. Do not be afraid. Let it be as it will be." Pippa and Jamie would see the smoke from the burning cottage. It would a warning to be cautious, to turn away.

A long tale. And Caela would never know the ending. That is how it was to be.

She hardly saw John Comyn any longer, nor felt the pain he inflicted. He finally threw her, still tied to her chair, to the floor with such force that the back of the chair broke. The ropes on her arms loosened. John Comyn started for the door. Flames were licking across the ceiling, coming close.

"This is your last chance" he said, turning back. "Do you want to die here, protecting a filthy brat and a murderer?" She didn't answer. Enraged, he slammed the door. Caela worked one hand from under her and reached for the locket that lay nearby. The roof was smoking heavily.

Their little cottage, scene of so many happy times. She had been given so many gifts. Her family had come to her, one by one, like stars into her bleak, dark life. Pippa and Jamie had given her something she had never even dared to desire. And then she had been given William, a tiny miracle.

She began to sing, although her ruined mouth could not form the words and her voice choked in her throat.

Oh rowan tree, oh rowan tree, thoul't aye be dear to me,
Entwin'd thou art with many ties, of home and infancy...

John Comyn of Buchan stood fuming just outside the door. Rain drenched the mountainside. He waited under the eaves, hoping she would call for him, would change her mind and beg to tell him what he wanted to know. Now, by every holy saint, did he hear her calling? No, she was singing! Her voice was rasping and horrid. He came back through her door in a fury. He pulled out his sword.

She recognized the end. The peace in her eyes drove him to insanity. His sword slashed and he stormed out just before the burning roof began to give way.

But he had gotten nothing. It was the way things often went for him. He had squeezed hard, but she, like so much else, had slipped through his fingers.

She was gone, like sand through his fingers.

The rain pounded relentlessly and the flames ate but half the cottage roof before turning to black smoke. John Comyn ran for his horse. He and his two henchmen tore at high speed down through the glen.

Far above them, a man on a pony came over the col between the mountains, whistling a tune in spite of the rain.

*T*he next day, Pippa spotted him first. She, Cuinn and Rob had just left Rob's ragtag army near the seashore, and were heading back up over the hills to the cottage. She was rather glad to be going home. Jamie had come to the caves the afternoon before and then left again for the cottage, hoping to surprise Caela when she arrived home. Pippa was glad to be joining them. She had worked hard to help Rob, but she had been away long enough.

Since she was leading the way, she was the first to see the solitary rider up on the mountain, framed against the grey winter sky. He was coming their way, swaying, barely able to stay in the saddle. It was very cold, but he seemed to be wearing nothing but a shirt and breeches.

The three of them stopped in their tracks. The rider was Jamie. From head to toe, he was black with soot. A blackened harp was roped across his saddle.

At first, she hadn't understood. The men raced ahead, dismounted and ran to him, but Pippa couldn't understand what had happened. Confused, she watched Jamie slip from the pony. His knees gave way. He sank into the mud. Pippa watched, horrified as he sank face down, down into the mud. His whole body was shaking. Cuinn and Rob knelt beside him. They turned to Pippa. Rob was saying something strange. What was it?

"...an accident." She was standing beside her pony. What did he mean? She couldn't understand. It wasn't true. It could not be true. No. The sound she heard coming from her own throat was the sound of pure agony.

*E*arlier, on the same day that John Comyn had visited Caela's cottage and just before suppertime, a wizened old fisherman walked down to the shore of the loch. Rain had been pelting the beach all afternoon and the wind was rising. He wanted to check on his fishing dory. At the sound of horses he turned to see three men, riding purposefully toward him. One horse was limping badly.

"Old man!" The one on the limping horse yelled to him. The old fisherman put his hands in his pockets and rocked on his heels until they pulled up in front of him.

"Who looks after horses on this island?" the rider demanded. "Mine took a bad fall coming down that wretched glen."

The old fisherman shrugged. "Most folk here don't keep horses. Only one who has a couple of 'em are the young Lord de Seta, and he ain't here. Neither are his constable." He refused to reveal that the young lord often brought in boatloads of horses. And he would die rather than tell where the young lord might have gone, though he had a pretty good idea where he and his friends were.

The man on the horse swore.

"What about his gardener?" He jerked his thumb toward Loch Ranza castle. "Tell me where he lives. The one with the eye patch." The fisherman knew immediately that he meant Dort and he didn't mind giving out information on the whereabouts of that scoundrel. He pointed.

"See that last hut down the beach? That're his. He probably are there now, drinkin' like a fish." He watched the three men ride away, then suddenly thought with regret of Dort's boy, Tom. He hoped, whatever those men wanted, that it wouldn't mean any trouble for Tom. Tom was Amie's boy. The fisherman wished yet again that God had taken her rotten husband instead of her when the coughing sickness went round, what was it now, almost eight, ten years ago?

*J*ohn Comyn dismounted in front of the hut. He had that day struck one woman, murdered another and burned her house down, but still the rage blazed inside him. He kicked open the door to Dort's house. One of the hinges broke and the door swung crazily.

There sat Dort, a jug of wine at his elbow, and John Comyn's silver coins spilled on the table in front of him. Dort's head swayed on his shoulders as he surveyed his intruder. He leaned protectively over his hoard and snarled. John Comyn moved closer.

"I hope you haven't spent any of that, because you're giving it all back."

"Oh no! I already tole 'xactly what yuz wanted ta know."

"No, you did not. I went all the way up there for nothing. And on the way down, my horse nearly broke his leg. That horse is worth ten times what you are. And yet I found no child."

"I tole yuz…She's there!" Dort half rose from his seat.

"She was not there!" John Comyn's fist crashed on the table. He scooped up a handful of silver. "I'm taking back my silver!"

Dort lunged drunkenly for the coins. John Comyn drew his sword.

"Look!" He held the blade to Dort's nose. His face cracked an evil grin. "Look at this. It's still bloody from the last person who stood in my way. And she was a woman! Aw, ain't that a shame now? You see what a formidable enemy I am? I have no mercy of any kind in me." Dort reared back, terrified. The table tilted and silver slid to the floor. "Pick those up!" roared John Comyn.

The rat-like way that Dort scrabbled for coins on the floor disgusted John Comyn, infuriated him. What a wretched parasite! The sword struck for the second time that day and Dort fell heavily. John the Black Comyn scooped his silver into a linen bag, kicking Dort's body aside to make sure he had retrieved every coin.

He stepped outside to his waiting men. Panting for breath and scowling fiercely, he surveyed the coast up and down. The rain was not letting up and no one was about. It was getting dark.

"Let's get off this godforsaken island." He and his men rode hard, in spite of his horse's injury, back towards the English garrison at Brodick Castle.

In Dort's hut, on the back of a shelf, John Comyn's richly bejeweled purse yawned open, empty save for one tarnished silver coin.

*A*fter a long time, Pippa became aware of where she was. It was night. There were people around, men. The scene before her gradually came into focus. They were sitting silent beside a flickering fire. She had returned to the caves. On the walls, ancient painted figures danced like devils across the stone, frightening to look at.

She could hear the waves booming against the shore outside. It sounded like a storm. Most of the men sat apart from them. She was curled on Cuinn's lap, his chin on her head. Rob was beside them, staring into the fire with a vacant expression. His cheeks were creased with concern. Tommy sat across the fire. She looked around for Jamie and saw him leaning against the wall. His black eyes were like holes, his face a mask. She said his name. She saw him slowly register her presence. She watched grief kindle anew behind his eyes. It welled up and slid out across his features. It pained her so, his grief.

Jamie held something in his hand. It caught the firelight. Gold. He saw her watching and held it up.

"That's Aunt Sebrina's."

Cuinn looked up sharply. "My mother's locket" he said, frowning.

"Your mother's? I found it.... It's partly melted from the fire." Jamie's voice choked. Fire. How had it happened? Grizel was always so careful.

"Let me see. Yes, look. We had Pippa's baby portrait painted for my mother."

"Why would it have been in Caela's hand?" Jamie whispered.

Cuinn was speechless.

"I didn't know my mother was planning to go up there" he finally muttered.

"I didn't find her there. Caela was the only one."

Cuinn lurched to his feet, spilling Pippa to the floor.

"You searched the ashes? There was only the one…"

"Yes, only Caela. And the dog. I searched thoroughly in case the baby…." He gestured bleakly.

"I've got to go to Loch Ranza. Something may have happened." Cuinn laced his boots.

"I'm going with you. I have to find my son." said Jamie, urgently.

"I want to go too." Pippa gathered up her mantle.

"No. You're staying here." Cuinn was firm. "There might be trouble."

"I want to see Aunt Sebrina." She wanted desperately to see Sebrina.

"No, Pippa. Absolutely not. Stay here with Rob until we come back."

Rob stood as well. "You're not to leave this cave, Pippa" Rob ordered.

"Warn the sentries, Rob, that something may be amiss. That fire may not have been an accident after all" Jamie said quietly. Rob turned back to Pippa with a fierce expression.

"I meant what I said, Pippa. Do not go out on any account. Stay here until we find out what is going on."

Pippa was infuriated. Rob's boots rang on the stones of the cave. Cuinn and Jamie took up their weapons and ran out. Pippa was deserted.

Tommy came to sit at her side. He brushed at her hair.

"What are you doing?" she flared at him. She had forgotten that Tom, at least, was here.

"You had a spider crawling across the top of your head."
"Oh. Thank you."
"What are they so upset about?"
"They found Aunt Sebrina's locket, I guess, on…" She couldn't say the words.
"With Grizel?"
She nodded. Tommy hunched and cradled his elbows in his lap.
"They think something happened to the Lady de Seta, too?"
"I don't know. Why would Grizel have Aunt Sebrina's locket?"
"You want to go back to Loch Ranza, then?"
Pippa nodded again. She sucked in a loud breath. "Rob won't let me. He always thinks he can tell me what to do." She beat on her knee with her fist.
"I could go for you."
"What good would that do me? I'd still be stuck here. I want to be with Aunt Sebrina."
"Tell the sentry you have to use the bushes to … you know …take a piss."
"Tommy!"
"Seriously. I'll go out first and sneak a pony out of the paddock. Meet me at the top of the hill. Cuinn will surely take the shore road to Loch Ranza. But I know a path up through the glen."

She gave Tommy a few minutes head start, then walked casually to an opening of the cave. Rob was nowhere in sight. She stepped outside. Out in the blackness the wind whipped the waves onto the shore.
"Miss, you aren't allowed out. I'm sorry." The sentry had been warned. He blocked her path.
"I need to use the bushes in private." The sentry looked at her and she made an urgent face. "Really, I've got to go. My insides are all upset. Please?"
The sentry bit his lip. Word had gone round that she had just been orphaned, her mother dead. Poor kid, he thought. They say

she hasn't shed a single tear. He didn't dare leave his post, but he could easily get someone else to go with her.

"You Harry, take her up there." The sentry pointed to a clump of bushes on the dark hillside. "Don't let her out of your sight."

Pippa groaned inwardly when Harry stepped forward. He wasn't much older than Tommy. She swallowed her embarrassment and waded uphill through the dry blowing grass. Above her in the dark, a figure was quietly leading a pony over the brow of the hill.

Harry was sullen. St. Fillian, spare me! he muttered to himself. So why does I get latrine duty? What, I look like some sorta addle-pated nursemaid? Harry clambered awkwardly up the steep hillside, cussing like a madman, arms flailing, ankles unsteady. This was the final disgrace. The last thing he wanted to do tonight was mind some ratty little wench who had bowel problems. The lads is nivver gonna let me hear the enda this, Harry told himself.

He was not supposed to let this kelpie out of his sight but she was up that hill faster than a stoat after a granary rat. He scrambled like mad to catch up with her.

"Moth'ragawd!" Harry swore, finally coming even with her.

Pippa rounded fiercely on him. "You're going to be sorry, you know, if you get too close." Harry gave her a mocking leer. "Stay here," Pippa barked. "Turn around and look the other way. And don't you dare listen."

He turned his back to her. "Just make it quick, would ya, Princess?" he blatted. "I'm not going to stand out here all night, ya know, freezin' me pintle off. I got better things to do than wait while some smelly little brat unloads a pile of ...."

Pippa would have hated Harry violently and forever if he had not been so endearingly gullible. He was still babbling away when she slinked over the top of the hill.

*T*om hadn't even had time to throw a saddle over the pony he borrowed. The ride would be uncomfortable. The night was stormy and dark. To avoid being seen, Pippa and Tom had to ride up through the glens. The route Tom chose to get back to Loch Ranza was arduously long and the trails were rough. They made very slow progress. They rode across Machrie moor to Iorsa Water, up along its course through the hills to Loch Tanna, and down into Glen Catacol, where a rainstorm caught them, wetting them to the skin. Pippa's arms went involuntarily around Tommy's waist for warmth. Still avoiding the coast, they climbed one last hill and finally saw Loch Ranza lodge below them.

"How are we going to get in without Cuinn seeing you?"

"There is a back staircase up to Aunt Sebrina's rooms."

"Really? I never saw it."

"The servants are supposed to use it but it's too steep and slippery so they just pile stuff on it for storage. I've used it lots of times for sneaking around and nobody has ever found me there."

Because Loch Ranza was so remote and the lodge was originally only meant for hunting parties, it did not have high protective walls like other castles. There were supposed to be watchmen on the bridge, but either they were dozing inside somewhere or they expected no intruders on such a stormy night.

Pippa and Tom rode at last into the yard. They weren't seen by anyone. They slid exhausted from the pony and led him into the stable, then splashed through the rain to the back door.

No one was in the dark kitchens when they crept in to find a light. Tom followed Pippa to the stone staircase that led up the back way to Sebrina's chamber. A stale, cold wind, having had the stairway all to itself for a very long time, was glad to pester them. They crouched, shivering and soaking wet, at the top of the stairs to listen.

In her room, Sebrina had hung a heavy tapestry over the stairway door, to keep out drafts, because no one used that passage anyway. Tom and Pippa could hear someone talking. The voice was muffled by the tapestry, but they could tell it was Cuinn speaking.

"She still hasn't wakened, Nancy?"

"Not yet, Sire."

"Mother? Can you open your eyes? Can you hear me?" A pause.

"She hears you. Look, she is trying to open her eyes." It was Jamie's voice.

"Mother, can you tell us what happened?"

Pippa's brow furrowed with concern when she heard Sebrina groan softly.

"It's all she's been able to do, Sire. She still hasn't moved her arms or legs and we can't get anything but moans out of her."

"You say no one knows how this happened?"

"No one saw anything, Sire. I'm sorry."

"But she went nowhere? She didn't leave here? Not at all in the last couple of days?"

"No, Sire. She was here the whole time."

"Did anyone visit?"

"I was busy in the wash room with laundry the whole entire day, what with so much extra because of the baby's clothes and all, and we havin'...."

"Nancy!" Cuinn was impatient.

"But Dickon could maybe tell you."

"Is he around?"

"I believe he's gone to bed, Sire."

"Can you ask him to come? I know it's late. I'll only keep him for a few minutes, but I must talk to him right away."

The steward soon came briskly into the room. "Good evening, Sire. I didn't know you had come home."

"Good evening, Dickon. I'm sorry to wake you. We're trying to find out how this happened. Nancy swears my mother hasn't left Loch Ranza. Is that true? Would she have gone up into Gleinn Eason for any reason?"

"No, Sire. But Nancy said you asked if she had a visitor."

Cuinn looked up sharply.

"Did she?"

"John the Black Comyn was here, Sire, for quite a while this morning."

"John Comyn, here? What in the world for?"

"He informed me most particularly that the English king had instructed him to search for Robert de Bruce, and I was not only to let him in but also to tell him everything I could. He was very abrupt with me, Sire."

"What did you tell him?"

"Of course, I had no idea what he was talking about. He was quite – I hesitate to say it, Sire, but he was really quite rude. Then he wanted to speak with Milady."

"Did my mother consent to see him?"

"Oh yes, she did."

"And?"

Dickon squirmed uncomfortably.

"I didn't hear their conversation. I don't want to place blame unfairly, but it was right after Lord Buchan left that we found Milady unconscious in the garden." He looked at her pale, vacant face in the bed. Cuinn's jaw clenched. "And one other thing, Sire. Lord Buchan also held a conversation with the gardener."

There was a little sound from behind the tapestry, but no one in the room seemed to take any notice.

"Buchan spoke with Dort? You saw them? Where did this happen?"

"In the garden, Sire. Near the place where we eventually found Milady."

"Did they talk for long together, Dickon?"

"I only saw them for a few moments. I confess I watched them from this window because I was nervous about having Lord Buchan about the place. He seemed so dangerously angry when he arrived. Sire, I can't swear to it, but it looked to me like something was passed between them."

"Between the two men? What do you mean? What kind of thing?" It was Jamie's voice.

"I don't know for sure."

"What size thing?"

"Small. Small enough to hold in one hand. It could have been a purse of money. I thought it probably was a purse."

"A purse? Then what happened?"

"I must say, Lord Buchan certainly left quickly after that. He seemed to be in a great hurry, urgent about something."

"Did you see which way Lord Buchan went?" Jamie asked tensely.

"Well, I did, actually. He and two others rode very fast, up into Gleinn Eason Biorach."

"The glen?" Jamie bellowed. He swore a filthy oath and kicked a chair over.

In the stairway, Tommy stood. He was very agitated.

Jamie spoke again.

"Where do I find this filthy traitor, this gardener?"

Tommy began to yell and pound the door. "Wait! Let me in!"

The men in the room whirled around. Cuinn strode angrily across the room and jerked the tapestry aside. He flung open the door and Tommy tumbled into the room.

"What are you doing here, you little runt?" Cuinn grabbed Tommy's arm, but dropped it as Pippa ran past him. "Pippa!"

She ignored him, ran straight to Sebrina's bedside and fell to her knees.

"Pippa, be careful! She cannot be moved."

Very gently Pippa encircled Sebrina's shoulders. Sebrina opened her eyes. Her face suffused with joy. Tears flooded down her cheeks. When Cuinn saw his mother's relief, he could scold no more. He ran his hands through his hair in exasperation.

"Keep these two here" Jamie ordered gruffly, pointing to Pippa and Tom.

"No!" yelled Tom. "You are not –-!" He lunged violently toward Jamie, but Cuinn restrained him.

Jamie grabbed the steward's sleeve.

"Come with me. I need you to point the way." He towed Dickon out the door.

From the edge of the room, Tommy craned his head to get a look at Sebrina. She looked deathly pale. Pippa had finally broken down and was sobbing her heart out.

Cuinn was mystified. Sebrina seemed so immensely relieved to see Pippa, uncommonly relieved. Had she been worried about Pippa, for some reason? Cuinn slowly began to piece things together. Dickon the steward claimed that John Comyn's visit was not a friendly one. He had been under instructions to find Rob. Who better for Edward the First to send hunting after Rob than Rob's worst enemy? John Comyn had spoken to their gardener, something had been passed between them, and John Comyn had ridden off into the glen. Dort the gardener was one of the few people in the world who would have certain information that would interest John Comyn. Very personal information that would induce the Black Comyn to set aside his hunt for de Bruce and send him riding into the glen and up to Caela's cottage. But he wouldn't have been looking for Caela, though by a twist of fate she was the only one he found there. Cuinn's head reeled. He suddenly realized that Caela's death was no accident. Her last minutes of life must have been horribly ugly. He leaned weakly on a table.

Then another dreadful thought came to him. What had Caela been forced to tell? Did she even know where Rob and Pippa had been that last night? He prayed she did not. Was John Comyn still a threat? Assuredly he was, and now that John Comyn knew about Pippa, she was in grave danger. Cuinn knew he had to get to Rob as fast as possible. He leaned over and put his hand on his mother's head, wishing she could tell what she knew. He didn't notice at first that Tommy had slipped out of the room.

When he did notice, he cursed. What had gotten into these children? They had no idea of the trouble they were causing. He would have to delay his message to Rob for a few minutes.

"Pippa" he roared, pointing his finger at her, "if I come back here and you are not sitting beside this bed, there is going to be hell to pay. Do you understand?" Pippa shrank back, her hand to her mouth. She nodded meekly. She would obey this time. Cuinn had never, ever spoken to her in that way. He ran from the room.

*H*olding a lantern aloft, Jamie ran through the rain to locate Dort's hut. He was insanely, violently angry. Gusts of wind tore at the flame in the lantern. He found the cottage that the steward had described, off by itself, the one furthest down the beach. It showed no light and its door, hanging by one hinge, banged back and forth in the wind. He pulled out his sword and stepped warily inside.

By the light of his lantern, he saw the body in a pool of dried blood, on the floor behind the upturned table. By the looks of things, the man had been dead since yesterday. He turned him over with the toe of his boot and held his lantern down to shine on the face. He remembered this man, but not with any warmth.

The mouth gaped open. The eye patch had pulled off, showing an empty eye socket that puckered grotesquely with the scars of an old wound. The face looked so ghoulish that he had to turn away, and when he did, a silver gleam caught his eye. Jamie bent to pick up a coin. The body moved. He had thought the man was dead. As it was, Dort was barely able to whisper.

"Tha's mine! Gimme it!"

"Where did you get it?"

"Give it ta me."

"Did John Comyn give this to you?"

"So what if he did?"

Jamie Douglas stared. He began to tremble from head to foot.

"Did you give him some information?"

"Yeah, so what of it? Lookit what he gave me." He gestured to the gaping wound in his side. Dort struggled to prop himself up on one elbow. He was breathing with difficulty. His single eye looked at Jamie from a creased and whiskery face. The gardener tried to speak, his words coming in short gasps.

"Why shouldn't I tell him about the brat? He has a right to know that his wife was false to him." The arm Dort was leaning on gave out and he sank to the floor. His wound was gushing blood again. "Tha' kid is spoiled rotten anyway, just like her pig of a father. She deserves…"

Jamie pointed his sword threateningly at Dort's chest. He, too, was breathing very heavily.

"One more stinking word out of you, you miserable pile of hideous offal,…" Jamie was stopped in mid-sentence by the sound of footsteps pounding through the rain. Tom ran shrieking up the steps. When he saw his father lying there bleeding and Jamie's sword pointed at his heart, he cried out.

"Papa!"

Dort's one eye was wild. He struggled to rise and reach toward his boy. Tom clutched his outstretched hand. The man's body began to convulse and his throat made gurgling sounds. In a few seconds it was all over for him. He fell dead to the floor. Tom's eyes were wide with horror.

"Papa!" Tom yelled again, shaking his father. "Papa!" Very gently, Jamie put his hands on Tom's shoulders. Tom screamed. He turned on Jamie, attacking him, viciously beating his fists on Jamie's face.

"You killed him! You killed him!"

"No, Tom, no!" Jamie could not hold him.

"You said he took a purse. He didn't! Can't you see? We have nothing. There is nothing here. Nothing! Nothing!" He tore at Jamie like a panther. Cuinn came running up the steps and saw them fighting. Jamie looked beseechingly toward Cuinn.

"Hold him! He thinks I killed his father!" Cuinn took one look at the dead body and tried to grab Tom's arms. It took both men to hold Tom down.

"Tom! Tommy, look! Jamie didn't do this. Look at this wound, look at the floor! See all that old blood? That wound was not made today. Yesterday, maybe. Jamie wasn't even here yesterday, you know that. Come on, lad. Back off! Jamie did not do this. His sword is perfectly clean, don't you see?"

"I would have killed him, if I had gotten here first" Jamie snarled. Tommy flung himself on Jamie again, kicking and punching.

"Stop it, both of you! Help me get him outside." They managed to haul the struggling boy out into the downpour and hold him down on the step. The drenching rain finally chilled him into submission. Tom stopped kicking. He let out one long, wrenching cry of pain. Cuinn watched helplessly, rivulets of rain streaming down his face. He tried to put his hand on Tom's shoulder.

"Come on, Tom. Let's go home." Tom jerked violently away, leapt up and ran off through the rain. Helpless, they watched him as he stumbled down the beach. Jamie fell back onto the step and dropped his head into his hands. Cuinn finally spoke.

"I have to tell Rob that John Comyn may be on this island. I've alerted our sentries. I don't know when I'll be back, Jamie."

Jamie stood. Cuinn gestured toward Dort's body.

"You'll bury him?"

Jamie took a couple of seconds to nod a stiff assent. What he wanted to do was pulverize the body and leave it on the beach for the shore birds to pick at, if they could stand eating such garbage. If it weren't for Tom, Jamie would have done exactly that. Actually, he didn't deserve even that much. The man was nothing but a pile of putrid entrails torn from the body of a diseased goat.

Cuinn pointed.

"The churchyard…"

"He doesn't deserve a churchyard."

"Put him there anyway. It's beyond…"

"I know where it is."

Jamie stomped inside, grabbed Dort's leg and the man's own shovel, bumped the body irreverently down the steps and dragged it through the rain to its final resting place.

*T*om finally raised his head from where it rested on his arm.

After a minute, he noticed the night sky had cleared. A handful of stars outlasted every storm. Again tonight, as always, they made a net of starlight across the heavens. It would be dawn in a couple of hours. The clouds were rolling away to the southeast and a light, cold wind fingered the opening in the hills at the end of the loch. The breeze found Tom where he sat on the beach and pried at his wet clothing. He slowly came to the realization that he was chilled to the bone. He had no cloak. He pulled his elbows in close and hunched his knees to his chest.

He was used to feeling lonely, oftentimes on the fringe. But now his father had left him and gone away. He was never coming back. Tom was left with no one.

He was almost sick with terror. His father had provided an anchorage. Flimsy though it was, it was all he had that was uniquely his. No one else's. Now he was adrift. He had nothing.

He winced and pulled his knees in closer. He had lost Grizel, too, another bond severed. She had been kind to him, more than kind, and he had been grateful for that. To Tom, the world suddenly seemed a dark and cruel place and he was lost in it.

Just beyond his feet, the tide pushed incessantly closer. Tom tried to get up and staggered a bit. There was such a weight on his chest that he could hardly stand. He straightened slowly and looked to the south. His house was there, but no light winked from the window. An empty body, the body of his father. That was all that was left in that house. Tom couldn't go there.

He started walking back down the beach. The lodge was dark too. He didn't want to go there, either. It would be impossible to meet James Douglas ever again and be able to quell the hatred he felt for the man who had murdered his father. Another thought stabbed Tom like a dagger: even Cuinn had stood up for Jamie. That, as much as anything, was tearing Tom to pieces. Cuinn had turned on him. Sebrina seemed close to death. Pippa....

The only place left for him was Rob's army. He knew Rob was watching for a fire signal from the mainland. If and when the signal came, the army would begin an assault on Turnberry, Rob's former home. At the same time, Rob's two brothers would sail down to Galloway and attack there.

Tom would have to ask Alexander de Bruce if he could sail with him. He had to get away from Jamie. He couldn't trust himself around the man. He was stabbed with a bolt of actual physical pain when he realized that he must have inherited his father's violent streak. He despised himself. In a single day, he had become an ugly, mean wretch of a person.

He looked up. He was standing, after all, near the step of his father's house. There was blood there, a trail of it. The door hung limp now and creaked softly in the breeze. Slowly, reluctantly, he was drawn up the steps. His father's body was gone but his life's blood stained the floor. Tom tried not to look at it.

The house was empty, the furniture was a shambles. He set the table upright and slid the two rickety chairs neatly beneath. He carried a bucket down to the shore and filled it with saltwater, then sloshed it over the floor. He began to cry again. He scrubbed and scrubbed at the bloodstains until he had worn out every rag he could find. The floor looked less gruesome. The fire had gone out in the fireplace so he threw the dirty rags on the dead ashes. His father's cloak hung by the door. He was shivering but he didn't want to put it on, or even touch it. Better his father should have it, in his cold grave, wherever it was. But Tom needed a cloak so he took it off the hook. There was very little else for him to take away with him.

He turned to look for the last time at his home. He wished the fire was still alight. If it were, he would have burned the whole place down. But if he had done that, he wouldn't have noticed the object that gleamed on the back of the shelf. He crossed the room again and took it down. No object so beautiful had ever been in their home before. He stared at it for a long time. Jeweled leather, with a crest displaying three sheaves of golden wheat. He realized why it was here.

He was suddenly nauseous, as though he had been hit heavily in the gut. Holy saints. He was stupid. Such a stupid idiot. He was devastated, burning with shame. He badly wanted to throw the thing, even the silver coin it held, into the fireplace with the bloody rags. He didn't want to keep it, yet could not let it go. He watched it fall from his hand into his bag. Then, head hanging, he put on his father's cloak and started for the road.

$\mathcal{F}$rom a high window of the lodge, Pippa had seen a figure walking on the beach. Thinking it was surely Tommy, she snatched up a woolen mantle and softly crept downstairs to let herself outside. She had already forgotten Cuinn's command to stay inside, but she had to be forgiven this time. She was thinking only of Tommy, and how he must be feeling.

She waited in the yard, knowing he would come home when he was ready. She pulled her hood close around her and watched for him. She walked out to the bridge and paced back and forth there, but he did not appear. She decided to walk down to the beach to meet him, looking to the right and left so she wouldn't pass him in the dark. When she came to his ramshackle hut, she stopped. The door, little enough protection as it was, had been kicked apart. She called but no one answered. Cautiously she went up the steps, still calling. She peeked in. It took only a glance to see that the place was empty. She had never been in Tommy's house. She was surprised at how rough it was. She went back out to the step and strained her eyes to see up and down the beach. The sky had begun to lighten. Tommy, if he was out there, was invisible. Pippa ran all the way back to the lodge, hoping, hoping fervently that he would be there. But he was nowhere to be found.

'$\mathcal{T}$was an ill wind that blew over Arran Isle, to be sure. But the proverb that promised somebody some good was to prove false in this case, for no good came to anyone that day or the next or the next. The pity was that, even when everyone was sure that good news had finally come, they were mistaken.

In the afternoon, later the same day, there was a knock on Pippa's chamber door. Alexander de Bruce, Rob's brother, was there. He looked at Pippa's chalky face and wondered if she had slept at all.

She couldn't meet his eye. She knew instantly why he had come and felt a pang of shame for disappointing someone she liked so well. She had disobeyed Rob the night before, and had run out of the caves without telling anyone where she was going. Alexander had surely come to reprimand her. She hung her head.

"Do you mind if I come in and sit a moment?" he asked kindly. "I have some good news, finally." He gave Pippa a hug. "But first, my condolences for losing Caela. Such a terrible thing. How are you faring?"

"I'm all right, thank you."

"I've just come from Sebrina. She's a bit improved."

"Yes, she can talk a bit today, and she is a little less dizzy. She says her hearing bothers her, though."

"It won't take her long to get back on her feet. She's a strong woman." Pippa nodded absently and Alexander continued. "I've come partly to see how you were and partly about something else. But I must tell you, we were worried about you last night. Very worried. Rob wanted to move the army to St. Mo Las, but he couldn't leave until he knew you were safe."

"I'm sorry, Alexander. It's just that…"

"You don't have to explain, Pippa. But please don't do that to us again." He decided not to mention that their biggest concern was that she, too, had met up with John Comyn. He wasn't sure that Caela had mentioned Isobel's husband to Pippa. He assumed, though, that she had fulfilled her promise to tell Pippa about her mother and father. He continued. "Fortunately Cuinn came back to the caves last night and told us you were safe, but you gave everyone a patch of trouble."

"I know, Alexander. I'm sorry. I wasn't thinking."

"Something good came of it after all. I've just been to tell Sebrina. Rob's army attacked Brodick Castle late last night and threw the English out. He was sure he would capture John Comyn in the process, but he missed him. But now Brodick castle will be

Sebrina's once more. She will be able to move back as soon as she's stronger. Isn't that good news?"

Pippa could not order her thoughts. She wasn't sure if it was good news or not.

"You mean, leave Loch Ranza?"

"Of course you never lived at Brodick. It's far grander than here. She's very excited about getting back to her home. And she tells me, too, that she will care for Caela's baby for the time being."

"Yes, a woman is coming in to help her."

"It helps set Jamie Douglas's mind at ease to know that." Alexander shifted in his chair. He smiled at her. "Pippa, I've also come with a proposition."

"A what?"

"A proposal. Your father would like you to sail back to the mainland with him. We are hoping to leave fairly soon. He would like to take you to your mother." Pippa stared at him.

"My mother?"

"I know this is a shock. But he feels that Arran is very unsafe for you, after what has happened to Caela. And it really is time you and your mother got to know each other."

Pippa's mouth was an O. What did he mean? What happened to Caela? Caela died because the roof of their cottage caught fire. Didn't she?

"I've spoken with Sebrina. I think, or I hope anyway, that I've convinced her that you would be safer on the mainland."

"Safer?"

"Arran is too small, you'd be too easy to find here. Sebrina will miss you, of course. But John Comyn is a formidable threat to you now."

"I see." Pippa's mind was spinning. John Comyn again. Who was he? She'd heard that name last night.

"Pippa, are you listening? You should start packing a few things. I'll take you down to St. Mo Las with me today. We sail for the mainland, God willing, sometime in the next couple of nights."

"Oh."

"Why don't you go and say good-by to Sebrina now and..." He was interrupted by a loud, insistent knock on the door. He had just risen to answer it when a soldier put his head into the room.

"Begging your pardon, sir, but the signal! It's come!"

"Cuthbert's fire signal?"

"Yes sir. You're to come to St. Mo Las immediately." Pippa could feel Alexander's excitement like a jolt of lightning.

"Wait for us in the yard. We're on our way."

Alexander closed the door on the messenger and held himself quiet for a moment.

"Well, the time has come. We'll finally be making our assault on the mainland."

"War, again?"

"Yes, beginning with our ancestral lands. Turnberry."

"Am I going to Turnberry?"

"You'll wait there until someone can take you to your mother."

"Are you coming to Turnberry too?"

"No, Thomas and I are leading a force to Galloway. This is going to be a two-pronged attack. On second thought, Pippa, I wonder if you could get someone else to ride with you to St. Mo Las to meet the boats? Someone you can trust? I'll also leave a soldier here to accompany you. But I'm anxious myself to get started immediately."

"Yes, I'll ask Dickon to go with me" she answered listlessly. A thick slurry of questions trudged round and round in her mind.

"You must hurry. Pack lightly and get on your way. We can't hold up an attack on your account, important as you are, Pippa."

"I'll be ready."

"Well, I hope to see you soon at Turnberry, my lass. Wish us luck."

"Good luck, Alexander" she replied automatically. He gave her another hug, looked into her face with concern for a moment and left quickly.

She had no choice. She was to leave Loch Ranza. First, Grizel and their cottage gone, now Loch Ranza, Sebrina, Baby William, Tommy, all. But to be with Cuinn. Finally, he was willing to be her father. She would be his daughter. A streak of satisfaction crossed her face. To go with Cuinn, to find out who her mother was. Pippa's feelings ran in every direction. She fingered the charm she always wore, the golden rowan tree on a fine chain around her neck. Then she stumbled across the room, trying to think what she needed to pack.

When Pippa rode down to St. Mo Las with Dickon, Loch Ranza's steward, neither of them could believe the bustle of activity there. But it was the fleet of boats, spread out across the bay, that simply took her breath away. There were nearly forty galleys hiding behind the beautiful Holy Isle. And here on land, there seemed to be so many soldiers! They milled around restlessly, working off nervous tension. Many were the rough Irishmen Pippa had seen at the cave. Even a few Hebrideans had come. Dickon's face broadened into a smile.

"This is wonderful!" he declared. "Look at that. Have you ever seen so many galleys together in your life? And all for Scotland!"

Alexander Bruce spotted them and rode up.

"Pippa, I'm glad you're here. It must have been difficult, saying good-bye to Loch Ranza and Sebrina."

Tears started in Pippa's eyes. She had had such a short time to be with Sebrina and Baby William for the last time. Well, she hoped it would not be the last time, but she didn't know when she would be returning.

"Your friend Tom is here. Did you know that?"

"Tommy! Where is he?"

"There won't be much chance to see him, I'm afraid. He's coming with me. And you're taking that vessel." He pointed. "I've arranged for them to find you a berth. It won't be luxurious, but it will only be for a night or two. Shall I say good-by to Tom for you?"

Pippa nodded and sniffled a bit. Suddenly this entire enterprise seemed like a very bad idea. Her only comfort was to be with Cuinn. To be with her father. She had to get used to calling him that. She tried to bring her attention back to Alexander. He was speaking again.

"I'll take my leave of you once more, Pippa. I wish you a good journey. We'll meet again at Turnberry."

"Good-bye, Alexander. Godspeed!" she called. She watched him ride away, so eager to be going off to battle. Her last good-bye was for Dickon. He ordered her little trunk carried down to the dock and watched her follow it. She turned back once to wave listlessly at him, then dropped her hand and walked on.

Just as she boarded, eighteen of the galleys got underway for Galloway. It was a stirring sight to see them all under sail, so full of hope for success. Tom must be on board one of those, she thought. I hope he'll be safe. She wished she could have had even a glimpse of him.

"Hello, Pippa. Do you remember me? I'm to show you to your cabin." Gilbert de la Haye, one of Rob's most trusted friends, was at her elbow. "We'll be leaving any time now. As soon as we're away, your father would like to see you for just a moment." Pippa smiled a little.

When Gilbert knocked on her door, she came out instantly and followed him to the deck. He pointed to the bow.

"He's up there" he said. She went forward, searching. There was only one person leaning on the rail, and that was Rob, looking towards the mainland. He turned and smiled at her with genuine pleasure. He watched the wind pulling on her red curls, loosening and blowing them across her temples. It stirred a memory. But he mustn't get lost in memory today.

"Pippa, I'm so glad you've decided to come."

"Hello, Rob. I was supposed to meet Cuinn here. Have you seen him?"

He squinted at her in confusion. "Cuinn?" he asked.

"He said to meet him here."

"Cuinn is sailing with Alexander, Pippa." Pippa looked to where the eighteen galleys were sailing into the south.

"What?" she cried. "No! Alexander told me to get on this boat." Her distress flared as suddenly as if someone had set a match to her. She let out a cry and ran to the rail.

"You said you wanted to sail with me."

"I said I wanted to sail with my father" she retorted fiercely. She beat a hand on the rail. She needed urgently to get to one of Alexander's vessels.

So. Rob rubbed his beard. She still didn't know.

"Pippa." Rob paused. "Pippa, I thought Caela would have told you before this. I am your father, not Cuinn."

She stared at him aghast. A long moment passed. Her stomach, empty as it was, turned over.

A page boy hurried up to them. Pippa's stare transferred to the boy.

"Your Majesty, you are needed by the captain right away."

"Tell him I'll be right there." Rob didn't take his eyes off Pippa. After another long moment, she looked up at him. She shook her head, frowning, and found her voice.

"Your Majesty?"

Rob nodded.

Pippa moved back to grip the rail with both hands. She had never been prey to seasickness before.

Her father, King Robert de Bruce of Scotland, put his hands briefly on her shoulders and left her to her thoughts. Behind her, the last light of day was dying and the black mountains of Arran Isle were disappearing over the rim of the world.

Rondel

February 1307
Near Turnberry Castle

𝓟ol the cook woke at the sound of light footsteps running across the deck. He had been told to take care of the one the men called "the lass". He was supposed to see that she was fed and stayed on board until the king and his army returned. For most of the day, Pol had watched the progress of the battle for Turnberry Castle. Once darkness came, all he could see were the blazing buildings that clustered outside the castle wall. He must have fallen asleep in the hammock out there. Now here she was, the lass herself, standing at the rail in the dark hours before dawn, watching the fire. He grunted and worked himself to his feet.

He hadn't meant to startle her, but he was a big man. He realized that he towered over her, and that she had no idea who he was. She drew away from him.

"Oh!" she exclaimed. "I thought everyone was gone." She had awakened to a silent ship, no pages scurrying fore and aft with messages, no soldiers jeering at each other, or rough Irishmen who abruptly cut off conversations when she came close.

"Good night. Your father, the king, tells me to watch for you. They have all gone off boat. Is big fire they make, no?" He pointed toward the burning town.

"It's terrible. Why are they doing that?"

The big man shrugged.

"This is war. They do this to win castle."

"Are they winning?"

"I think yes, because King Robert make the fire. This is bad for the English."

"Fires are terrible things. Terrible." Pippa shuddered.

"Would you like food? I am very fine cook, you must know."

"No. Thank you, though. I'm not hungry."

Pol shrugged again. Anyone foolish enough to turn down his food was beyond help.

"Just come down to Pol when you want food. I am Pol." He patted his broad chest. "Pol. And you are …?"

"I am Pippa."

"Peepa. Your father say you must stay on boat, Peepa. Don't go off. You understand?"

"Yes, I understand."

He nodded and walked off.

A cold breeze from the north had begun to clear Pippa's head, but misery still sat like a rock on her chest. She had slept a bit, finally, but didn't feel rested. She wondered how long it would be until morning. Over the harbor, a thousand stars peeked through smoke and cloud.

The men must have gone ashore while she slept. Soot drifted over the deck, and faint sounds of battle. On shore, every roof of the town seemed to be aflame. She wondered if Rob had been caught in the fire, or Gilbert de la Haye.

She was still angry at Rob for deceiving her, for tricking her into leaving Loch Ranza. She could be home with Sebrina and Baby William right now. She longed to be at Loch Ranza more than anything. Perhaps Rob would take her back there when he was finished with this fighting business today. She would ask him. Since he was the one who brought her here, he should take her back.

She heard heavy footsteps and Pol was back at her side.

"I forget. Your father say you help Pol with food tomorrow."

"Me?"

"You must do this because not enough help for cooking. I am sorry. You are king's daughter. But work must be done."

She looked away.

"You are this girl who lost mother, yes?"

"Yes. Well, she was my guardian."

"Ah, not so bad then?"

"She was like my own mum."

"Ah, so very bad then. I have hurt here for you." He pressed his heart. The man spoke with an accent. Pippa could barely understand him. "I forget again – your name?"

"It's Pippa."

"Ah, yes. Peepa."

"You're not a soldier, Pol?"

"*Tiens*! No. With these hands? I can not fight." He rolled his eyes. "I am cook. Very special cook." He leaned his hefty arms companionably on the rail. "In Scotland, not so special. But in my land, cook is very important. More important than soldier."

"Where is your land?"

"I come of Brix. Flanders, same as King Robert's family. Um, your family, too, I think so, yes?"

"Yes. I guess so."

"We are Norman peoples. Very special to be Norman. Do not forget this. You too, very special. Not of Scotland. Bah! Too..." He rolled his hands in eloquent circles, then shrugged. "I not know."

"Don't you like it here?"

"No, not good here. I go back to my beautiful home soon."

"You're homesick?" Pippa understood exactly how he felt and she hadn't been away from home for even a full day.

"Sick? Not sick. Pol never sick."

"But you miss your home?"

"Yes, yes. I go back soon. In spring."

"That will be nice for you."

Pol tilted his head and shrugged.

"Yes, but when you taste Pol's food, you will wish he stays here. So now good-bye. I go to get food ready for when others come back. Later you will eat."

"Maybe."

"Sure. Must eat. Pol's food is very good. Good night, Peepo."

"No, it's Pippa."

"Of course, Peepa. Good night."

"Good night, Pol."

He began to walk away, then turned and called to her.
"Papee! Don't forget, you help Pol with food in morning, yes?"
"Maybe."
"This would be good for you. You work and forget all troubles." He touched his forehead in a salute and went below, whistling to himself.

"And my name is Pippa" she muttered. She slumped against the rail and watched the blazing buildings for a while. The night was cold, though. She went back to her bunk but sleep did not come again.

$\mathcal{P}$ol did not forget her. Before it was light he banged on Pippa's door and summoned her to his galley kitchen where he put her to work packing scores of bannocks that he had baked two days ago. They were hard as rocks now. She loaded them into bags and carted them up onto the deck. Pol had been right about one thing: she had no time to think about her troubles.

Messengers arrived. The bannocks were needed, and ale was to be brought ashore, lots of ale.

"The fight, it goes well?" Pol asked.

One of the messenger boys pulled off his cap. "Hoot! Me stomach thinks me throat's been cut! Give us one of these would ye?" He helped himself to a bannock. "Saints preserve us, Pol! What's this yer callin' food? Jock, best you don't put that thing in yer gub until ye've dunked it in some ale. You'll break both the tooths ye got left."

"But the hunger is on me somethin' fierce!"

"Give us a mug of ale, would ye, Pol? These here bannocks 're goin' ta need a good long soak."

Pol shrugged.

"This is food of Scotland. Always hard like stone. Not Pol's food."

"Don't yammer ta us about Pol's wonderful food. We been eatin' it, or tryin' to, fer weeks."

"I not like this talk. No ale for you. You are not friend to Pol!"

"Not friend? Not friend? Pol, I'm hurt. I'm hurt you should say that. That do hurt, don't it Jock?" He bent over, sniggering.

"You men load cart now. No more talking. But first tell me, was fighting good?"

"Fightin' was good, but we've not won the castle yet. Made pretty short work of the garrison though. Nothing left of it."

"What happened to all the people?" asked Pippa.

The boy guffawed. "Nothing left of them, neither!"

Pippa was shocked. They had killed all the people in the town? Were they killed by Rob's orders?

He was despicable. She hated him.

A cart waited to take them across the timber bridge to the other side of the river. Pol took his seat on the cart with the majesty of a king ascending his throne. From there he snapped orders to all and sundry, and had worked himself into a truly foul mood by the time everything was loaded. When the bannocks and ale were properly stowed, they trundled off toward the castle. Pippa wasn't sure she wanted to go along, but waiting alone on the boat didn't appeal to her either. She climbed aboard.

Light was just coming into the sky. The first beams of morning sun touched the mountains across the bay with gold. Pippa realized they were her mountains, the mountains of Arran Isle. Tears rolled down her cheeks. Why did Rob make her come here? She was dear to no one here. She wanted so badly to go home.

Though she longed to be elsewhere, she found herself intrigued by everything she saw. Toward the north stood the graceful turrets of Turnberry Castle, the home of Rob's family before it was confiscated by King Edward. It sat high above the water, with an immense sea door that gave entrance to its walled harbor. It was beautiful, and the largest castle Pippa had ever seen. On a field near the castle were at least a hundred men and their horses, all busy setting up camp. Men on foot ran here and there, dodging men on horseback, men shouting orders, others setting up the tents. This was Rob's army, Pol explained, setting siege to the castle, trying to force it to surrender. More men worked near the burning buildings. Figures moved through a screen of dark smoke. The wind blew much of the smoke to the south, but still it swathed every cold hollow and poured constantly, black as pitch, from the ruined buildings. Such an enormous amount of destruction. Not a single building outside the castle walls was left standing. The soldiers said there had been no survivors.

Pippa worked all morning, passing out food and drink to the men. They were filthy and tired but bragged endlessly of their victory, or rather, their partial victory.

"Did ya see the wound I give to that last boggin' Englander?" demanded one. "He'll never forget me, I'll tell ya that!"

"You! You was nothin' but a big sook, you was!"

"Was not! I warn't afeared a-tall. Not me!"

"You shoulda seed me! Even after I was hit, with my shoulder all gowpin', I could still pull the bow, strong as ever. You never seed arrows fly that fast. One of 'em, bam! I gots 'im right in the face. Right in the face! That English is gonna be hackit-lookin' for his whole life, thanks ta me. If he lives."

On and on, they delighted in recounting every gory detail of the fight. Pippa wanted to crawl away somewhere and would have, if they hadn't given her so much work to do. She helped some of the men who were bleeding. She could do nothing for those who were hideously wounded. All the soldiers were exhausted. Not one was too tired to complain about Pol's bannocks, though. He, in turn, kept up a constant stream of angry retorts.

"I make your own food of Scotland. At home, we not feed this to pig, or else he gets glued up inside." Pol's apple-round cheeks were flaming pink. "But in Scotland, you eat this every day. This is what make you nasty."

"Yeah? Well why is it, just the once, Pol, you can't feed us well as you feed your pigs, eh?"

Pol loosed a torrent of words, all in French, that few of the peasant soldiers could understand, and none of them bothered to answer.

They set about caring for the wounded, and labored until well into the afternoon. Pippa was reeling with fatigue. Rob appeared, took one look at her white face and pulled her aside.

"Pippa, we're going to find you somewhere else to stay for a few days."

"Can I go back to Loch Ranza? Please, Rob?"

"I simply don't have time to take you there. I'm sorry. Go with Geordie now. He will row you back to the boat to get your trunk. Then come back and meet me here."

$\mathcal{R}$ob was waiting when she returned. A page strapped her little chest of belongings to her horse and they rode out of the camp, accompanied by six soldiers. Rob rarely traveled alone when he was on the mainland.

Smoke still poured from the ruined buildings as they passed. Pippa slowed her horse but Rob pulled up beside her, blocking her view.

"Pippa, best you don't look over yonder."

She leaned to see around him. "What is it?"

"It's not a thing you want to be seeing, take my word for it."

She insisted on looking, even after he warned her, and truly, she wished she had not.

"The horrors of war, lass, the horrors of war. You have to do something with the dead. You can't just leave them lying about, you know."

"You didn't have to kill them in the first place. How could you burn up a whole town like that? The women and children? Their homes?"

"It wasn't a town. There were no children there. It was a garrison, a place where soldiers live. English soldiers."

She was too angry at Rob to answer. She thought he was revolting.

As for Rob, he understood she was feeling the strain of the last few days. She looked exhausted. He let her be.

They rode until late afternoon, in the opposite direction that Pippa wanted to go, farther and farther from Arran Isle. To Pippa, used to the mountains of Arran, the terrain was easy. The winter ground was bare. When they crested a small rise, Rob paused. Below them was a beautiful stone building washed in the lavender light of evening. Pippa saw towers, pointed arches, an old stone cross. On the lawn, bare trees, thin as ink strokes, spread into the sapphire sky.

"Where are we?"

"Crossraguel Abbey. It's a monastery that our family built for the Benedictine monks. You'll be safe here until we capture Turnberry. That should only take a few more days, Pippa, and then I'll come back for you."

Rob banged the iron knocker on the huge door. A monk peered cautiously from a grated opening and he and Rob exchanged a few words. When he swung the door open they stepped into a cavernous stone hall. The door boomed shut behind them. Grey silence filtered over them like a dove settling on her nest.

They were told to wait. In a small niche off the hall was a prie-dieu and a statue of a saint. Candles flickered. Pippa was surprised to see Rob kneel there. She sank onto a stone bench and watched him through narrowed eyes. He bent his forehead to his folded hands. To whom did he pray, after all the killing he had just done? Or were his prayers just for himself? She looked past him, along a dark colonnade supported by intricately carved stone pillars. Everywhere her eye rested there was a beautiful piece of carved stonework, from the floor all the way to the top of the vaulted ceilings. The last light of day slanted through tall narrow windows. It was very beautiful, so peaceful. Armies and fighting seemed far away. She wished Caela were here with her.

The black-robed prior was so soft-footed, she didn't hear him approach. He waited until Rob finished his prayer, then embraced him gladly, like an old friend. From her bench she watched them speak together. The prior looked in her direction and nodded at something Rob was saying. Rob turned to Pippa.

"Pippa, this is Prior William. He has agreed to give you shelter here until I come back." He grasped the prior's arm affectionately. "As soon as we escort Henry Percy and his men out of Turnberry and back to their English rat holes, Father, I'll send word."

"Please, I implore you, Robert, choose your battles with caution. You must live to fight another day. Scotland needs you. We all need you. Promise me you'll remember this?" Rob smiled and nodded. "In the meantime," continued the prior, "don't fuss yourself. Your young lass is in good hands. Godspeed, my son. May the grace of God go with you." They embraced again and the prior made the sign of the cross on Rob's back.

The prior beckoned to Pippa and led her down the colonnade to a staircase that took them to his chambers in the east tower. She followed him in a daze of exhaustion. He asked a servant to find someone called Anna, and when Anna came, she took Pippa to a small room furnished with a bed and a table. She looked askance at Pippa's stained clothing.

"Shall I have a tub filled for you, *ma petite*?"

"A bath? That would be lovely" answered Pippa.

A warm bath! After a long soak, Pippa went directly to bed, finally able to surrender to sleep. She didn't move until the next morning.

Someone had left a slice of bread and honey beside her bed, which she devoured hungrily. Well-rested at last, she left her room and found the staircase. At the bottom of the steps, she heard voices in the outer hall, dissonant, rude voices in a peculiar accent, splintering the quiet. Curious, she crept to the doorway. Facing her was Prior William. He spoke with three men in mail shirts. They held their helmets under their arms. Their leader was having a heated conversation with the prior.

"No, I'm sorry Sir Henry!" Prior William was saying. "You know I cannot let you search here. Wars and fighting have no place in a monastery. We protect everyone, good or evil, who enters here."

"But it is not I who insists on searching, my good monk. It is the King of England himself."

"I, however, answer to the King of Heaven, Sir Henry. As does, I needn't remind you, even England's king."

Prior William looked up then and spotted Pippa. He froze in alarm. He gestured to her with the slightest motion. Pippa began to back away. The leader of the mail-shirted men turned, sensing her presence, and stared in surprise. She saw his face harden. He was tall. His pale eyes, like two shards of ice, sat close to a zig-zag nose. He frowned and pursed his thin lips. Pippa turned away as the argument continued. She sensed a dark, heavy presence in that room. She felt sorry for the gentle prior.

She wandered glumly from corridor to corridor until she found a door that led outside. Beyond was a courtyard.

The dark doorway was a threshold, not to a place but to some other plane of being. When she stepped over it, she stepped out of the world, out of time, and at last, far from sorrow.

It beckoned as if waiting for her. The courtyard, its garden, the morning light, everything had been waiting. Even though it was winter, this garden, surrounded on all sides by high walls, was sheltered and warm. Like a balm, sunshine poured from the sky. It soothed her aching spirit. All thoughts slipped from Pippa's mind like minnows through a net. Stillness floated in on damselfly wings.

Two black-frocked monks were turning the soil. Small fruit trees were scattered here and there. It had rained in the night and the bare branches twinkled with sunshine diamonds. Silver glistened every twig and a tiny rainbow hung in every crystal droplet. On the far side of the garden there stood a pretty dovecote and beehives. Little finches were fidgeting on the rim of a stone birdbath, arguing in dainty voices. Pippa watched them with pure delight, the first she had felt in many days.

Truly, if there were secret places of enchantment hidden anywhere on earth, she had just stepped into one of them. There was something in the air here, something exquisite. She breathed it in, something cleansing. A heavy burden slipped from her shoulders but she felt unbalanced without it. Her strength drained away. She almost felt too dizzy to stand. She squeezed her hands tightly, trying to hold herself together.

It was then that she came. She touched Pippa's hair very gently, with a warm hand. Pippa lifted her head. Caela was here beside her. This was what she wanted, to have Caela back again, and she had come. They were together, in that place between worlds where neither could remain for more than a moment. One touch and they were separated again. The great gift had been given, though, that one unforgettable touch.

The two monks who gardened there turned as one just then, and they smiled at Pippa so beautifully that she had to press her folded hands to her lips. They left their shovels and came to stand near her, perfectly quiet, waiting until she had collected herself. She held her handkerchief to her eyes.

"I'm sorry. I didn't mean to interrupt your work." She hiccoughed, and laughed with embarrassment. "I don't know what happened to me. Something strange .. "

"No, please dear lass, no need for apology. Many a person has been lifted by the spirit of this garden" said one of the monks.

"It feels like a ...another world."

"It is indeed a holy place." The monks folded their hands into their black sleeves and beamed.

"It's beautiful. I wish I could stay here always."

"Have you seen the chapel? It's very lovely too."

She drifted after them, light-headed. They left her in the chapel and she sat there for long time, thinking about Caela. Strange to say, it suddenly seemed appropriate to use her real name, though she had never called her that in life. Grizel was gone. She knew she must accept that. She was gone forever. But Caela would be part of her always.

When Pippa left the chapel she felt almost whole again. It was wonderful that she had found a place that gave comfort to her wounded spirit.

But enchanted places are fragile, and the hurts of the world bite deep.

*P*itch dark, it was the middle of the night. Someone was calling her name, shaking her urgently. The woman, Anna, hunched over her in a white shift, wild with terror, her hair in a riot.

"Get up, get up. *Vitement!* Come quickly. No time to dress. Take your blanket." She hauled Pippa from her bed.

"What is it?"

"Hide, we must hide. Run. *Allons-y!*"

They fled down a dark hall. Sounds came from the courtyard. Pippa stopped short. Screaming. A man was screaming there. Anna turned around and pulled Pippa in another direction. Booted feet were running down the hall behind them. They could hear sounds of fighting outside. Anna grabbed Pippa's hand and they ducked into a narrow, dark stairway. They had to feel their way. The stairs circled round and round, steeply downward. Through a door, onto a dark lawn.

Many men on horses, cold dim moonlight. Huge swords, glinting silver. The swords slashed without mercy, though the monks were completely defenseless. Steaming clouds of breath puffed from mouths contorted with pain, then no breath. No breath at all. Bodies dropped to the frozen ground. Cries of anguish, cut short. Pippa whirled in confusion. The grass was covered with frost. Bodies in black robes lay everywhere. Black blood oozed over the white grass. Pippa and Anna both cried out and began to run, trying to get as far away from the abbey as they could.

"The swamp. This way" Anna panted. There was cover there, if only they could reach it. They ran for their lives. Anna began to fall behind. She doubled over, holding her side. Pippa turned back.

"Take my hand."

"No, you go!"

"Please!"

"No! Don't wait! I come, I come."

Pippa leapt barefoot from hummock to hummock of frozen grass. She spotted a clump of bushes. Leafless though they were, they were the best protection she could find. She flung herself down behind them and huddled beneath her grey blanket, panting furiously. She had to cover her ears. The sounds of fighting were horrible. She peeked out. Anna was nowhere to be seen.

Even though her hands were tight over her ears, she still heard it, and felt it as well – the enormous crash. The earth shook under her. It was beyond imagining. What could have struck such an enormous blow? She kept as low to the ground as she could and peered through the darkness. As she watched, an entire stone wall near the east tower buckled and fell to the ground.

The beautiful abbey was being destroyed. A huge device, as tall as four or five men, had been dragged in, a device made for destruction. It hurled boulder after boulder into the stone walls. The stonework crumbled, the walls buckled and came crashing down. The violence of the blows rocked the earth to its roots. Another contraption threw balls of flame whistling through the air. Broken wood caught fire.

Pippa wanted to scream. Why were these soldiers doing this? Where did they come from? And why destroy this exquisite place? Of all the places in the world, why this abbey?

The moon was blind to everything below. It rode clear across the heavens and still the soldiers battered at the abbey. Pippa's mind could take no more. She began to shake with rage. She couldn't remember ever in her life feeling such fury. She wanted a sword. She wanted a bow, a club, anything. But she was helpless. There was absolutely nothing she could do. Crouched on the icy ground, she prayed that morning light would never come. She feared so dreadfully to see what lay before her.

*H*er prayers did not hold back the dawn. Morning came.

Crossraguel Abbey was nothing more than a smoking ruin. But for one tower and a bit of a wall, it had been leveled to the ground.

Trembling with misery and cold, Pippa raised herself slowly. No one moved anywhere. Not a single person. She crept stiffly from her hiding place.

So many dead.

She picked her way among them, the unspeakably ruined dead. White, still faces, black robes in disarray. Across the lawn, a white shift fluttered but the body that wore it was still as stone. Pippa had to find out if Anna ... she stumbled over to her, looked and dragged herself away. How was it that Pippa was the only one left alive?

She stepped her bare feet carefully among the burned wreckage, and found a seat on what had, just yesterday, been a stone bench. She was shaking with cold. Her blanket was thin. She pulled her blue feet up under her and wrapped her arms around her knees. The courtyard was unrecognizable. Something more than just a building had been destroyed last night. The rapture she had felt here a few days ago? Gone. The kind, smiling monks who knew that beauty would give comfort? All gone.

$\mathcal{P}$ippa felt a light mist of rain on her face. She lay on the hard stone bench, where sleep had finally overcome her. Her head felt sore when she tried to raise it. Had the rain wakened her?

"Pee-paa!" Someone was calling. "Peepa?" She saw Pol the cook half-running, picking his way over the broken walls. His arms flapped over his head like the wings of an excited bird.

"I find her, I find her!" he shouted. Pippa sat up, dazed and bewildered.

"Look at you. You are a mess, Peepa! Let me help you."

She held out her hands and leaned on his arms.

"They're all dead, Pol!"

"I know, *cherie*. This is terrible."

"I couldn't do anything to stop them" she choked. "I couldn't help anyone."

"No, no, but of course. These were bad mens."

"I had to run away. I wanted to fight but I had no sword." She was sobbing uncontrollably.

"What could you do, Peepa? You are too small."

"Yes, but…"

"Shh, shh. Don't cry. *Cherie, ma cherie.* Shh."

Rob, ashen with shock, came stumbling across the piles of stones. He groaned in disbelief when he saw the thin little figure in Pol's arms, wearing nothing but her shift in the February rain.

*T*hat night, late, Pippa and Rob dismounted quietly in a stable yard. Pippa's mind was a dull blank. She had no idea where they were, except that they were ever further from home. Pol had stayed behind at the abbey with the men of Rob's army, to help bury the dead. But Pippa and Rob had ridden hard all afternoon and evening to get here. They had not used roads, but had ridden through forests by day and then across the winter fields when darkness came. Rob seemed to know precisely where they were going. Far behind them, Crossraguel Abbey was a mirage that shimmered on the edge of imagination.

Now they were in a stable yard outside a big timber-framed house. Even in the dark, it looked imposing.

"Wait here" Rob whispered, and handed her the reins of his horse. "Stay back, out of sight." He grasped the blanket that she wore as a hood and pulled it forward to hide her face. Underneath she still wore only her tattered shift. Her feet were wrapped in black rags torn from a dead monk's garment. She drew the horses into the shadow of the barn.

Rob crept up to a window and quietly tapped a rhythm. Almost instantly a woman appeared and opened the window a crack.

"*Qui va?*" Who's there?

"*C'est moi, ma rose.*" It's me, my rose.

"*Viens, immediatement.*" Come immediately.

Rob sprinted to a dark door and slipped inside as soon as it opened. Pippa waited, leaning against the horse for warmth.

Finally the door opened again and a sleepy boy came out to take the horses. Rob leaned from the doorway and beckoned.

He pulled Pippa into the house and they entered a warm, softly lit room. It was beautifully furnished and subtly fragrant. A woman was pulling shutters across the windows. When she turned, Pippa saw that she was quite lovely. She moved gracefully, crossed to a table and closed the ledger book she had been working in. Then she leaned on the table and looked at them both. Rob moved to her side but she turned away and put the table between them. She did not invite them to sit down, nor did she waste time on courtesies. When she finally spoke, her voice was gentle and low-pitched.

"You know the king's men are looking everywhere for you, don't you, Robert? I can not let you stay here. I'll give you something to eat, but I don't want anyone, especially the children, to find out you were here tonight."

"Christian, it would only be for one night. Please. We'll be gone, out of your way tomorrow. We'll sleep in the barn if need be."

"Robert, I'm telling you, the English come through the villages and search every house without a moment's notice. It's too dangerous." She crossed her arms and frowned. "Isn't there another place you can go?"

"I am heading north, to take Pippa to her mother. She went in that direction a couple of months ago. The last I heard, she was at Kildrummy."

"Kildrummy? How can you ...? Oh, Robert." She shook her head and came across the room. "And, of all your women, my darling, which would be mother to this lass, I'm wondering?" she asked archly. Gently she pulled the blanket back from Pippa's head. She sucked in her breath and raised Pippa's face with a finger under her chin. "No. Don't tell me, Robert." She looked at him with disgust. "She's the very image."

"Christian, I beg you—"

"And your great plan was to take her off to her mother?" She spread her hands and looked imploringly at him. "Robert, I'm thinking there may be some things you don't know yet. You haven't heard..." Rob frowned and stiffened, and the lady leaned on her table. She sighed. "All right." She bowed her head and spoke softly. "All right, I'll give you a place to stay, but you're not to set foot outside by day. The children are never to know you're here, much as they adore you." She glanced at Pippa. "And you'd better be gone at the setting of the sun tomorrow evening. I'm sorry, Robert. It's the best I can do."

"We thank you, Christian."

"Ai, well, you might not thank me for what I have yet to tell you. Come with me."

She leaned into a room to speak to a woman there, then took them outside past the barn. She unlocked a tiny tumble-down cottage that stood empty beside a field and let them in. Rob started a small fire while Pippa found blankets for the beds. Christian of Carrick came back with water for washing and the serving woman carried a tray of food.

"No candles, if you please. The firelight will have to do." Christian drew Pippa close to the fire and looked critically at her, sizing her up.

"Here, my lass. Try these clothes on. These boots might fit. You must be freezing cold."

"Thank you." Christian helped her into a tunic. Pippa recognized beautiful fabric when she saw it, and this tunic was of very finely woven wool.

"This is a bit big, and no wonder, you being no bigger around than a broom straw. If I give you a needle and thread, can you alter this yourself tomorrow? Do you know how to sew?"

"Yes, I can take it in. Thank you very much." Christian handed her a ribbon.

"This should help to get that mop of hair tied up." While Pippa washed her face and plaited her hair, Christian caught Rob's eye.

"I've got bad news, Robert" she whispered. She gestured with her head in Pippa's direction. "Should this one be hearing it?" Rob's knees buckled. He sat down and looked gravely at Christian.

"Pippa's had enough bad news as it is lately, but you might as well tell us everything. She'll hear it eventually anyway. Is it news from Galloway? My brothers attacked there about six or seven days ago."

"The attack never happened, Robert."

"What?"

"You left Arran because you thought you saw a fire signal, but your man Cuthbert did not light that fire. Someone else did. Cuthbert knew it wasn't safe for you to leave Arran yet. As soon as your brothers sailed into Loch Rìoghaine, Dougal Macdougall was there to capture the entire fleet." Rob sat up straight, his expression dazed. "Everyone was captured. Macdougall beheaded several of the leaders on the spot. Your brothers Thomas and Alexander were sent to the king at Carlisle."

Pippa cried out. Alexander, that sweet man! Cuinn? What had become of Cuinn? And Tommy? Tommy was with him. Had they been beheaded? It was not possible! Pippa sank to the floor, her hand tight over her mouth.

"The word is that Edward is planning to execute both your brothers. They may already be dead." Christian looked away. "I'm so sorry, Robert."

Neither Rob nor Pippa could do more than stare at her in disbelief. Half of Rob's army captured, half his plans in ruins. Not one brother, but two, probably dead already.

"The other news is worse, I fear."

"Worse?" Rob's voice was hoarse. "Go on with it then."

Christian sighed.

"Last month, Castle Kildrummy was taken. Your brother Niall..."

"I heard he was captured. What ransom do they ask?"

"No ransom. He was executed. Cruelly executed."

"No! Not our Niall! What about my wife and daughter? My sisters? They were with him."

Pippa looked up. Rob had a daughter, another daughter?

"They got away to Tain with the Earl of Atholl. He got them safely to St. Duthac monastery, but…."

"Thank goodness."

"No, wait. No. The Earl of Ross lives near there. He found out they were at the monastery and turned them over to the English."

"They can't do that! They can't forcibly remove someone from a monastery!" Rob shouted. "They can't violate the sanctuary of a holy place!" He smashed a fist onto the table.

"The earl claimed he was getting revenge, Robert, for the two men of the Comyn family that you murdered in another holy place last winter."

There it was again. Rob, a murderer. Was it this that started all their troubles? Was it all because of Rob?

Rob cried out and threw himself backwards on the chair. "What have they done with my family?"

Christian sighed again and shook her head. "Your wife is being held prisoner in a manor house in Holderness. She's not badly treated, mostly because she has powerful English relations. Though you, of course, are not counted among them."

"My sisters are there with her? And my daughter, surely."

"No, Robert. Your sister Christian is in a nunnery in Lincolnshire." Rob nodded and closed his eyes.

"Your sister Mary hangs in a cage from the walls of Roxburgh castle."

Rob's eyes flew open.

"What? A cage?"

"In all weathers. An object of ridicule by all the English people who have taken over that castle."

"Is that some kind of punishment for being Christopher Seton's widow?"

"Probably. The king did surely hate him. He probably still hates him, even though he has already sent him to his death. And, I might as well tell you," Christian glanced at Pippa to watch her reaction, "Isobel MacDuff got the same treatment as your sister.

Her cage hangs from the walls of Berwick." Oddly, she saw no response on Pippa's face. Did the lass not know?

"Animals!" roared Rob. "These are noblewomen! They're treating them like animals!"

"Isobel's husband, John Comyn, begged the king to execute her, but Edward thought, and probably rightly so, that this punishment would be worse than death."

Pippa looked at Rob in alarm. His face had gone absolutely gray.

"And Marjorie?"

"Your daughter was to be put in a cage in London, but they finally took pity on her, but a lass of twelve years, and moved her to a room in the Tower of London."

Rob began to weep.

A daughter Marjorie, Pippa thought, just a bit older than she was.

"And the Earl of Atholl, who was traveling with them. He was executed as well."

"They can't execute an earl! It's not legal."

"They did. And in honor of his high nobility, they built his scaffold especially high. His head is on a pike on London Bridge, alongside all the other Scotsmen."

Rob crumpled in his chair. Christian watched him sobbing like a child with his face buried in his arm. She rose and put her cheek against his shoulder.

"I'm sorry to bring such terrible news, Robert."

After a moment, Christian came to kneel beside Pippa.

"How about you? Are you going to be all right, lassie?" Pippa nodded dumbly. Christian gathered her in her arms, then led her to a bed by the fire and tucked her in. She stood beside Rob for a moment. When he didn't look up, she stroked his hair and walked to the door.

"Let me know if you have need of anything, my darling." She left them alone until late the next afternoon.

*C*hristian brought them some dinner. Pippa had eaten little in the last few days but still, she wasn't very hungry. Christian sat with them while they picked at their food. She leaned her elbows on the table and smiled.

"I have a little good news. Someone rode in just a while ago. I think you'll be glad to see him. He's just getting cleaned up." She was interrupted by an impatient knock.

"Ah, here he is."

Cuinn de Seta put his head into the room.

For a moment, Pippa stood in shocked disbelief. Then she leapt at him and nearly knocked him over. He hugged her tightly. Why she began to cry, when she felt so relieved and happy, was a mystery. Tears just seemed to come pouring out of her lately. Rob jumped up and grasped Cuinn's free arm with a strong grip. They were all crying now, even Christian.

"How many others got away from Loch Rìoghaine?" Rob asked eagerly. Cuinn wiped his face and shook his head.

"None, Rob. None that I know of."

"Tommy?" Pippa asked.

"I never saw Tom again. I looked for him for two days. I'm sorry, Pippa." The dull weight that Pippa had been carrying returned.

"When they attacked our ships, I dove over the side. I grabbed a dead body that had fallen overboard and drifted along underneath it until I could work my way to shore."

"How did you find us?"

"I had no idea I'd find you here. I bought a horse and only came to Carrick because I thought Christian might have news of you. I never dreamed you'd be here with Pippa."

"We were on our way to Kildrummy."

"That was your plan?"

Rob turned to Christian of Carrick.

"You've told Cuinn everything, Christian?"

She nodded.

"She told me" said Cuinn. "She told me about Crossraguel Abbey as well." Cuinn stood there shaking his head for a few moments, then collected himself. "We need to focus on those new plans, Rob. Right away. Do you have any idea who destroyed the abbey?"

"Henry Percy escaped us at Turnberry. It could easily have been him."

Pippa looked up.

"Is he called Sir Henry? Does he have very light-colored eyes and a strange accent?"

"An English accent. Yes, he does, Pippa."

"And a nose...?" She made a squiggly motion with her finger.

"That's Percy. Why? Did you see him that night?"

"He was talking to the prior the first morning I was there. He sounded angry. He wanted the prior to let him search the monastery."

"I knew it! He sacked the abbey out of revenge. He thought I was there. So he had every man killed, looking for me!" Rob grabbed at his hair in desperation.

So many deaths, Pippa thought angrily, laid at your feet.

"Please, Robert, you mustn't ... " began Christian.

"Oh, be assured we are leaving here, my love" Rob interrupted harshly. "Not a doubt about it. We won't trespass on your kindness any longer. We'll join the rest of my men. I know where they were heading."

Christian put a patient hand on Rob's arm.

"Now just wait a moment. What I am trying to say, Robert," said Christian. "is that I'd like to do something to help you. I could spare forty of my fighting men. Would that help your cause at all?"

Rob relaxed a bit.

"More than you can know, Christian. We'd be very grateful."

"Well, if it's battles you are looking for, it seems you have your work cut out for you." She turned to go. "Just wait until dark to take your leave, and go quietly. That's all I ask. I'll tell the men to be ready."

Before they left, Rob pulled Christian aside.

"Christian, I uh ..."

"Will I be seeing you again before the heather blooms, Robert? I feel badly about sending you away. The children miss you so. You know that, don't you?"

"I'll return when I can. But I have a favor, another favor, to ask." Christian of Carrick raised an eyebrow and folded her arms. Rob plunged on in spite of her expression. "It's Pippa. She has no one, now, to go to. Could you take her...?"

"Robert, how can you even ask? How would I explain her to the children? Explaining you is enough of a trouble."

"I see."

"I am sorry. But I have to draw the line somewhere."

"I realize that."

"Oh Saint Brigid, give me strength to put up with your shenanigans." She put her hand on her forehead. "I hate to say 'no', Robert, but it's got to be this way. I wish it could be different. Whatever will you do with the lass?"

"Well, considering how very like her mother she is, I could probably make a pretty fine soldier out of her."

"If she's anything like her mother, I'd say it won't be long 'til she's giving the English a fair bit of trouble." Christian tossed her head spitefully. "In fact, if the English know what's good for them, they'll run the other way while they've got the chance."

"It's not like you to be unkind, my love. You're upset. We must be putting too much strain on you. But don't worry, we'll be on our way soon." He kissed her hand tenderly. "Thank you again for hiding us, my Christian. I'll add a stone to your cairn."

"I'm afraid your cairn will be built a long time before mine, my darling." Christian of Carrick swept through the door and slammed it behind her.

Glen Trool
March, 1307

Cuinn, Pippa and Rob left Carrick after sundown but they didn't get far that night. With the forty men Christian had lent to Rob, they could not move easily through territory that was almost all hostile to them. Fortunately, Rob seemed to know his way down through narrow valleys and up trails hidden in the woods.

When it began to get light, a scout came back with the news that English troops were camped just beyond the next hill.

"We'll sleep here for a few hours" Rob said to Cuinn. "Ride with me to the top of that hill so we can get a look at them."

"I don't think we should risk that. Far better to trust the scout."

"These scouts are practically useless, Cuinn. I can't get reliable information out of any of them."

"If only Tom were here. Saints in Heaven, I miss that lad a hundred times a day. He could have weaseled in and out of that camp in a heartbeat."

"Ai." Rob sighed.

"But you're going to have to find someone you can rely on, Rob. It's too dangerous for you to go out on your own."

They posted plenty of sentries but didn't dare light fires with the enemy so close. After a cold and skimpy meal they huddled in their blankets on the bare ground. Rob had too much on his mind to sleep. He had finally found a scout willing to try to get into the English camp and when the boy came back Rob got up and grilled him at length.

When Rob returned to his blanket, Cuinn was still awake.

"Did you get anything out of the scout?"

"Not much of any use. He thought they had about a hundred horse and the same number of foot soldiers."

"So they've got us outnumbered at least three to one. He couldn't get any idea of where they are headed?"

"He was afraid to get close to them."

"You're not going to attack, are you?"

"We don't have enough men."

"They would wipe us out. And we can't afford to lose even one more battle. You're going to have to choose your battleground carefully from now on."

"Someone else recently said the same thing to me."

"We could slip past these English and move on to meet the rest of your army."

Rob yawned and nodded. "Ai."

"And I've had another idea, Rob."

"Hmm?"

"You know those women we caught last year, who were spying on us while they pretended to sell thread and take on mending jobs? Let's try the same thing."

"You want to put on a gown and a veil, Cuinn, and sell thread to the English lads?"

"No, ya great large bampot. How could I do that? I left all my gowns on Arran." Rob snorted. "But Pippa could do it" Cuinn continued. "She can sew. She could go into a camp as a seamstress and eavesdrop for an entire day, and no one would ever suspect."

"No, it's not safe, Cuinn, and frankly, I'm worried about her. She's been through a lot. It's been hard on her."

"Let me talk to her. She's tougher than you think. She went into Brodick Castle, remember, and got that silver out."

"But Tom was with her then, God rest his soul. She's just a wee lass yet."

"If I may be so bold, please tell me how old your second wife was when you married her, eh? Not yet fourteen?"

"Marrying me at age thirteen is a little different from going to war at age thirteen."

"Ha! You flatter yourself. It is not that different! Many a lass has been wed and is raising a bairn or two, when she is only a little older than Pippa. She's not such a wee one anymore, Rob."

"You're making me feel old." Rob yawned again.

"Let me talk to Pippa. We don't have much choice. We've got no food, few friends even in our own country, and we're trying to take on the entire English army."

"All right, but if Pippa's not keen on the idea, we'll have to drop it."

She was not keen on the idea at all, but somehow Pippa found herself, two days later, carrying a sewing basket and a little stool into a camp full of enemy soldiers. She had at first pleaded that she would be paralyzed with nervousness, but Cuinn was persuasive.

She really didn't even want to be with Rob's army. But here she was, her stomach feeling like lead and her eyes wide with fear, offering to mend clothing in a feeble little voice. Only the image of the ruined Crossraguel Abbey, so vivid in her mind, gave her the motivation she needed to work up her courage.

She had told Cuinn how bitterly angry she was.

He said that would be her strength.

She told him that Rob's war-like ways made her sick.

He said Rob could see things, could envision a future that she could not.

She said she didn't understand.

Cuinn told her Rob was a great man. She would look back, one day, and it would all make sense. In the meantime, they needed her help.

"I'll do this, but only because you asked me" she had said.

"Do this for Scotland" he replied.

But Scotland meant little to her. In the end, she did it for Cuinn.

So here she was. She was stunned to see how many soldiers there were in the English camp. Rob's army was much smaller in comparison. She was able to spot the big tents that Cuinn described as belonging to officers, and she headed that way. She walked slowly up to a group of men. They glanced down at her with frowns. She cleared her throat.

"I'll do your mending" she squeaked. "Mending and sewing. Need anything mended, masters?"

In an hour, she had more work than she could handle. She sat on her little stool and opened her sewing basket, straining her ears all day to hear every scrap of conversation. She could hardly understand a word these men spoke. She thought, at first, they were speaking in a foreign tongue. It didn't sound like English and it certainly wasn't Gaelic. Finally she realized that it was English they were speaking, but with a strong accent. It took her a while to get used to it.

The next day she went back again with a task even more dreadful. This time she was supposed to do more than just eavesdrop. Cuinn asked her to engage one of the English soldiers in conversation, and casually mention a rumor that Robert de Bruce was camped in Glen Trool. She was so nervous she could hardly sew.

When she left the enemy camp at dusk at the end of the second day, Cuinn met her at the edge of the woods.

"How did it go?"

"Well, when I first arrived in the morning I told one squire that a shepherd had seen Rob's men in Glen Trool. Before noon the whole camp had heard the story. They are getting ready to attack tomorrow."

"Now aren't you the clever lass?"

"There are such a lot of English though, Cuinn. And they have all kinds of weapons. We should tell Rob we need to get out of here while we have the chance. Just get out."

"Don't even think like that, Pippa."

"But I'm scared."

"Don't be frightened. This is going to be one battle we're going to win. Come on, let's tell Rob your news." She mounted the pony he was holding and they rode away, melting into the shadows of the forest.

$\mathcal{P}$ippa could not understand why Rob and his men were rubbing their hands in anticipation. The English were coming, they were on their way. Rob is daft, she thought, completely daft. She was positive she was the only one who realized what they would be up against. She had seen the size of the English army. The Scots didn't stand a chance.

"Our sentries killed a couple of their spies" Gilbert de la Haye told Rob.

"Good. We need to surprise and confuse them. That's our first defense," said Rob.

"We're going to shock the bobbies off 'em!"

"The trenches are ready?" Rob asked.

"Ai, and lots of them. We covered them so their horsemen won't see them until they fall into them. They'll lose a lot of men before they even get into the glen. Our foot soldiers will be ready to ambush the rest who do get through" Gilbert said, "there on that narrow strip of ground on the edge of the cliff."

"That'll put their bowels in a knot. It's high above the loch here, too, so if they try to turn back, they'll either have to run down their own men or fall over the cliff."

"And their big horses will be useless on this rocky ground. We're going to win this one, Rob."

"You've piled some rocks up on the side of the hill, for the foot soldiers to throw? Get the archers up there too, among those trees, so they can pick the rest off as they come into the glen" Rob suggested. "Our small folk should climb over the hill and wait on the other side, out of the way."

The small folk were the people who traveled with the army but did not fight. Pippa was one of the small folk now. Pol the baker was another.

"Peepa, *cherie!*" he exclaimed when he saw her. "You are back safe from English."

"How are you, Pol?"

"You know, I am tired of living outside in cold. It's very nasty here."

"Soon it will be spring."

"I go in spring, back to my home. Ah, back to warm sun. You eat food yet? How 'bout I make you special?"

"We can't cook now. We have to move your cart to the other side of that hill first."

"What, that big hill? I climb there? No, no! Too high! My nose can not get the air." He clutched his chest and wheezed dramatically.

It seemed he did, though, have enough air to issue commands. He managed to get hold of Pippa and he nabbed two skinny boys who didn't get away fast enough. He ordered them to hitch up his mules. But no one did anything to his satisfaction, and Pol showered them with abuse.

"He's a bit nippy, ain't he?" said one boy under his breath.

"That's sayin' it mild" said the other. "That great numpty is gonna get a chibbin' one of these days, if I find him hangin' about."

"Yeah, well, give him one fer me too, right in the...." He gestured. The other boy laughed. In the end it took the two boys and three strong men to get Pol and his cart of supplies over the top of the hill.

$\mathcal{P}$ippa hardly slept that night, not only because the ground was cold and hard. She couldn't stop imagining the long lines of English soldiers headed toward Glen Trool, with their heavy swords and lances, their huge bows, and maces and clubs. At Crossraguel Abbey she had seen how much destruction could happen in only one day. Would Cuinn still be alive tomorrow night? Would she?

All was ready for battle early the next morning. Rob asked them all to kneel on the ground before first light while he said a prayer, and then each soldier took his appointed position. Their faces were grave. They adjusted helmets and tightened armor, those that owned any. Rob's order of silence was strictly enforced. All was quiet in the dark glen. Scouts had spotted the English army, marching toward them and bristling with weapons.

Pippa wrapped herself in a blanket and crawled beneath Pol's cart for safety. Several of the small folk were huddled there. The battle at Crossraguel Abbey replayed itself endlessly in Pippa's mind, the crashing and the screaming, on and on. She began to shake. One of the older girls put her arm around her.

"Cooch down here with me, lass." Pippa squirmed closer to her. "Yer afeert, are ya? Yer lookin' kinda peely-wally."

Pippa nodded.

"Look, I got this dagger." The girl pulled a long blade from her boot. Its edges were rusty. "You bide with me. Dinna fuss yourself. Ain't nobody gonna get close to us." Pippa wanted to believe her, but she had seen crazed soldiers on the rampage. What good would one rusty dagger be against men like that?

There! She could hear them. They all listened intently – the faraway rumbling of a hundred horses on the move. The steady tattoo of drums beat on their ears and splintered their confidence. The rumbling was growing louder, nearer. It halted all of a sudden. The English waited on flat ground for the Scots to present themselves for battle. Hundreds of heartbeats pulsed against the silence. There was not a Scotsman to be seen.

Pippa buried her head under her cloak. What was happening on the other side of that hill? She could hardly get her breath. Not a note of birdsong welcomed the day. The whole world held its breath.

Then, like a violent thunderstorm, a great battle cry rent the sky over Glen Trool. The small folk gripped each other in fear. They heard the shattering crash of men and weapons and horses. Pippa curled into a ball and covered her ears.

They stayed there, huddled beneath the wagon, for hours. How long would they have to wait before they found out what was happening? The fighting at the Abbey, Pippa remembered, had gone on for an entire night. On and on they waited, worn and weary with fear.

Then they heard another great roar, the cries of many men. It was agony. Pippa looked out from beneath the wagon. Messenger boys were running full tilt over the top of the hill. They were running away! In terror she crawled from under the cart and began to run too, downhill, as fast as she could.

"Wait, Peepa!" She looked back. Pol was waving to her, beckoning. "Come back!" All the small folk were jumping for joy. "We win! Come back. King Robert wins!" She could hardly believe her ears. "Yes, come! Help with food."

The small folk were giddy. The victorious soldiers were rowdy wildmen. And they were hungry. They had had no food since last night's sparse supper. Now they demanded food and drink, and Pol had to work quickly to get it ready. By good fortune, their soldiers had captured the English supply wagons. Their eyes bulged when they saw they were full of food, so even Pol felt like celebrating. For the first time since he had come to Scotland, he cooked a meal in the tradition of his country. He felt it was only fitting. The day's battle was Rob's first victory in years. The entire camp was jubilant and today they would finally have a feast.

*W*inter days were lengthening. When the meal had been cleaned up, it was still light. Pippa climbed up to a high spot on the steep slope of the glen. It reminded her of home. And she wanted to sit quietly in a place where the fighting had not reached, where the ground was not trampled to mud and the grass not stained with blood. The sun was dropping behind huge grey clouds that piled over the loch, and a wind was rising. She gathered her cloak around her and found a place to sit so she could watch the activity below. Rob's flag, a red rampaging lion on a yellow-gold field, beat noisily over the camp. Beneath it, some men still searched the battlefield for wounded comrades. Some looted the pockets of the dead.

So many dead men and horses, such a hideous sight. Swollen bodies rocked on the waters of the loch, staring sightless into its depths. She wondered if Tommy ... She shivered. Was he floating in Loch Rioghaine? Had this been his fate? Where was his body now? She would never know. She would never lay a flower on Tom's grave. She clamped her hand over her mouth and rocked frantically back and forth.

It was impossible to imagine that there had come a winter dawn that had not been greeted by Tom the gardener's son. And yet, that dawn had come and gone. Had Tommy given her some sign of his passing? One morning the rising sun had run its long fingers over the world, searching for the golden-cheeked lad who lived beside a loch on Arran Isle. Maybe it had found him. Maybe it had been drawn to him by one last spark of vitality. Was it so slight a spark that even the sun could not warm it into life?

Pity the dead. Pity the living. How many other anxious women and children waited in far away places for men who would never return? Fathers and brothers, beloved sons and husbands? Most would not even be able to name the day that began their mourning. Nor would they ever know the place.

Wherever Tom's body lay, she hoped he was covered from the wind and rain, that someone had laid him in the earth, laid him gently in the earth, so he wouldn't lie forever beneath the eye of an indifferent heaven.

Downhill below where Pippa sat, Rob's army was still celebrating even as they worked. They gloated over their revenge on the English. Pippa had had enough of death, but everyone else was glad, and Rob was elated.

Rob knew that this victory was badly needed. Today his little army regained some faith in him, and he in himself. Sitting around the fire when the long day finally came to an end, they all cheered him and cheered Pippa as well, for going into the English camp and, in effect, bringing the enemy to Glen Trool. She was taken aback when she realized that she too had a part in this destruction. It was all very confusing.

"Peepa" said Pol, proudly, "I bake you a treat special." When he placed a delicate confection in her hand and she took her first bite, she couldn't help grinning from ear to ear. The pastry was the lightest, flakiest she had ever tasted. Pol regarded her seriously.

"This smile! First smile you ever do, Peepa" said Pol. "This I am happy for. You like food of my land?"

"It's wonderful, Pol."

The foot soldiers watched from a little distance. Today they had been well fed for the first time in weeks. They had had a good day and a good feast, but they just could not leave well-enough alone.

"Hoot, Pol. You got some bonnie little treats for us?" hollered one of them, amidst the catcalls.

"Och, ai. Pol can cook after all. And here I thunk him were just some old blow-hard."

"Not as good as me old maw used ta cook, though!"

Pol's face turned bright red.

"Bah! Scots not know real food. When summer come, Pol is not cooking here anymore. Pol goes home." He inclined his head and listened carefully to see how many of them protested.

In the summer, wondered Pippa? I thought he was leaving in the spring.

$\mathcal{R}$ob decided they were safe resting in Glen Trool for another day before they moved north. The morning after the battle, sentries brought three peasant farmers into their camp.

"We're all wantin' to fight in your army, if you'll have us, my lord." Big, brawny men, they were sent immediately to speak with Gilbert de la Haye.

"You'll join us?" he asked.

"Better to die fightin' with yuz than let King Edward torture us and hang us and do every other terrible thing."

"Sure we'll fight. We'd be worse off if Edward catched us, and that's the truth" said another. It began to look as if King Edward's threats were having the opposite effect from what he had intended.

Three more brave men for the army. It was a lucky day. That afternoon, the sentries intercepted a young nobleman who had been searching through the glen. His family lands had been stolen by King Edward and he was itching for revenge. He had heard that Robert the Bruce was near. He brought a dozen knights with him and a wagonload of supplies. Had the tide finally begun to turn in their favor?

"We can move the army north tomorrow" Rob told Cuinn as they bedded down that night. "But I will not be going with you. I've got to go east to Roxburgh and Berwick."

"You're going to Berwick to see Isobel MacDuff, aren't you?"

"Yes, and my sister, if I can get in."

"You'll never get into Roxburgh. Can I come with you?"

"Cuinn, my man, don't tell me you're still in love...is Isobel still...?"

Cuinn sighed and nodded. He pulled his blanket up to his chin and watched the clouds retreating to the other side of night. Rob looked at him with concern. "She won't be the bonnie, light-hearted lass she once was," he said softly, "after hanging in a cage for all this time."

"Somehow, that just doesn't matter to me, Rob."

"You know, I'm thinking Pippa should come with me, to see her mother."

"Ah, Rob, do you really think she should? It won't be a nice sight."

"She may never get another chance to see her, that's my thought. The king could change his mind, get his tail in a knot over something, and execute Isobel at any time."

"But Rob, it will be bloody traumatic for us to see her. Do you want Pippa's first and last sight of her mother to be a broken woman in a cage? Isobel might be raging insane by now. No, Rob. Please don't take her."

"It will be good for her. Pippa still doesn't understand what this war is about. She thinks I am a murderer and fighting for my own advantage. I want her to see how the English have beaten us down, so she'll know what we are really up against."

"Aw, think about it, mon. It's difficult for a child —"

"You said yourself she wasn't a child anymore," Rob reminded him.

"But she hasn't had a chance to see how things are. She doesn't know that the English take all our crops and tax money, and won't let us trade. What does she know about Edward taking our men away to fight and die in his continental wars? Pippa hasn't been touched by any of this."

"She has lost Caela and Tom. She's been touched by this war, Cuinn."

"Maybe she can avoid it, escape the misery. Maybe if we can keep our children away from all this, then there will be some sweetness left in the world."

"I want her to know there is evil in the world, and that we have to fight against it. She will have to fight against it. Let her see how King Edward is hammering the Scots. Maybe she'll stop hating me and hate him instead."

Cuinn shook his head. "It's a mistake, Rob. You're teaching her to hate."

"It's all very easy for you, isn't it, Cuinn?" Rob shot back angrily. "You don't have to prove anything to her. She already worships you." Rob turned abruptly away, pulling his blanket over his head.

*A*nd so they set off for Roxburgh the next day, Cuinn, Rob and Pippa. They took ten men with them. Even with that much protection they dared not ride on the open roads by daylight. They dressed plainly and rode warily through the night on poor horses. Pippa was glad she had been asked to go along, though she hadn't been told where they were going. She guessed it had been Cuinn's thoughtfulness that allowed her to be included on this little jaunt. He knew she would appreciate being away from fighting men for a change.

Just as Cuinn predicted, they were not able to get anywhere near Roxburgh Castle. It was too dangerous. It was in English hands, of course. Sited between two rivers, it was supremely well-guarded. All Rob could do was to stare in silent fury at the place from upriver. His face was stony and he breathed heavily. He had so wanted to see his sister, and give her a word or two of hope to ease her pain and loneliness. He wanted her to know he was sorry. But they were forced to ride away, and his sister, hanging miserably in a cage, never knew they had been there at all. On they rode, to Berwick-Upon-Tweed.

They split into small groups and entered the town of Berwick on their skinny palfreys. It was cold and raining lightly but it was market day and people needed to trade and barter in spite of the weather. They slipped into the crowd and rode through the gate in the turf wall. English voices surrounded them on all sides, speaking with the strange accent to which Pippa was finally becoming accustomed.

From a distance, the town of Berwick was imposing. It sat high on a hill that commanded views up and down the river. It was by far the largest town Pippa had ever been in, but up close it was noisy and it stank to high heaven. Pippa covered her nose with her scarf. The streets were thick with mud and refuse that was churned to slurry by the market day crowds. Piles of horse dung and reeking garbage were everywhere.

Edward the First had tried to make Berwick an English colony, but some Scots had managed to stay on and make a living there. For protection against the rest of the country, Edward had built an enormous wall that stepped down the hill, all the way from the town to the river. The townspeople had nicknamed it the Breakneck Stair. In spite of this impressive defense, Robert the Bruce, the most sought-after outlaw in the land, managed to ride right through the gate.

Pippa, Cuinn and Rob rode through the streets without speaking. Pippa was feeling more lively than she had in days, turning this way and that and eager to see everything. Rob was grim and silent, Cuinn very nervous. The men stopped suddenly. They were staring.

Pippa almost missed it, the cage made of wood and iron, hanging over the street. She pulled her horse back.

A woman sat inside, alone. Pippa could just see her skirts, filthy and soaking wet from the rain. This must be the woman King Edward was punishing. Oh, what a pity, Pippa thought, that any woman had to endure this. Rob and Cuinn were watching the woman. Pippa glanced at their faces. They looked stunned.

Curious, Pippa maneuvered her horse so she could see the lady better. It was strange to see a woman in a cage. Nearly everyone who passed stopped to gape at her. Many mocked her with coarse jokes. The woman sat perfectly still, staring at her lap, responding to no one. Her red hair was tied back with a piece of old string and hung in a thick plait down her back. King Edward was wrong to punish a woman in this way. How much malice did he have in him? Did such a malicious man deserve to be king?

She heard Cuinn speak in a whisper.

"Iseabail."

The woman started slightly. She turned her head slowly, as if she were unused to moving. She looked down at them. Loss, terrible loss was etched upon her face. The lady's grey-green eyes studied Rob's face beneath his hood, then lingered on Cuinn's. Her eyes moved to Pippa. She frowned suddenly. Her mouth opened. The lady rose shakily and gripped the bars of her cage.

Pippa went numb.

No one had to tell her. She stared back, in shock.

The lady's face contorted. A silent scream, useless, wrenched itself painfully from the place within her where her child had lived.

She could not take her eyes off Pippa.

Pippa was thunderstruck. She watched the green eyes fill with tears. The lady collapsed to her knees. She stretched her hand down through the bars of her cage, reaching. A sob tore her throat and she pressed her face hard against the bars, straining, urgent.

Pippa rose in her saddle. She raised her hand high. She tried to link hands with the woman. She could not reach the outstretched fingers. Pippa began to cry too, great gulping sobs.

She couldn't do it.

Here, at last, was her mother, her own mother. But she was unreachable.

Rob leaned over and struggled to lower Pippa's arm.

"Don't" he warned quietly. "Don't."

Pippa snatched her arm from his grasp. This was her one chance. It was impossible, though. She couldn't reach.

She heard a shout and a ball of wet dung hit the bars of the cage. It splattered the lady's white face. Pippa gasped and pulled away but the lady ignored it. A couple of boys jabbed mocking words at her. A heavier dungball rocked the cage. Sharp, jeering words. Cuinn turned his horse to face the hecklers. He stared in fury. His grey eyes had turned almost whitehot with rage.

Rob tried to pull him back. "Don't!" he said again. "We must go. We're only making things worse."

Cuinn ignored him. He moved his horse slowly in the boys' direction. They began to throw garbage at him now, taunting, guffawing. Cuinn came on and drew his sword. Pippa cried out. She had seen Cuinn angry before, but never vicious. The boys stopped to gape at him, then began to stumble backwards. Cuinn's horse picked up its pace. Mud flew from its hoofs. People turned to stare.

Everything happened at once. The boys turned and ran, slipping in the mud, knocking people over. Cuinn cantered after them and disappeared in the crowd. Rob grabbed Pippa's reins and turned her horse back the way they had come. She twisted to see the lady one more time, over her shoulder. They couldn't leave! The lady still knelt, weeping bitterly.

"Let's get out of here. Come on!"

"No, please Rob!"

But they did leave her there.

Down the street, a group of English soldiers had gathered beneath a porch roof. They looked up as the riders trotted past but the rain discouraged them from paying much attention. Rob and Pippa cautiously slowed their pace but continued directly to the gate. They left Cuinn to his fate and clattered across the bridge, away from town.

The lady in the cage had risen and stood straining, watching their backs riding away from her for as long as she could. Watching, for only the second occasion in her life, her daughter, her beautiful daughter.

And now began her real punishment.

*P*ippa and Rob left the road and entered the woods where his men were gathering. Worried and impatient, they watched the road for Cuinn. Pippa sidled her horse over next to Rob's. She could not look him in the face.

"What is her name?" She had heard him mention the lady in the cage, but couldn't remember her name.

"Isobel. Isobel MacDuff."

"Isobel."

"Yes."

"She is being punished like this because of you?"

Rob sighed. He had been hoping Pippa would have a different outlook now.

"I guess you could say that. Yes, a lot of it is my fault."

Anger gripped Pippa like a vise. She knew she wasn't being reasonable but she couldn't stop.

"Is she your wife?" she asked, contemptuously.

"No." Rob fidgeted. "She is married to John Comyn." Pippa had heard that name too. John Comyn.

"Why didn't she —?"

"What is keeping Cuinn?" Rob blurted angrily.

"I'll go back to find him."

"No, wait Pippa! Here he comes. Finally!" They moved deeper into the trees to wait for him.

"What happened back there?" Rob scolded when Cuinn joined them. "You didn't do anything rash, I hope. They were just ignorant lads, Cuinn."

"They were very ignorant. The two I caught are much smarter now."

"I'm not even going to ask."

"Don't" said Cuinn shortly, and turned and rode back to the road without another word.

Eventually they caught up with him. Rob rode slumped in the saddle. Pippa's back was stiff and straight. Furious, frustrated, she made a decision. She pulled her horse closer to the men and tugged insistently on Rob's sleeve.

"You're not going to leave her there. We can't leave her there." Rob turned to look at Pippa. That expression on her face – she looked exactly like Isobel at her most stubborn.

"I'm not leaving her there" Pippa said again.

"Pippa, we can't hope to rescue her. The punishment would be death, a long, drawn-out and very painful death for her, for all of us. King Edward would relish the chance to invent a horrible torture for anyone in my family."

"So if I weren't part of your family, everything would be different? I wouldn't have to fear King Edward?"

"Every Scotsman should fear King Edward."

"You are the one who did this to her, but you won't rescue her? Well, I can't let her stay there, Rob. I'm going to get her out."

Rob bent his head. He watched Pippa give her horse a kick and pull ahead of him. If a giant claw had raked across his heart, he couldn't have felt more pain.

May 1307

*B*y the time spring came, though, Pippa realized that she was truly helpless to rescue Isobel MacDuff after all. She vowed to herself that she would watch for an opportunity, but it never seemed to come.

She spent less and less time in Rob's company and he did nothing to change that. In front of his men, Rob was still the great commander, always ready with a word of encouragement, trying never to put his men in unnecessary danger. And they were devoted to him. But in private Rob hardly ever laughed. He was overwrought, he poured endlessly over maps, and checked lists of supplies repeatedly. He slept little.

By May, Rob's army had moved north to Loudon Hill. Again they lured the English to fight on difficult ground. Again they ambushed them on a narrow strip of land and watched them mow each other down, trying to retreat. The carnage among the English foot soldiers was awful to see. It was a rout, and Rob's little army had another miraculous victory, then three days later, yet another. Several top English lieutenants began to invent reasons to flee Scotland and head back home to England rather than meet Robert de Bruce on the battlefield.

"*M*ending, mending and sewing." Pippa swung her basket and walked toward a group of English soldiers lounging on a riverbank. They were only a few years older than herself, about the age Tommy would have been. She put that thought away immediately and tried to size up the group in front of her. Often she got as much information from the foot soldiers as she would from the knights. She called to the boys, imitating an English accent.

"Need any mending done, sirs?" She pulled her face into a winning smile.

"Eh, little maid, you can fix me shirt for me. I'll just get it, if you'll wait."

"Hey, George, give her those breeches a yours what split wide open t'other day! Whew! That were a sight for sore eyes!" All the boys laughed at George's beet red face.

They offered Pippa a good morning's work. She settled her stool near them and took up her stitching mechanically. Her real work was listening. It didn't take long for the soldiers' conversation to turn to Robert the Bruce.

"Me master is plain fed up with The Bruce, that bloody sneak" said one. "He don't never have the nerve to come out on open ground and fight like a man."

"He don't never stay out in the open, neither. Ye don't even have a chance to get yer lance lowered and he's gone agin. Disappeared."

"Did ya hear tell that Archie's men chased him into the woods and…"

"I'll tell ya what happened to Archie's men. The Bruce bamboozled 'em, that's what happened. There was The Bruce, right in front of them, and the idiots lost 'im. Bloomin' cowards, they is."

"Warn't their fault! He dragged 'em down a path what went straight into a gully. Archie tole me. No one kin take a horse over that kinda rough ground."

"Them Scots have them little horses. Some kinda dirty little Welsh beast. They not s'posed to have 'em, neither. Where they gettin' 'em, is what I wanna know."

"It's a good job the Bruce's army is small. We're gonna cream 'em one a these days. All we hafta do is git ahold of them. What's he got, less than a couple hundred men? I never seed more than that."

"What I wanna know is, how is they always ready for us, whenever we meets 'em? They always know what we're gonna do, even before we know. I can't figure how they do that."

"They got spies er somethin', ye think?"

"You nit. How's a spy ever gonna git in here, past our sentries?"

"Ai, that are so. If they did git in, they'd nivver git out."

Pippa stitched and sewed and stitched and sewed.

*A*t each dusk she returned to Rob's camp. She walked out of the English camp before sundown, pretending to head for a house or a village. Cuinn was always waiting faithfully, hiding in some dark corner. They would ride into the woods, checking carefully to make sure Pippa had not been followed, and then they would disappear.

If ever they had an evening with little to do, Pol would bring Pippa's meal on a thick trencher of bread, and she would eat beside Rob's campfire. Rob was a great story-teller, and his men often asked for a tale from him. In spite of herself, it became a favorite part of Pippa's day too. When she got to know the men better, they sometimes coaxed a song from her. She missed Jamie's flute, though, and Caela's harp. She still missed Caela's harp terribly, but it, and the beloved hands that played it, were lost to the world.

By the time spring showered the land, their food supply had run out again. There was little food to be had anywhere in the east of Scotland. As often as not, there wasn't even any they could steal. Everyone in the land was thin and hungry. The countryside had been ravaged by the English time and again for so many years that farmers had lost more crops than they had been able to save. Their food stores and barns were almost empty. Pol began to complain bitterly, though the men never did. Pippa could never figure out, though, why the men were strangely silent about their empty stomachs, until one rainy afternoon.

They had had thunderstorms all day so she stayed in camp. She had spent the afternoon in Rob's tent because it was warm, patching together the raggedy clothing belonging to some of their own soldiers. She heard someone splashing through the puddles outside and Pol burst in, soaked to the skin. His apple cheeks were pink and glistening wet.

"See, Your Majesty?" he cried triumphantly. "Look, the boys caught rubbits! These I will roast for you tonight, my lord. Just for you, special. And Peepa, too. I have wild onions found…"

"Rubbits?" asked Rob, looking up from his map table. Pol held several grey furry creatures up by the ears.

"Meat! Hunh hunh hunh! I will make you feast tonight, Your Majesty."

"Pol, I appreciate your offer, but the men need meat too. Can you put these in the stewpot?"

"What? What do you say? Truly? The stewpot? Bah! My Lord Bruce! No, no! That would be terrible. Roast rubbit would be so tasty-ish. Mmm-mm! Stuff him with wild onions! He would be…" Pippa's mouth was watering. Rob was unyielding.

"No Pol. This meat must be shared. Put it in the stewpot."

"You want I cook rubbit stew?" Pol squeaked, incredulous. "But, Sire…"

"Rubbit stew" said Rob firmly.

Pol was disgusted.

"Haugh! This is …what is word? Holy Mary, I not know…" He took his creatures and muttered his way out.

Rob's men had been subsisting on watery broth for two weeks. They never forgot that stew. It was such little kindnesses toward the common soldier that turned The Bruce into legend.

*T*he army headed north. They besieged Dunstaffnage Castle, home of John Macdougall of Lorne. Here Rob finally caught the man who had captured his brothers in Loch Rìoghaine and turned them over to the English king for execution. In Pippa's mind, he was Tommy's killer too. The very name of John Macdougall made her shake uncontrollably. He would suffer badly at Rob's hand, she was sure. What terrible punishment would Rob choose for him, she wondered?

She could hardly believe, when the word got round, that Rob had decided not to execute John of Lorne. Instead, he had negotiated a truce with him. His enemy! Their enemy! Rob and their enemy were to work together against King Edward. After what he had done to Rob's family, Pippa could hardly believe that the lord of the great Macdougall clan was going to be allowed to live.

What could Rob be thinking? She was disgusted with him. She wanted to hate him because he was a murderer, a savage warmonger. She wanted to hate him because Tommy's death was his fault. But here he was, extending the hand of forgiveness to a person who had hurt him most dreadfully. Pippa didn't want to admire Rob for any reason, no matter how generous he might be. Most of all, she didn't want to acknowledge that he would ever be worthy of taking a parent's place, of taking Caela's place in her heart. Never.

In her bitterness, she became one of the war's wounded.

When her heart spoke back to her, she tried not to listen. When had she turned into a hateful savage, it asked her? For answer, she put her face into her hands and wept.

The army was again moving further north. More castles were taken. In many battles, because of Rob's cunning tactics, they lost very few of their own soldiers compared to losses on the other side. It was well that this was so, as the English army vastly outnumbered the Scots.

In spite of its superior numbers, the English preferred to take a castle with very little fighting. They would surround it and let no one come in or go out until, sooner or later, the castle would run out of food and drinking water. Sometimes this would take months, sometimes years. They simply waited until everyone inside was starving, sick or dead and their only hope was to surrender. When a castle was besieged, there was rarely a happy ending.

Such long-term methods were not Rob's style of taking castles. He preferred to rip little pieces from the English impudence and eat their pride in small morsels.

He trained his men to dissolve into small groups and vanish just when a massive English attack was beginning. And Rob was brilliant at choosing his battlegrounds. The Scots would disappear in all directions, into hills and forests and ravines where no army could maneuver. But the English, in the confusion that followed, trampled their own men, or were met by a hail of boulders from a hillside, or found themselves lured into a swamp, floundering helplessly.

Rob often won castles through trickery. He might sneak soldiers inside their walls, hidden in hay carts or disguised as market folk. Then he would attack from outside and the castle guards would end up fighting Rob's soldiers both outside and inside the walls.

Jamie Douglas gave his men black cloaks, those Caela had dyed, and at nightfall, wearing the cloaks to hide their gleaming armor, they could sneak right up to the walls of a castle.

After capturing a castle, Rob always burned it to the ground.

"Why are you destroying everything? You don't have to burn all this down" Pippa would rant.

"If I left the castle standing, the English would move right back in again as soon as we were gone."

"But all the people..."

"Let them move back to England, where they came from."

Rob's tactics also made good use of Pippa. As a mere lass, she could get into castles and towns shepherding a few sheep, and walk out with a drawing of the battlements or information about the late-night changing of the guard.

Amongst all her exploits, only one was a failure and it was a sore disappointment to Jamie Douglas. He had given her a hedgehog. A very dead and stinking hedgehog. She was to enter a castle yard and simply drop it into their well.

"It will poison the water. The whole place will be sick or dead in four days. That's when we come swooping in" explained Jamie gleefully.

He sent Pippa through the gate. She led a cow that was covered with every kind of filth, in order to disguise the stench of this hedgehog.

She didn't feel comfortable with this task. Hesitantly she approached a well in the busy yard. She leaned on the edge of the well, twisting and untwisting the button on her satchel. A casual flick of the wrist and the hedgehog would be down the well, the job done. The cow she had been leading looked at her expectantly. Pippa watched the townspeople, every one of them as thin as last year's cornstalks.

A gaggle of boys scuffled barefoot in the dirt nearby, banging sticks together in mock sword-play. Pippa watched them for a few moments.

They were puffed with boyish bravado. Bang-bang went their sticks. Their cheeks were pink and gleaming with perspiration. They badgered each other, screeching, taunting, daring one another to cut off the head of the dreaded Black Douglas before supper. Such skinny, dirty little boys. Pippa had to smile. Such funny lads. And so young. Too young to die.

She stood up, shouldered her satchel and pulled on the cow's rope. She turned on her heel, walked out through the gate, and threw the hedgehog back into his hedge. She envied him. He hadn't died making war on his own kind.

In July of that summer, a most amazing piece of luck fell right into the lap of Robert the Bruce. Edward the First, the malevolent king of England and the Hammer of the Scots, died while leading an army to Scotland. On his deathbed the king commanded his son, Edward the Second, to promise to continue the fight. His son, however, was more interested in his love life than in leading an army. As soon as his father died, he ordered his army to remain in Scotland. But he departed, and didn't return for three years.

Without the support of their new king, suddenly the English army in Scotland was at a disadvantage. Even though they blustered and swaggered and tried to convince themselves that they were still powerful, their confidence began to wane. Soon that endlessly long and deadly creature, the worm of fear, slithered into their midst and began to gnaw.

So for all that summer and into the autumn of 1307, Robert the Bruce won castle after castle. And finally, after years of mistrust, he was winning the hearts of the Scottish people as well.

A year before, they said he was only trying to make himself rich and powerful. Now, almost overnight he became wildly popular, practically a legend. Last winter everyone said he had stolen the crown of Scotland. Now they began to believe that he deserved it. He became a king in more than just name, and what is more, a king beloved and a great hero. The people took his cause to their hearts at last, and began to help him whenever they could, offering shelter, food, and even their beloved sons. His army grew with every victory.

And then Robert the Bruce fell ill, deathly ill.

November 1307
Northern Scotland

*I*n wartime, the sick are often abandoned, simply left behind.

It was difficult to carry a sick or wounded man, and his gear and his horses as well. It would force the entire army to move too slowly. It would endanger everyone. Robert the Bruce, however, would never be left behind by his men. They loved and respected him, and his army carried him faithfully and without complaint, whenever they were forced to move.

Pippa heard murmurs about Rob all over the camp. The men were afraid for him, she knew. They paced in and out of his tent all day and whispered in tense little groups with their heads down. They greatly feared they would lose their beloved leader. If he were to die, many said, Scotland would never gain her independence. He alone could command with such a light and caring hand. He alone shored up all their hopes. It was for him they knelt in the mud and prayed before every battle. Without him, they would lose the bond that kept them all together, and all their years of fighting, all the years of dying, would have been for nothing, wasted.

Pippa did not want to think about Rob dying.

Rob's closest advisers got together and decided that he had slept on the hard ground and gone without food long enough. He had pushed himself about as far as a man could go. And his guilt weighed heavily. It sat cruelly upon him and was crushing the life out of him.

"The guilt is eating him alive" said Gilbert de la Haye, Rob's close friend. "He blames every death on himself."

"I think the sea air would do him good" Cuinn told him.

"What sea air? Where can we go? There is no seashore near here that is safe" Gilbert answered.

"Slaines. If we could get him to the Castle Slaines, on the east coast, where food is more plentiful and..."

"That's enemy territory. The Comyns would have every man in Buchan and half the English army surrounding Slaines in no time. They would starve us out."

"If we don't get him to a place where he can rest, even for a short time, and get him some decent food, death will come for him anyway."

Cuinn had his way. They moved as quickly as they could, before any word could leak out. The King of Scotland, a pathetically sick man, was carried on a litter to the coast. But, just as Gilbert foresaw, it wasn't long before they were surrounded by enemies. Pippa stood on the wall of Slaines castle and watched the armies gather. John Comyn was the first one there. He brought his forces and set up a siege. He sent word immediately to the English and they came in great number to support him. They didn't press their advantage, however. They didn't bother to attack. It was winter. Why risk their lives? They could wait for starvation and disease to do their work and then attack in the spring.

"Pippa?" Cuinn leaned over to look at her face. She sat outside, alone on the bitter cold parapet, staring at the waves that boomed against the castle wall. A lonely wind wailed out of the sea. She hadn't even heard Cuinn approach. "Rob wants to speak to you."

"Rob!" She was surprised. She hadn't visited Rob in the three weeks since they'd arrived at Slaines. "Is he all right?"

"Well," Cuinn's brow creased with worry, "you should come and see for yourself."

He held the door while she entered the room. Pippa did not care for the smell in that room. She approached the bed slowly. She tried not to look shocked. Where was the big, broad-shouldered man she had known? A long bony figure lay there, his face grey. Her heart sank. Rob turned his head with effort.

"Pippa?"

"Yes, Rob. It's …it's me." She gulped. "How are you feeling?"

"I haven't seen you in so long." He had only enough strength to lift his hand to her. She moved her leaden feet toward the bed. Gently, she touched his hand with one finger. His index finger locked with hers.

"Yes, I know, Rob. It's been a while. I'm sorry, I …" She had been heartless.

"Pippa, I want to give you a task. Cuinn will have to tell you about it. I hope you'll feel able to do it for us."

"I'll try."

"I'm sorry to ask it of you, but you are the best person to send. You've been so helpful to our cause. And such a good… a good…" Rob's head fell wearily to the pillow.

"It's all right, Rob" she said finally in a small voice. "I'll do whatever you ask."

"I also, … I wanted to tell you something…" He gasped, hardly able to speak. "The English nobleman we took prisoner…" he coughed, "a few weeks ago? I tried to exchange him for your mother. For Isobel."

Pippa felt herself shrink. She had been heartless, demanding so much of Rob.

"King Edward would not even consider … my request. I'm very sorry."

Pippa could say nothing. Her throat was squeezed tight.

"There's more I wanted to…" He was having great difficulty breathing. Pippa looked at Cuinn in panic. He signaled for Gilbert to come in, and quickly pulled Pippa outside.

"He's not very well, is he?"

"No, Pippa. He hasn't been well for weeks, as you must surely have heard."

Cuinn was walking away from her. Was he angry? Was he ashamed of her? She ran after him.

"Rob said you had something for me to do?"

Cuinn turned back and looked at her. His face was sad, whether for her or for Rob, Pippa couldn't tell. He leaned against the wall and looked at the floor.

"You know, there were fifty people Rob could have exchanged for that English nobleman. He wanted to trade for one of his soldiers, but he asked for Isobel MacDuff, only to make you happy."

"Oh."

"You couldn't even thank him?"

"I didn't realize... I'm sorry, Cuinn."

"You don't have to apologize to me."

Pippa was stunned into silence. Shame ate at her heart.

Cuinn said nothing either, and his silence cut the very breath from her body. She had no idea how to put things right.

It was a long time before Cuinn roused himself to speak again.

"We need you go into John Comyn's camp to see what you can find out."

"Right away?"

"Yes, tomorrow. But we want you to stay there until you get some good information. It may take a couple of weeks."

"Weeks?"

"You'll have to take a tent, whatever you need to look like a traveling seamstress. Try to get close to Comyn. Let us know how determined, how watchful his men are. Tell us everything you can about their guards, and if there is any quarreling amongst them, any unrest. Let us know if there is a good time for us to break out of here."

"Break out? Why?"

"We've eaten up almost all the food. It was fine at first, but we'll starve if we stay much longer, and Rob's life is hanging by a thread as it is. As you just saw. He needs nourishing food and a healer, if we can find someone."

"How do I get word back to you?"

"Someone will visit you from time to time. In disguise, so you'll have to be watchful."

"You?"

"Maybe me, maybe someone else. Keep your eyes open."

"What should I do about Rob?"

"Pack some belongings" he said over his shoulder, as he walked away, "and just do what needs to be done."

She stood alone, looking miserably after him.

$\mathcal{P}$ippa's first day in John Comyn's camp did not begin on an auspicious note. But as sometimes happens, she feared the situation would be worse than it turned out to be.

It had been difficult getting out of Slaines castle, down through a secret tunnel to a wild cliff where massive waves hurled and smashed themselves against the rocky path. She was supposed to remember the way back in, but it was confusing. She wasn't sure she could find it again by herself. Then, once outside the castle walls, it was painful watching Cuinn turn to go back. He had abandoned her.

She carried only a small tent, a bag of clothes and food, her sewing basket and her little stool. She had long ago lost track of how many English camps she had worked in. She had learned how to spot the earls' tents. They were by far the largest in the camp. Their bright banners snapped in the wind. She headed in that direction and almost immediately was given a job mending a squire's surcoat.

"I've torn the trim here."

"I can fix that."

"I'll add another ha'pence to your fee if you do a nice job."

"Do you mind if I sit near your fire?"

"You are most welcome."

Perhaps because she was just a girl, and a very quiet girl, the men hardly took notice of her. She bent over her stitching and listened to the talk flowing around her. A pair of grooms curried gigantic horses on the other side of the fire. When the earls went inside for their mid-day meal, she pulled her stool as close to the grooms as she dared.

"Whoa, there!" A groom struggled with a huge horse. "I say, help us, Flin! Grab his reins, would ye? Take it easy, fella. Easy!" The warhorse snorted violently.

"Sure yer antsy, fella" the groom crooned to the horse. "I know. Ye got nothin' ta do all the day, ain't that right?"

"He's itchin' for a good fight, he is."

"So right. He bit Gurn day 'fore yesterday. Och, took a chunk right outta him. Jes plain bored, he is, jes plain bored. Ain't ya, fella?"

"Well, and it's cuz there ain't no action. Wha' d'ya expect?"

"Wanna hear my thinkin'?" The man looked around secretively. "I'm thinkin' the earl is utter scared. He's got more men than the Bruce, but he's afeert to attack."

"And the Bruce's army is shrinkin' smaller by the day, is what I'm hearing. He's sick, is why."

"No. You kiddin'?"

"Ai. Serious sick, is what I heared."

"Mayhap we're on the winning side of this war after all."

Pippa's needle wouldn't go where she wanted it to go, on account of her heart pounding so violently.

When the squire came back for his surcoat that afternoon, he was so pleased with her work, he sent two of his friends to Pippa. She had done about all she could for the day, though. Daylight was short, the weather cold, and she still had to set up her tent. She began to gather her things.

The rainstorm came so suddenly, it surprised everyone. Soldiers ran in all directions and ducked into their tents. Pippa found herself alone in the cold pouring rain, standing beside someone else's smoking fire with her tent rolled up and slung across her back. Where was the camp for the small folk?

Someone splashed through the mud behind her. A woman ran by, holding her cloak over her head. She stopped suddenly and turned back to Pippa.

"Do you need a place to stay?" she called over the roar of the rain.

Pippa glanced around and gestured to herself.

"Me?"

"Come on, come to our tent." She beckoned and ran on. Incredulous at her good luck, Pippa followed most willingly. They ran until they came to an area where smaller tents clustered. Pippa followed the woman into one of them. They pulled their soaking wet hoods back and regarded each other, smiling. The woman was much younger than Pippa had thought, about fifteen or sixteen years of age, she judged. She watched her turn and hold out her arms. Pippa hadn't noticed a man in the corner, seated on a cushion. On his lap was a baby whose grin displayed a pair of pearly teeth. The child reached for his mother and laughed and kicked. The woman caught him up in her arms. He smiled shyly at Pippa. She went to him and touched her finger to his chubby fist. She was suddenly flooded with thoughts of Baby William at Loch Ranza. He must be about the same age as this boy, almost a year old now.

The woman introduced herself. "I'm Loise and this is Baby Robbie." She looked toward the man. "This is my father, Kevon."

"I'm Penelope." The name came readily. Pippa had used it before.

"Can we call you Penny?"

"Everyone does." She had practiced her English accent, but she could not guess, from the other woman's speech, where she had come from. Loise handed her baby back to Kevon.

"Let's hang these wet cloaks over here and see what we can find for supper. You're welcome to join us, though our food is poor."

"I have some bread and sausage here. We can share it."

The woman stopped in surprise.

"Meat?" said she and Kevon together. They both stared. Pippa pulled out a loaf and unwrapped the sausage that Pol had given her. Kevon caught himself staring and swiftly offered Pippa a cushion.

"It's very kind of you to ask me to eat with you."

"I noticed you working here this morning. Are you new in camp, Penny?" asked Loise.

"Yes, I haven't even had time to set up my tent."

"I thought as much. Please, stay with us tonight. It will be crowded but at least we'll be warm."

"I'd appreciate that, just for tonight."

"Are you planning to stay in camp for a while?" asked Kevon.

"As long as there is work."

"Oh, yes, there should be lots. The last seamstress left two weeks ago. She was tired of starving."

"But I smelled meat roasting all afternoon. I was hoping it was dinner."

"It may be dinner, but not for us."

"Who is it for?"

"The earls and the knights dine well. Their dogs eat better than the rest of us."

"Don't they cook for the whole camp?" They looked at her in surprise.

"Wherever did you come from, lass?" asked Kevon.

"Well…the last camp I was in…" Pippa had blundered. Did not all commanders share the food with their armies? "It was down near Glen Trool."

"Mayhap you should have stayed there. You've come far."

"And where are you from?" Pippa asked. Loise looked at her and then away.

"Originally from Berwick-Upon-Tweed" said Kevon. "My business is selling wool, or was until the English blockaded our shipping."

"But you sound like you're English" Pippa said to Kevon.

"I was born there, but I live here now. My wife, Loise's mother, was Scottish. She came from a long line of healers and taught Loise her skills. She passed away these four years ago."

"I'm sorry for that."

"Thank you, Penny."

"Are you selling wool here in this camp?"

"N-n-no." Kevon paused and looked at his daughter. "It's a long story. The English heard that Loise was a physician and brought her here under duress."

"What does that mean?"

"We're not here because we want to be" explained Loise. "We wanted to stay in Berwick – because of the baby, you understand, but the army needed someone to doctor the wounded and brought me here to do that. I had no one to care for Robbie so my father was forced to come along also. They gave us no choice."

"And the baby's father? Is he here too?"

"No" said Loise. "That's a long story too. For another evening perhaps. Penny, I have to feed the baby and get to bed. I get up early in the morning. Did you bring a sleeping blanket?"

Pippa spent a comfortable night in Loise's tent, and less lonely than she had expected when she set out that morning. She listened to the rain drumming on the roof and the next thing she knew, it was morning.

$\mathcal{T}$he rain was over but it was very cold. Pippa shared what remained of her bread in the morning. Kevon helped her set up her tent next to theirs and showed her the fire that was shared by the little community of folk. They had very little firewood, so they took turns tending a communal fire. It was too dark to sew in her tent, so Pippa pulled her stool as close as she could to the fire and began her mending.

Word soon got out that there was a new seamstress in camp, and the soldiers brought her plenty of work. She worried that, sitting far from the earls' tents, she wouldn't get much information to give to Cuinn, but there was actually a great deal of activity in this part of the camp. They kept the horses just beyond the small folks' tents, so she was able to listen to the chatter of soldiers coming and going down the lane next to their fire.

She had been there for a few days when, one morning, she stopped stitching for a moment so she could rub some warmth back into her fingers. As always, she looked in vain for Cuinn or someone she knew. She was just wondering how long she could last in this freezing weather when angry voices interrupted her thoughts. Four soldiers were dragging a man into the camp. His hands were tied and they were not treating him gently.

"Get the earl. He'll wanna talk to this one" snarled one of the soldiers. "You two, stay here and keep an eye on him."

Pippa turned her stool so she wouldn't have to look in that direction. She soon heard the soldiers returning but tried to ignore them. For the next little while she was vaguely aware that they were questioning the man across the way, but she didn't pay much attention until she heard the crack of a whip. The man was struck several times. She glimpsed his bleeding back and looked away again. By the tenth lash, she could stand it no more. She piled her work into her basket and went to find Kevon and little Robbie.

"Do you mind if I come in?"

"Please, you're more than welcome, Penny."

"I can't stand to listen to them torturing that man out there."

"That is mild compared to some of the things they do" Kevon answered. "I just wish they didn't have to do it so close to our tents. I'm sure they do it on purpose to scare the rest of us."

"Would you like something hot to drink? Perhaps I could brew some peppermint leaves?"

Kevon smiled.

"Ai, lassie. Aren't you just the little ray of sunshine?"

"You sound just like a Scotsman, Kevon." He laughed.

Pippa stood out by the fire, watching her kettle of water and keeping her back to the activity across the lane. It was quiet there now. Pippa's pot of water was nearly boiling. She folded her arms and looked toward Slaines castle. For the first time all day, she thought of Rob. Her throat tightened and her mood felt suddenly fragile. Was he still alive, she wondered? She wished she could find some bit of information in this camp, something worth passing on, that would give her an excuse to sneak back into the castle. But until she had something interesting to tell, she would have to stay where she was.

In the next few days she heard no news from Slaines castle and she had no news for them, so she stayed on with Loise and Kevon. They fell into a routine. Pippa began to feel like part of Loise's family. She contributed the pennies she earned from her sewing and they were very grateful for the food they could buy with it, if there was any food to be had at all. They had been hungry for weeks.

Loise thought it was too cold, and possibly unsafe, for Pippa to sleep alone in her tent, so she spent the nights with them. They began to use Pippa's tent for storage. Loise had a very large wooden chest with an iron lock that held her possessions. Her dearest treasures were her herbs and medicines as well as some very sharp blades and saws. Pippa chose to remain in ignorance about those particular tools though Loise seemed to value them highly. They certainly had a lot more room in the sleeping tent after they dragged that chest out, though it was so heavy that Kevon needed Pippa's help to move it.

In the afternoons, when her fingers were too cold to sew any longer, Pippa was delighted to take over the care of Baby Robbie. She tried not to think about Caela's baby, back in Loch Ranza with Sebrina, but his little dark-headed image would pop into her mind at the strangest times. And images of Sebrina, as well. Her fond smile. Very gently, Pippa would close the door on those thoughts. She never spoke of anything in her past and neither Loise nor Kevon asked. They never mentioned their former lives either. It was, in its way, a comfortable relationship. No one trespassed the boundaries of privacy. Pippa was content to be among kind people and asked for nothing more. They had found themselves a harmonious corner of the world in the midst of an ugly war, and they were making the best of it.

$\mathcal{W}$alking back to her tent late one afternoon, Loise stopped across the lane. The prisoner who had been brought in a few days before was being tied to his post once again. One soldier held him upright while another tied his wrists. The prisoner had no shirt and had obviously had a very difficult afternoon.

Loise put on her softest manners.

"Good evening, my friends."

"Evenin', Lady."

"Had any luck with this one?"

"Nah. The earl couldna get nothin' outa him."

"Two or three more days of being out in this cold, and he'll be ready to talk." She laughed. "It wouldn't be any trouble for you to keep him going for a couple more days, would it?"

"Nah. They said they wanted him alive. He must be good for some kind of, I dunno, somethin'."

"You're absolutely right. I expect you two know a great deal about these things."

"Well sure. Been doin' it fer long enough. Had lots of 'xperience."

"Oh good. So you know, then, that the earl could get more out of this man if he were treated a little better?"

"Wha?"

"Yes, I've seen that happen in other camps. If you give him a coat and some food, he'll actually soften."

"That true?" asked one.

"You fink so, Lady?" asked the other.

"I do, chaps. I really do. Confuse him, be nice to him. Look at him. He's nearly ready to start co-operating. Soften him up a bit and you'll see. Maybe you can find him something warm to wear? Without telling the earl, of course. Our little secret."

"I ain't too sure" said one, glancing for support at his companion.

"Bran, you gots ta 'member this lady wuz the one what helped Dick wif his arm."

"Ai, poor Dick's arm."

"C'mon, we can find a coat for 'im, if she say so."

"Mayhap it'll soften 'im up an' he'll talk."

"The earl would appreciate you two for that, I'm sure."

"Yeah, I suppose that may be."

"Oh, I'm sure he would. And see that he gets a little food" Loise prodded them.

"Sure, yeah okay."

"You can manage that, can't you? Just a little? Of course you can. You know what else? Maybe you could lower his arms a bit when you tie him. It's very painful when they're tied so high."

They adjusted his bonds.

"That's better. Now you'll get some results. I can't tell you how glad I am to see that you lads are more clever than some people around here." Loise caught the prisoner's eye. Then she put a hand on the arm of each English soldier.

"I respect you gentlemen. You are both very kind and decent men. You know that, don't you?" She smiled at them as she turned to go. "I'll remember you both. If ever you need doctoring, anything at all, just call on me."

"Fank you, my lady."

"Good night, chaps."

Two such foolish, nearly toothless grins, stretching between two pairs of prominent red ears, had seldom been seen in that camp.

"She's a beaut!" said one soldier with a sigh.

"Ai" breathed the other. "Very sonsy!"

"If ever I..." wished the first.

"Haugh" snorted the other. "Don't even fink it. Ye'd fink ye'd died an' was standin' at the door ta Heaven, were that to happen."

"Ai, that's so, that are. If ever...."

Although the armies at Slaines occasionally exchanged volleys or met in small skirmishes, the war seemed to stagnate. Autumn had turned to winter and Pippa stayed on in the English camp, as Cuinn instructed, waiting to make herself useful when the time came.

Whenever Pippa was free to care for Loise's baby, Kevon would take the opportunity to go out to scrounge for food for them. One dark afternoon, just before Christmas Eve, he came home from a nearby village and triumphantly presented a meat pie.

"Look, Penny. What do you think Loise will say when she sees this?"

Pippa's eyes widened.

"Where did you get it?"

"I bought it from a crofter's wife, for a very pretty penny, I can tell you."

"Oh, Kevon. This will be delicious. I can't wait."

They watched eagerly for Loise to come. She rarely finished working in the hospital tent before dark. She had to care for men who had been wounded in skirmishes or during practice sessions. There was no shortage of work for her. On this afternoon it was dusk and snowing lightly when they finally saw her walking wearily down the lane between the tents. She seemed lost in thought. Pippa was eager to surprise her with the meat pie, so she stewed with impatience when she saw Loise stop to speak to the prisoner. He seemed to be the only prisoner the English could get their hands on. At Loise's insistence, he had been given a coat, but he remained bound by the wrists day and night. Sometimes they took him away. They always had to carry him back on a stretcher.

Watching Loise bending over to talk to the man, it suddenly struck Pippa that she herself should have taken more interest in him. She had been so busy putting on her English persona that she had forgotten he was probably a Scotsman like herself. And a lonely Scotsman, among many enemies. A sharp stab of shame, becoming all too familiar, made her wince.

On this night, Loise stopped to speak to the prisoner and then looked quickly around. She opened her satchel, pulled out some kind of medication and dabbed it on a cut that gashed his cheek.

Pippa felt the clutch of terror, wondering if Loise would be caught helping him. She tried to call her away.

"Loise, come and see what Kevon found for supper."

"Something good?"

The prisoner had turned, or tried to turn to look across at her. Pippa beckoned Loise away.

Inside their tent, a smile lit Loise's tired face when she saw the pie. They divided it and mashed a little bit for Baby Robbie. Loise sliced her portion in half.

"What are you doing?" asked Pippa.

"Taking some to that man."

"What man?"

"The one across the way."

"The prisoner?"

"He's starving, Penny. Go ahead and eat. I'll be right back."

When she returned, Pippa and Kevon had added some of their portions to hers.

"You are going to get into trouble if they find out that you're feeding him" Pippa insisted.

"She thinks she can do whatever she wants here" said Kevon.

"They know they can't be too hard on me. They need me too much."

"It is true. The men seem to respect you, Loise." Pippa looked at her pretty face and abundant shiny hair. Small wonder that men were at her beck and call. But it was her talent for healing, more than her appearance, that was very much in demand throughout the camp.

"The men give me a wide berth now. It wasn't that way at first."

"What did you do? Put the pox on them?"

"I carry this bodkin." She pulled a dagger out of the sheath at her belt. Its razor edge gleamed in the lamp light. "I had to threaten a big beast of a knight with it on the very first evening we were here. The next day he was badly wounded in battle and I wouldn't treat him. His men begged but I refused, and I told them why."

"What happened to him?"

"He died." Loise shrugged. "I haven't had any trouble since." Pippa was shocked – Loise, always so compassionate, certainly had a tough side. And for an Englishwoman, she had the strangest attitude.

Loise's baby crawled onto her lap, distracting her with his adorable smile.

"We have a little dried peppermint left. Is someone going to boil water? Penny?"

"Yes, the water's on the fire."

The next afternoon was so frosty that Pippa had to sit in the tent to do her mending. Still, she had trouble keeping her fingers warm enough to hold a needle. After a while she could hardly move them at all. She put her work away and put some broth into a pot to warm for supper. She pulled the hood of her cloak tight around her face. A light snow began to fall again.

She had no sooner taken the pot out to the fire when her attention was caught by a commotion across the way. She earnestly wished that prisoners could be kept somewhere else.

At any rate, she could hardly ignore the activities over there this afternoon. Some high-ranking lord was bullying the prisoner while his soldiers watched. After days of being left out in the cold, the poor man had no fight left in him.

"Are you ready to tell us what we want to know?" demanded the lord. Pippa could not hear what the prisoner replied.

The lord swung a club. Pippa could hear it pound against the man's back.

"Is Robert the Bruce still alive?" The club thudded into his body again. Pippa shrank beside her fire and looked away.

"That is enough of that, Sire! I have warned you about that kind of treatment." Pippa looked up. Loise had come to stand between the earl and the prisoner. "This man can take no more of your punishment. You will kill him. And I told you not to tie his arms above his head like that."

"You are obviously confused, Mistress, about who is running this army. I will say what punishment will be meted out." The earl, not a very tall man, puffed himself up, but the top of his head still only came to Loise's chin. She managed to look regal in a shabby brown cloak, while his impressive tunic, emblazoned with three golden sheaves of wheat, seemed some sort of poor disguise. "Go on about your business and leave me to take care of mine."

"No, I will not work in a camp where simple morals are not observed."

"I have heard of your threats in the past, Mistress. They do not work with me."

"If you are wounded in the next battle and I refuse to help you, my Lord Comyn, you will change your mind."

The earl exhaled in fury.

Pippa stood up slowly. Lord Comyn? Was this John Comyn? If so, he was the one who had married Isobel MacDuff, her own mother, who now hung in a cage in Berwick. He would be the man who had requested –no, begged– that her mother be executed.

"Two can play at the game of threats, Mistress." The earl turned to his men and spoke as softly as a snake rustling through grass. "I'm told this woman has a child. Bring it to me."

"I ... do not know where her tent is at, my lord."

"I do" said the other promptly. "It is right across the way."

"Kevon!" Pippa called, warningly. The two henchmen came striding across the lane toward Loise's tent.

"Get out of the way!" They pushed Pippa aside like a bag of meal. One man grabbed her hood and a handful of hair with it, and held her to the ground. The other ducked into Loise's tent. He seized Baby Robbie from his grandfather's arms. When Kevon fought the man, he was struck down with a single savage blow to the side of his head. He fell groaning to the ground. The soldier held Robbie by the back of his jacket and, swinging him like a basket of apples, he carried him to the earl. The baby braced his hands and feet stiffly outward and screamed in terror. Loise stood still as a post but Pippa could see she had her hand on the hilt of the dagger in her sash.

Pippa was not aware of how many times Loise had seen infants brutally murdered in order to force parents into submission. Panic must have gripped her to her very core but she stood quietly. The baby screamed and twisted, reaching in vain for his mother's arms. His little face was bright red. Watching him struggle, a rush of white-hot anger burst through Pippa's body. She fought desperately to get up but the soldier yanked viciously on her hair and forced her to her knees again. She struggled to see what was happening.

She watched this lord, this John Comyn, take the baby from his soldier. The child flailed, howling like a Storm Hag. His mother watched silently, not moving a muscle. A few of the small folk had come out of their tents when they heard the commotion, but they, too, were silent. They stood well back, a tense and angry wall of people.

John Comyn slowly slid his dagger from its sheath. He held it casually in front of the child's face.

"Will we have any more trouble from you, Mistress?"

"No, my lord" answered Loise, without a single sign of emotion.

"I believe I shall make certain of that" replied John Comyn, unable to resist goading her to anger, now that he had the upper hand. Before he had finished his sentence, the prisoner, tied by the wrists though he was, stamped hard on the calf of the soldier nearest him. The man crumpled and fell onto one knee, and immediately received a second kick from the prisoner, this time in a more tender spot. He fell backwards and knocked John Comyn off his feet.

Like a flash Loise caught the baby, still screaming, and fled with him toward her tent. The soldier who held Pippa pushed her sideways, and lunged to catch Loise. Pippa grabbed the man by the ankle just in time, and he sprawled hard on the ground. Loise evaded his outstretched hands and Pippa, without a second thought, scrambled to her feet and clubbed him over the head with his own staff.

"Take the baby, Penny!" Loise ordered Pippa. "Hide!" She drew her dagger and ran back toward the prisoner. Pippa ducked behind the nearest tents and zigzagged deep into the middle of the camp. The sympathetic small folk were waiting to help her. They bustled her into a tent. Several of them seized the soldier that Pippa had bludgeoned and dragged him away. It was only later that Pippa found out the rest of what happened.

Running back across the lane, Loise saw John Comyn turn ferociously on the prisoner. His dagger flashed.

"No!" screamed Loise.

His blow was never delivered, however. From out of nowhere came a swift, long, black-feathered arrow. It slammed into Comyn's shoulder, just to the left of the nape of his neck. He arched backwards and stood as if frozen. Slowly, he sank to his knees.

"Help me, help me!" John Comyn cried to Loise.

She regarded him coolly.

"Take him to his tent."

"Get this thing out of me! Get it out! It burns!" He was crying pitifully.

"Go to your tent, Sire. I'll get my medicines and come to you there" Loise said, tonelessly.

John Comyn's soldier, still bent in severe pain himself and entirely befuddled, took Comyn's arm. He limped him away, supporting his lord as best he could with an arrow sticking in his shoulder.

Loise was out of danger, at least for the moment. She looked around in bewilderment. She couldn't see the archer. The only person in sight was a rather tall but deformed old woman, scuttling away to keep out of trouble. Hastily, Loise said a few brief words to the prisoner, then ran back to her tent to help her father.

If Pippa had been nearby, she might have recognized the black feathers on that arrow. The prisoner definitely recognized them. For the first time in many days his battered face wrung out something resembling a smile.

Loise found her father hurting, but not unconscious. She begged him to get a few belongings together while she began a frantic search for her son and Pippa. She ran from tent to tent, all through the community of small folk.

A groom waited in the shadows. He touched Loise on the arm. He had idolized her since she set a broken leg for him the previous summer.

"Jock! You surprised me! I'm looking for my son."

"He is safe in my tent. The seamstress lass is with him."

"Hurry! Take me there, please!" Only when her son was in her arms did Loise break down. She rocked him and held him so tightly he started to kick in protest.

"We must get him away from here, Penny. I'll not have him made a victim by that horrible man." She pulled herself together. "Jock, will you go ahead of us, to make sure the way back to my tent is clear? I expect John Comyn's men to come for me at any time."

"I hope they haven't taken Kevon already" worried Pippa.

"Saints preserve us! Let's go quickly."

Jock crept ahead and gestured to them to follow when it was safe. They found Kevon holding his battered head.

"You must get out of this camp as fast as you can" Jock warned Loise.

"Jock, I'm so grateful for your help."

"Anytime, my lady."

"Do you mean that?"

"I mean it absolutely. I would be a cripple now if it weren't for you." Loise pulled him aside and spoke quickly to him.

"I'll be back soon" he promised, and left.

Loise turned to Kevon.

"Father, you must take the baby away" she said. "Please? Can you do that?"

"I was thinking the same thing. But I don't dare go home to Berwick. Comyn's soldiers may come looking for us. I'll go to Aldon in Edinburgh. Here's his address." Kevon scribbled a note. "You'll find us there?"

"I will." Loise tucked the note into her bodice.

"Take some coins" offered Pippa.

"We'll pay you back, Penny."

"I don't dare buy a horse until I'm far from here. They could trace me more easily. I'll have to go on foot for the first day."

"Father, I'm so sorry all this falls on you."

"I'll be glad to get Robbie away from this place. And what will you do, Daughter?"

"I haven't the faintest idea" said Loise with a little catch in her voice. She kissed her son good-by and hugged her father and they disappeared into the night. Kevon counted it as a good thing that the snow, an unusually early storm, had not let up.

Loise turned to look at Pippa and Pippa could see her pain. A plea for help was written all over her white face.

"I'll start packing."

"Thank you, Penny" Loise said, fervently. "You're a godsend. Put as much as will fit into my big wooden chest. Here is the key. I will be right back."

"Where are you going?"

Loise merely waved and slipped cautiously out of the tent.

Pippa ran back and forth between the two tents, packing as much as she could into the chest. She was in her own tent when she heard a commotion and men's voices in Loise's tent next door. Some second sense warned her to duck behind the big chest. She crouched tight against it. Moments later her tent flap was flung aside. There was a pause.

"No one here. Move on" someone ordered. Pippa waited a few minutes, then crept outside. Loise's tent had been slashed with knives and knocked to the ground. She stood there in shock for a moment. It was only a miracle of chance that she had not been inside when the soldiers came.

"Pip."

Her head came up. Had she imagined someone had called her name?

"Pippa."

Not a single person in this camp knew that name. Cuinn must be somewhere nearby. She looked around eagerly, moving away from the light of the fire and straining her eyes to see into the shadows. She could see no one.

"Over here."

Pippa recoiled. How had the prisoner known her name? She moved a little closer, frowning warily, but refused to cross to his side of the lane.

"Pippa, it's me, Tom."

It was a severe blow. Her breath was knocked out of her.

Tommy. Tommy wasn't dead? Pippa bent double and smothered the scream that welled up. But it would have been impossible for a sound to escape her anyway. Her heart was jammed so hard in her throat that no room was left for her voice.

She looked quickly in all directions. No one was about on such a snowy night. She flew across the lane. Still, she could not believe. This tall man –Tom was a man, practically. So skinny. Hair grown long, past his shoulders. Not a trace of an impish smile on his wounded face.

It was Tommy. Pippa held his shoulder and didn't know whether to laugh or cry.

"Pippa, can you help me? Can you tell Cuinn...?"

"I'll get you out of here, Tommy."

"No! Get Cuinn. Tell him..."

"I will get you out. Just wait." She had no knife. The sharp blades she had seen in Loise's chest, they would cut Tommy's ropes. She ran to her tent.

It seemed to take forever to saw through the cords that bound Tommy's wrists, but she managed it. When Tom's arms came down, he cried aloud in severe pain.

"What's the matter?" She hadn't expected him to remain leaning on the very post he'd been tied to. He moaned pathetically.

"My arms, they hurt so much I can't lower them" he groaned. She put her arm around his waist.

"Come on, Tom. We have to get away …"

He stifled a scream. She was squeezing his broken ribs. She finally coaxed him to start hobbling toward her tent. She had just gotten him inside when she heard Jock return. He had brought a small cart and a good-sized mule. She stepped outside but didn't dare mention Tommy to him.

"Jock, where did you get this cart?"

She could see Jock's blush even in the dark.

"It's my own cart. Mistress Loise said you would pay me for it. I'm sorry to ask."

"You can have all my money. I hope it's enough."

Jock left her a couple of coins. "No, no. This is plenty. Thank you, little maid." He too melted into the night. Pippa looked in dismay at her thin purse. Her supply of coins had nearly disappeared.

What had become of Loise? Pippa wondered. Had she gone back to help that filthy vermin, John Comyn? There was a rustle of fabric and Loise herself came to crouch behind the cart. Pippa couldn't tell what she was carrying bundled in her arms. She was afraid to tell Loise that, wherever they were going, the prisoner had to go as well.

"Loise, in your tent…" Loise crept over and lifted the flap. The prisoner stood there, leaning on the chest.

"Good work, Penny!"

Pippa was surprised at her reaction. She seemed to accept Tom's presence as a matter of course.

"Can you find us a loaf of bread, Penny? Go to the baker's tent. She owes me a favor."

"Will you take care…?"

"Don't worry. I'll take care of him. Hurry, go!"

When Pippa returned, she had a small bag of food. Loise stood alone in the tent.

"Help me get this chest on the cart."

"The prisoner? Is he in the chest?"

"Heavy!" panted Loise. "Push!"

The two of them struggled mightily and finally worked the heavy chest onto the cart. Even a person as skinny as Tommy weighed more than Pippa imagined.

"Let's go."

"How will we get out of here with him in the chest? The guards will look in there for sure."

"Sh-h." Loise snapped the reins and the mule lumbered into action. They headed toward the edge of the camp.

"Are we going to –"

"Don't talk to me just now. I'm thinking."

Pippa slumped in her seat, worry gnawing at her. An ugly suspicion flared at the back of her mind. Loise. Why was an English woman helping a Scottish prisoner escape? Pippa sat up straight. Reward money? Would Loise be paid for handing Tom over to someone?

*T*heir cart was heading for the road. But first they had to pass the guardhouse. A lantern flared up ahead and Pippa found herself panting.

"Just sit quietly. I'll talk to the guard" Loise ordered.

Two sentries waddled toward them, thumping their lances on the ground.

"Aw-righty, what's this we got 'ere? Why, why it's a lady! Lookit 'ere, Dribell. A lady. And they's two of 'em, ackshully. See that?"

"Awright, git down here." Dribell bawled to Loise. She dropped to the ground. "You too" he motioned to Pippa. "We wants ta git a look at ya. Come 'round 'ere."

Pippa stood close to Loise. Loise reached secretly for her hand. Dribell held his lantern high. His smaller companion began hopping in glee.

"Ooo! Lookit! Bonnie, this one. We kin have a bit a fun here, Dribell."

"Shut yer gob, Chut. What's yer business, Lady?" Dribell stuck his face alarmingly close to Loise's, then turned to swat the other sentry. "Git away from me. Geesh, ya don't have ta stand under me armpit!"

"I wuz jis helpin'."

"I don't need yer help."

"They gonna need questionin', Dribell. I kin help with things what need lookin' into."

"In a pig's ear! I'll do the questions, ya bampot." He smacked Chut soundly on the side of the head. Chut mewed like a kitten and shrank back. Dribell turned back to Loise. "The night's baltic with this storm, Mistress, right baltic. Where d'ye think yer goin' in such weather?"

Pippa groaned inwardly. This was going to take a long time. She looked nervously back toward the camp. All seemed quiet there, so far, but that would change when the English found their prisoner gone.

Loise was unhurried.

"I'm a physician."

"Eh?" grunted Dribell.

"She's a sufficien'" Chut explained.

"I work for the earl. He sent me to look after his sick mother. She's in one of the great houses down the way."

"Eh?" Dribell squinted near-sightedly at Loise, pushing his face closer. She made a visible effort not to back away. Pippa gagged at the smell of him. "What earl?"

"The earl of Buchan." Loise spoke slowly and patiently.

Dribell turned to Chut and smacked him again.

"I said keep away, ya boggin' troll!" And back to Loise. "Now, how do I know yer speakin' the truth?"

"I have a note to prove it."

"Lessee it then."

Loise took a long breath, opened her cloak and very slowly reached into her bosom. The men's heads came together. They were nearly cheek to cheek as they watched. Their powers of concentration had never been keener. Their very eyes bugged out of their heads. Neither one breathed. Unhurriedly, Loise drew out the paper her father had given her with his address written on it. She held it before them. They sighed in unison. Their faces were pictures of vacuous contentment.

They both reached for the note, their hands accelerating like windmills in a hurricane.

"Gimme that!" Dribell slapped Chut.

"I jis wanna touch it whilst it are warm!" Chut hit him back. Dribell punched him in the face. Chut, with blood dripping from his nose, countered with a blow to Dribell's bulging abdomen.

"Ooogh!" grunted Dribell.

"Gentlemen, please! Would you allow us be on our way? This is an emergency. There is a sick mother out there."

"The earl really gots a mither?"

"So his mither's sick, yer sayin'? Whadja do with that letter, Chut?"

Chut answered nasally, squeezing a rag to his bleeding nose.

"I don't gots it! You tooked it!"

"No." Dribell bonked Chut on the head.

"Yes, you did too" countered Chut in a small, hurt voice. "Ooo, lookit. She gots it her own self."

"Lady, we can't read nohow" Dribell confessed. "What it say?"

Loise pretended to read.

"It says to let us through. The earl's mother is contumacious and needs care." She looked at them. "Poor woman."

"That so? Ai, dint yer sister have a touch a thet?" Chut turned earnestly to Loise. "Her tongue turned black and, phewf, ya shoulda smelled her breath."

"Heh." Dribell nodded and scratched his jaw. Pippa rolled her eyes beseechingly at Loise.

"Guess we better let 'em go, eh, Dribell?"

"I'll say what happens, ya ugly fachan! Guess we better let yuz go, Lady."

"Thank you. Thank you very much." Pippa jumped back into the cart and watched Loise arrange herself carefully on the seat. Loise fidgeted in the most annoying way before she lifted the reins. Pippa was driven nearly to distraction. It was taking forever to get moving.

Then Dribell called to her again.

"Wait a minute. We gots ta look in that box."

Loise turned slowly to face them.

"It's only my medicinal herbs."

Dribell scratched his jaw.

"Awful big for a bit of medicinals."

"It takes many different medicines to treat people."

"Yeah, that's prob'ly true."

Loise looked back toward the camp.

"Please, we're in a dreadful hurry. If anything should happen to the earl's mother, he will string us all up, you included."

"Ai Dribell, I fink she's right, ya know. Let 'em go."

"Wheesht, ya idiot. I do the talkin' here. Hmm. Maybe yuz better git along then, Lady."

"Thank you." Pippa sighed with relief and Loise lifted the reins for the second time.

Then they heard it, unmistakably. A horseman was riding out from the camp. Pippa's heart lurched. She turned on her seat again. Loise stared straight ahead.

Dribell and Chut lifted the lantern high.

"What is his trouble?" The horseman could barely sit up straight.

"Whoa. Is he blootered er somefin'? I fink he's blootered, Dribell."

"Ai, too much a the drink, I'm afeert yer right. 'Ere! Who goes there?" The horseman walked his horse up to them. His surcoat showed him to be one of the earl's men.

"The light" he said, weakly. He pulled his hat protectively over his eyes when Dribell held the lantern up.

"Had a bit of a nip tonight, did ya, mon?"

The soldier nodded and groaned.

"I have a message from the earl." He spoke slowly, with difficulty. "You're to check everyone who comes through."

"Oh! Somebody missing?"

"Seems so. Have you checked that chest?"

"Well, uh, sure" hedged Dribell.

"Yoo ain't neither!" affirmed Chut. "I tole him ta open it, but all it takes is a bonny face on a lass like this 'un here, and he git talked outa it. He nivver opened it, not once." Chut dabbed his nose righteously with his nasty rag.

"It's got a lock" said the soldier. "Get the key." He swayed precariously in the saddle. Panic slammed Pippa like a physical blow. She wished devoutly that the soldier would fall off his horse and break his neck.

"We told you, we're in a hurry" Pippa screeched. "There's a sick woman up there." They all ignored her. "The earl's mother!"

What was wrong with Loise? How can she just sit there like that? She doesn't have to give them the key.

"No," yelled Pippa. "There's no time to open this!" She stood up and put her arms protectively across the top of the chest. "No time!" she screeched.

"What's her matter, eh?" asked Chut suspiciously. "Get that thing open, Dribell. Me finks she's hidin' somefin'."

"Shut yer pie hole, will ya, Chut? I'll say what's what! Git that lantern closer. I can't see the bluddy keyho'e."

The key grated in the lock. Pippa sank to her seat. Her heart was beating furiously. They had come so close to getting away. Her thoughts were in a muddle. She could think of no way to distract them. Loise had a knife. Pippa wanted to grab it.

The lid of the chest creaked open and Tommy was done for.

"Hmm." Dribell poked around inside. Pippa felt like crying.

"Whut's unner that there blanket, Dribell?" Dribell poked it with his lance. Loise didn't move a muscle. She stared straight ahead. Pippa began to whimper. The tension was too much.

"Don't stab him!" screamed Pippa. She whipped around to glare at Loise, who had put a calm hand on her arm. Dribell squinted up at her.

"Awright! Take it outa there" he ordered. Chut pulled the blanket aside.

"Nuffin' here but more bottles. Lookit all these crumply li'l leaves." Pippa was aghast. What had become of Tommy? She stared at Loise, who sat still as a statue.

The soldier's horse danced nervously and the man lurched in the saddle.

"Where did these ladies say they were going?" he asked. He was so drunk, he could hardly pronounce his words.

"They sez the earl's mither is sick as a dog. The one is a healer. She sez the earl sent her."

"Why didn't you say so?" demanded the soldier. "We'd better get moving. Close that chest up and let them go ahead. On second thought," he coughed.

Pippa nearly howled with anxiety.

"Please, just let us go!" she pleaded. The soldier continued with his tiresome orders.

"I'll accompany them" he affirmed, "so there will be no more trouble. Thank you, men. You've done a fine job." He tried to lift his hand to his cap but could barely raise his arm without swaying sickeningly. Dribell and Chut, however, cranked out their finest salutes, proud as peacocks, their chests swelling in their frayed jackets.

"Right very chuffed we is, Sire. Fank you for your kind words" puffed Dribell.

"Move on, if you please, ladies." Pippa sank to the back of her seat, bitterly cursing their bad luck. What in the world had become of Tommy? Where was he? Maybe he was hiding underneath the cart?

Now Loise lost no time in snapping the reins. The mule moved slowly down the road, a white ribbon of snow between lacy black trees. The soldier walked his horse in front of them. Pippa glared at his back with hate.

When the sentries' lantern was a tiny prick of light far behind them, Loise pulled on the reins.

"Whoa, there!" The cart stopped and the soldier turned his horse back. Pippa sat up. She could tie him up while Loise held him at knife point. He was obviously in no shape to fight. They could overpower him easily.

Loise leaned over and put her arms around him. Pippa's mouth dropped open. Loise, in league with the English after all! Of course! She should never have been so trusting, so stupid! Loise had set a trap and Pippa had walked right into it. Somehow Loise had found out that Pippa was Scottish. They would take her prisoner. What would they do to her? No one would ever know what had become of her.

"Careful. Just take your time" Loise said gently to the soldier. She held his horse steady. The soldier put an arm on her shoulder and Loise helped ease him onto the seat of the cart. Pippa watched, numb as a fencepost, while Loise, with great tenderness, helped the stupid drunkard.

"Get that blanket out of the chest, would you, Penny? I mean Pippa." Pippa stopped in mid-stride.

Yes it was clear, Loise knew everything. How long had she known? Pippa had believed that she herself was the one with secrets, the clever one, fooling everybody. But apparently Loise was far ahead of her. Now Pippa was in deep trouble. Her hands started to shake. She could not lie her way out of this one. In a helpless stupor, she fumbled in the big chest. The knives, Loise's knives! Where were they?

"Be quick, Pippa!"

Would Loise murder her and leave her body beside the road? Her mind had hit a blank wall. She had no idea what to do next, except to obey orders.

"Spread the blanket back there so he can lie down."

Pippa's head was jangling. She watched Loise loosen the soldier's surcoat. His head rolled backwards. He looked at Pippa over his shoulder and she frowned down at him.

"Hey, Pip" he said softly. Tommy, his soldier's cap askew, gave her a rough imitation of his old grin and Pippa dropped weakly to her knees.

When they had gotten Tommy somewhat comfortable in the back of the cart and given him the bag of food, they started down the road once again. It was a dark night and the snowfall was getting heavier. Loise had trouble steering the cart away from ruts.

"Sorry, Tom" she called back over her shoulder. "These bumps must be really painful." Tom didn't answer.

"He's asleep already."

"He's exhausted. I'll have to fix his bandages soon, but let's get as far away from the camp as we can."

"Where are we going?" asked Pippa dully. Her nerves wouldn't be able to take much more excitement.

"I haven't the faintest idea" said Loise for the second time that night. "Down the road, I guess. Just down the road."

Snow fell in heavy white veils now. Pippa and Loise were silent, too occupied with keeping the cart on the road to ask the questions that each had for the other. They huddled miserably in their hooded cloaks but the snowfall became so thick that Pippa had to walk beside the mule to show him the way. The wind blew fiercely from the sea, across the dunes of Sand Loch. There was not a tree to be seen, nor indeed, anything but snow, blowing snow.

When the road finally entered a forest, the going became easier. It was very dark amongst the trees and the snow continued to fall, but at least the narrow white road was marked out. They were protected from the wind. Pippa could take her seat on the wagon again and let the mule find his own way. She reached back and brushed the snow from Tommy's sleeping form.

"If only we could find a nice warm place to stay" said Pippa wistfully.

"Maybe we'll come to a village. Do you have any money left?"

"Only a little."

"Look, there is an open place ahead. Is that a crossroads?"

Pippa sat up.

"I think I see …oh, oh."

"Oh no. I see them too. I do not believe our bad luck. How many are there?"

"Three of them." Three big men, sitting on very large horses, waiting at the crossroads. They had obviously seen the cart.

Had the earl sent them by another route? Pippa and Loise didn't stand a chance against them. Their mule, strong as he was, could never outrun those horses, even if he weren't knee deep in snow. Pippa's courage sputtered and went out. She could not take anymore.

"What do we do now?" she sobbed.

Loise bit her lip.

"I don't know. They've seen us. I'm not ready to give up yet, though. You mustn't give up either. Stay steady, my pet. We'll think of something."

The horsemen were riding slowly towards them. They broke into a trot. Pippa prodded Tommy awake, more from panic than from any hope that he could help, in his condition. Loise pulled their cart to a stop. There was no escape. One of the men pulled ahead of the others and then leapt from his horse and ran towards the wagon.

"Loise?" he called.

She dropped the reins and jumped to her feet with a little scream.

"Gil?" She leapt from the cart into his arms. They embraced and didn't let go, while the other two riders drew alongside. Pippa was standing too, in total confusion yet again, ready to make a run for the woods. But how could she run from the English and leave Tommy behind? Tommy, on the back of the cart, was struggling to raise himself on one elbow.

One of the horsemen called her name.

"Pippa?" She stared into the darkness. The snow made a nearly solid curtain, all but obliterating his form. He rode around to her side of the cart. She nearly lost her balance.

"Cuinn!"

"Jamie is here too, and Gilbert de la Haye."

"It's you!" Pippa hugged them, laughing hysterically. Her mind thrashed helplessly in a whirlpool of confusion. "And l-l-look!" she stuttered. "Tommy is with us."

"Oh, you took Tom! We looked everywhere for him. Tom is here, Gil!"

"Is Gilbert Loise's brother?" she asked.

"That's her husband."

Pippa found that very comical. She laughed so hard she fell back onto the seat. Cuinn watched her for a moment, incredulous.

"Hoot, you are in a bad way, lassie. Better let me drive" said Cuinn. He gave his horse to Loise to ride and he climbed onto the cart. "There's an inn up ahead, on the river beside the ford. We'd better get moving. Buchan's men will be along soon, looking for all of you."

He put one arm around Pippa. She collapsed into a helpless, snuffling heap and fervently wished that this day would come to an end.

*T*hey took the left fork at the crossroad. It took them out of

the forest and straight into the howling wind. The snow blew so heavily they could hardly see. In a very short time, though, they could make out lights ahead. It was an inn, The Sign of the Bell. It materialized out of the storm like a mirage.

They drove into the stable yard and two lads came out to take their horses. Loise asked Pippa to see that her wooden chest made it safely inside while she helped Tom limp slowly upstairs.

A girl, sturdy as a stone oven, brought them a kettle of hot water and left it near their fire for washing. She promised to bring whatever dinner she could find. Loise asked for a bowl of wine for soaking bandages.

"Pippa" called Loise, "come and watch how I clean the cuts on Tom's back, so you can do it next time."

"Why? Where are you going?"

"I want to go on to Edinburgh tomorrow, to find my father and my son. Can we, Gilbert?"

Her husband came and laid a hand on her shoulder.

"I'm sorry, love," he said, "but the king needs you right now, more even than our son does." Loise looked at him in alarm.

"Rob is still alive?" asked Pippa. She was surprised at how relieved she was to hear that. She had been convinced that she didn't care.

"He's feeling a little better. He's on his way to Strathbogie right now. We want to meet him there tomorrow."

"What? How did he get past the English army?" Loise asked, then stopped. There was a knock at the door. Cuinn peeked into the hall and opened the door wide. The stout girl from the kitchen had brought a tray of covered dishes. The girl stood immobile in the doorway, beaming at them as if bedazzled.

"Now that is a big doorful of a girl!" whispered Jamie. Gilbert snickered quietly.

"Come in, my apple-cheeked beauty" said Jamie. He rose to take the jug of wine from her and she set her tray on the table. "And what might you be called, my sweet?"

"Marfa." She lowered her head, unable to say more, and looked up at him expectantly. She gripped the edge of the table as though she was afraid of tipping over.

"Marfa! A right bonnie name. So Marfa my sweet one, are there many travelers at the inn tonight?"

"No, Sire. Just yourselves." She giggled nervously.

"Splendid. You know what I wish, Marfa?" He leaned companionably on the table too. Marfa shook her head, her eyes fastened on his. "I'm wishing you would turn anyone else away, should someone come along tonight." She giggled again, uncertain what he meant. She looked around at the rest of them. "Would these two silver pieces make it worth your while to do that?"

She looked doubtfully at his coins.

"I'd have to ask me dad."

"I'll add another coin if you'll just tell other travelers that there is no one here at all. That you're closed for the night." He took her hand and put three large coins into it. She looked at the coins, then up at him. "What do you think, Marfa? Could you do that for me?"

"Ai, all righty then."

"And send someone to wake me immediately, if you do get any visitors. Otherwise we'll be leaving early tomorrow. You'll be good enough to give us a bite to eat, Marfa, before we leave in the morning?"

She nodded, waiting timidly. Jamie went to open the door for her and she finally got the hint, released her hold on the table and left, a look of dejection on her face that Pippa couldn't decipher. The door closed after her.

"You'll have to sleep in your clothes tonight, lassies, in case we have to make a fast get-away" Jamie advised them.

They pulled their chairs to the table and began to eat.

"Food! This is wonderful!" Jamie took a bowl of soup over to the bed for Tom.

"It's been a while since we've had a hot meal" said Cuinn. "How have you fared?" he asked Loise.

"We've managed, haven't we Penny?"

"Pippa" she reminded her. Her mouth was crammed with food but she talked on anyway. "How did you know we were on the road? And I thought you –" she looked at Loise, perplexed.

"Neither of us knew much about the other, it seems" said Loise. "I thought you were English, Penny, but with some kind of peculiar accent."

"Is it okay to tell her?" Pippa asked Cuinn. He nodded.

"Ai, tell her all."

"My name is Pippa. Rob sends me to spy on the English camps."

"Rob –?"

"She means Robert de Bruce."

"Did the English really force you to work for them, Loise?"

"Yes, they did. My father really is a wool merchant, or had a business, anyway, before we were captured. That was just after I last saw you, Gil" she said to Gilbert de la Haye.

"I hadn't heard from you for two months, Loise. I was wild with worry. Then Jamie came back from the English camp one day, swearing he saw you and the baby."

"You were in the camp?" Pippa exclaimed, gaping at Jamie.

"You didn't see me? The old woman selling meat? 'Good meat for sale, laddies! Pathetically bony hares! Scrawny pigeons!'"

"Jamie made such an attractive hag. Kind of oversized, though. You must have noticed him?" Cuinn joked. "He was keeping an eye on you, Pippa."

"I knew you were there." They turned to the bed where Tom was making a weak effort to join the conversation. "That was your arrow in John Comyn's shoulder."

Jamie's face contorted. "Aagh, I missed his rotten neck by a finger's width!" he said darkly. "I should have at least hit him in the sword arm. I assume he's still alive?"

"He was, the last we knew" said Loise.

"That foul scrap of diseased vermin! I should have poisoned that arrow."

"You saved my skin tonight, Sire. I'm grateful" said Tom quietly. "And, Sire..." He was almost in tears. "I want to apologize for what happened the last time we met. What I said to you. Back on Arran."

Jamie jumped up with outstretched hand and went to Tom's bedside. They made a long handshake.

"Say no more, Tom." Jamie's voice was hoarse. "It was a dark, dark day in both our lives."

"What are you talking about?" asked Pippa. Somehow she had lost the thread of the conversation. "And what is John Comyn to you, anyway, Jamie? Why do you hate him?"

She was interrupted by another knock on the door, this one soft and furtive. Jamie leapt up again. Cuinn and Gilbert stood as well. Marfa was there, looking very agitated.

"Sire, there's men outside, just knocking on the door. My dad said to take you to the hidin' place."

"How many men?"

"Four of 'em."

"Marfa, you are the bonniest lass in all of Scotland, without a doubt. Don't worry. Only four of the blighters? We can take them easily."

He gestured to Cuinn and Gilbert and they slipped into the hall behind him. Marfa put her fist to her mouth in fright. Jamie motioned her back into the room and closed the door. She plopped heavily onto a chair. Pippa and Loise huddled together on Tom's bed and stared at the door.

They heard voices, someone yelled, then there was a clash of weapons. In a very few minutes, the door was flung open. The women shrieked, but it was Cuinn, Jamie and Gilbert who burst into the room again. Loise ran to Gilbert.

"Thanks to you, my dear Marfa" roared Jamie, "we are all safe and sound. That was such a skoosh. We didn't even break any furniture. There's a little blood on the floor, is all."

Marfa rose smiling, looking at Jamie with doting eyes. Gilbert clapped Jamie's shoulder.

"There's nobody like Jamie Douglas in a fight, and that's the truth!" He was yelling too. They were laughing and still panting from exertion.

Marfa's eyes popped and her mouth dropped open.

"Is you?" she breathed. "Is you the Black Douglas?"

"My enemies call me that, but not to my face."

"Oh holy mither."

Marfa took a step back and tripped over the chair she had just been sitting on. Floundering, and still not taking her eyes from Jamie, she backed out of the room. They heard her running down the hall.

"You have either made her night very special, or ruined it completely, Sassanack" declared Cuinn. "Was that awe or fright on her face?"

"Why it was sheer adoration, ya filthy galoot." Jamie took a swipe at Cuinn's head.

"Adoration? You puffed up, oversized sparrow turd! I doubt that!"

"Yer a big jealous creep. You'll pay...."

"Boys" admonished Loise. "We'd better get a bit of rest. We're all tired, and we have a wounded man here who needs peace and quiet."

"Sorry, Tom" said Cuinn, but too late. Tom was again fast asleep.

*T*hey left for Strathbogie before morning light. The snow was deep and wet. They drove the big draft mule as fast as he could manage. The storm had quieted but the sky was dark and heavy, even after daybreak. They were the only souls abroad on the white landscape. Loise wanted to be as close to Gilbert, her husband, as possible, so he drove the cart and she sat next to him. They had piled straw to make a fairly comfortable bed for Tom in the back.

Pippa rode horseback with Jamie and Cuinn. Since their pace was matched to the cart, they could talk easily. Pippa had so many questions, she didn't know where to begin.

"Jamie, do you hate John Comyn too?"

Jamie tilted his head, but was unable to answer. She started to repeat her question.

"I heard you, Pippa. I was trying to think of what to say." He was quiet for a minute. "You might as well hear the whole story. Don't you think she should, Cuinn?"

"I can tell her, Jamie."

"Go ahead, mon."

So Pippa heard the long story of Isobel MacDuff from the beginning, when she first sailed to Arran Isle more ten years before, invited by Cuinn to stay at Loch Ranza Castle until her baby, Pippa herself, was born.

Pippa was quiet for a while.

"But why does Jamie hate John Comyn?"

"That's a little more difficult to talk about."

"Did you once love Isobel, Jamie?"

"No, truly, Caela was the love of my life, Pippa. I'll tell you. I'll try to tell you what we think happened. It seems John Comyn somehow finally found out about you. Maybe a year ago, it was. Found out that Isobel had a baby and that child was living on Arran. We think he was probably searching for Rob, came to Loch Ranza, and found out accidentally that you existed. He must have seen your portrait in Sebrina's locket somehow. We may never know. But we think that Sebrina's gardener, Tom's father —what was his name, Cuinn?"

"Dort. Speak softly though, Jamie. Don't let Tom hear ye. "

"Ai. Well, Dort, it seems, took money from John Comyn, and in exchange must have told him that you lived up in the glen with Caela. He went up there to find you, but as luck would have it, you were with us, down at the caves on the shore. He found Caela, though. He ..." Jamie shook his head. Tears wet the cheeks of the formidable Black Douglas.

"What Jamie means is that we don't think the fire was accidental, Pippa, the fire that killed Caela."

"So John Comyn set the fire?"

"It looks that way."

"I wish you had killed him with your arrow last night, Jamie!" All the misery of Caela's death was as fresh as though it had happened yesterday.

"So do I, Pippa. So do I."

"So why was Tom apologizing to Jamie last night?"

"Tom found Jamie confronting his father that night and they fought. Tom thought Jamie had killed his father, but he hadn't. It was John Comyn that killed both Dort and Caela. But Tom didn't understand and that is why he went off and joined Rob's army. He was with us when the MacDougalls captured us but I never found him again. I thought he was dead. By some miracle, he turned up at Slaines a few weeks ago, and was out scouting with me when he was captured by the English. You know the whole story from there."

They rode in silence, heads hanging.

Pippa finally asked "Isobel knew I was living with Caela?"

"Oh ai. It was Rob's thought that you would be safest in a remote place. When you were born he promised Isobel he would keep track of you and that was why he visited you fairly often. As you got older, there were even plans made for Isobel to come and take you away."

"Really?"

"Needless to say" said Jamie, "Caela would have hated to lose you."

Pippa couldn't answer at first. She blew her nose.

"I never wanted to leave her. Nor you, Cuinn, and Aunt Sebrina. Did you think I did? I wouldn't have gone with Isobel. Not ever. But I did want to know who my mother was. And why she left me."

"It's only natural, Pippa. We should have told you long ago, but we were afraid." Cuinn tried to turn their mood. "You know what I've been thinking? If you still want to rescue Isobel, here's the very person who could do it." Cuinn pointed to Jamie.

"Truly? Do you think we can?"

"Ach, just leave that to me" declared Jamie. "It's my specialty. As soon as we get to Strathbogie, I'll introduce you to someone who can help us." Here was a ray of hope. Pippa began to feel better.

"One more thing" Cuinn said. "You should know that your mother didn't name you Pippa. She named you Eshne. If things had turned out differently, you should be called Eshne de Bruce."

"Eshne?" This was a surprise. "Where did I get the name Pippa?"

"Well, as a red-faced, squalling infant, we thought you looked like a little pippin apple" Cuinn laughed. "But a cute one, mind you, a cute little apple!"

"A squalling infant? Oh, thank you very much. Maybe I'll keep the name Penny, after all."

*W*hen they reached Strathbogie, they found Robert de Bruce in slightly better health. His men were cautiously optimistic. Loise examined him and immediately prescribed some cleansing herbs and Rob soon felt well enough to rise from his bed for an hour or so each day. When he began to come down to the fireside of an evening, to listen to the music of Jamie's flute, they really began to take heart.

But again they began to run low on food. The countryside could barely feed the folk who lived there, much less an entire army. It was time for them to move on, down to the Earl of Garioch's castle known as the Bass, where the River Urie met the Don. Here food would be more plentiful.

Buchan's forces put up a half-hearted resistance when Rob's army pulled out, but a few weeks later their fighting spirit returned. They began to move toward their enemy again, down towards the Bass.

Meanwhile, the spring days became warmer. Pippa was happy to see that Tom, too, began to heal. His bones began to knit back together. Scars took the place of open wounds, and, though he hobbled a bit, he began to feel like his old self, with one change. For some reason he had acquired a yearning to play the flute.

"Blowing a flute will be good for your chest" Jamie declared. "It will help you get your strength back." He gave Tom his old flute and the two of them would go off whenever they had a chance, to practice together for a couple of hours. They became close companions, and for Tom, the friendship was all the sweeter for taking the place of an old enmity.

After they had gotten settled at the Bass, Gilbert de la Haye rode to Edinburgh and brought back Loise's father, Kevon, and his little son Robbie, named in honor of Robert de Bruce. Pippa was once again brought into their family, and Loise bloomed with happiness, having all her loved ones around her at the same time. She had plenty of sick and wounded soldiers to attend, but in the evening she and Pippa would sit by the earl's fireside together. On some nights, they almost forgot about the war outside their walls.

The day that Pippa met Sim of Ledehouse was the first day she felt real hope of rescuing Isobel MacDuff. Before joining Rob's army, Sim had worked in a shop where he invented and fabricated all kinds of metal tools. He had become great friends with Jamie Douglas. They both delighted in concocting clever plans to defeat the English. On many an afternoon the two of them could be found in a stable that Sim used for a workshop down in the castle town. There they'd be working with their heads together, leaning over a drawing or a work table, puttering away on what they called their inventions. Jamie took Pippa down there with him one afternoon, and Sim listened sympathetically as she explained her wish for rescuing Isobel MacDuff.

Sim worked as she talked but his eyes began to glow and his eyebrows waggled up to his hairline.

"Och, that could be done, easy as pie" Sim declared. "I'm working on a portable ladder at this very time, for scaling castle walls." He showed Pippa a drawing. "We could lift one of these up to the edge of that woman's cage, ai, couldn't we, Jamie lad?" Sim turned to Jamie. "Look, you could lift 'er up there on the point of a lance, hook it onto the cage floor, and get that poor lady down. You'd have to work out a scheme to distract folks, James, but an escape would be the work of a moment."

"A skoosh?" Pippa asked, hopefully.

"Very easy. A skoosh, ai, truly!"

At last, Pippa had a hope of realizing her wish. They would be able to get Isobel MacDuff out of that cage and away from Berwick. She went straight to Rob's chambers with the good news, and was glad she found him up and around that afternoon. Her heart sank, though, when she heard his response to her idea.

"I absolutely forbid you to set foot in Berwick, Pippa" he told her.

"Rob, it's all planned. It will work perfectly."

"No, I've explained this to you before. If you're caught, you will be used as bait, nothing but a worm on a hook, for the English to get at me. They'll dangle you under my nose and they'll not give a pence for what becomes of you. You simply cannot imagine the suffering they would put you through."

"But the old King Edward is dead and..."

"That may be so, but I have many enemies in the world, Pippa. You know this very well. It would only take one of them to figure out who you were, and you'd be lucky –lucky!– if they only put you in a cage. Can't you understand that? You've seen for yourself, more than once, the tortures they use. I am going to tell Cuinn and Jamie as well, that you are forbidden to go to Berwick."

Bitterly disappointed, she complained to Tom that Rob had put a stop to her plans.

"At least you tried to help, Pippa" Tom replied. "You've done all you could, lass."

"I just feel someone has to do something for her, you know? We came up with a good plan to save her. Why is he trying to stop me?"

"You can't keep blaming Rob for not letting you do the impossible."

"It's not impossible. I have to do this for my mother. She has no one, I have no one now. Why is Rob so selfish, that he doesn't see that?"

"He's not selfish, Pippa. You should never say that."

"Doesn't he see that she has been hanging in a horrid cage, ridiculed every day of her life for almost two years?" Her voice cracked. "Can't he understand the pain she is going through?"

"Of course he understands. Rob, of all people, knows pain. He knows how she must suffer."

"He might, if he ever stopped to think about anyone else. But he doesn't."

"I dinna believe you're talking like this!" cried Tom, reverting to his old slang. "Rob has an entire army to worry about, Pippa. He cares deeply for his men. If he didn't, he would have lost their respect a long time ago and his army never would have won the battles they did. And he cares deeply for Scotland. He is trying to pull us all together again. That is a lot of people to care for."

"He doesn't care for me!"

"Oh, quit whingeing and grow up, why don't you, Pippa?"

"I'm not whingeing!"

"You're whingeing and complaining like a wee child!"

"I am not! It's true. Rob doesn't care for me!" she insisted, though with less conviction.

Tommy glared at her.

"If that were true, he wouldn't care whether you went to Berwick or not. Don't you see that?" She started to protest but stopped with her mouth hanging open. Tom was really angry. "Is it just that ye like to feel sorry for yerself, or are ye completely blind, Pippa?" Tom got up and walked away in disgust.

His words hit her like a blow. She actually felt dizzy. But when the spell of light-headedness faded, her vision began to clear.

*I*t was on a spring evening, pouring down with rain, while Pippa and Loise were sewing by a big warm fire, that Gilbert de la

Haye appeared with a very dazed look on his face. Loise put her sewing in her lap.

"You're looking like the cat that got into the cream jar" she said.

Gilbert scratched his head vigorously.

"Gil? What's happened?"

"A great day for Scotland! Rob once made a promise to some of the lords who have fought for Scotland. He told us he would give us castles as rewards. So I'm a land-owner again, Loise. Rob has given us Slaines castle!"

Loise stared at him, speechless.

"Slaines, can you believe it, Loise? I have land of my own once again."

Loise could not say a word. Gil came and took her hands and pulled her to her feet.

"We'll rebuild, help the townspeople get back on their feet again. And being right on the sea, it will be possible for your father to start shipping wool to Flanders once more. Loise? Are you happy?"

"Oh my soul, Gil!" They danced a little dance.

"We'll have a home for the baby." Loise twirled giddily.

"For all our babies."

"Why were you chosen to get Slaines?"

"Rob promised me a reward last fall, remember?"

"You saved his life."

"He said he'd find a property for me. I was afraid he had forgotten but he never did. And he so appreciates the care you give him, Loise. He says you've saved him."

"This is wonderful news, Gil!"

"I'd better get back to him. I just wanted you to be the first to know." He kissed her and ran out, leaving her standing in shock in the middle of the floor.

"Do you believe it, Pippa? Slaines!" She laughed. "It's where I first met you. You must come and visit us there often."

"I'm happy for you, Loise."

"Rob has been such a wonderful friend." She sat down again and looked at Pippa guardedly. "You don't agree, I know. He's been wonderful to Gil. I really don't see why you hate him so much."

"I don't hate him."

"You don't appreciate him."

"I always thought, well, I thought he was mean."

"You mean ruthless?"

"Ai, that. Fighting, forever fighting. All he ever thought about was war. And I thought he didn't care what happened to anybody but himself."

"He had a vision, a dream. There was no way to achieve it with half-measures. It has to be all or nothing for a soldier. Of course some things had to be sacrificed, but it doesn't mean he didn't care."

"I understand him better now, how very serious he is."

"He has to be, doesn't he? War is serious business."

"I see that now. I'm going to try to be…"

"Friendlier?"

"I guess."

"More like a daughter?"

"Well, maybe."

"If my son grows up to act as cold as you do, Pippa, I'll be heartbroken."

Again Pippa felt as though she had been struck. Loise bit her lip, afraid she had provoked her. Instead Pippa jumped up and threw her arms around her, clinging like a barnacle. Loise pulled her away and held her by the shoulders.

"I know you are sorry you have treated your father that way."

Pippa nodded. Tears dripped down her cheeks. Loise hugged her again.

"You'll feel better after you've talked to Rob."

Pippa nodded again, but unfortunately put off going to see him that night. By the next day, it was too late.

May 1308

At their posts on the battlements of the Bass, the castle guards heard the fighting, even before they saw it. They ran to the top of the palisade and looked down the hill in dismay. A lone rider galloped across the bridge with news. Gilbert de la Haye was summoned.

"I must tell the king" he cried when he had heard the message. He stormed into Rob's quarters. Loise, mixing some of her potions there, looked up sharply. Gil barked out the news: David Brechin, an ally of John Comyn of Buchan, had made a surprise attack on the castle town, killing some of their soldiers and several townspeople. Brechin's men had come riding across the river and into the town so suddenly that the sentries were completely unprepared. Anyone that had been in their way had been mercilessly cut down.

"John Comyn must have ordered this."

"Doubtless, Sire."

Rob rose immediately and began to dress.

"Your Majesty" protested Loise. "I must forbid..."

"Do not forbid me!"

"You're not well enough, Sire!"

"I appreciate your concern, but this news is better than any medicine. It is by far the best potion I have been given. Buchan could not have chosen a better way to heal my ills. Help me with this mail shirt, will you, Gil?" Rob was so weak, he could barely lift the heavy chain mail.

"Rob, I agree with Loise. You'll set yourself back by weeks if you try to go out."

"I'll need my horse brought. The shirt, please, Gilbert." Gil puffed out a sigh and eased the chain mail shirt over Rob's thin frame. "Call my lieutenants. I refuse to sit by and let this happen." Loise looked at Gil in frustration. The king had spoken. They were powerless.

The castle yard was in chaos. People from the town and soldiers who had survived the attack were running up the hill and over the bridge, seeking shelter behind the castle's palisade. Fortunately, John Comyn's army, which was to have joined Brechin's attack, had not arrived, or the damage would have been much worse. David Brechin's small army had been forced to withdraw, furious that John Comyn had never shown up to support them.

Rob stood contemplating the scene below. Loise ran down to help with the wounded.

Rob turned to Gilbert.

"We counter-attack right away. The English are camped just down the road by Barra Hill, I'm told. Rally the men."

Frowning, but without a word of protest, Gil swung around to obey.

A bit earlier, before all this happened, in a stable down in the castle town, a little Welsh horse called Ffion had worked himself into a dither. He whinnied impatiently. He tossed his head at the men who were bent over a table nearby, but they ignored him. All the other horses in the stable had been taken out for field practice. But Ffion was forced to stay behind. He had pulled a tendon three days ago, and, being a very valuable animal, was supposed to rest until it was healed. He had tried to convince the men that he was still as strong as ever, but they had made up their minds. No matter how much protest he made, he was ignored, even by the other horses. They had paid him no attention at all as they trotted merrily out of the stable. Not one gave him a backward look. So much for friendship, thought Ffion bitterly. He was a herd animal. He could not bear to be left alone.

He made another appeal to the men hovering over the worktable. They'd listen to him this time! He flung his head back, screaming, and kicked at the gate to his stall.

"What is the matter with that horse?" asked Pippa, who had walked down to the stable with Jamie Douglas and Sim of Ledehouse.

"He's angry at being left out of field practice today."

"Why didn't they take him with them?"

"I think he's got a bad leg or something."

Pippa left the table where Sim and Jamie were revising some drawings they had made. She walked toward the horse.

When Ffion saw the little person come toward him, he began to dance eagerly.

"You're upset, aren't you boy?" She patted his nose. "What's your name?"

I'm Ffion. What kind of man are you, so very small?

"You've got a bad leg, do you?"

Not all that bad. They should have taken me with them!

"Poor horse."

If you have a treat, that would help. What's in here?

"Hey, leave that alone! What are you looking for?"

The big men always give me something to eat.

"Stop it! Don't do that. It's not my fault that you have to stay inside."

"Careful, Pippa" warned Jamie Douglas. "Those hobbies can get nippy."

"What's all this?" Sim of Ledehouse looked up sharply at a commotion out in the stable yard.

Ffion's ears perked and then laid back flat. He called a warning to the men.

Something is happening!

The small person began to walk away from him, but Ffion hated to be left behind again. He reached out to pull the little one back but only managed to catch a mouthful of the beaded net that held her red hair.

"Stop that, you brute!" Pippa grabbed at her hair net, but too late to keep her unruly mop from tumbling out.

If you let me out of this stable, I'll take you with me, if you like.

"You are a wicked horse. Look what you've done to my hair!"
Jamie and Sim jumped up when they heard screams.
"Get down in that basement!" Jamie ordered Pippa.
"What's going on?"
"Just get down there and stay there until we come back for you!" He lifted a door in the floor and shoved Pippa through it. She ducked and stumbled down a wooden ladder. Jamie closed the door on top of her.

She was in the dark, all by herself. The sounds of a terrible struggle throbbed overhead. People were screaming, children crying, feet pounding. She didn't realize she was hearing David Brechin's attack on the town.

She stayed there until all was quiet again. Pippa crawled up the ladder and opened the door a crack. No one was about. She clambered through the opening and dusted herself off. The street seemed quiet, until she heard the wail of a child. The agony in that sound took her back immediately to a glen on Arran Isle, the awful day she had found out about Caela. She ran in a panic from the stable.

Down the alley across the way, a little boy crouched next to a woman lying in the street. Pippa ran to him and knelt beside him. She put her hand on his hot little back. He was perhaps five or six years old.

"Mama!" Convulsed cries were torn from his throat. "Mama!"

His mother lay on the street, very badly wounded. In one arm she clutched a bunch of rags soaked with blood. Pippa could tell she was close to death. Her eyes were huge in her white face. She saw only her little boy. Her head began to jerk uncontrollably. She was unable to get a breath, but her eyes never left her boy's face until the moment her head dropped to the ground and she saw nothing.

The little boy pulled on her limp hand and stamped his feet in a frenzy of sobbing. Pippa wanted to draw him away, but realized he had only a few moments before he would have to give up his mother's hand for ever. She stared at the bundle of rags the woman held for a long time before she grasped what it was. A tiny baby. One stroke of a sword had killed both mother and child.

Pippa was too shaky to stand. She was filled with nauseated loathing for the animal that had done this. Another woman came to the door of the house.

"Davie!" she cried with relief. The little boy looked up. The woman's eyes went from his wet red face to the still bodies of his mother and baby brother. The woman reeled and clutched the doorway. She came slowly forward, bending to see, not believing, both hands on her mouth.

"Oh no." The woman dropped to her knees. Pippa backed away. It was only right to leave them to their grief.

Thunder rumbled ominously in the distance. In a stupor Pippa stumbled down the street. There were many dead bodies, still clutching the baskets and jugs they had been carrying. Townspeople, killed in cold blood, not a weapon to be seen. Was it John Comyn's army that had done this? She knew they were camped nearby. She lurched dizzily and the dusty street spun round and came up to hit her hard.

She was on the ground. She tried to raise her head. It was thundering without pause now, louder and louder.

Then Pippa realized it wasn't thunder at all. It was horses, many horses, and men dressed for battle. She got up and staggered to the end of the street. Rank upon rank of horsemen passed. People scrambled into doorways to get out of their way.

Pippa's breath caught in her throat. There in their midst, snapping in the spring breeze, was a golden banner, a red rampaging lion! The arms of the King of Scotland, Robert de Bruce.

"The Bruce! The Bruce!" people cried to him.

Rob had gotten off his sickbed to take revenge on the English. He would put everything right! Pippa's heart soared. Foot soldiers and archers followed the horsemen, looking determined and proud. The women of the town cheered them with tears in their eyes. One by one, townsmen left their doorways and joined them.

Pippa could do nothing less. So much emotion boiled inside her that she knew it would be impossible to just stand and watch.

All at once she understood what it meant to take up a weapon and fight in spite of danger.

She ran back to the stable. Ffion the horse looked up sharply as she came in. He pranced with excitement when she reached for his bridle. She had gotten him saddled before she stopped to ask herself what she would use for a weapon. She looked desperately around the stable, knowing it was not likely that anyone had left a sword behind. Back in a corner she did find a bow and a quiver of arrows. It had been a long time since she had pulled a bow.

She was testing her strength on the bow when she heard footsteps. A wounded soldier limped into the stable and hid behind the door. He must not have noticed that she was watching him from the back of the barn. After a second he peered cautiously into the street. Pippa had seen the livery he wore many times in John Comyn's camp. An English soldier! He must have been wounded and left behind when his army withdrew from the town. His leg was bleeding badly.

Ffion the horse whinnied his advice.

Watch out! There's trouble here.

The soldier, hearing the horse, turned eagerly, and then noticed Pippa, standing with a bow and arrow in her hand. He pulled his sword slowly from its scabbard.

"Don't give me no trouble. Just stand aside. Get outa my way. I needs that pony" the man snarled. His accent was distinctly English. He began warily to cross the floor of the barn.

The horse tossed his head in anger. Who are you calling a pony? retorted Ffion.

"Stay back. This is my horse." Pippa's hands tensed on the bow but she didn't move. The man stopped, his posture threatening. He raised his sword.

"Get outa my way." He lunged at her.

Pippa pulled the bowstring to her cheek and loosed the arrow before she had time to think.

The next thing she knew, she was panting hard, trying to get a breath. At first she could not figure out how her arrow had gotten stuck in a man's chest. There he lay, on the floor at her feet. She stared at him, dumbfounded. She had killed him. She had killed a man. She dropped the bow.

Ffion stamped restlessly.

Hoot, little one, let's get going.

The horse's protest brought her to her senses. Gingerly she pulled the dead man's helmet from his head. His hair was soaked with sweat. She chided herself for being too fastidious, but she wiped the inside of the helmet with her skirt anyway. She pulled it over her own head. It was very large. She took it off, found a bit of string on Sim's worktable, and tied her hair into a twist. When she stuffed her red mane into the space inside the helmet, it fit a little better. She still needed a weapon. The dead soldier's sword was so heavy she could barely lift it. She pulled a dagger from the man's boot and opened the gate for the horse.

"I sure hope your leg holds out" she said to the horse as they left the stable.

Ha! snorted Ffion the Mighty. Just try to stop me!

At the edge of town, Ffion caught the scent of his kindred, not far down the road. Nothing and no one could have held him back then, and he ran like the wind, straight onto the battlefield.

Pippa had seen many battles in the past year, but she was unprepared for taking part in one. She had never been so intimate with the very moment of death. This wasn't the aftermath of war, but the horror itself, in the making. On both sides of her, in front, behind her, combat was ugly, loud and terrifying. Faces were grotesque, distorted. Men were bellowing with determination, shrieking with pain. Ffion dashed straight into the midst of it all. He refused to be held back and he swept Pippa along with him. Men and horses on all sides were alive one moment, dead the next. The clamor was overwhelming, confusion everywhere.

Ffion charged in this direction and stamped in that direction, trying to tempt his rider to engage the enemy. But now Pippa was confused. She could not recollect what she had intended to do here. All she could see was a sickening clash of metal and flesh. What part had she thought she could play? Her mind spun in panic, until, that is, across the field she spotted a red plume and a surcoat embroidered with three golden sheaves of wheat. Suddenly her purpose was absolutely clear. She gripped the little dagger and, urging Ffion in that direction and beating his sides with her heels, she unfurled her lust for vengeance like a giant sail. She tore across that field and gambled everything she had for revenge.

John Comyn of Buchan's army had not gotten to Inverurie in time help David Brechin in his attack on the town. Comyn was supposed to have been there, and Brechin was furious that he was not. But it wasn't entirely Buchan's fault. He needed more time, time to decide. Should he join the battle? He had hesitated.

He wasn't sure he could persuade his men to do what he needed. Many times his orders would be ignored. Although his temper was notorious and his punishments fearsome, he did not inspire obedience.

Some of Buchan's soldiers were paid to fight, but he did not pay them enough to earn their loyalty.

He had turned other men into unwilling soldiers by pulling them off their farms and forcing them to fight. But he did not value them enough to earn their respect.

Today, he needed to urge them to fearlessness, but they smelled his fear.

To raise his own courage, he had dressed resplendently in his red surcoat. Three golden sheaves of wheat glittered on his chest. He would impress everyone. His helmet carried a red plume signifying that he was their great and unmistakable leader.

His army saw a coward hardly taller than a boy.

"The Bruce is sick and all but dead!" he shouted. "He cannot even rise from his bed! Without him, his army has no spirit for fighting! I can, and will win the day against them. I can defeat the forces of Robert de Bruce because he is too weak to stand against my might. His army will run at the very sight of my strength!"

Strung out along the road to Inverurie, Buchan's men looked at each other. Stories had haunted their campfires, whispered behind shielding hands. Stories of the legendary Bruce, clever and fearless, and at his side, the vicious, the dreaded Black Douglas. No, if half the stories were true, it would not be an easy battle. It was insane to underestimate these Scots.

Down the road, the army massing against them was riding hard. The English were horrified to see, waving defiantly in the wind, the red and gold banner of Robert the Bruce. It came toward them without faltering. It came on, and across the fields they heard the cry of battle. The king had come, and he did not look half-dead to anyone.

The word spread quickly back through the ranks. It was indeed Robert the Bruce riding beneath that banner and the black plume of the Black Douglas was right beside him. Buchan had lied to them again. The knights gripped their lances. In their pride, they tried to ignore the twisting in their guts. The foot soldiers panicked, but proud they were not. To survive, they had learned to trust their gut feelings. One after another, they turned and ran.

The horsemen of the two armies swept together in titanic fury, but even at the first bloody clash, Buchan's army had begun to fray at the edges. Men looked over their shoulders and saw retreating backs. Their support was evaporating. Their courage wobbled, their sword arms weakened. Buchan tried to hold the line. He rallied a few knights and urged a charge, closing in on a knot of horsemen. He picked out a small rider from among the enemy and bent all his concentration on him. The boy was headed straight for him. Buchan felt vastly relieved. He had found someone his own size.

Buchan's war horse thundered across the field. John Comyn of Buchan drew his huge broad sword and swung it high over his head. He closed with the rider, so young, just a lad, really, but Buchan didn't care.

He swung his sword and missed. The boy's ruddy little horse had turned right in front of him, at the very last moment. And now his own horse – what was wrong with his horse? He was faltering. The beast stumbled and Buchan's head whipped backwards inside his helmet. He and his horse hit the ground hard. A long red gash across his horse's chest was spouting blood and Buchan floundered awkwardly in his armor, trying to get his feet out of the stirrups before he was caught beneath the dying animal.

Enraged, he turned just in time to avoid the dagger thrust of his opponent, aimed right at his unprotected face. He grabbed the boy's saddle as he rode by and jerked hard on it. The rider fell. Buchan ran to give the final thrust. The boy jumped to his feet so fast, though, that Buchan barely had time to raise his sword. But he almost laughed when he saw that the dagger was the boy's only weapon.

Then, instead of advancing toward Buchan, the boy did a strange thing, though it certainly had its effect. He tore his helmet from his head.

Buchan gaped at the red hair. Lots of red hair came tumbling, tumbling down to his waist. For a boy, too much red hair. And, for some distance across the battlefield, that red hair blazed like a beacon, enough to turn at least one person's head.

Buchan was caught under a spell. He was staring into fierce green eyes. A cry of pain burst from his throat before he could stifle it. He was paralyzed, and could hardly hold onto his sword. It was his wife standing before him. Isobel! But so young. His head was thick with confusion. Why was she so young? No, oh dear God, no! It was not his wife.

The world tilted and he swayed on his feet. In that instant, the girl lunged at him. He screamed in rage, straining with every fiber of his being to strike her, to smash her breath from her body. She had no right to exist. He forbade her to live.

Buchan's reactions were dulled. The girl was quick and so close to him that he couldn't get his sword up in time. But just before she reached him he managed to beat the side her head with the flat of his sword.

She fell. He had wanted to pierce her heart. He would! He would pierce her heart, though he was already certain that his face had been the last thing she ever saw.

But he— now he had been stopped by something. He looked down. An arrow had lodged just under his heart. Where had this come from? His head was clouded. He couldn't see. Stupid with shock, he tried to pull on the arrow. A white-hot flame seared deep in his innards.

He looked up. Where was someone who could help him? A man, no, a boy who was barely a man, dismounted and dashed toward him. His bow was drawn, another arrow pointed at John Comyn's throat. He knew this young man from somewhere. John Comyn stumbled backwards and fell. Sweating, grunting with pain, he stared up at the second arrow pointed at him. Then, looming monstrous over the boy's shoulder, the face of James, the despicable Black Douglas appeared. The sword belonging to the Douglas was poised.

"What have we here, Tom?"

"Nothing but a pile of garbage."

"This ain't garbage. This is what drips from the bowels of dying pigs."

"Look what he did to Pippa."

"I see. So which of us gets to wipe this putrid hog turd off the face of the earth, Tom?"

The Douglas stopped abruptly. The boy had stayed his sword arm.

"Do we have to put him out of his misery?"

"No. Not at all." replied the Black Douglas.

"Let him suffer then."

"A stomach wound. He'll feel it for a good long time before he dies." His spittle landed on John Comyn's cheek.

The boy reached into his tunic. He drew out a jeweled purse, decorated with three golden sheaves of wheat. He let it fall from his hand onto John Comyn of Buchan's bloodied chest. One tarnished silver coin slid out and thudded into the dust. Buchan looked stupidly at it. A forgotten act of violence, come back to haunt him.

The Black Douglas looked warily about, guarding while the boy lifted the body of the red-haired girl. They backed away and left John Comyn lying there.

Buchan could not catch his breath. Would no one help him? The battle still raged across the field. Buchan lurched to his feet, swaying precariously. He tried to call for help. He coughed and wiped blood from his lips. Finally, someone was there, steadying him, lifting him awkwardly onto a horse. Holy saints, the arrow flamed so deep inside him! In a stupor, Buchan fled the battle field and what was left of the army fled with him, chased every pain-wracked step of the way until they reached Fyvie Castle.

Victory that day went again to Robert the Bruce.

Loise cried out when they brought Pippa's body into the hospital tent.

"What was she doing on the battlefield?" she raged.

"Setting all her demons to rest" said Tom.

Loise examined the swelling on the temple and down the side of the face and neck. Her shoulders sagged. She called for cold compresses wrapped with lemon balm, but knew they were practically useless. Still, she had to do whatever she could. More and more wounded men came in, but Loise kept a constant eye on Pippa.

The afternoon waned, the flood of wounded began to slacken. Loise stretched her back for a minute and then bent again to the torn young man lying before her. When Rob and Gilbert burst through the door of the tent, though, she handed a cloth to the woman working with her.

"Press that against here, would you, Sera? Keep it there, tight, until I come back."

She looked sorrowfully at the white-faced men and pointed to where Pippa lay. Loise and Gilbert stood aside and watched Rob move slowly to Pippa's cot. He leaned his arms on the edge, breathing heavily. When he finally raised his head, his eyes met Loise's. She couldn't bear the look on his face.

He ground his teeth. "Is there no hope?" he asked.

"There is always hope, my lord. It is all we have, in the end."

"But..." His voice faltered.

"We're doing everything we can." She could not bring herself to say more. "You must get some rest, Sire. You have barely recovered yourself."

A growl crescendoed from his throat and he knocked a stool over and stamped one of its legs to splinters.

He had sensed the familiar dark presence. Again and ever again, here stood the Lady. Would she never leave him be? Lady Victory, holding out her hand to him. She wanted payment and, as ever, as always, he was forced to compensate her. She never gave him an inch, pressing, pressing him heartlessly to the wall. I spare no one after all, she whispered to him. Not even a king. And certainly not a king's daughter.

Rob's face, when he turned to Gilbert, was not a face so much as a map of grief. He measured his words carefully in a trembling voice.

"We are going north to Buchan territory, Gilbert. We will kill them all. Not a single member of the Comyn family will escape. There won't be a Comyn left in the whole of Scotland. No man, no child left alive. Not a house. Not a barn." He leaned over Pippa's still body one last time. "Tell the men, Gil." He stalked out.

Loise found herself trembling. She stood close to Gilbert and turned his face to hers.

"You must go?"

"I must."

"Come ye back to me, Gil, as soon as ever ye can."

"I will, my love, I will." And then he, too, was gone.

Loise gripped Pippa's limp hand. Stay with us, my girl, she prayed. Please, please stay with us.

What was there to do but wait? So Loise sat down and she waited. She could watch like a hawk, night and day, and she did. She could pray to every saint she knew. She let no one else touch Pippa. She let nothing and no one come near the motionless girl but her own healing hand and her own strong spirit, coaxing, crooning, wooing her back to life.

July 1308

After the victory at Inverurie, Robert the Bruce laid aside the duties of kingship for a time and took up a struggle of his own. For two decades he and the Comyns had carried on a raging blood feud. Such a long time for hate to fester. In the kiln of this burning hatred, his good judgment had been seared over and over. The one thing Rob knew was that the fight would not ever go away, no matter how many battles he won. Meanwhile, the dead wandered his dreams night after night, beloved family, dear friends who had been brutally killed in this war. The sight of their long, grey faces stalking his dreams wrung his heart and he could get no rest. He wakened every night in the small hours, thrashing and drenched with sweat. Nor did dawn bring any surcease from grief.

The dead finally convinced him. He had to make sure, absolutely sure, that no member of the Comyn clan would ever again rise against the Scottish monarchy. He was finished with hope – hoping that the feud would evaporate, hoping that he could work against it. No, he must destroy it.

So the Bruce dragged his army north. Utterly without mercy, throughout all of Buchan territory, at every castle and farmhouse, he slashed, burned and murdered ruthlessly. Peasants fled for their lives that summer, running to the hills with only their children and what few cattle they could salvage. Comyn family members, those that hadn't escaped Scotland already, died in scores by his sword. It would be fifty years before that part of Scotland would build a community again, but many hundreds of years would pass and still The Bruce's brutal retaliation would be remembered. The Harrying of the Comyns, the storytellers called it. Rob might forgive members of other clans. He might come to treat them as equals, if not friends, but the Comyns, no. They would lose everything. The few that had escaped already were dispersed to the four corners of the known world, for all of time.

When there was no living thing left standing in Buchan, Rob turned south. He knew he hadn't ended the pain. His dead family did not come back to him. His living family did not suffer any less. But now at last Scotland would be able to stand strong and independent from England. He gathered his men and went home. Scotland would have her king again and he would do the best by his country that he possibly could.

Tom the gardener's son was sick of war. He wanted no part of this wholesale slaughter in Buchan, and told Rob so. He had something else in mind altogether.

"Instead of going north with you, I'd like to go to Berwick, Sire" he said. "Pippa would have wanted me to do this, and I think it can be done."

"I have to advise against it. Of course I can't forbid you, but Tom, if you're caught, there will be no mercy for you. And I will be losing yet another valuable man. It would be an utter waste."

Tom blushed. "I'm chuffed, Sire, that you would say that. But I think I've got me a good plan. I'd like your blessing, is all, Sire. It would mean a lot."

Rob rose and came around the table to where Tom stood.

"And you have it, Tom, in thanks for all you've done for your king."

"I would do it all again in an instant, my lord." He started to kneel but Rob gripped both his shoulders. Little Tom was now tall enough to look Rob in the eye, the king and the gardener's son.

"I look forward to hearing good news from you, lad."

"Thank you, Sire. I'll let you know as soon as I can."

Tom spoke as though he was working alone. He had been instructed to do so by James Douglas, Sim of Ledehouse and Cuinn de Seta, but they were all in this together. The next day, the four of them rode into Berwick town.

For three days they did nothing but watch. The English woman who guarded Isobel MacDuff was a terror. They hated her before the end of the first day. If the milk of human kindness had ever coursed through this woman's veins, it had turned rancid a long time ago. Her body had a shape as feminine as any fireplace poker. Indeed, a bad choice of forebears had robbed her of any physical attractions at all, and her nastiness did nothing to transform them. She gave Isobel not a moment of respite.

Her name was Gillian Bagley.

For three days the men listened to her taunting Isobel, sneering at her, denying her meals or use of the privy. Now that the men had their plan ready, their determination was at fever pitch.

*M*istress Bagley had just left Isobel in her cage and gone inside to her own room. A headless arrow zipped between the bars and lodged near Isobel's feet. She started violently, then noticed the thin cord attached. She looked furtively over her shoulder and began to pull the cord. A small package slithered across the floor of her cage.

It had been a long time since there had been any change in Isobel's routine. Finding this package nearly made her nauseous with excitement. She hid it beneath her tunic and dropped the arrow into the street. She felt actually giddy with anticipation, and didn't see that a man picked it up a moment later. Finally, when it was time for Mistress Bagley's afternoon nap, Isobel got up the courage to open the package. It contained a tiny, very sharp saw blade no longer than her finger, and a note telling her to make cuts in the outer side of three bars at the corner of her cage. She was to cut nearly, but not all the way through the bars, and she was being given three days in which to accomplish this. She could signal her agreement with this plan by dropping the note to the street when the lady in the blue gown passed underneath.

Isobel looked up. There was indeed a lady in blue trundling in her direction. Her manner of walking was surprisingly ungraceful. Who could she be? Isobel stood, crushed the note into a ball and dropped it between the bars. The lady, quite a good-sized wench, picked it up and went on her way with a merry wave. She was no one Isobel recognized.

Isobel hid her little saw in the palm of her hand and scraped it on the edge of a heavy wooden bar. It would take her some time, but she was determined. She had to remind herself not to rush. She would give herself away.

Her heart beat wildly.

Tom, from behind a chimney on the roof across the street, grinned and ducked back into an attic with his bow and arrows.

*T*hree days later, a couple of shepherds entered the town at the head of a flock of female sheep. They herded the ewes toward the center of town. It must have been a big day for sheep in Berwick because, at a different gate, two more shepherds entered with their flock, all rams. An odd coincidence. Jamie Douglas, wearing a dirty hat and a brown shirt, watched the sheep from his seat on a hay wagon at the end of a street. He could see Isobel's cage a short distance away. He spoke to his dogs but they were already taut with anticipation. Jamie kept the dogs in place.

And, who would have thought it? Merely by chance, the other flock of sheep appeared at the other end of the street. Sim of Ledehouse, dressed in clothes very like Jamie's, pulled a similar hay wagon into place and held tight to his dogs at the other end of the street.

So. The males of a particular species were about to meet the females. Mother Nature had paid this particular piper and she was calling the tune.

The dogs knew their work very well. They pawed impatiently at the ground. When Jamie and Sim loosed their holds on them, they went to work. The flocks swerved together. Ram instinct battled ewe judgment. The females began to panic, the males became confused. Some turned back, others ran ahead. The dogs sent them one way, they turned and ran another. The street became a melee, a carnival, a riot. Sheep chased sheep, dogs chased sheep. The people on the street ran after them all, certain, at the outset, that all the lowly creatures could be brought under their control. As the animals tore through the town, however, that notion began to disintegrate. Soon, the street was empty, but for two brown-shirted peasants and their wagons.

The two wagons pulled up to block the entire street, one at each end. Somehow, what with all the commotion, each accidentally dumped its load of hay. A clever invention of Sim's, a device that tilted the beds of the wagons, had somehow misfired. Yes, accidentally of course. There was a huge pile of hay from one side of the narrow lane to the other, at both ends of the street. It would be the work of a morning to clean it all up.

Tom, at his post on the roof, laughed uncontrollably. Cuinn came running from a doorway, carrying a lance. Impaled upon its point was a ladder, also of Sim's invention. Cuinn slid its prongs neatly between the bars of Isobel's cage and hooked it to the floor. He was up the ladder in a flash. With his fist, he easily knocked out the three wooden bars that Isobel had cut for him. He gripped her arm. She looked warily at the ladder. She was so unused to physical exertion that she hesitated. But, being Isobel, she teetered for no more than a moment.

An unfortunate moment, as it turned out. Gillian Bagley had been awakened by the noise in the street and rose to check on her victim. She clambered into the cage, grabbed Isobel's hair from behind and put a knife to her throat.

Her little raisin eyes looked menacingly at Cuinn.

"Get away or she's a dead woman!"

Fonk! An arrow tore right through her gown and grazed her derriere. Well, one would call it a derriere if one were kind. Anyway, a shallow cut opened back where a derriere is usually found.

"Aagh!" she cried, and grabbed her sagging backside.

In that instant of pain, Isobel drove her elbow backwards, deep into the middle of Gillian Bagley's bony ribcage. She followed that with blows of her fists, hammering Gillian Bagley's face. Mistress Bagley hit the floor with a thud and still Isobel pounded at her.

Cuinn had to force himself to stop gaping so he could pull Isobel away.

"You can beat the old hogbeast to a pulp another day. Get down the ladder, will you?"

Isobel crawled through the bars of her cage and clambered to her freedom. Mistress Bagley, with the wind knocked out of her and a searing pain in her backside, found she could not even get up to follow, but Cuinn was right behind Isobel. He used his lance to lift the ladder down and they ran toward Sim, who had his wagon waiting behind the pile of spilled hay. Sim flicked the reins and the hay wagon lumbered off, heading for the town gate. Jamie, still at the other end of the street, turned his wagon and drove in the opposite direction.

From the empty cage, or empty but for one hogbeast of a woman, hideous cries followed them, threatening death to a peasant in a brown shirt. But in a matter of moments, both brown-shirted peasants would be driving empty wagons.

On the back of Sim's wagon, Cuinn handed Isobel a pair of breeches and a tunic.

"Quick, take off your clothes!"

"Merciful Heaven! It's forever the same with you men, isn't it?" Isobel retorted, opening her bodice.

"I notice you didn't have to be asked twice."

"I've been in that cage for two years. I'm desperate. Even you look good." Isobel has to be forgiven for being saucy. Finally free after so long a time, she was a bit overwrought.

"My, my, you've learned sweet gentility in these years, my lady. Is this my thanks for rescuing you?"

"You call this a rescue, standing nearly naked in the middle of town, on the back of a hay wagon?"

"Well, my delicate blossom, it's the best we could manage. I suggest you hurry. Townspeople up ahead. If you'll get yourself into those breeches, we'll jump down into the street and walk amongst them. You'll have to try to walk like a man, all the way to the town gate."

"Waddle away, my prince. I mirror your every move."

"Put this hat on, sweet dove, and say nothing until we are out of town. Not a word. Your voice somehow sounds like a woman, though you have the tongue of a serpent." They both, it seems, had a bit of a saucy streak.

Cuinn helped Isobel climb down from the wagon and motioned for Sim to turn up a side street without them. He turned back to Isobel and saw her eyes brimming with tears. She was dressed as a man so, against every desire, he felt that he ought to refrain from putting his arm around her.

"Och, I'm sorry, my lady. That was a terrible thing to say, especially after you so heroically pounded your jailor to Bagley pudding. Tell me you'll forgive me."

"I would love to hug you right now, Cuinn my darling, and tell you how mad I am with love for you, but dressed like this, it would look a little funny."

"Well, dry your tears and share this jug of ale with me. Then we can act as silly as we like."

"Thank you, my bonny prince, thank you. So all the kisses I'm going to shower upon you? They'll have to wait for later?"

Cuinn stopped in his tracks.

"Life passes so quickly" he said, greedily. "Why wait?"

Envoi

August 1308
Loch Ranza

*A*way out on Arran Isle of a summer afternoon, the old woman, Ailliol, rested her crippled back against the trunk of a murmuring rowan tree and turned her blind face to the sky. At long last, she was saying 'farewell'. She sensed that her time was over, that she would no longer be needed here. Ailliol was over one hundred years old and had accepted her fate long ago. She had already given instructions about the rowan staff she had inherited, and now she settled herself to wait for the Riders of the Sidhe, the Fair Folk on their beautiful horses.

And after a time the air was filled with humming, like a swarm of bees. A breeze came up, and Ailliol could hear gay voices and harnesses jingling amongst the trees. There they were! She could see they had brought a riderless horse, with a saddle of silver gilt. Ailliol stood up and swept a thick fall of hair from her face. She watched them, smiling. Then she was amongst them. Their bright faces were exquisite, so dazzling that at first she had to shade her eyes. They welcomed her warmly and held the grey horse for her as she swung into the saddle. And when the moment ended, Ailliol had disappeared and was never seen on Arran again.

*N*ow it was high summer. White cloud castles in the sky built themselves again in the loch below, and gulls sailed between the two, sliding across the wind with nary a beat of a wing. Their sharp yellow eyes looked for a perch from which they could spy on Loch Ranza castle because people had returned there. Once again the old grey stones rang with the sounds of coming and going. To the tone-deaf ear of a seagull, this was a kind of music.

*E*arlier, back in the spring, Pippa had been so frail that Loise the healer and her father, Kevon, had outfitted a carriage with a bed that would carry Pippa all the way across Scotland. They were taking her back to Arran Isle. She had wanted so badly to go. They weren't sure she would survive the trip but there was nothing else they knew to do for her.

They took a ferry to Arran Isle and Sebrina de Seta welcomed them joyously at Brodick castle. Sebrina had returned to her old home after the English had been evacuated, and she was raising Jamie Douglas's baby, William, there.

But Pippa, who had never, except once, been inside Brodick, could not orient herself to a new place. Everything was strange to her, confusing. She was not thriving. She grew ever thinner, languishing, not getting stronger as they had hoped. Her bewilderment and frustration were so painful to Sebrina that she decided that the whole lot of them should move to Loch Ranza lodge. At least until Gilbert and Cuinn came home from the war, they would move back to the little castle, she and Pippa, Loise and Kevon, and the two toddlers, Baby William and Loise's Robbie. It was only after that move, when she was on familiar ground once more and the beloved music of Loch Ranza sang in her ear, that Pippa finally began to heal.

*S*he awakened feeling certain that she would be having visitors that day. At mid-morning, she walked cautiously out to the garden. She felt for the bench and sat listening. The gulls called and little wavelets plopped onto the shore, but no visitors arrived. She wasn't there for long, though, when she heard the crunch of a footfall.

"Dickon?"

"How did you know it was me, Miss?"

"Have there been any messages this morning, Dickon?"

"None, Miss. Were you expecting something?"

"Someone is coming today. I feel sure of it."

Dickon smiled knowingly. He had lived on Arran all his life and believed the old superstitions.

"Then it will surely happen, Miss. Until they arrive, would you care for something to eat?"

"I'm starving." Pippa rose uncertainly.

"Here is my arm. Oh, you mustn't forget your staff." He placed it in Pippa's hand.

"I don't really need a staff, as long as I can lean on you."

"But Miss, it is a venerable relic. A treasure. You must keep it with you always. It is over four hundred years old."

"I don't know why it came to me."

"Ah, do you not? You will, Miss, in time. You will."

*B*y mid-afternoon, Pippa was becoming impatient. She went to a window and leaned out. The breeze, soft and fragrant, was summer's touch at its most beguiling. It blew stray curls across her cheek. She listened, but she heard only the songs of the loch, nothing more. However, the premonition was so strong, she knew beyond doubt that it was true. Someone was coming, someone she held very dear. But there was a shadow. One would be missing, someone dear would be missing.

She turned from the window and fumbled for the rowan staff. It had steadied her more often than she liked to admit. Even though the dizzy spells were less frequent now and her balance was improving, it was still comforting to have the stout stick at hand. And it kept her from banging into things quite as often as at first.

There they were at last. Voices! She was certain she heard them now. Down on the beach, no, perhaps in the garden. She sat on the window seat, placed the rowan staff to one side, and waited. When the door opened she half-rose and held out a hand. He was there in an instant and her heart overflowed.

"Cuinn!"

"You're looking so much better, Pippa."

"I'm so glad you came! Who else is here?"

"Well, I've brought someone to see you."

"Who is it?"

"It's me." A husky voice. "It's... it's Isobel MacDuff, Eshne." Their fingertips just touched, faltered. Uncertainty arced between them. It was difficult to know the heart of the other.

But the pull was too strong and their arms reached for each other. Their bodies fit together as snugly as they had from the very beginning. Pippa felt tears drop onto her neck.

"Let me have a look at you, Eshne. I'm glad to see you are wearing this necklace." Isobel fingered the little rowan tree charm and smiled at Cuinn over Pippa's head. "Cuinn gave it to me the year you were born. Did you know that?"

"No, Caela never told me. Do you want it back?"

"Maybe I'll ask Cuinn to get me one just like it."

"I knew it!" Cuinn declared. "You ladies are going to become very expensive pets."

Isobel cradled Pippa's face in her hands.

"Sebrina tells us you want to stay here at Loch Ranza. I would really like to stay with you."

"You would?"

"I'd like it so very much. But tell me what you think. Shall we give it a try, Eshne?"

"Maybe. If only..."

"If only what?"

"It's..."

"Tell me."

"If only you could call me Pippa. I just... I'm used to Pippa."

Isobel laughed.

"I hardly think I could deny you anything at this stage. Pippa. I'll get used to it."

Cuinn spoke up.

"Let's not forget! There's someone else here too."

One more person here, and still one missing. Who?

Pippa heard the hesitant footsteps. Rather large feet, by the sound. Someone caught her outstretched hands by the wrists. She had known all along he would come. She hugged him tightly.

"Tommy."

"Hello, Pip."

"It was Tom that rescued Isobel, Pippa, just as we had planned."

Pippa heard the big feet shuffle.

"I didn't do it all by myself."

"Ai, but you did insist on getting it done. He even got Rob's blessing, Pippa. By the way, Rob would like to visit you sometime this fall, and Jamie too, if you're feeling up to it."

Rob would come someday. Her father would come and she could make amends.

"I would love that."

"Oh, and I ...I brought you a little present here, Pip." Tom tugged her gently across the room and placed her hand against taut strings. "Here, sit." He pushed a stool against the back of her legs. She sat and he guided her hands.

The harp spoke at the merest touch, small quivering notes. She rested her forehead against it and a hundred pictures came to mind. She heard Tom come to sit beside her.

He began a tune on his flute. Her fingers trembled. Her throat was squeezed so tightly that it ached.

And then she found her part in Tom's song. Their melodies spun round and spiraled up together like two butterflies. They sailed up over the blue loch, lifted on the breeze that whispers in the rowan leaves, and drifted out beyond the end of the world, weaving a long, long tale into one silver gossamer thread.

Postlude

When, in 1306, Isobel MacDuff (usually known as Isabel MacDuff) placed a crown on the head of Robert de Bruce, she helped set in motion a chain of events that make the centerpiece of this story. She was indeed married at the time to John Comyn of Buchan, but whether or not she was one of de Bruce's lovers is open to question. It is true that Edward I did exact revenge upon her as described, as well as upon the other women of de Bruce's family, and this punishment was fully endorsed by Isobel's husband, but her real history after her capture is murky. No one knows what actually became of her.

Family and many friends of Robert de Bruce who were mentioned in this book were authentic historical figures, including, among others, Jamie Douglas and his son by an unknown mother, Gilbert de la Haye, and Christian of Carrick and her two children. And it is true that John Comyn of Buchan was wounded at the battle near Inverurie. He fled to England and died of some unknown cause within a year, possibly as a result of a wound received in that battle.

As for the involvement of the folk of Arran Isle in the Scottish Wars for Independence, tales tell that Robert de Bruce watched the legendary spider in the caves on Arran and thus was encouraged to continue his battles against the English. It is said that he landed at least once at Loch Ranza castle. Loch Ranza has not been proposed as the destination of the mysterious journey he took before his death but it is believed he traveled in that direction. It is also accepted as fact that Alexander de Bruce and his brother set sail from Arran for their fateful encounter in Loch Ryan, or Loch Rioghaine, as it was then known. James, The Black Douglas landed on Arran Island too, and did take Brodick Castle from the English. And of course, as stated at the outset, Loch

Ranza castle really does sit brooding in its loch, and jealously guards its secrets to this day.

But the other characters in this story are just that and no more, though to call them fictitious is somewhat wrenching. However, neither Pippa nor Eshne de Bruce ever existed, though no one can say that with certainty about the old seer, Ailliol. Tom the gardener's son, Cuinn and Sebrina de Seta, Caela MacDuff, and Loise the healer are part of a tale that ends right here.

Or maybe the whispering rowan trees tell you differently. Perhaps you can hear them counsel you to ignore the dreary caterpillar who believes that all stories have endings, who sees nothing beyond the chrysalis. If so, then hold out your hand. One day, surely, the butterfly will alight there.

And you too will see what the Master sees.